# THE *Scorpion* CODE

This book is a work of fiction. Names, characters, businesses, organizations, places and events are either a product of the author's imagination or are used fictitiously.

**THE SCORPION CODE**




ISBN: 9781976505034
First Edition: October, 2017

For my wife, Amie, whose consistent and loving support brought this book to life.

# Chapter 1

October 20, 1861 – 3rd Ward, Washington City

The sex was good but, then again, sex with whores always was. It was free of the complications of sex with someone you might care about. Sex with whores allowed a man to be free—free to be exactly who he was and free to be who he wasn't. There were so many whores in this rotten City that a man could reinvent himself every day, twice a day, for the rest of his natural life and never see the same woman more than once. That particular aspect of the City suited John Haney just fine. In fact, the ability to reinvent himself and disappear in this godless town is what had kept him alive for so long.

John stretched to loosen his tight muscles but the iron headboard resisted against his enormous frame. So instead, he laid there in the soft mattress and felt the warmth of the fire on his face. The fire was an extravagance, as was the pleasure of sleeping with Ellen Wolfe all night, but he'd earned it. The plan he set in motion was almost complete, and that called for a celebration. There was simply no better way to celebrate than with Ellen.

Unlike most of the loose women in this City, Ellen wouldn't take just anyone into her bed. Her discerning taste made the men who did make it into her chambers feel special. Feeling special made them loyal and willing to pay Ellen's rather exorbitant prices. But then, Ellen's performance made every man forget what he'd paid and gladly come back for more.

John turned his head to shade it from the warmth of the fire. His stomach tightened in anticipation of Ellen's touch. He pictured her long red hair cascading down her porcelain skin and over her breasts. He rolled onto his side, his body rigid for the touch of her skin. But when he opened his eyes, disappointment washed over him. Ellen wasn't there. He lifted his head off the pillow.

Across the room, Ellen's naked figure padded over the wooden floor to her wardrobe where she slipped a nightgown over her head. John smiled. The gown was made of a sheer blue silk that accentuated her taught nipples and the patch of red hair between her legs. Ellen crept silently across the room towards the fire and John's smile faded. There was something in the way she moved that felt out of place.

When Ellen reached the chair beside the fire, she stopped and turned towards the bed. John closed his eyes, assuming the part of a tired and satisfied customer. Seconds later, he cautiously peered across the room to see Ellen holding his heavy overcoat. His brow furrowed and, as Ellen searched through the pockets, a second wave of disappointment crashed.

It was all too common for whores to prey upon their sleeping customers. There were limits to the depths of any client's purse and most women felt they deserved a little something extra for their services. When their clients were stupid enough to fall asleep, they often took what they deserved.

Still, John was surprised. As Ellen searched each pocket, his surprise turned to concern. He wasn't concerned about money. The money wasn't really his after all, and it came in limitless supply. The tension spreading across his body arose from somewhere far removed from money.

John's life depended on reading people and judging them correctly. There was simply no room for mistakes. Clearly, watching her comb through his things, he had misjudged Ellen Wolfe. But to what extent? Was she after money or something else entirely?

Ellen searched the last pocket and slid the coat through her hands to lay it back on the chair. Suddenly, she stopped. Shifting her gaze, she stared down at her hand, which was still gripping the bottom of the coat. She rested the top of the coat on the chair and squeezed the fabric along the bottom. Feeling the object for a second time, Ellen flipped the coat over and examined the inner lining.

The dancing mixture of light and shadow made it difficult to see. Ellen stepped closer to the fire and studied the lining in the orange glow of the burning cedar. Turning the coat, a small and almost imperceptible opening appeared beneath the lining.

John Haney slid his hand beneath his pillow and gripped the handle of his knife.

Ellen twisted the coat and the lining separated from the outer fabric to reveal a small pocket. Ellen's heart beat wildly. Instinctively, she looked over her shoulder. John's hand was under his pillow but his eyes were closed and his breathing steady. She turned back to the light of the fire and, holding the pocket open with one hand, she swept her finger inside.

Instantly, her finger pressed against something hard. Blood pounded in her temples and her hands began to shake. Frantic, she twisted at the fabric until a small scroll of paper appeared at the mouth of the pocket. Ellen grabbed the scroll and crouched down to study it in the firelight.

The paper was wound as if it had been rolled tight around a pencil. Holding the edge of the scroll, Ellen stopped and glanced back at the bed. Her customer was still resting comfortably with his hand beneath the pillow. Relieved, she turned back to the scroll.

She had long wondered at the secrets that lay hidden beneath the surface of her client's convincing exterior. Now, she held those secrets in her hand. She would finally know who John Haney really was.

Ellen pulled at the end of the scroll and the paper began to uncoil. Her breath caught in her chest as she anticipated the revelation hidden inside. Pulling further, she unrolled the paper and began to read. She quickly scanned the text and confusion swirled in her mind. Her eyes darted around the room, searching for understanding. She read the scroll again but it only confirmed what she already knew. John Haney was exactly the man she had feared.

Just then, something moved behind her. Ellen gasped, knowing there was only one thing it could be. Before she could turn, an arm as hard as iron grabbed her and pulled her to her feet. The scroll slipped from Ellen's grasp and fell deep into the ashes as a massive hand tightened around her jaw like a vice.

She twisted her body and flailed at her assailant but the arm around her chest constricted further. Her lungs compressed and she strained to breathe. The vice-like hand snapped her head back to expose her soft porcelain skin and the veins throbbing in her neck. Ellen forced a scream through her clenched teeth. Death itself had her in its grasp.

Suddenly, a glint of steel flashed in the firelight. Adrenaline and fear coursed through Ellen's veins as she prayed that her eyes had deceived her. Then she felt it—the cold steel of Death's blade pressed gently against her neck.

"You've found more than you were looking for, my dear." The voice was colder than the blade and sent a chill down Ellen's spine. "Reading that scroll won't change a thing. What's done cannot be undone."

The words hung heavy in the air for a long moment. Then, the grip around Ellen's chest tightened as the silver blade swung high into the air. "But that this blow might be the be-all and the end-all here."

Ellen fought to draw the breath that she knew would be her last. And then, with every ounce of her being, she forced the air from her lungs. A blood-curdling scream pierced the air. The panicked shrill echoed across the room and tore through the walls.

A second later, the scream was punctuated by a rapid staccato from somewhere across the room. John glanced at the door but Ellen's eyes were fixed on the knife suspended in mid-air.

"Ms. Ellen?" came a muffled voice through the door with another series of rapid knocks. "Ms. Ellen, you okay?" The voice was strong and masculine.

John looked down at Ellen and then back to the door. He had to make a decision. The police would likely ignore the discovery of a dead whore but a double murder would demand justice.

Slowly, he lowered the knife and loosened the grip that had held Ellen Wolfe on the edge of death. Sensing her fate had changed, Ellen quickly grabbed John's arm and pushed it away. But before she could move, John grabbed her again and spun her in place. For a long moment, he held her in his gaze—his cold black eyes conveying a message words could not describe.

A heavy sound from across the room broke the spell. They turned as the dull thud of a shoulder slamming against the door sounded again. John pushed Ellen to the floor and grabbed his pants from the nearby chair. Another thud at the door and the crack of the doorframe sounded as he threw on his pants and boots. John seized his shirt and coat from the chair. Gripping his knife, he arrived at the door just as it broke free from the frame.

John's arm tensed in anticipation, prepared to strike anyone who got in his way. The door swung open and light from the gas lamps in the hall illuminated the man whose very presence had unwittingly brought an end to John Haney's short life. When John saw his face, a surge of anger welled inside. How could he have allowed a man like this to stand in his way?

Blood surged through his veins as he clenched the knife. He could do it. He could kill this man right here in the doorway and the world would be better off for it. But John had to get out. In one form or another, he had to survive and killing this worthless man could jeopardize everything. Still, something had to be done.

"What's your name, boy?"

The man stared directly into John's coal black eyes. "Josiah."

It was then that John noticed the man's right ear, or, at least, what was left of it. "A one-eared nigger," he said, disgusted. Still holding the knife, John extended his arm and pointed at the man. Josiah's gaze was locked on the murderous eyes but something about the man's finger briefly caught his attention.

"You're gonna die for what you've done tonight, boy." The man's voice recaptured Josiah's attention.

Josiah stared deep into John's eyes as a tornado of pride, regret, fear, and anger raged inside. He could kill this man. He could kill him with his bare hands. But in this twisted City where justice drew a clear distinction between black and white, Josiah's neck would be in a noose by morning. He had to let him go. Josiah narrowed his gaze and he smiled inwardly. There were other ways to deceive justice.

Suddenly, the tense stare that had frozen on John's face began to thaw. He shook his head. "You know what?" John asked as he lowered the knife. "I changed my mind." A knowing grin spread across his face as he brushed past Josiah and stepped into the hall. "I've got something better than death for you." John walked calmly down the hall towards the stairs. "Something far better than death."

Josiah watched as the man descended the stairs and disappeared from view. Turning back, he saw Ellen Wolfe standing in the doorway, her naked body clearly visible through the sheer silk fabric.

Josiah respectfully diverted his gaze to the floor. “You okay, Ms. Ellen?”

Without a word, Ellen Wolfe closed the door.

# Chapter 2

October 22, 1861 – 3rd Ward, Washington City

Levi Love pulled at the wool collar and scratched his neck. Surely the irritation would subside once the coat was properly worn in. Under normal circumstances, he would take the damned thing off but, as it was, the coat was mandatory. The United States Congress had recently outfitted officers of the Metropolitan Police with new uniforms, which left Levi with little more to do than scratch at the bothersome wool.

Whether out of laziness or a pure lack of imagination, Levi wasn't sure but Congress had approved a uniform design that was virtually identical to those of New York City. The pants and coat were constructed of rough wool that had been dyed dark blue. For the colder months, a light blue overcoat was deemed sufficient to combat the driving wind and snow.

Levi didn't really mind the uniforms. Raising police visibility had made his job easier, if only by a measure. What Levi minded was that the uniforms only allowed for minor variations in the stature of those who wore them. Officers could, at their own expense, have Charles Quigly or some other suitable tailor make the necessary modifications. But Levi had decided against the expenditure in hopes that the new wool would ultimately relax and make an allowance for his broad shoulders.

The only variation to the New York City uniform was the badge that hung on the coat's upper left breast. The silver shield depicted the U.S. Capitol building not as it was today but as it was intended to be. Gone were the piles of building materials and the scaffolds rising out of the half-finished dome. In their place stood the completed building with the Statue of Freedom sitting high atop the magnificent edifice. Levi glanced down at his shield with an uneasy smile. Given the recent news from the battlefield, the whole idea of a completed Capitol seemed rather optimistic.

Levi breathed a heavy sigh as a familiar boredom began to set in. The sixth precinct station house was nothing more than a small, rectangular building with a long front desk facing the door and four jail cells along the back wall. There was just enough space between the front desk and the cells for a table, storage locker and some open space for handling prisoners.

Save for the prisoners, Levi was alone. In the early hours of the morning, Sergeant Corbett had received a message that spurred him to drop his coffee cup and run out the front door with Corporal Townsend close behind. On his way out, the Sergeant had paused just long enough to say, "You stay here, Lover." It was a nickname that Levi despised but, in truth, he was happy to stay behind. There was only one thing that could get Sergeant Corbett moving that fast and Levi wanted no part of it.

The seat of Levi's pants began to itch, so he stood from his stool at the front desk and scratched at the wool. He adjusted the glazed leather belt around his waist and the rosewood club hanging at his side tapped his leg in response. Combing his fingers through his thick brown hair, Levi crossed the room to check on his prisoners.

Washington City had once been a quiet, almost boring town. But the first shots of war at Fort Sumter sent a shockwave through the heart of the country and completely changed the face of the City. In less than a year, the Army had moved in and the City's population doubled. Soldiers poured in from all over the Union, and an insatiable appetite for gambling and female companionship poured in with them. Overnight, enterprising women set up shop all over town and the number of taverns quadrupled. Alcohol flowed like water. And, to add fire to the fuel, guns were suddenly available on every street corner. The shots at Fort Sumter had transformed Washington City into a haven for violence, vice, and crime.

Everyone agreed that something had to be done and the formation of the Metropolitan Police had been a tacit admission to that effect. But with only 160 officers for a City of over 100,000 people, police work was like swatting flies on the piles of shit that littered the City streets.

Levi reached the back of the station house and peered into the first cell. There were no windows, so the cells remained dark even in broad daylight. No matter. The smell emanating from the other side of the iron bars confirmed that Roland Mills was still there.

Roland was one of many town drunks who spent most nights competing for space with the feral hogs on Louse Alley. There was something about Louse Alley's particular blend of mud and feces that had always attracted the hogs. It wasn't the mud, the feces, or the alcohol that made Roland a danger to the public—it was the hogs. They'd push into his space one too many times and he'd go directly to the first police officer he could find to start a fight. From time to time, the fight earned him an evening in a jail cell and away from the hogs.

Levi paced slowly by the next two cells to see that their occupants still wore the bloodied mark of his rosewood club. Yesterday afternoon, Levi had been walking his beat along 10th Street when the two men burst out of the Star Saloon in a brawl. Levi stood by and was content to allow the men to wear themselves out when an arm emerged from nowhere and pulled him into the fray. The rosewood club flew from Levi's belt and made short work of it all. Seconds later, the two men lay bloodied and unconscious in the middle of the street. Levi commandeered a nearby wheelbarrow and carted the men to the station house.

There was no doubt the occupants of the first three cells had all gotten what they deserved. But as he approached the man in the fourth cell, Levi's convictions grew thin. Levi had been raised to believe two things: the law is the master of society and God is the master of everything. Levi wasn't sure what that meant for Amos Green. Late last night, Sergeant Corbett had locked the man away for the crime of disobedience—a crime Amos committed by refusing to go home when his master called.

The law said Amos Green was the property of Mr. Clement. Levi's conscience told him to obey the law. And as for God? From the state of things, Levi could only guess that God was still trying to work that one out. Still, arriving at the wall of iron bars, Levi couldn't help but fear that jailing Amos Green represented everything that was wrong with this City, and everything that was wrong with himself. But there was nothing he could do.

Levi peered through the bars to see Amos sitting quietly against the back wall with his legs drawn up and his hands clasped together. "You thirsty?" Levi asked through the bars.

A moment passed before a voice spoke from the dark. "No, sir. I'm just fine right here."

Levi nodded silently and walked back to the front of the station house where he resumed his post at the desk. Reaching into his pocket, he removed a small coin and turned it in his fingers. In 250 BC, the Carthaginians struck a series of gold coins depicting the goddess Tanit on one side, and a rising sun on the other. Levi's cousin, Allan Pinkerton, had given him the coin on the night Levi's father died. The coin was worth a small fortune but it was also the only thing Levi had to remember his father and the tragic mistake that had led to his death. And for that, the coin was the most valuable thing he would ever own.

Turning the coin through his fingers, the memory of a beautiful woman in an elegant dress emerged in his mind. Sunlight filtered through the window and cast her long hair in shadow and light. Her amber eyes held Levi motionless as the woman slowly reached for his hand. Levi's heart faltered as he willed his hand towards hers.

Suddenly, the memory vanished when the front door of the station house burst open and crashed into the wall. Levi jumped and his coin clattered to the desk as a black man with a bloodied face appeared in the doorway. A heavy shove from somewhere outside caught the man off guard. Stumbling forward, the man's foot caught on the pinewood floor and he began to fall. Levi shot to his feet and it was then that he noticed the man's hands were bound tight behind his back. With nothing to break his fall, the prisoner landed hard on his face and skidded to a stop on the rough floor.

"Get him up," boomed Sergeant Corbett from somewhere outside. His voice was rough and scratchy from years of heavy tobacco use.

Corporal Townsend stepped through the door and grabbed the man by the back of the arm. Townsend's eyes were wild and his smile manic as he yanked the man to his feet. A familiar pit formed in Levi's stomach. He'd seen that look before.

Townsend cleared his sinuses and spat. A mixture of mucus and tobacco juice clung to his heavy beard before dripping to the floor. He spun the man to face the door as Sergeant William Corbett stepped inside. Corbett's barrel chest and thick arms stretched at his uniform.

Corbett closed the door and the noise from the City streets faded into the background. His hand hung on the doorknob for a long moment before he turned and stepped across the entryway to within inches of the new prisoner.

Corbett stared at the man for a long moment, his eyes deep-set and calculating. Then, the grizzled goatee around Corbett's lips parted and he opened his mouth wide. His foul breath hung in the air as he stuck out his tongue and slowly licked his hand. Confusion shone in the prisoner's eyes as Corbett raised his moist hand high in the air. A menacing smile spread across

Corbett's face. Suddenly, his hand came down hard. The prisoner tightened his jaw to prepare for the blow. But just as Corbett was about to strike, his hand stopped and hovered an inch away from the man's eye. A broad smile spread over Corbett's face. Slowly, he moved his hand to his own head and pressed the heavy mixture of saliva and tobacco juice deep into his perfectly parted hair.

The prisoner's face twisted in confusion and disgust. Corbett bellowed a raspy laugh that filled the room. On cue, Corporal Townsend echoed Corbett with a high-pitched cackle that sounded like a pack of hyenas.

Corbett bent over and slapped his leg before turning to the front desk. His eyes were still narrowed from laughter and Levi almost missed the flicker of a glance Corbett shot to the surface of the desk. Levi's blood surged as he followed Corbett's gaze down to the gold coin that was sitting out on the desk for the world to see. Levi's hand shot out to cover the coin but he feared it was too late.

"Get him inside," Corbett ordered, his gaze lingering on Levi's hand.

Townsend pushed the prisoner towards the interior of the station house but the man held his ground. Townsend's tall and lanky frame was no match for the much thicker, much stronger prisoner. Sensing defiance, Corbett turned to see the prisoner staring straight ahead. The muscles of the man's face danced beneath his skin as he clenched his jaw tight. Corbett looked at Townsend and waited.

Townsend's rosewood club appeared in a blink and crashed down on the prisoner's shoulder. Pain shot down the man's side like lightning and his knees buckled. Townsend stared down at the man with a maniacal smile that faded as the man regained his footing and resumed his stare.

Corbett had seen enough. He grabbed the prisoner with his thick hands and gave him a shove that sent the man stumbling past the front desk and into the open space in front of the cells.

"What has this man done?" Levi asked, finally regaining his voice.

Corbett stood just inches from the prisoner. He watched as a drop of fresh blood trickled down from the cut above the man's eye and hung on his jaw. Corbett circled the man slowly. "You hear that, boy?" he said. "Officer Lover over there asked you a question." The man stood silent, his jaw still clenched. Corbett continued his slow circle.

"Corporal Townsend?" Corbett shot. Townsend stepped forward, eager to get involved. "Would you tell Officer Lover what this *man* has done?" He spat the word *man* as if it was something distasteful.

Townsend spoke rapidly. "This here nigger and three of his friends stole a wagon and tried to sneak out of town." He licked his lips, hungry for what was to come.

"That's right," Corbett agreed. "Now three of them boys belong to Mr. Jackson, so we know they'll be taken good care of. But this one here," he poked the prisoner, "this one here was working in town on loan from Mrs. Peterson." Corbett stood within an inch of the man's face. "But that just wasn't enough freedom for you, was it." The prisoner stood as if carved from stone. "I got eyes and ears all over this town, boy. Ain't no one moving your kind around here without my permission." Corbett began circling again. "What's your name, boy?"

There was a long pause as the man considered whether to answer. "Mayo," he finally said. His voice was unwavering.

Townsend's cackle echoed around the room. "You hear that, Sarge? Skin as dark as night and someone done went and named him Mayo."

Corbett glanced at Townsend and he instantly fell silent. "We got us a little tradition here in the Sixth," Corbett said, turning back to Mayo. "We like to give our guests a name that is a little bit more descriptive, don't we Corporal?" Townsend nodded, unsure if Corbett wanted him to speak. "So what do think we call this one?"

Townsend's face screwed up as he struggled to find something clever in the barren landscape of his mind. Suddenly, his eyes went wide. "How about chocolate?" he suggested.

Corbett shook his head. "We used chocolate last week. Now we've talked about this. We can't go using the same name over and again. Don't you know? Mayo and his kind say they're *individuals*. We should respect that. Mayo here needs a name of his own."

Townsend stepped close and he squinted hard at Mayo's face. A moment later, his eyes shot open. "How about Raspberry?"

Corbett bellowed. "Raspberry!" he said through his raspy laugh. "I like it." Corbett put his nose up to Mayo's neck and drew a deep breath. His nostrils flared. "You know what?" he said as he stood back to give Mayo another look. "He even smells like a raspberry. Hell, he may *be* a raspberry."

Townsend cackled like a hyena as Corbett circled Mayo for a final time. "You know what I think?" Corbett asked. "I think there's only one way to find out if this here prisoner is a man or a raspberry."

Townsend's laughter faded and he looked confused. "How's that, Sarge?"

Corbett faced Mayo once again. "We're gonna have to see if you bleed like a raspberry." Corbett waited for that familiar first drop of fear to cross Mayo's expression but it never came. Mayo's jaw clenched and he stared straight through Corbett as if he wasn't there.

Accepting the challenge, Corbett backed away. "Corporal Townsend?"

"Yeah, Sarge?"

Corbett licked his hand and pressed his hair down. Satisfied everything was in order, he dropped his hands to his side. "Hang him up."

Townsend pounced at the command and pushed Mayo to the nearby wall where a pair of manacles hung from an iron chain. Moments later, Mayo's hands were shackled over his head. Townsend turned and the familiar crack of the Sergeant's leather whip sounded from across the room.

"You know how many lashes I can give you, boy?" Corbett asked. "Thirty-nine." He said, with a crack of the whip. "So sayeth the Bible," *CRACK!* "So sayeth the law." *CRACK!*

"Now, you don't know me, Raspberry but I'm a caring kind of man and I like to do a bit of good where I can. It's times like this that I see a public service can be done." Corbett stared down at the leather whip as he pulled it slowly through his hand. "How high can you count?"

Mayo's eyes narrowed, unsure what to say. Corbett looked up at him and his voice went cold. "How high?"

"Thirteen," said Mayo.

Corbett nodded. "Thirteen," he repeated as he thought it over. "Tell you what," he finally said, "today you're gonna learn a new number." *CRACK!* "Yes, sir. Today you're gonna count to fourteen."

Just then, the front door crashed open and broke the spell that had transfixed Levi to the scene across the room. He turned to the doorway to see a man in a pair of filthy overalls with a thin and scraggly kind of beard that can only be grown by the young. "Someone help me!" he said. "I found me something at the Canal!"

An instant later, Levi was almost knocked over by the smell that trailed in behind the man. Then Levi made the connection—the filthy clothes, the Canal, and the overwhelming smell of shit. This man was what polite circles called a scavenger. It was a scavenger's job to clear blockages in the open sewers that ran throughout the City.

"What you waitin' for?" the scavenger asked. "Come on!"

Levi turned to the Sergeant for instructions. "I ain't going nowhere with that shit digger," Corbett said. "You go see what he's carrying on about."

Levi grabbed his overcoat from a hook on the wall and quickly rounded the front desk. He was relieved to not witness the dark scene about to take place. But as he left the station house, a wave of guilt followed close behind.

# Chapter 3

October 22, 1861 – 2nd Ward, Washington City

John Haney arrived at Rhode's Tavern earlier than the agreed upon time. He had learned some time ago that being the first to arrive at any meeting gave him a certain advantage. So when he stepped into Rhode's, he was not surprised to see that Edman Spangler was nowhere in sight.

John closed the door behind him and blinked heavily to help his eyes adjust to the dim lighting within. Most taverns around town had installed gas lamps some years ago but not Rhode's. Talbot Rhode was a man who liked the old ways of doing things. As the war began, he felt the old ways slipping through his fingers, which only incited him to tighten his grip. Talbot Rhode fiercely resisted progress of any kind. It would be a cold day in hell before gas lamps lit the bar at his tavern.

Talbot's attitude towards progress didn't harm his business. In fact, his staunch adherence to the old ways had turned his establishment into a sanctuary for like-minded men. From the start, Rhode's had thrived on the slave trade. Buyers and sellers often found that conducting their business over a bite of stew and a pot of ale helped to ease the transaction. And Rhode's had the best stew in town. There, under the flickering candlelight of the tavern tables, papers were signed and the fates of the souls of men were sealed.

Congress had banned the slave trade in Washington City a decade before, but the news had yet to reach the dark corners of the tavern. For as long as it was still legal to own a slave, there would be places for men to meet and engage in the trade, or in any other activity that may further their cause. At the moment, it was exactly this type of men that John Haney needed.

As John passed the bar and made his way towards the back of the tavern, he was surprised to see that most of the tables were empty. Just then, an eruption of cheers and whistles filled the air. John looked to the far side of the room to see a circle of men five or six deep. Pints of ale held high in the air sloshed over the rim and onto the crowd as another cheer broke out of the center of the ring.

If Rhode's was best known for its Southern sympathies, its cockfighting pits were a close second. Cockfighting was a widespread obsession amongst the men of the City. Such men argued endlessly about the various breeds and proper fighting weights. They spent years raising their prized birds only to strap finely tempered steel around their legs and throw them into a pit to watch them hack their rivals to death.

A chorus of cheers and boos erupted from the pit and money began to exchange hands. The fight was over but John Haney hardly noticed. Cockfighting had never really interested him, and besides, he had much more pressing matters on his mind. He sat down at a table in the back of the tavern where he could see the front door and the rest of the room. A candle at the center of the table cast an orange halo and illuminated the dark stains of ale and tobacco that had set deep into the wood.

"What can I getcha?"

John looked up to see a rough looking barkeep cleaning a beer mug with a rag that could have used some cleaning of its own. "I'll have a Schell's," John said and returned his gaze to the front door. The man disappeared and John retrieved his pocket watch. Spangler was late.

The barkeep returned and set the pint hard on the table, sending a good measure of the dark beer over the edge of the mug and onto the wood. Just then, the front door opened and a man stepped quietly inside. John grabbed the pint and sipped at the foam while he studied the man over the top of his mug.

He was average in height with dark brown hair and a goatee that was barely longer than the three-day growth covering the rest of his face. He wore a heavy overcoat and a tan, felt hat that looked as if it had been crossed over by a wagon train. The hat was pulled down tight but failed to cover the deep indention in the middle of his forehead that appeared to have been made by the errant swing of a ball-pein hammer.

The man traced a direct path to the back of the tavern and slid onto the bench opposite John. The light from the candle cast half the man's face in shadow, which only accentuated the dent in his forehead.

"You're late," John said.

Edman Spangler shot an uneasy glance around the room. "Couldn't help it," he said. He leaned nervously across the table. "I think someone was following me."

John took a sip of his beer and licked the foam off his upper lip. He set the mug back on the table. "No one was following you."

Spangler was eyeing John's pint when the barkeep appeared. "What can I getcha?"

"He doesn't want anything," John said. Spangler's mouth hung open for a moment before he finally closed it and waved the barkeep away. "Well?" John asked impatiently as soon as the barkeep was out of earshot.

Spangler glanced over his shoulder. "I just got back from the Armory."

John's eyes went wide. "And?"

"Everything's ready."

"No one suspects anything?"

"Nope," Spangler said. "At least, I don't think so." John shot him an icy stare and Spangler quickly corrected himself. "That Armory's a tricky place to get in and out of but no one's seen nothing."

John nodded his approval. "And did you ask around about me?"

"Sure did. Asked everyone I could trust," Spangler said eagerly. "No one's heard or said a word."

John took a sip from his mug and smiled inwardly. It seemed he had managed to contain the damage that Ellen Wolfe had dredged to the surface. Still, there was no way to be certain. And there was too much at stake for unnecessary risks. That one-eared freedman had poked his nose where it didn't belong and had done him in. This would be the last day John Haney walked the streets of this detestable City.

"So do we do it?" Spangler asked nervously.

John held his mug up and studied it in the candlelight. "Do it tomorrow."

Spangler slapped the table and stood to leave. "Edman," John called. Spangler turned back towards the table. John continued studying his mug in the light of the candle. "Do it first thing in the morning."

Spangler's mouth fell slightly open. This wasn't part of the plan. And the consequences, well they were unthinkable. "In the morning?" he asked, hoping he had somehow mistaken what John had said. "You sure? There's gonna be women all over the place by then."

John turned his gaze from the mug to Spangler. Even in the dim light, his black eyes were piercing. "Do it in the morning," he said, punctuating each word.

Spangler gave him a quick nod and retraced his steps across the tavern and out the door. With Spangler out of sight, John pulled a pencil and a small scroll of paper from his pocket. Glancing up at the ceiling, he mentally composed the message he was honor-bound to send.

# Chapter 4

October 22, 1861 – 7th Ward, Washington City

"You're gonna need that wagon," the scavenger said as Levi closed the door to the station house.

Levi followed the man's gaze to the side of the building where he saw the Sixth Precinct wagon hitched to a pair of brown horses. With its wooden frame and open bed, it looked just like every other wagon around town. Its only distinguishing feature were the large spoke wheels, which, for some unknown reason, had been painted red.

"What do we need it for?" Levi asked, stepping around the scavenger to get up wind of the wretched smell.

"Can't say for sure," the man said. "But you're gonna need that wagon."

"What's your name?"

"Albert."

Levi glanced at the wagon and then turned back to the scavenger. "Okay, Albert," he sighed, "Let's go see what you've found." Levi climbed up the side of the wagon and sat on the bench. The metal springs shifted under his weight.

Albert dropped his shovel in the back of the wagon and the blade rang as it clattered to the surface. Suddenly, the bench shifted again and Levi looked to see Albert settling in beside him. Levi hesitated for a moment before slapping the leather reins. The wagon jumped to a start but moments later Levi pulled the horses to a stop. The smell was simply unbearable.

"You're going to have to ride in the back," he said.

Albert looked over his shoulder at the cargo space. “Like a prisoner? Or a hog?”

Levi felt a pang of guilt until he glanced at the man’s overalls and the globs of smeared shit that had worked deep into the fabric. “I don’t care what you ride like,” he said, “you just have to do it back there. Or you can walk along side. It doesn’t matter to me.” A passing breeze directed Albert’s scent Levi’s way. He winced. “What matters is that you don’t sit here.”

Albert appeared wounded. “Fine then,” he said as he climbed over the back of the bench and sat on the hardwood bed.

With the seating arrangements settled, Levi asked, “Where are we going?”

“Virginia and Capitol,” Albert said. “To that little bend in the Canal.”

Levi was afraid of that. He hated the Canal. The reins slapped against the horses and Levi headed north. The wagon bumped and squeaked as it forged over the deep ruts in the street. Jostling in his seat, Levi debated for the thousandth time which one he hated more: the bumpy hard-packed streets of the dry season or the impenetrable mud of the wet.

Bouncing along 9th Street, Levi hardly recognized the City. After Ft. Sumter, President Lincoln had called for 75,000 volunteers to defend the Union. The first militias arrived to find a City that was unprepared for them in every way imaginable. A severe housing shortage forced the troops to bivouac in public buildings. Soon, the Treasury and Patent offices were overwhelmed and the men moved into the Capitol to set up camp in the legislative chambers and the rotunda. When the Capitol filled to capacity, villages of white canvas tents sprang up in Franklin Square and spread out to every open space available. After occupying every blade of grass in town, the troops spilled out of the City into the surrounding hills.

As dramatic as these changes were, there was something deeper that had shifted in the City's foundation. In the early months of war, the City and its occupants knew their cause was just, and that God was on their side. Confidence was so high that when word spread a battle would be fought in nearby Manassas, Virginia, a carnival atmosphere broke out in the streets. Hundreds of families packed their picnic baskets and settled in on the hillsides of Manassas overlooking the battlefield. They wanted their children to witness God vanquish the enemy. But God had other plans and the Union Army suffered a crushing defeat. By early evening, the feelings of an inevitable Union victory were a distant memory. Fear and doubt clawed at the City's soul. The South could win this war.

Levi turned right onto Pennsylvania Avenue and the streets suddenly came alive. Halfway between the White House and the Capitol stood Center Market—Washington's largest emporium where anything and everything was for sale. Butchers, tanners, tailors, and merchants of every kind lined both sides of the street. And then there were the gun shops. Guns had poured into the City with the incoming army and were available on every street corner. There were so many guns that dealers had trouble getting rid of them all. Passing by one of the shops, Levi read a sign that was echoed all over the City: "Pistols! Pistols! Pistols! Of every variety. Sold low." But guns and dry goods weren't the only attractions. The Market District was also home to dozens of theaters, restaurants, saloons and bawdy houses, which drew as many people as the market itself.

Nearing the market, the streets were choked with traffic and Levi guided the wagon carefully into the throng. With no sidewalks to separate out the pedestrians and no established lanes of travel, the City's streets were an all-out free-for-all, operating with an every man for himself attitude. Merchants pulled carts of wool and boxed goods in every direction. Endless trains of Army supply wagons rolled along the avenue as women in hooped dresses waited for an opening to cross the street. Two soldiers burst arm-in-arm from a nearby saloon shouting "On to Richmond!" Someone fired a pistol in the air, setting off a chain reaction all the way down the avenue.

A knot of people and wagons collected in the center of the road and Levi slowed the horses to a crawl. When he finally reached the other side of the confusion, he saw a cow standing calmly at the front of the traffic jam chewing its cud and wondering what all the fuss was about. Levi felt like an ant on an angry mound as he kept the wagon moving at a cautious pace.

"I tried to be a police officer, you know?" Albert said over the din of the avenue. "The second I heard they was forming a department, I went right down there and signed up. I hadn't hardly said a word before they was kicking me out the door." The wagon hit a rut and Albert bounced hard on the bed. He winced in pain. "Yeah," he said, rubbing his tailbone, "I bet you got to have some kinda luck to get a job like you got."

The truth was, Albert was right. But Levi had no intention of discussing how he had obtained his job with this scavenger or anyone else.

At the far end of the market, Levi slowed the wagon to allow two men pulling a donkey to cross. "Damn! You smell that?" one of them asked as they passed the back of the wagon. "Smells like shit!"

Levi glanced back at Albert, who shrugged it off. "I hear that a lot."

Turning onto 3rd Street the chaos of the Market District faded and the rhythmic rattle of the wagon returned. "So when you couldn't get a position with the police, you decided to scavenge?" Levi asked.

Albert shook his head. "Nah. I tried lots of other things first. But I got no education and there's too much free work in this town."

They reached a clearing in the surrounding trees and Levi looked up to see some of that free labor toiling high above the open dome of the Capitol building. Slaves built most of the public buildings in the City but Levi knew their labor wasn't truly free. A price would be paid for the work they had done—in this life or the next.

"Then I read an advertisement in the paper," Albert said, breaking into Levi's thoughts. "Well," he said, reconsidering, "someone else had to read it to me, but I saw it there in black and white. It said, 'Good labor needed for public service.' Yessir, I'm a public servant," Albert said with a certain amount of pride. "You know that for every seven square foot of sludge I pull out of the Canal I get twenty-five cents? That's twenty-five cents guaranteed by the government of the United States!"

Levi wasn't sure what to say, so he chose to stay quiet. They rode in silence until the rhythmic clang of horse hooves on metal signaled they had reached the 3rd Street bridge.

"There she is," Albert said. Levi looked back to see the scavenger's brown toothy grin. It was the kind of smile a father might give his newborn son. Levi turned to see the place he hated more than any other in the City—the Washington Canal.

Ill-conceived from the start, the Washington Canal was intended to help develop the City by easing the transport of goods to its center. But with a complete lack of funding, and an equal measure of common sense, the engineers had merely built a three-mile ditch of stagnant water that trapped the pollution and disease of an overcrowded City.

"How much farther?" Levi prodded. He'd had enough of this adventure already.

"Just up there," Albert said, pointing to a bend in the Canal. Levi looked ahead to see an open field hosting the usual collection of white canvas tents. "You can stop up there by them tents."

Levi pulled on the reins and the horses slowed the wagon to a stop. He locked the brake into position and Albert hopped out with shovel in hand. Delaying the inevitable, Levi took his time climbing down from the wagon. By the time he reached the ground, Albert had already crested the embankment that shielded the Canal from view.

"You want to see this or not?" Albert asked, gesturing with his shovel to the other side of the levee.

"I'm coming," Levi said, rounding the wagon. He crossed the dirt road and stepped into the field of tall grass that ran along the edge of the embankment. Half way across, something caught his eye. A light breeze passed over the field and the tips of the tall grass danced in unison. Levi gazed across the shifting grass but there was nothing there. Just then, the wind shifted to reveal two lines of bent and broken grass. Levi fixed his gaze on the lines. Beginning at the dirt road by the bridge, the parallel lines ran directly across the field to where he was standing. He had seen such tracks countless times and there was little doubt they were made by a horse-drawn wagon.

Levi quickly scanned the area. Save for an overabundance of weeds and grass, the field was completely empty. What was the wagon doing out here? Levi returned his gaze to the tracks, which continued on from where he was standing and ran directly to the bottom of the embankment.

"Hey!" Albert called. "What you waiting for?"

Levi looked up to see the scavenger standing atop the embankment and directly above where the wagon tracks ended. A sense of foreboding fell across the field as Levi walked to the end of the tracks and slowly climbed the embankment.

Reaching the top, Levi caught his first glimpse of the Canal. His stomach lurched at the sight and his hand instinctively flew to his face. It was here, in these stagnant waters, that the accumulated filth and excrement of the entire City came to rest. The offensive mixture collected in the bend of the Canal and sat in a permanent state of semi-solution that baked and putrefied in the sun. The contamination infected the surrounding air, which was thick and rancid. The smell was dizzying and Levi almost wished he was back at the station house.

Albert was unfazed. "Look there," he said, pointing the shovel at the sludge.

Levi's gaze followed the blade's direction but he didn't see anything but human waste and latent disease. "What the hell are you pointing at?" he asked, dropping his hand from his face. It wasn't doing any good anyway.

Albert shot him a confused look. "You got shit in your eyes?" he asked. "Right there!" The shovel blade shot out again.

Levi followed its direction. This time, the blade hit its mark. Emerging from the black, Levi saw what had sent the scavenger running for the police. It was the unmistakable form of a human hand. A long moment passed before Levi spoke again. "Is that a woman's hand?"

"Hell if I know," Albert said.

"Well didn't you try to get it out of there?"

"Sure as hell didn't," Albert replied. "I hit the leg with my shovel and damn near shit myself!" Albert smiled at his own wit but Levi wasn't amused.

Levi pointed into the sewage.

"What?" Albert asked.

"Get in there and dig it out!"

Albert rolled his eyes and rolled up his sleeves before wading into the muck. Levi watched as the scavenger went about the business of extracting a corpse from the vilest place on Earth.

After ten minutes of digging and pulling, Albert threw up his hands. "I don't think I can get this thing out on my own," he called from the putrid waters.

There was no way Levi would step foot into that Canal. He looked around for ideas. "Hold on," he said and went down the embankment to the wagon. Peering into the bed, he saw the long rope the police used to restrain their more reluctant prisoners. He grabbed the rope and returned to the top of the hill.

"Here," he said, throwing one end into the Canal. "Tie this to the body. We'll pull it out with the wagon."

Levi ran back down the embankment and kicked at a feral hog that had taken up residence at the back of the wagon. "Git!" he warned the hog, which trotted hastily out of the way. Levi tied the rope to the hitch and climbed up to the bench. "Ready?" he yelled towards the Canal.

"Ready!" came Albert's muffled voice.

Levi slapped the reins and the horses began to pull. The wagon rattled down the road until Albert yelled, "That's good."

Levi drew on the reins and locked the brake. Looking over his shoulder, he saw Albert standing beside a blackened mass at the bottom of the levee. A swell of reluctant excitement and intellectual curiosity rose in Levi's mind, as it always did at the start of an investigation. *Who was this person? What was their story?* And most importantly, *if it was murder, who had done the killing?*

He hopped down from the wagon and followed the rope across the road and into the grass. Drawing closer to the body, his heart beat faster and his mind sharpened to a razor's edge. The trail to truth and justice began at the end of the thick braided line.

Nearing the end of the rope, the dark and muddy mass began to take shape. The body was lying on its side and folded nearly in half by the pull of the rope that was still tied around its waist. Long flowing hair, thick with heavy silt, stuck to her skin and obscured her face. Circling to the other side, Levi saw a pair of fashionable boots emerge from beneath the hem of a long dress. The fabric was expensive with gold feathers woven against a green background.

Levi's eyes slowly traveled the length of the body. He peered carefully through the layers of mud and filth but found no immediate signs of a struggle—no tears in the fine dress or blood soaked into the fabric.

Continuing his inspection, he saw the woman's arms laid out in front of her one on top of the other. Pale white hands with delicate fingers appeared at the end of the sleeves. The hands were young and vibrant and lifeless. Levi furrowed his brow and crouched beside her. Reaching down, he carefully moved the top hand so that he could see the one underneath.

"Look at that," he thought aloud.

"You find something?"

Levi turned in surprise. He had almost forgotten Albert was there. "She's wearing a ring."

Albert jumped around the body to take a look. Seeing the thin gold ring, he was instantly disappointed. He should have searched the body before calling the police. That ring was probably worth a hundred square feet of Canal shit, and he'd missed it. "So what?" he asked.

"It's a bit strange, isn't it?" Levi asked. "If she was murdered, why wouldn't the killer take the ring?"

The thought hadn't occurred to Albert and his face twisted in confusion. "Yeah," he agreed. "Why not take it?"

Levi stared at the woman's face, still covered in silt and hair. *What had led to this woman's death? And who had condemned her body to the bottom of the infected Canal?* Slowly, he extended his hand—hesitant to remove the hair that protected the woman's identity and defended the last of her dignity. Brushing the hair aside, a pair of deep auburn eyes met his gaze.

Levi gasped and fell backwards. He looked away and for a moment he lost his breath. *This isn't possible,* he told himself. *It can't be.*

Then, forcing his eyes back to the woman's face, he saw dark traces of blood around her lips. Levi struggled to collect his emotions and force air back into his lungs. He didn't want to look. He didn't want to know. But he had no choice. Leaning down, Levi gently opened the woman's jaw and peered into her dark mouth.

"My God," he said in a whisper.

"What?" Albert said, craning to see what was going on. "What is it?"

"Someone's cut out her tongue." Levi sat down beside the body giving Albert his first glimpse of the woman's face.

"Holy shitballs!" Albert said. Levi turned to see Albert pointing excitedly at the woman. "I seen her before!"

Levi looked up at Albert in surprise. He too had seen the woman before.

# Chapter 5

October 22, 1861 – 2nd Ward, Washington City

John ducked out of Rhode's Tavern and cut down F Street. The message he had written after his meeting with Spangler would soon be on its way across the Potomac. Having given the final approval for the operation, John Haney had done everything he could do. Tomorrow would redefine fear in this City. There was no turning back. And that meant John Haney was more a liability than anything else.

John kept a watchful eye as he wove his way through the usual collection of merchants and tradesmen along F Street. Newspapers from all over the Union had set up shop along this stretch of the street, which was known as Newspaper Row. A wagon hauling a heavy load of paper slowed to a stop behind the New York Herald printing house. The driver hopped down and began loosening the ropes that held the load in place. John instinctively tracked the man in his peripheral vision. The driver was just a tradesman delivering his paper but John watched him anyway. In this den of thieves and spies, you could never be too careful and you were never safe.

Washington City had always operated with a Southern mentality. For its entire history, slaves had been openly traded in the City and it was common to see coffles of chained men and women being driven through the streets. The law had recently banned the buying and selling of slaves within the City limits but owning slaves was still perfectly legal. When the war broke out, many of the City's slave owners and sympathizers fled to the safety of the Confederacy. But just as many stayed.

The Union Government did its best to identify the remaining traitors but the infiltration was too deep and too broad. From lowly unskilled laborers to leaders in society, there were those who wished nothing more than to see the South take back the City, and the country. The presence of such men and women in the heart of the Union's war efforts put the Confederacy at a great advantage. By the time the first shots of war were fired, a secret web of connections allowed Southern spies to operate seamlessly throughout the City. A crucial anchor point in the web was Charles Quigly.

Turning onto 14th Street, John was halfway down the block before he saw the bright red letters marking Quigly's Tailor Shop. Over the past decade, Charles Quigly had established himself as one of the finest tailors in the City. Everyone who was anyone had at least one of his perfectly tailored suits hanging in their wardrobe. Quigly's patrons were the richest and most powerful of the City's elite. Members of the lower classes never shopped at Quigly's, which made John Haney feel all the more conspicuous.

Approaching the shop, John passed a narrow alley running alongside the clapboard building before coming to a stop beneath Quigly's bright red sign. He leaned casually against the side of the building and took one last look around. A paperboy across the street bundled copies of an evening edition, while a nearby banker appeared in his doorway to swat at a feral hog with a stick. No one seemed to notice the spy leaning casually against Quigly's Tailor Shop. With everything in order, John slipped down the narrow alley and made his way to the back of the store.

The alleyway was dim and cold as the last of the day's sunlight dissolved over the horizon. John turned the corner at the back of the shop to find a plain wooden door with a brass handle. He crept up the stairs and slowly turned the knob. The door opened with a soft creak and John stopped to listen. Everything was still and quiet. Then, muffled voices sounded from the front of the shop. John listened a moment longer and then pushed the door further. Just inside, a pine box filled with new spools of thread sat inconspicuously on the floor. John smiled.

He stepped quietly inside and closed the door. Standing in a long hallway with curtained rooms on either side, he took a deep breath to steady his nerves and mentally rehearse the scene he'd played many times. With his head clear, John picked up the box of spools and walked down the hallway towards the voices at the front of the shop.

"Mr. Quigly?" John asked as he entered the elegant showroom at the end of the hall. Bolts of wool and silk of various colors lined the oak shelves along the back wall. Display racks exhibited Quigly's finest shirts, suits, and frock coats. On the far side of the shop, a long glass case displayed top hats, shoes, and canes for ready purchase. With the stock on hand, one could emerge from Quigly's a completely new man.

Scanning the room, John saw Charles Quigly crouched beside a withered old man with an impressive white mustache. "Mr. Quigly?" John asked again. "Delivery for you, sir."

Quigly turned to see John holding the box of spools. "Yes, yes," he said through a mouthful of pins. "Just put them in the back." Quigly's words were dismissive but his eyes told John that everything was ready.

"Yes, sir," John said, turning on his heels and walking back down the hallway. Quigly instantly renewed the conversation with his customer to keep him occupied.

At the end of the hallway, John put the box of spools back where he found it and stepped into the last dressing room. He pulled the canvas curtain across the doorway and checked to ensure it was tight against the frame. Closing his eyes, he blocked everything else out and just listened. A burst of muffled laughter from the showroom signaled all was well. It was time to get to work.

The dressing area was a simple wood-paneled room with a bench on one side and a mirror on the other. John sat on the bench and tugged his boots off. Kneeling down beside the bench, his hand swept the underside of the polished wood until it found a curved metal handle. The handle led to an iron rod that ran through a series of metal knuckles, much like the hinge on a door. The mechanism was simple but it ensured no one moved this particular bench without knowing precisely what he was doing. Gripping the handle, John pulled on the well-oiled rod.

A light click signaled the bench was free from its mooring and John quickly moved it to the opposite wall. He glanced over his shoulder to confirm the canvas curtain was still tight against the doorframe. At this point, even a passing glance from the outside world would mean disaster. John turned back to the wall and searched along the floor where he found two small holes that had been previously concealed by the legs of the bench. He knelt down and pushed his index fingers into the holes. His pulse was racing. Pulling at the holes, a long section of the wood paneling shifted. Pulling further, the paneling broke free from the wall to reveal a darkened compartment. John leaned the panel against the opposite wall and turned back to see what Quigly had prepared for him.

There, hanging neatly on a wooden rod, was everything John Haney needed to end his life. The black suit was perfectly tailored and made of tightly woven wool that felt like silk. A white shirt and black tie hung beside the suit. Everything was clean and pressed. On the shelf below, a set of polished black dress shoes sat beside a new pair of socks and a top hat. As always, Quigly had thought of everything.

John stripped off his clothes and piled them on the floor. In this moment, standing naked in front of the compartment concealing his deepest secrets, the man formerly known as John Haney was completely vulnerable. His heart pounded in his chest as he pulled the new clothes from the rack and slipped them on. Donning the fine wool coat, he turned to face the mirror.

The clothing had done more than alter his appearance—it had changed his demeanor. He stood much straighter now, projecting the confidence that comes with wealth and refinement. But still, somewhere in the edges of the reflection, familiar traces of John Haney remained.

Turning back to the closet, he retrieved a small leather pouch hanging from a nail on the back wall. He reached inside and removed a glass bottle and what looked like an artist's paintbrush. Opening the bottle, he dipped the brush into the thick liquid. The hint of alcohol hung in the air as he spread the clear adhesive on his face. With the application complete, he pulled a thick beard from the leather pouch and pressed it firmly into the glue. A final search of the bag produced a pair of wire-framed glasses. Grabbing the top hat from the closet he turned to face the mirror.

The transformation was astonishing. The only remaining hint of the man he used to be were the coal black eyes hidden behind the round glasses. But it didn't matter. John Haney was a tradesman with neither the means nor the connections of the man in the mirror. John Haney was dead and Edward Huff had returned to the streets of Washington City.

Turning back to the room, Edward threw the old clothes into the closet and replaced the wall panel and bench. He checked the room to ensure everything was in order before stepping through the canvas curtain and out into the hallway.

"Good afternoon, Mr. Huff," Quigly said as Edward entered the showroom.

"And to you, Charles," Edward replied with a touch of his top hat.

The bell on the door rang as Edward pulled it closed and stepped out onto 14th Street. The sun had dropped behind the horizon, leaving a collage of pink and orange in its wake. Edward reached into his waistcoat pocket and checked his gold watch.

"Edward!" came a familiar voice from just down the street. "Back from the wilds of Colorado, I see."

Edward looked up from his watch to see the tall figure of Wilburn Jackson. His eyes were full of a youthful energy that stood in sharp contrast to the rest of his body. Wilburn glanced at the sign over Quigly's shop and smiled. "How much of your fortune have you shoveled into Charles's pockets this time?" he asked with a feigned sense of practicality. In actuality, his steel and railroad investments had made him wealthy beyond measure. Wilburn had spent several good fortunes at Quigly's himself.

Edward smiled and shook his head dismissively. "Just a trifle," he said. His diction was polished, educated, and as far away from that of John Haney's as could be imagined. "I was considering a new cane but decided against it."

"Yes, well his selection has been a little thin of late," Wilburn agreed. "The war may soon put us all in rags. Are you off to the Willard?"

"As luck would have it, I am."

"Well then, shall we walk together?"

Edward glanced down at his watch again before tucking it back in his pocket. He swept his hand out in front of them. "After you," he said. The timing could not have been more perfect.

# Chapter 6

October 22, 1861 – 7th Ward, Washington City

"What?" Levi Love asked, looking up at Albert. The scavenger was still layered with a toxic mixture of filth and excrement but Levi paid it no attention. "You're saying you've seen this woman before?" Levi didn't want to believe it.

Albert nodded. "Sure have."

Levi stood so that he could look the scavenger in the eye. "Where?" he demanded.

Albert suddenly looked sheepish and a hint of pink appeared through the smear of silt on his cheeks. "I seen her one time up at Venerable's place." Albert looked down at his feet and then added, "Or, at least, I tried to see her."

"Venerable's?" Levi asked, unsure that he had heard the man correctly. He glanced down at the beautiful and soiled woman lying at his feet. He considered the intricate embroidery of her dress and the delicate hands at the end of the sleeves. The woman was refined. Elegant. Suddenly, an uninvited memory of the woman laughing in the sunlight forced its way to the surface. Levi quickly shook it away. There was no way this woman would be seen anywhere near Venerable's but Levi had to be sure. "You mean the whore house?"

"Yep," Albert said. "I just seen her there a couple weeks ago."

"You're sure?" Levi asked again, a crack forming in his disbelief.

Albert kept his eyes pinned to his feet. "Once you've seen a face as pretty as that, you don't never forget it."

Levi looked down at the woman and knew it to be true. He would certainly never forget her face, or anything else of her image.

"You say you've seen her." Levi continued. "You mean you've *seen* her?" He emphasized the word *seen* to imply a more carnal vision. Levi still found it difficult to believe this woman could be a prostitute.

"Nah," Albert said. "But it weren't from a lack of trying." The scavenger hesitated but Levi's intense stare insisted that he continue. Albert obliged. "I'd had a good day at the Canal clearing out nearly thirty foot of shit. That's thirty foot in one day!" Albert looked at Levi to see if he was adequately impressed. He was not. "Anyway," Albert continued, "I got everything measured right and the government handed me a brand new dollar bill and a little change on top. I was walking along and wondering what I might do with it all when I looked up and saw Venerable's front door right there in front of me.

"I stopped right there and said to myself, 'Albert, what you need is a good tumble.'" He nodded his head firmly as if his conclusion were unassailable. "So I walked right through the door and there she was. She wasn't at the bar fiddlin' with the men like them other whores. No, sir. She was sitting in one of them chairs in the back. And do you know what she was doing?" Albert screwed up his face. "Reading! Can you believe that? And I thought, 'Albert, that's the kind of whore your momma would be proud of.' So I walked right back there and tried to bed her.

"But you know what? She wouldn't take me," Albert said in wounded disbelief. "She said I needed a good washing before she'd even think about it. Well, I ain't never seen nothing like her before so I ran out to the Tiber and threw myself right in."

Tiber Creek was one of the many waterways in the City that the incoming army had turned into an open sewer. No one in their right mind would wash in the Tiber but Levi saw no point in discussing personal hygiene with a scavenger.

"I shook myself dry and went back in there but she *still* wouldn't let me wiggle in. I couldn't believe it—a whore with standards."

Albert belched something foul and then shrugged the whole thing off. “Man at the bar told me she was known to turn down gentlemen with pressed shirts and top hats. So it weren’t just me that she told to take a jump in the creek.”

Levi’s mind shifted from Albert’s wounded pride to an image of the woman sitting at a café table in a fine dress, her amber eyes drawing him near. “Do you know her name?” Levi asked softly, as the memory vanished in a fog.

“Sure do,” Albert said.

Levi waited but Albert just stood there. “Well?” Levi prodded.

“Well what?”

“What the hell is her name?” Levi demanded. There was little doubt as to why this man was reduced to scavenging for a living.

“Oh that,” Albert said. “That there is Ellen Wolfe.”

At the sound of her name, Levi’s eyes began to well and he quickly turned away. He walked slowly down the embankment and looked out over the horizon. A watercolor of pinks and blues appeared in the evening sky. He stared into the distance as his memories played against the colored clouds.

The ringing of the bell on the tea-shop door. The brush of her hand against his own. The feeling that gripped his body at each glance of her amber eyes. It was a feeling like none he had ever had. It was love or, at least, he had thought it was.

Levi stopped in the tall grass and turned to look at Ellen's lifeless body. She had been young, vibrant, and full of dreams. But everything she was, or would ever be, had been taken from her in an instant. Levi set his jaw. Perhaps he didn't love Ellen Wolfe but he wouldn't allow her murderer to simply fade into the background of this merciless City.

Walking slowly towards the body, Levi focused his mind on the facts at hand. If Ellen Wolfe truly was a prostitute, finding the murderer would be significantly more difficult. Lust had invaded every corner of this City. It resided in every tent in the field and in every chamber of government. Depending on how entrepreneurial Ellen had been, virtually any man on the streets of Washington could be a suspect. At least, any man other than this scavenger.

Levi reached into his pocket and retrieved his gold coin. Turning it in his fingers, he paused beside the embankment to consider another question hovering in his mind: How did Ellen Wolfe's body end up here? Margaret Venerable's bawdy house was on P Street—nearly three miles north of the foul blockage that had entombed Ellen's body. The Canal itself was motionless and stagnant, meaning there was no current to wash her down stream. Perhaps she was killed nearby and simply thrown into the diseased waters out of convenience.

Following this thread, Levi turned in place and scanned the field of canvas tents across the road. The camp was largely deserted, save for a few cooks preparing a meal over an open fire. The soldiers were likely participating in the endless military drills that occurred behind the Capitol. Could the killer have been a soldier? When full of men and guns, encampments such as the one across the street were loud and chaotic. A soldier could have easily killed this woman and dragged her to the Canal.

But that didn't answer what Ellen Wolfe was doing this far away from Venerable's in the first place. If what Albert said was true, Ellen had high standards. It seemed unlikely that she would bed down with a pack of soldiers in a canvas tent. There were no shops or entertainment in this part of the City and no other reason for her to have been anywhere near this remote field of soldiers.

Levi's eyes fell upon the wagon tracks that cut across the grass and another thought came to mind: Perhaps the body was placed here to make it look like a soldier committed the crime. His mind lingered on the idea and then gave it up. At this point, it was impossible to know.

Reluctantly, Levi stepped through the grass and crouched beside the lifeless woman at his feet. Though he was certainly no expert, Levi's cousin had taught him the basics of how to examine a body and determine a cause of death. A quick scan of Ellen's soiled figure revealed three obvious wounds at the throat, chin, and tongue.

His eyes drifted to the deep incision that ran across her neck. Levi got down on his hands and knees to steady himself and leaned in close. Pulling a handkerchief from his pocket, he gently removed the layer of silt and mud on her neck and studied the wound. The edges of the opening were clean and well defined with no bruising or abrasion along the surrounding tissue. He stared at the layers of skin and muscle as a hazy picture of the murder weapon began to take shape.

The object used to slash Ellen's throat must have been very sharp. The lack of tears along the edges of the incision indicated the blade was straight and without a serrated edge. Levi stared at the cut, willing it to provide further information but slashing wounds such as this left little trace of the weapon or the man wielding it.

Levi tilted his head to get a better view of the wound beneath Ellen's chin. The hole was narrow and just over an inch in length. The slit was defined by a precise V-shape on one end and a blunted square on the other. A heavy bruise surrounded the wound and formed a purple halo that covered her jaw and extended down to her neck.

Levi pushed off the ground and stood. His eyes travelled back and forth between Ellen's neck and chin. The stab wound beneath the chin told a story that the slash on the neck did not. Levi had learned that skin would often retract upon removal of a blade. At just over an inch long, the length of the hole indicated the blade was likely an inch and a half or two inches wide. The shape of the wound pointed to a knife that was sharp on one end and blunt on the other. It was more likely a Bowie knife than a dagger.

The bloodstains around Ellen's mouth caught Levi's eye and a cold chill spread across his body. A simple question came to mind: Why? Any one of the three brutal injuries would have killed Ellen Wolfe. Why would the murderer slash her throat, stab her beneath the chin, and then take the time to remove her tongue?

The answer came almost as soon as Levi had asked the question. This was no ordinary murder—it was passionate and vengeful. Ellen Wolfe had done something to enrage this man.

Oddly, this conclusion brought Levi some hope. Anger of such depth came only from the hearts of the betrayed or the deeply depraved. Levi hoped for the former but one thing was certain—Ellen Wolfe either had an emotional connection with her killer or she'd had the simple misfortune of bedding a murderous lunatic. Either way, the list of potential suspects had shrunk from the City's entire male population to something slightly more manageable.

"We gonna just stand here all night?" erupted Albert.

Levi broke from his thoughts to see the scavenger rubbing his arms to keep warm in the last remaining rays of sunlight. "Come on then," Levi said. "Let's load her into the wagon."

# Chapter 7

October 22, 1861 – 2nd Ward, Washington City

Edward Huff strolled along 14th Street keeping pace with his companion. Wilburn Jackson's eyes and heart may have been full of vigor but his legs were not. Their conversation wandered from upcoming social events to the rising cost of goods and the Confederate's endless blockade of the Potomac.

"They're trying to choke this City to death!" Wilburn concluded as they turned right on Pennsylvania Avenue and the Willard Hotel came into view.

In 1853, President-Elect Franklin Pierce had made the Willard his home while awaiting his inauguration. Every evening, Pierce spent hours in Willard's lobby sipping fine whiskey and holding court. A grand tradition was born. Though Pierce was gone, Willard's lobby remained as *the* place for the rich and powerful to gather and exchange ideas and gossip. The doors were technically open to the public but, for all practical purposes, Willard's lobby was a private club. Only those with wealth and connections were granted entry. Edward Huff had both.

Bellmen in matching green liveries and gloved hands opened the Willard's doors and allowed the distinguished gentlemen to pass. The grand lobby was a cavernous space with oak paneled ceilings and thick marble columns. A sea of men in black coats and top hats stirred about the room holding glasses of whiskey and wine. A thin veil of tobacco smoke drifted overhead.

Edward quickly scanned the room to see that the crowd had organized itself in the traditional manner. Groups of men collected in tight circles throughout the lobby. The size of the circle was dependent upon the topic of conversation and, more importantly, the wealth or status of the man at its center. After spending many months in Willard's lobby, Edward knew the smaller circles tended towards gossip, whereas the larger ones focused on politics and the war effort. From time to time, Edward had collected interesting information from the gossip circles but it was highly inefficient. Tonight, he was anxious to re-establish certain connections—there was simply no time to waste on gossip.

Edward turned his attention to the larger circles. The man he wanted to see would most certainly be discussing the war effort. Peering through the shifting crowd, he noticed a large and rather solemn group in the back corner. He decided to start there.

"I say, Edward," Wilburn said, "there's someone back here that I'd like you to meet." He grabbed Edward's arm and led him in a direction that was opposite of his intention.

Along the way, Wilburn spotted the red coat worn by a member of the wait staff. Tapping the boy with his cane, he said, "We need a drink, my boy. I'll have an Overholt but I presume my friend Mr. Huff would prefer a Maker's." Wilburn turned to Edward, who confirmed the order with a nod. In Edward Huff's opinion, drinking whiskey from Pennsylvania was akin to blasphemy. If it didn't come from Kentucky, it simply wasn't whiskey. Turning back to the waiter, Wilburn raised his cane and pointed over the top of the crowd. "We'll be over by the fireplace." The boy nodded and disappeared.

"This way, Edward," Wilburn said, pushing deeper into the room. Seeing no gracious way to decline, Edward followed Wilburn towards the marble fireplace. He would make his introductions and then politely bow away from whatever socialite Wilburn intended him to meet.

Approaching the fireplace, they encountered some resistance at the outer edge of the large circle. Wilburn raised the ivory handle of his cane over the top of the crowd. Almost instantly, someone bellowed, "WJ!" The conversation stopped and the circle parted to make way for the man holding the cane.

Following Wilburn to the center, Edward caught his first glimpse of the man commanding such a large audience. It was Abraham Lincoln's Secretary of War, Simon Cameron. Edward smiled inwardly. Perhaps this wouldn't be a useless meeting after all. He should have known better. You simply never knew whom you might find drifting in the currents of Willard's lobby.

"I'd like you to meet a friend of mine, Edward Huff," Wilburn said, gesturing grandly in Edward's direction. "Recently returned to us from the wilds of Colorado."

Edward gave a slight bow of his head and extended his hand. "A pleasure, sir."

Cameron grasped his hand and held it firmly. "Edward Huff, you say? From the Huff family in Georgetown?"

Cameron had instantly made the connection to Edward's carefully constructed alias, which wasn't too surprising. Simon Cameron was known for his love of money and his love for a good conspiracy. "The very same," Edward said.

"Ha! I knew it," Cameron said, pulling Edward in close and putting his arm around him in an abrupt show of friendship. "Edward's family are the trickiest of all devils," Cameron explained to a rapt crowd. "They were among the first to move to Georgetown in the gold rush but then they found something even better—silver." He paused to glance at Edward, whose face shone with a respectable amount of modesty. "The Huff's quietly purchased damn near all of Argentine Pass. Rumor has it the Argentine has enough silver buried beneath it to purchase every kitten at every cattery in the City."

A light laughter spread around the circle until someone asked, "Have you heard any news from Ball's Bluff?" The crowd instantly fell silent so as not to miss a word. The battle at Ball's Bluff had been fought just forty miles west of the City but news from the field had been slow in coming.

The smile on Cameron's face faded and he released Edward from his grasp. "It is not good, gentlemen," Cameron said with a heavy sigh. "Reports are still coming in but it appears we may have lost nearly a thousand men in all." A brief murmur rose as Cameron continued. "The idea was to simply determine if the Confederates were occupying Leesburg. How hard is it to send a few men across the Potomac and back?" The blood now boiled in Cameron's face. "A task apparently too difficult for our General McClellan. I will be speaking to the President about having him removed." At this, the crowd broke into a flurry of conversations.

The news was astonishing. The North had suffered another crushing defeat and better yet, Cameron was going to request that Lincoln relieve McClellan from his command! Edward's heart swelled knowing that tomorrow's operation at the Armory would be yet another blow to the wretched Northern Army. The South was surely winning this war.

The Southern blockade of the Potomac was breaking the Union's back. Supplies in the City were running short and the cost of goods was on the rise. The Confederates had the North by the throat. But it wasn't time to celebrate—it was time to squeeze.

Edward studied the men in the circle until he saw the golden epaulettes marking a senior naval officer. Leaning in, Edward asked, "Have you by chance seen Commander Glasson this evening?"

The officer broke away from his conversation. "Commander Glasson left about a half hour ago."

"Any idea where he's gone?" Edward asked.

"The Commander had an urgent appointment across town," the officer replied with a conspiratorial smile.

"Ah, yes. Of course he had," Edward said with a wink and a tip of his hat. "Thank you, sir."

The officer turned back to his conversation and Edward Huff made his way to the bellman at the front of the lobby. "Have my man bring about my carriage," he ordered.

Moments later, a black Brewster and Company coupe rolled to a stop in front of the Willard. Quite literally a coach cut in half, Brewster's new coupe provided comfortable seating for two. It had glass windows over the shining wooden doors and a large windshield directly behind the driver's bench. The rear wheels were slightly larger than the front, which gave the Brewster an appearance of speed even at a standstill.

A man hopped down from the bench and opened the door. "349 Maryland," Edward said as he stepped into the richly appointed carriage.

"Right away, Mr. Huff," said the coachman. The carriage jumped to a start and Edwards closed his eyes. His trusted driver would deliver him precisely where he needed to go.

# Chapter 8

October 22, 1861 – 3rd Ward, Washington City

Levi Love pulled the heavy wooden door to a close and his hand hung on the latch. It wasn't the first time the old shed behind the station house had been used to store a body. Levi had found an old blanket to cover Ellen Wolfe's remains and allow her to finally rest. It was the best he could do. Her body would be safe in the shed until the undertaker's wagon came by to collect her in the morning. And as for her soul, Levi simply didn't know.

He cut across the covered porch in front of the police station and began his long walk up 10th Street. Metropolitan Police regulations required officers to walk their beat at least once a day. Given he had spent most of his shift dredging Ellen Wolfe from the depths of the Canal, Levi had yet to cover any of his assigned territory. Tonight, he was eager to get started. His beat took him to the far end of 10th Street and directly in front of Margaret Venerable's bawdy house.

The lower half of 10th Street was a commercial district filled with shops, theaters and restaurants. The street was always busy but the character of the traffic changed as the evening hours wore on. Merchants carting boxes of dried goods were slowly replaced by sleek carriages carting the wealthy and the powerful. The herds of cattle ambling to slaughter were exchanged for courting couples out for an evening stroll.

At the corner of E Street, Levi noticed a tuxedoed gentleman and his wife walking arm-in-arm. Suddenly, a pack of street children appeared from nowhere and surrounded the couple. The man tried to push through the band of ruffians but was forced to a halt by sheer numbers. A boy around the age of ten stepped forward with a filthy face and tattered clothes. "You got any money to spare?" It was more of a demand than a question.

“Yeah,” chimed another small voice, “give us a nickel.” This roused a chorus from the remaining gangsters.

“Give us a nickel! Give us a nickel!”

“Look at his pretty clothes,” someone said. “He’s got more than a nickel to spare.”

This got them all thinking. Finally, a voice cried, “Give us a dime!”

“Yeah! Give us a dime!”

The children were so determined to land their prize that they didn’t notice Levi until he was already upon them. “Get out of here!” Levi said, brandishing his club without any intention of actually using it.

Several of the children turned at once. “Oh shit! Police!” In a blink, the gang ran off in different directions and disappeared into the dark.

Levi looked up to see the woman clutching the silken bodice of her dress as if her heart was failing. Her husband put his arm around her and pulled her close. “Those boys are animals!” he exclaimed. “They should be locked up in the workhouse and put to use!” The couple pushed past Levi and hailed the nearest carriage.

Bands of roving children were common in Washington City. The endless supply of cheap labor had depressed wages and pushed many families past the breaking point. With parents unable to provide enough food, children were often turned out of their homes and made to fend for themselves. The children were hungry and cold and Levi saw no use in locking them away in the public workhouse to starve and likely freeze to death. The City streets at least gave them the chance of survival.

Levi continued along 10th Street where a series of gas lamps cast their bright yellow glow onto Ford's Theater. Patrons collected in tight bunches of top hats and lace to discuss the upcoming performance. As Levi approached the crowd, he saw a man shake the hand of another.

"Charles!" the man said. "I didn't think you would make it."

"I nearly didn't," Charles replied. "Impossible to get tickets. You know I had to pay almost two dollars a seat? And even that only got us a place in the Dress Circle!"

"Outrageous," replied his friend. "But worth it," he added with a wink.

"I wouldn't have missed it," Charles agreed.

Members of the upper class loved the theater, mostly because it allowed them to see and be seen. Typically, the entertainment value of the play was a secondary concern, which was what made the scene in front of Ford's so unusual. Wondering what all the fuss was about, Levi glanced at the sign over the door to see that Laura Keene was in town to reprise her role in Our American Cousin. Levi hadn't heard of the actress or the play.

He skirted around the crowd and the commotion of Ford's Theater faded into the background. Levi strolled in the blue-gray light of the moon and enjoyed the growing quiet as he passed St. Patrick's Catholic Church at the edge of the commercial district. The gothic stained glass cast a welcoming light and Levi pictured Father Joshua Whitfield working tirelessly within to save the soul of a soulless City.

Passing the alleyway that ran along the far side of the church, Levi heard a shuffling of feet and a groan in the dark. In an irony that was not lost on anyone, St. Patrick's Church marked the City's boundary line between morality and sin. It was here that prostitutes who had fallen to the lowest rung of their profession plied their trade in the muddied recesses of the City's alleys.

There were several classes of prostitutes in the City. At the top were those who worked in one of the ten elite brothels, known for their crystal chandeliers and refined clientele. There, as the saying went, the best cuts of women were served alongside the best cuts of meat. Middle and lower-class houses were more difficult to distinguish from one another. With names like The Wolf's Den, Madame Wilton's Private Residence for Ladies and The Devil's Own, the uninitiated were often uncertain what type of house it was until they were given the price for their evening's entertainment. The women who had managed to secure a place in any established house were fortunate, for it was the poorest of souls who were forced to sell their wares in the darkened alleyways. There was simply no other place to go in this unforgiving City.

Levi stopped at the corner of 10th and P where a sign announced his arrival at Venerable's. The house was a two-story clapboard with a small porch and an aged coat of white paint. A handful of men gathered out front for a laugh and a pre-coital drink of watered down whiskey. Levi stepped onto the porch and the conversation ended abruptly. The men eyed Levi closely, unsure of his intentions.

Prostitution wasn't technically illegal but it did operate in a gray zone that enabled police to make arrests, or even to shut houses down, when political and social pressure demanded. This gray area of the law allowed police to do as they pleased inside the brothels, which meant Madams and customers alike gave the Metropolitan Police a wide berth.

The men on the porch stood aside to allow Levi through. Nodding at the men as he passed, he opened the flimsy wooden door to a hive of noise and activity. A familiar tune rang from a piano in the back and filled the air that was already thick with tobacco. Just as Levi stepped inside, a man at a nearby table fell off the bench and landed face first on the pinewood floor. A roar of laughter erupted from the surrounding tables, temporarily drowning out the piano. Just then, a loud clatter from across the room broke through the laughter as a man at one of the gaming tables abruptly stood and sent his chair tumbling to the floor.

"That's bullshit!" he yelled, throwing his cards on the table. "That Jack was mine!" He stared down at the man to his right and a tension arose between them that went unnoticed by the rest of the establishment. Levi put his hand on his stick but the moment passed as the man turned away from the table and stormed across the room to order a drink.

Levi followed the man and found an opening at the opposite end of the bar. Waiting to catch the bartender's attention, Levi couldn't help but feel the presence of the man sitting next to him. The man's weathered face and greasy black beard were partially obscured by the leather collar of his overcoat. Levi narrowed his gaze and watched as the man grabbed his glass with a hand that was as rough as his coat and swirled the last drops of whiskey at the bottom.

"Can I help you?"

Levi turned to see a man in a striped shirt and thin mustache standing on the other side of the bar. He was rubbing a glass with a rag and looking nervously around the room.

Levi looked down to see the man with the black beard was staring at him. It was then that Levi noticed the leather patch over the man's right eye.

"Is something the matter?" the barman asked nervously, regaining Levi's attention.

"I need to see Madame Venerable," Levi said.

The barman continued wiping the glass as if he was trying to rub a hole in it. "Um," he stammered, "what should I tell her this is about?"

"Tell her it's about the death of Ellen Wolfe."

The barman nearly dropped the glass and his mouth hung open in disbelief. "What?" he asked. "Ellen? Ellen's dead?" The barman blinked and shook his head. "No. It can't be. There must be a mistake."

Levi's stomach turned at the confirmation that Ellen truly did work here. He leaned into the bar. "I assure you there is no mistake," he said firmly. "Now go get Madame Venerable."

The bartender set the glass down and quickly rounded the bar. The man with the black beard swirled his glass and continued staring at Levi with his remaining eye.

Levi put his hand to his stick and turned to face him. "Do we have a problem?" Levi asked.

The man held his stare for a long moment. He was not intimidated. His eye suddenly shifted to something over Levi's shoulder and then he silently returned his gaze to his glass and went about his swirling.

"You asking for me?" came a deep voice with only a hint of femininity. Levi turned to see an enormous woman stuffed in a silk dress that was stretched to its limits. "I run a clean business around here and I don't want any trouble."

Levi made a quick scan of the room. It was hard to imagine how anyone could describe Venerable's as a clean business. "I need to talk to you about Ellen Wolfe."

Venerable's skin grew pale. "So it's true what Billy said then," she gestured towards her barman. "Ellen's really dead?"

"She's really dead."

Venerable cast her eyes to the floor and nodded her acceptance. "Follow me," she said. Without waiting on Levi, she turned towards the back of the room and headed upstairs.

At the top of the stairs, there were six bedrooms fronted by an L-shaped balcony that overlooked the tavern below. Levi followed Madame Venerable along the walkway and past a pair of scantily clad women advertising their availability. Venerable reached for the black iron knob of the third door and pushed it open without warning.

A man with his pants halfway down jumped at the unexpected intrusion. He spun in place but his legs got tangled in his pants and sent him crashing to the floor. With the man scrambling to recover himself, Levi saw further into the room where a woman with thick blonde hair lay completely naked on the bed.

"What the hell?" asked the man, buckling his pants while still laying on the floor.

"Get out, George," Venerable ordered without so much as glancing to the floor. Her gaze was fixed to the woman on the bed. "We need to talk."

George got to his feet and grabbed his shirt from a nearby chair. "I done paid for my poke. Do I get a free one or something?"

The look on the Madame's face made it clear there were no free pokes at Venerable's. George attempted a menacing stare at Levi as he pushed by. It was clearly safer to blame the interruption on a police officer than Madame Venerable. When Levi turned back to the room, the woman inside had slipped on a cotton gown and was sitting nervously at the edge of her bed.

Levi stepped inside and pointed to the chair. "May I?"

The woman nodded and Levi pulled the chair closer to the bed. There were many police officers who felt their authority was sufficient to get any information they needed by simply demanding it. While brute force certainly had its place, Levi tended to start interrogations such as this with a softer touch. If that didn't produce the proper results, there was plenty of room for brute force later.

"My name is Levi Love," he said, extending his hand.

The woman shifted on the mattress to reach for his hand and the iron bed frame let out a feeble squeak of resistance. "Christine Brandy," she said in a soft voice that conveyed the uncertainty of her situation.

"He's here to talk to you about Ellen," Venerable said rather harshly. "You tell him what you know, you hear?"

Christine looked confused. "What's happened to her?" Seeing the look on Levi's face, she shook her head. "No. It can't be. He did it, didn't he? He killed her." Levi looked to the floor and then back at Christine. Her eyes welled and a tear rolled down her face.

"Who are you talking about?" Levi asked as gently as he could. "Who killed her?"

Christine shook her head. "I don't know," she said, fighting back her tears. "I don't know who it was. I just know she was scared." Christine buried her face in her hands and began to cry.

Having the police around was bad for business and Madame Venerable was anxious to get Levi out the door. "Stop your crying and tell him what you know," she ordered.

Levi turned and shot Venerable a look that told her to keep her mouth shut. She glared back at him. No one bossed Madame

Venerable around in her own place but she kept quiet nonetheless.

"Take your time," Levi said, turning back to Christine. She looked up at him and wiped her tears. "Just tell me what happened."

"I don't know, exactly," Christine started. "A few nights ago, Ellen knocked on my door. It must have been two o'clock in the morning but she was shaking and crying. I'd never seen her like that before. I sat her down on the bed and she just kept saying 'I knew who he was. I should have never got involved with him.'"

Levi sat forward in the chair. "Who was it? Who was she so scared of?"

Christine shook her head. "I told you, I don't know. I asked her but she wouldn't say. She told me it was safer if I didn't know."

"But it was one of her customers?"

Christine nodded. "It was. But I don't know which one." Christine began to cry again.

"It's okay," Levi said, placing a comforting hand on her knee. "Did she tell you anything that could help identify who the man was? What he looked like? How often she saw him? Anything?"

Christine looked over at Madame Venerable and then back to Levi. Christine obviously had something to say that she preferred Madame Venerable not hear. "Give us a minute," Levi said, glancing halfway over his shoulder.

"You want me to leave?" Venerable asked, incredulous.

Levi turned to face her. "Yes. I want you to leave."

Venerable narrowed her eyes at both of them and stormed out of the room. Levi waited a moment to ensure she was gone and then turned back to Christine. His eyes invited her to continue.

Christine stood and walked to the other side of the bed. "She wouldn't tell me what it meant," she said, reaching under the mattress, "but she gave me this." Christine stepped around the bed and held out her hand.

Levi glanced down to see that she was holding a tiny roll of paper. He took the scroll and pulled it open. His brow furrowed. The writing made no sense.

STAF GGOG LCQB LMRN WURR
NKBB WZWK RWBS ATAV S

"What is this?" Levi asked.

"I don't know," Christine said. "Ellen told me to hold onto it for her."

"What for?" Levi asked. "It doesn't mean anything."

"I don't know," Christine repeated. "She just said if anyone came asking about it that I should tell them to go find Josiah."

Levi was confused. "Josiah?" he asked.

Christine nodded. "He's a carpenter that works around here. He's a colored man but you'd know him if you saw him."

"How's that?" Levi asked. There were thousands of colored men in this City.

"He's a big man with a beard and most of his right ear has been cut off," Christine said, reaching up to her own ear. "Ellen said Josiah had the key to understanding what the letters on that scroll mean."

Levi looked down at the scroll trying to make sense of Ellen's instructions. How could a colored, one-eared, and likely illiterate carpenter hold the key to understanding what the letters meant? Levi looked up at Christine. "Did Ellen mean to say that Josiah could read this paper?"

Christine shrugged. "I guess so," she said. "But it doesn't matter. You won't be able to find him," Christine added.

"What?" Levi asked. "Why not?"

"He was taken."

"Taken? What do you mean *taken*?"

"I mean a bunch of men surrounded him and took him." Christine started to cry. "He was standing right out there on P Street."

"Who took him?" Levi asked. The threads of this conspiracy were growing thicker by the moment.

Christine cast her eyes at the pinewood floor and shook her head. When she turned her gaze back to Levi, her face was covered in fear. "Bad men," she said in a whisper. "Men who would never let a man like Josiah get in their way. It's useless, Mr. Love. Josiah's gone. Won't no one ever see him again. And that's everything I know," she said. "Honest."

Levi stared at Christine for a long moment. Her eyes begged him to believe her. Levi nodded and stuffed the scroll into his pocket. "It's okay," he said. "I believe you."

Just then, someone pounded on the door. "You done in there?" demanded Madame Venerable. "I got a business to run."

Levi looked around the room and back to Christine. "Sounds like you need to get back to work." He stood and put the chair back where he found it. "Thank you for your time," he said as he headed for the door.

"Anytime," Christine said before he could leave. Levi turned to see Christine twirling her hair. "You can come see me anytime."

Levi smiled politely. He had never taken a whore in this City and he never would. He opened the door and disregarded Madame Venerable's complaints about lost profits as he walked down the stairs to the tavern below. The barman watched Levi closely. When it appeared the policeman was leaving he turned to a teenaged boy behind the bar and whispered in his ear. The boy stared at Levi to get a good look at him and then darted around the bar and out the back door.

At the other end of the bar, the man with the greasy beard and eye patch set down his empty glass and followed Levi out into the night.

# Chapter 9

October 22, 1861 – 7th Ward, Washington City

The sleek black carriage pulled to a stop at 349 Maryland Avenue and a man in a black suit promptly opened the door. “Good evening, Mr. Huff,” the man said. “Nice to see you again.”

Edward Huff smiled as he stepped down from his carriage and into one of the worst neighborhoods in the City. Broken down wooden shacks littered both sides of Maryland Avenue and housed the poorest laborers in Washington. But it wasn’t the dilapidated housing that made Edward smile; it was the beautiful, two-story brick building that sat amongst them.

“Nice to see you as well, Henry,” Edward said as he stuffed a dollar bill in the valet’s hand and stepped up onto the grand front porch that wrapped around the building.

Of all the whorehouses in Washington City, Mary Ann Hall’s was the finest. Constructed well away from the red light district north of the Canal, Mary Ann had created an isolated fantasyland for her elite clientele. Congressmen, bankers, industrialists, and anyone else who could afford her lavish services always found their way to Mary Ann Hall’s. Edward Huff was glad to be back.

He stepped through the heavy oak doors and into a windowless antechamber. An ornate chandelier cast the room in a bright yellow glow. “Good evening, Mr. Huff,” said a man just inside the door. “May I take your coat and hat?” Edward surrendered the items and waited patiently while the man disappeared into the nearby closet. “Right this way, sir,” the man said upon return.

Edward followed him to the other side of the antechamber where he opened the interior door and swept his hand out to invite Mr. Huff inside. Edward crossed the threshold and entered into a world of luxury that he hardly believed existed on Earth.

The house was exquisitely furnished. Mahogany dining tables were set with silver-plated candlesticks and porcelain dishes. There were felt-covered gaming tables near the back and plush lounges filled the corners of the room. Near the door, a long, polished bar stood in front of an extraordinary collection of liquor from all over the world. In a City where the finer things in life were increasingly difficult to come by, Mary Ann had never failed to answer the demands of her clientele.

Mary Ann Hall carefully orchestrated her operation to provide her clients with an evening of luxury and intimacy while extracting as much of their money as possible. Men in handsome suits and tuxedos enjoyed the attentions of Mary Ann's *intimates* while dining on Beef Wellington and drinking the finest wines in the City. Afterwards, clients were encouraged to enjoy the gaming tables and a cigar before retiring upstairs. Even there, the ladies were trained to order a bottle of champagne or wine before getting down to the business at hand. If a man was looking for a cheap quickie, he wouldn't find it at Mary Ann's.

Stepping inside, Edward was instantly greeted by a beautiful woman in an embroidered silk dress. "It's nice to see you again, Edward," she said, handing him a crystal tumbler with a healthy splash of Maker's Mark. "Compliments of Mary Ann."

"Delightful to be seen again," Edward said, taking the glass. The woman gave him a shallow curtsy. "Margaret," Edward said before she could leave, "I wonder if you might know where I could find Commander Glasson."

Like all of Mary Ann's intimates, Margaret had been trained in the art of discretion. A client's secrets, desires, and whereabouts were almost never shared. But Margaret knew Edward and Glasson were friends and that Glasson would be pleased to see him. And pleasing the client was always the top priority. "You've just missed him for dinner," Margaret said, "but I believe he's in the Nicholas Room."

Edward's eyes instinctively traveled to the heavy oak door at back of the room. "Ah, of course. Thank you, Margaret."

The Nicholas Room was a private area at the back of the house where Mary Ann's most important customers could indulge themselves in seclusion. It was where the truly rich and powerful relaxed amongst friends over a glass of port and a game of cards. Edward had spent countless time and money at Mary Ann's before finally securing an invitation, but it was worth the effort. The deepest secrets of this forsaken City were stored in the Nicholas Room.

"Good evening, Mr. Huff," said the man standing by the door. Edward nodded and tucked a dollar bill in his gloved hand. "Thank you, sir," the man said as he opened the door to the most exclusive room in the City. When it came to opening doors, Edward had always found that money was far more effective than the heel of a boot.

Similar to the front of the house, the Nicholas Room had felt gaming tables and lounge areas where ladies entertained the men who were sitting out a round of cards. Edward laughed inwardly at the irony. As the patron saint of prostitutes, Saint Nicholas was supposed to rescue women from taking up the world's oldest profession. Scanning the room, it was clear that rescuing prostitutes was the last thing on anyone's mind.

"Edward!" came a booming voice over the quiet conversation in the room.

Edward turned to see the wide smile and even wider frame of Commander John Glasson. The gold epaulettes on Glasson's shoulder danced as he waved Edward over to his table. Edward crossed the room and met the man with a firm handshake. "I see you're back in town," Glasson said excitedly. "I hope your trip to the mountains proved profitable."

"It went as well as could be expected," Edward said with a glimmer in his eye.

Glasson leaned back to get a better look at his expression. "You've found another fortune!" Glasson laughed. "By God, I can see it in your eyes! Come," he said through the tail of his laughter. "Have a seat."

Edward took the open chair and Glasson introduced him to the other players at the table. In addition to the Commander, there were two of the City's largest bankers, a Congressman from New York and the young heir to the Bellefontaine railway fortune.

"So," Edward said, "what are we playing?"

"Five-card," said Glasson. Union soldiers had recently invented five-card stud and Edward had developed quite a knack for it. A devilish grin crossed his face.

"Now, Edward," Glasson said. "Do take it easy on us. We've set a ten dollar limit and have no intention of raising it."

Edward raised his hands in surrender. "I'm just thankful you've invited me to play."

With the table limit confirmed, the dealer threw out the first round of cards. Edward casually observed Commander Glasson out of the corner of his eye. The combination of alcohol, cigars and women had the naval officer in a relaxed and pliable state but Edward had to be cautious. In this room of traitorous men, patience was his only ally. He would see where the conversation started and then direct it exactly where he wanted it to go. Edward checked his cards to see a pair of kings.

"So Commander," said Congressman Briggs, "you were telling us of Ball's Bluff."

"Yes," Glasson said glumly, "I've just returned from a trip up river. My men counted over one hundred bodies that had washed ashore. But news of how the battle ended is scarce."

Edward couldn't believe it. Luck really was on his side tonight. He had his opening. "I've just had a conversation with Secretary Cameron," he said casually as he glanced at his cards. The table was instantly silenced. Edward looked up from his cards to see that all eyes, including the dealer's, were on him. The lingering silence only tightened his grip on the conversation and he let it hang for a moment longer.

When Glasson appeared ready to burst, Edward continued, "The news from Ball's Bluff is not good, gentlemen." Edward's tone was solemn and controlled. "It appears that we may have lost a thousand men and lost the battle as well." Several of the players looked down at the table as if the need to pray had overcome them. "But that's not all the Secretary said," Edward continued. "He places the blame for the loss entirely on General McClellan and said he would be speaking to Lincoln about taking his command."

"You're not serious," said Commander Glasson. "Take McClellan's command?"

Edward looked down and nodded in disbelief. "It seems the administration has little tolerance for failures in military leadership." Glasson's face turned white as a ghost. The hook was set. "Come now, John," Edward said. "You needn't worry. The Union Navy is doing a fine job on the seas."

"What about the blockade?" It was the brash young heir at the far end of the table. "It seems to me the Confederate Navy has this City withering on the vine." He turned to Commander Glasson. "Aren't you the commander of the Potomac fleet? Aren't you to blame if this suffering continues?" The man's tone hinted that he was more concerned about the cost of his suits than the tides of war.

"Well, I," Glasson stammered and Edward jumped in.

"Sir, I would remind you that you are speaking to a hero of war. This fine man commanded the USS Perry against three frigates, including the Confederate privateer Chotank, which is now resting at the bottom of the sea. No one in the entire U.S. Navy is more capable or qualified to break this infernal blockade!" Edward's blood was up and he slammed his hand on the table for good effect. "I would stake my life that Commander Glasson has a plan to send those traitors to God and country straight into the Devil's arms!"

Edward turned to Glasson who had regained his color and his composure. He sat up straight, as if a rod had been thrust down his spine. "As ever, my friend Edward is correct. A plan is in place and the blockade will be broken!"

A smug look crossed the young heir's face as he turned his cards over to reveal a pair of jacks. "Agh," Glasson said in disgust. He threw his cards on the table and stood. "I believe I need a break from play. Edward, would you care to join me?"

Edward stood and glared at the heir. "Gladly," he said, folding his hand and sliding his kings to the dealer.

# Chapter 10

October 22, 1861 – 7th Ward, Washington City

Edward followed Commander Glasson out of the Nicholas Room to the bar at the front of the house. Glasson ordered two Maker's Marks, which the bartender promptly delivered. The service at Mary Ann's was impeccable.

"The petulance of young wealth is nearly too much to bear," Glasson said, thinking of the smug look on Bellefontaine's face.

"In my experience," Edward observed, "those who don't earn their own wealth are ultimately suffocated by it."

Glasson chuckled and held up his drink. "Well we can be thankful for that!"

They clinked glasses and Edward took a long sip as he calculated how to guide the conversation back to the Union's plans to break the blockade. He decided to proceed with caution. "How are things at the Yard?" he began. The Washington Naval Yard was the largest naval and manufacturing installation in the Union. "Are you finding it difficult to keep up with the sudden demands of war?"

"We're keeping up," Glasson said confidently. "But we're having to expand. We've added a new furnace, which will soon double our iron production. And that means twice as many balls, plate, and anchors with which to push back these Southern scoundrels. We've also expanded into things of a more," Glasson paused to search the ceiling for the right word, "*experimental* nature."

Edward's heart pounded and he sipped his whiskey to mask his excitement. There was a true art to gathering intelligence, which often arrived in disparate pieces and fragmented thoughts. An operative had to know which fragments to collect and which to leave behind. Collecting a single piece of bad information could color the entire picture in the wrong light. There was no doubt that the doubling of the Navy's iron production was information worth collecting. The vague mention of Union experiments was less clear. Perhaps it would fit into a larger picture and perhaps not. The game was still young.

"All this expansion means we're on the constant lookout for skilled labor," Glasson continued. "We've hired every ironworker, ship builder, and carpenter we can find and we're still short handed."

"It seems an awful lot to manage," said Edward.

"It certainly is," Glasson agreed. "The only way to manage it is with whiskey." Edward glanced at his glass and raised his eyebrows. "Nothing as good as Maker's Mark, I assure you," Glasson explained, "but the stuff arrives every morning in fifty barrel lots."

And just like that, Edward's opening appeared. "Fifty barrels a day?" he asked as if the sum was too great to fathom. "How ever do they get the supplies through the blockade?"

Glasson sipped his whiskey. "Ah, Edward. You really never were much of a seaman. A complete blockade of a port is almost impossible. Some of the smaller schooners can make it through by simply out maneuvering the Southern guns. Even larger ships can sometimes make it through if the conditions are right. But mostly, getting a larger ship to port is like threading a needle with a ball of yarn. Many of the ships simply don't make it."

"That's exactly the problem," Edward said. "The blockade is tearing at the morale of this City. It simply does no good for the nation's capital to be cut off from the sea. There must be a way to stop it!"

"There is a way," Glasson said. He leaned in close and cut his eyes around the room. "We have a solution, Edward," he said in a near whisper. "The President has ordered some extraordinary measures. Truly extraordinary. It has taken us some time but we're almost there." Glasson's eyes danced with excitement.

Edward's heart beat heavy in his chest. He had Glasson pushed to the edge and the answers Edward needed were just within his reach. He stared into the amber whiskey at the bottom of his glass hoping Glasson would answer the question left hanging in the air. But the silence between them remained too long. The moment was slipping away. Edward didn't know whether to push further or to hold back but he had to decide.

"Well," he finally said, careful to keep his voice down, "what have you got for us, John? What's the solution?"

Glasson thought for a moment but then suddenly stood up straight and cleared his throat. "I may have already said more than I should. Top secret and all, you know."

Edward silently cursed himself but he was determined to squeeze every drop from the conversation. "Of course, of course," he said. "I understand the difficulty of your position. If you can't tell me what the solution is, perhaps you can at least tell me when I might see it. I've grown tired of paying double for my drink."

Glasson smiled and raised his glass. "I can tell you this: if things go right, you shall never see the solution at all."

Edward lifted his glass to meet Glasson's and drank. The Union had gone to extraordinary measures to try and break the blockade but Glasson's cryptic comment only obscured what those measures were.

"Now," Glasson said, draining the last of his whiskey, "how about we return to the game and relieve young Bellefontaine of his winnings?"

Edward knew he had gotten all he could from Commander Glasson tonight. It was time to leave. He pulled a gold watch from his pocket and frowned. "The journey from Colorado has done me in," he said. "I'm afraid another game would only increase Bellefontaine's fortune at the expense of my own."

"Right then," Glasson said, patting his large belly. "I shall have to slay the beast myself. Have a good rest," he said, turning toward the Nicholas Room. "I'm sure to see you at the Willard."

Edward drank the last drop of Maker's from his glass and stepped out into the cool October night. He needed a safe place to sit and think. Suddenly, an idea came to mind. Edward smiled and called for his carriage.

# Chapter 11

October 22, 1861 – 3rd Ward, Washington City

Levi Love left Venerable's whorehouse—the conversation with Christine Brandy consuming his thoughts as he retraced his steps down 10th Street. Christine had provided some useful details about what had happened, but hopes of quickly finding Ellen Wolfe's murderer were as dark as the Canal that had taken her body for its own.

Ellen had gone to Christine in a panic. She knew the man she had just seen would one day take her life and she had to tell someone. But to protect her friend's safety, she refused to tell Christine the man's name. Instead, Ellen handed her a meaningless scroll of paper and said the police should talk to the one-eared, colored man named Josiah. But Levi couldn't talk to Josiah because an unknown group of men—probably slave-catchers—had snatched him right off the street and taken him God knows where. Levi knew that when a colored man was taken from the streets of Washington City, he was rarely seen again. Levi had reached a dead end.

Levi's stomach growled as he waited for a carriage to pass before crossing C Street. He hadn't eaten since before the Canal, which seemed like a lifetime ago. An image of the blackened waters and the butchered face of Ellen Wolfe flashed in his mind. He blinked to wash the gruesome scene away and opened his eyes to see the gold-lettered sign of Harvey's Oyster Salon hanging overhead. Levi smiled for the first time all day.

When the Harvey brothers first opened their Oyster Salon in an old blacksmith's shop, there was little demand for their peculiar offerings. Now, just three years later, the two brothers found themselves swamped by customers demanding oysters. Business soared when the fad took hold in the U.S. Army, who often ordered the creatures in five hundred gallon lots.

To keep up with demand, Harvey's supply ships were forced to run the Southern blockade daily, regardless of the risk. Just last week the Evening Star reported rebel guns had taken down one of Harvey's schooners, the Mary Willis. All souls, and all oysters, on board were lost but the Harvey brothers were determined. They ordered their supply ships to continue running the gauntlet and the raw oysters continued to arrive at the corner of 10th and P by the wagonload. Oysters were an obsession of wartime Washington and Levi Love was no exception.

Levi stepped into Harvey's Oyster Salon where the gleaming, hundred-foot-long bar—the longest in the City—was crowded with customers. Twenty men scurried around behind the bar cracking oysters on demand and scalding them in steaming caldrons. Levi stepped through a crowd of soldiers and found his way to the far end of the bar where a few open seats remained.

He had just sat down when a sweaty clammer appeared on the other side of the bar. "How many?" he asked, wiping his hands on his apron.

"A dozen," Levi said.

The clammer quickly retreated to the steam cauldrons and a burst of laughter from the soldiers up front drew Levi's attention. He looked down the length of the bar to see the soldiers slapping one another on the back and raising their glasses for another drink. Suddenly, the knot of blue uniforms loosened and a man pushed his way through. Levi's stomach constricted and his pulse raced as the man emerged from the crowd. He had a greasy black beard and a leather eye patch over one eye. It was the man from Venerable's bar.

The man stopped and slowly scanned the restaurant. Levi slipped his hand from the bar and placed it on his stick. He watched closely as the man slowly scanned the length of the bar from one customer to the next. Reaching the end, his eye found Levi and stopped cold. The man's eye narrowed and he stared at

Levi for a long moment. Levi's pulse quickened. The man's presence at Venerable's, and now at Harvey's, could not be a coincidence. He was after Levi and, chances were, he was after blood. Beneath the bar, Levi gripped the handle of the rosewood baton and slowly unhooked it from his belt.

The man tightened his jaw and his greasy beard shimmered in the yellow light of the chandelier overhead. With his eye locked onto Levi, the man walked directly towards the end of the bar. Levi's muscles coiled and his breath grew steady as the man rounded the corner. If the man wanted blood, he would surely see some of his own. The greasy stranger came to a stop and glanced down to see Levi's firm grip on the hardwood club. Slowly, he leaned over to within an inch of Levi's ear.

"I know what you're looking for," the man said. His voice was rough and his breath fetid. Confused and disgusted, Levi tried to lean away but the man pressed in. "You're looking for that one-eared negro."

Levi's eyes widened. The man stood and, seeing the utter confusion on Levi's face, he let loose a crazed laugh that sounded like a lamb being taken to slaughter. Levi recoiled as the man's laugh revealed three blackened teeth hanging loosely from his otherwise abandoned gums.

"His name is Josiah," Levi said over the man's laughter. "What do you know about him?" Levi was anxious to get the conversation over with.

The man stepped around Levi and sat in the next empty chair. "I'll start with a dozen," he said. His information clearly came with a price.

Just then, the clammer appeared with Levi's order and set it on the bar. Levi looked at the bearded man and then down at the steaming tray of oysters. His stomach growled. Reluctantly, he slid the tray across the bar in front of the man. "You better have something to say," Levi said.

"Oh I got something to say alright," he said, digging greedily into the first oyster.

"How about we start with your name," Levi suggested.

"Name's Cordell," he said, slurping a second muscle from its shell. "And I know where your colored man is." He smiled to reveal bits of oyster clinging to his lonely teeth.

Levi looked away. "How would you know that?"

"I was there that night. I seen it all." Another oyster vanished into the beard leaving beads of juice behind.

Levi had no reason to believe a word that came out of this man's decayed mouth. But if Cordell really knew where Josiah was, then the hunt for Ellen Wolfe's killer was on. For the moment, Levi had little choice but to indulge the man and his appetite. "Alright then," Levi said, "where were you and what exactly did you see?"

Cordell finished the last oyster and pushed the tray of empty shells to the far edge of the bar. He turned and stared at Levi in silence. Further details required further payment. A clammer appeared, as if on cue. "Another dozen for my friend here," Levi said with at look that all but dared Cordell to order another.

Satisfied the order was in, Cordell continued. "I was sitting on Venerable's front porch drinking my whiskey and dreaming of cunny. That one-eared carpenter was out there banging on the clapboard when a covered wagon drove around front kicking up all kinds of dust. By the time the dust cleared, four men done hopped out the back of that wagon and snatched your boy right off the porch."

Cordell chuckled and shook his head. "That boy's a fighter though, I'll tell you that. He didn't go quietly. He was kickin' and swinging the whole way until they got him good and hog-tied. Weren't much he could do then. Them boys threw him in the back of that wagon and tore out of there. I swear I could hear that negro screaming all the way down P Street."

Stories of slaves getting pulled off the streets were all too common in the City. Levi had witnessed Sergeant Corbett do it countless times. If the slave wasn't actually a fugitive, Corbett would stuff him in the cellar behind his house for a day or two and make him one. Then, Corbett would return the slave to its master and demand a finder's fee. It was just one of the many savage ways in which men were brokered for money in this City. But Josiah wasn't a slave and there was no finder's fee to be had.

"You know Josiah's a freedman," Levi said indignantly. "Why didn't you do something?"

Cordell looked at Levi as if he'd just sprouted a horn. "Now what am I to do against four men?" he asked but he didn't wait for an answer. "I couldn't do nothin' against them boys." Just then, the clammer slid the second tray of steaming oysters across the bar. Cordell eyed it hungrily. "Besides," he added, diving into the first shell, "I knew who them boys were and where they were taking your negro. Didn't even need to get off my chair to know that."

Cordell sucked down three muscles in a row. "Well?" Levi prodded impatiently. "Who the hell were they?"

Cordell faced Levi and sucked a bit of meat off his tooth. "Them's William H. Williams' boys."

The name hit Levi like a punch in the gut. He sat back in his chair and let out a heavy sigh. A master at running slaves, William H. Williams was the largest and most ruthless slave trader within two hundred miles of Washington City. Ten years ago, the law banned the sale of slaves in the City but Williams simply took his operation underground. Instead of selling his slaves at Center Market, Williams sold them from dozens of cellars and makeshift prisons hidden around town. Williams constantly moved his stock around the City, using his network of secret dungeons in an endless human shell game. Better to fall off the face of the Earth than to be picked up by William H. Williams.

Levi sat up and collected himself. The longer Josiah stayed with Williams, the deeper and darker his hole became. "You said you know where they took him."

"Sure do," Cordell said. He sucked another oyster from the shell. "Took him to Roby's."

Roby's was a rundown tavern not too far from the Capitol that was known for its hatred of the Union. Levi threw a dollar on the counter and stood to leave.

"Whoa," Cordell said, grabbing Levi's arm. "Where you going?"

"Where do you think?" Levi asked. "I'm going to Roby's."

"You're going to Roby's, by yourself, at night, looking to free a slave captured by William H. Williams?" Cordell barely got the question out before he expelled a laugh that sounded like bleating goat. When Cordell finally recovered himself, he said, "I've got good word they're pushing your boy to the Deep South. These days it takes time to make a move like that—even for William H. Williams. Best you go in the morning."

"What if they've moved him by then?" Levi asked.

Cordell shook the question off. "Don't you worry," he said. "He'll be there in the morning."

Levi looked down at Cordell and a nagging question came to mind. "How do you know all of this?"

Cordell stood and wiped his mouth with the sleeve of his leather coat. "This City's rotting from the inside out," he said. "There's always schemes. There's always lies." He stopped to look Levi straight in the eye. "And there's always spies."

# Chapter 12

October 22, 1861 – 4th Ward, Washington City

Edward Huff rapped his cane on the roof of the carriage and the driver reined the horses to a stop. Opening the door himself, Edward stepped out into the wealthy residential enclave at the corner of New York Avenue and H. The crisp October air chilled his lungs as the carriage clattered off and disappeared into the night. Then, setting his cane to ground, Edward followed the long string of gas lamps that marked his path along this affluent stretch of H Street.

Opulent mansions lined both sides of the road and housed the City's wealthiest bankers, politicians and industrialists. Edward had met most of these men either in Willard's lobby or over a game of cards at Mary Ann Hall's but he had no desire to see any of them tonight. If someone happened to recognize him, Edward had a ready excuse as to why he was wandering H Street at this hour of the night but it would be far better to avoid such complications. For the delicate business at hand, it was best to go unnoticed.

Edward strolled along H Street and admired the passing homes until he saw a three-story brownstone with a bright red door. He glanced over his shoulder to ensure he was alone before turning down the dirt carriageway running alongside the mansion. The path grew dark as the light from the gas lamps on H Street began to fade. Edward slowed his pace to compensate for the dark and uneven surface of the carriageway until he saw a pair of thick oak gates at the back of the property.

Edward stopped at the gates and glanced back up the carriageway towards H Street. A haze formed around the distant gas lamps as a fine mist began to fall over the deserted lane. Certain he was alone, Edward knelt down and began tracing his fingertips around the bricks at the bottom of the wall. His pulse quickened with anticipation. On his third attempt, he hit his mark—a small hole in the mortar just large enough for man's finger. Inserting his finger into the hole, Edward pulled on the brick until it broke free from its mortar to reveal a small cavity. He thrust his hand inside. The hole was damp but small and he easily found the item hidden within. Grabbing the object, he stood to examine it in the moonlight.

The waxed leather bag had been folded over twice and tied with a string. Edward squeezed the leather and felt the resistance of the object inside. He untied the string and cupped his hand before turning the bag up. The leather case relinquished the item, which fell gently into Edward's palm. Looking down, a thin smile spread across his face. The iron key was exactly where it was promised to be.

Stepping to the oak gates, Edward slid the key into the lock and gave it a turn. The mechanism resisted at first but finally gave way with a heavy clack. Edward held his breath as he gently tested the gate, but the hinges complied without a sound. Edward slipped quietly through the opening and into the estate.

The moon cast a silver light across the yard and the small formal garden behind the mansion. Standing inside the locked gate in his top hat and coat, Edward felt as out of place as he looked. If he was caught now, no amount of lies could explain away his presence. He glanced across the back of the property where a clapboard carriage house stood at the end of a gravel path. With time against him, Edward hurried down the path to the wooden door on the side of the carriage house and stepped quietly inside.

The carriage house was pitch black and Edward fumbled around on a nearby table until he found a brass lantern and a box of matches. The match ignited with a hiss and Edward touched the flame to the lamp's oil-soaked wick. A halo of orange light grew from the center of the lantern and reflected off the massive carriage that filled the room. Edward skirted around the end of the carriage to find a wooden ladder leading to the loft above.

Grabbing the ladder with his free hand, Edward started his climb. When his full weight hit the bottom rung, the ladder let out creak that stopped him in his tracks. For a long moment, he stood stock-still and just listened. The only sound was his own heart beating hard in his temple but something in his gut told him to be cautious. Slowly, he shifted his gaze to the top of the ladder.

Was someone waiting for him on the other side of the darkened hole above? Had he trusted too many people? Had someone sold him out? Edward's palm sweated against the frame of the ladder as he thought of all the consequences. But every moment he spent in this City had consequences. There was simply no other way.

Edward set his jaw and continued the climb. Nearing the top of the ladder, he reached over his head and set the lantern at the edge of the landing. Then, heart pounding, he slowly pushed his head through the opening and peered into the space above. Edward breathed a sigh of relief. The loft wasn't full of Union soldiers waiting in the dark. The only thing waiting for him was a dusty old trunk in the middle of the room.

Edward pulled himself into the loft and got straight to work. He opened the trunk to find a well-worn set of workman's clothes and a brown cotton bag. Stripping down to his underwear, he quickly changed into the clothes and slipped on the pair of leather work boots. He folded his black suit neatly at the bottom of the trunk and looked into the mirror on the underside of the lid. With the glasses and top hat gone, his transformation was well underway but the beard would have to go. Edward pulled on the sideburn and his skin stretched in fierce resistance. Pulling harder, he opened his mouth in a silent scream until the bond finally broke and the beard peeled away. It felt as if half his face had peeled away with it.

Looking back in the mirror, he no longer saw Edward Huff. He saw only the lowly wagon maker, Nicholas Turner. Edward had gathered valuable intelligence from Commander Glasson and he certainly had more work to do. But tomorrow's operation at the Armory required a tradesman, not a wealthy silver miner from Colorado. So it was time for Edward Huff to sleep and Nicholas Turner to rise.

With everything in place, Nicholas grabbed the brown cotton bag from the trunk and dumped its contents on the floor. A bound stack of cash fell out first, followed by the clatter of a thin knife in a leather sheath. Nicholas smiled. He strapped the knife inside his boot and covered it with his pants before stuffing the cash in his pocket.

Throwing the cotton bag into the trunk, Nicolas closed the lid and threw the latch. The driver of the carriage below would ensure the trunk arrived safely back at Quigly's, where its contents would be cleaned, pressed and made ready for Edward's return.

Nicolas climbed down the ladder and retraced his steps across the moonlit yard and through the gate. Walking quickly down H Street, the grand stone mansions soon gave way to the plain wooden houses of Washington's working class. The mist hanging in the air cooled Nicholas' face and dampened his clothes as he turned onto 6$^{th}$ Street. Passing beneath a row of immature oak trees, he reached the end of a series of row houses where a flight of stairs led to Mary Surratt's boarding house.

Nicholas breathed a sigh of exhaustion. There were no more taverns, no more card games, no more changes to his identity. To survive tomorrow, he would have to be at his best. There was nothing he needed more than the comforting hospitality of Mary Surratt and the warm bed that she provided.

# Chapter 13

October 23, 1861 – 7th Ward, Washington City

Carrie Fleck hurried to the gate at the U.S. Arsenal on Greenleaf's Point. She had made the mile journey from her one-room home as fast as she could but she was still fifteen minutes late. Her three-year-old daughter Elizabeth caught a fever that had been lingering for days. Once again, Carrie had stayed up all night nursing her but the fever refused to break. Lingering fevers could be deadly but Carrie had to work. Without money for food or heat, death was certain to find her darling Elizabeth.

Carrie had asked her neighbors if they would watch over Elizabeth during the day but they had their own work and their own problems to deal with. So Carrie returned to Elizabeth's bedside feeling more alone than she knew possible. Elizabeth was all she had in this world. She held her daughter's hand and asked for her promise not to get out of bed until Carrie returned from work. Elizabeth nodded weakly and Carrie rushed out the door.

Seeing the state she was in and noting the time, the soldier guarding the Arsenal's gate waved Carrie through without delay. The U.S. Arsenal occupied the entire peninsula at Greenleaf's Point and was the largest storehouse for munitions in the Union. Carrie cut across the vast central yard towards the buildings and storehouses on the other side. She passed row upon row of shining new cannons and rifles stacked together like teepees until she finally arrived at a plain A-frame building known simply as Workhouse D.

Carrie took a moment to catch her breath before reaching for the knob and quietly opening the door. Before she could step foot inside, a man in a blue uniform grabbed her arm and pushed her back into the yard.

"Do you know what time it is?" Carrie regained her balance and looked up to see her supervisor, Corporal Lofland, staring down at her. "You're late," he said.

"I know," Carrie said, forcing herself not to cry.

"You know how many women would be glad to have your job?"

Carrie looked at her shoes and nodded.

"Well then?" Lofland snapped. "Why are you late?"

"It's Lizzy," Carrie said, her tears breaking through against her will. "She woke up with a fever in the middle of the night. I tried my best to get here." She began to sob. "I'm sorry I'm late. It won't happen again. Please, Corporal, don't let me go. We won't be able to eat."

Then suddenly, surprisingly, a crack formed in Lofland's hard exterior. "Has the fever broke yet?"

Carrie looked up at Lofland and a tear rolled down her cheek. She shook her head.

"I've got a little girl myself," he said in a low voice. "Damn near lost her to the fever last year." Lofland looked down at Carrie for a long moment. "I tell you what," he finally said. "You pack forty casings and I'll let you go home for the day." Carrie couldn't believe what she was hearing. A thin smile surfaced through Lofland's thick beard as he opened the door. "Now get in there and get to work."

Carrie's eyes lit up. "Thank you," she said and then went straight inside.

The long room was filled with a central wooden table surrounded by twenty women hard at work. The workhouse was quiet as a tomb. Corporal Lofland hadn't ordered the women to sit in silence—it was the work itself that demanded absolute concentration. The women in Workhouse D were packing *case shot*—the most terrifying weapon in the Union's arsenal and the most dangerous to those who assembled it. Having seen what the weapon could do to a field full of young men, Carrie was convinced the Devil himself had a hand its design.

Case shot was made of a hollow iron ball filled with seventy-five smaller balls and a bursting charge nestled inside. The heavy ball was loaded into a cannon and hurled over four hundred yards before the internal timer ran out and the bursting charge exploded. When fired properly, the bursting charge would explode over the head of the opposing infantry column, propelling the iron shot indiscriminately in all directions and laying waste to anyone in its path.

The black powder used to make case shot was so highly combustible it could erupt through simple friction. Once packed tightly into the bursting charges, the powder was absolutely lethal. Workhouse D was silent because the women's lives depended on it.

Carrie hung her cloak on the wooden peg behind her chair and grabbed an empty powder tin. With the look of a small watering can, the tin was used to store a measured amount black powder and gently guide it into the cotton bags that formed the bursting charges. Every woman in Workhouse D started her day with a trip to the powder house to fill her tin.

Carrie stepped through the side door and crossed a short breezeway to a wooden storehouse. She opened the door to see kegs of black powder stacked three high and two deep. On the far wall, fully packed bursting charges were stored in wooden crates that reached up to the ceiling. The site had become so familiar that Carrie often had to remind herself that she was standing in the deadliest place in the entire City.

Following procedure, she went to the far end of the storehouse where a powder keg had been tapped and set out on a table. She placed her tin under the keg and carefully removed the cork stopper near the bottom. Black powder hissed like falling sand as it fell from the keg and slowly filled her tin. When the powder reached the top, Carrie quickly replaced the stopper but, oddly, the hissing sound carried on.

Carrie furrowed her brow and checked that the stopper was firmly in place. *Where is that hissing coming from?* She turned her head to locate the source. Setting her tin on the table, she slowly followed the sound across the room to where the powder kegs met the crates of bursting charges. Carrie stood on her toes to look over a stack of crates. The sound was getting louder.

She narrowed her eyes and peered into the dimly lit space on the other side of the wooden crates. A black cord as thick as a pencil ran from beneath the crates to a small hole in the exterior wall. The menacing hiss grew louder and faster. Suddenly, Carrie's eyes grew wide as the black cord and the strange hiss collided in her mind. She had opened her mouth to scream when a white-hot spark flew through the hole in the wall and shot down the black cord towards the bursting charges.

In that instant, she knew her life was over. An image of Elizabeth waiting patiently for her mother to return flashed before Carrie's eyes. It was the last time she would see her lovely Elizabeth.

A concussive wave of heat and light hammered Carrie in the chest like a battering ram. And then everything went dark.

# Chapter 14

October 23, 1861 – 4$^{th}$ Ward, Washington City

Nicholas Turner stared at himself in his bedroom mirror at Surratt's boarding house. The thick brown hair that had been slicked back and hidden beneath Edward Huff's top hat was now exposed and combed loosely to the side. The tailored black suit and top hat were gone and in their place, a simple cotton shirt and the wool pants of a humble tradesman. He stared at his reflection for a long moment. The change of clothes had somehow made his handsome features more accessible. Finally, he opened his eyes wide and set his jaw. Edward Huff was gone. Only Nicholas Turner remained.

The staircase creaked as Nicholas stepped into Surratt's first floor common area. The room was modestly furnished with a settee by the far window and two well-worn, but comfortable, wingback chairs by the fire. Nicholas had just lowered himself into the chair nearest the fire when a woman pushed in from the adjoining room.

"I thought I heard you come down."

Nicholas turned to see the plump figure of Mary Surratt. Wearing a plain woven dress, and with her hair pulled back in a bun, the woman had made no effort to look anything but ordinary. The only things that weren't ordinary about Mary Surratt were her eyes, which were sunk deep in their sockets and conveyed a sincere lack of intelligence.

"It's so nice to have you back," Mary said, offering her guest a cup of hot coffee. "Can I fix you some breakfast?"

Nicholas took the cup. "What time is it?"

"Quarter past seven," Mary chirped, as if there wasn't a care in the world.

Nicholas was wondering if there was any news from the Arsenal but Mary's tone indicated she hadn't heard a thing. At just a quarter past seven, Nicholas had plenty of time and decided he may as well eat. "I'll have some breakfast," he said.

Mary smiled and left for the kitchen. Nicholas returned to his coffee and stared peacefully into the flames until the clunk of heavy boots on the hollow floor pulled him from his thoughts. Nicholas glanced up to see a skinny man with slicked back hair and the kind of stringy mustache worn only by the recently pubescent. It was Mary's son, John.

The rhythmic clunk of John's pacing continued until Nicholas had had enough. "What do you want, boy?" he asked, his eyes still buried in the flames.

"I ain't no boy," John said defiantly. "I'm a man and I've been watching you."

Nicholas turned and ran his eyes over John's lanky figure before returning his gaze to the fire. "I don't fancy skinny boys like you."

John looked confused. "No," he protested, "I mean I've been watching you come and go from here for weeks. Sometimes coming, sometimes going."

"Well that's the natural way of comings and goings, ain't it?" Nicholas asked, coolly. John Surratt had obviously inherited his mother's brains.

"I mean I think you're up to something," John said. "Whatever it is you're up to, I think it's big. I think it's real big and I'm gonna be a part of it." The demand hung in the air but Nicholas simply stared into the fire and sipped his coffee as if it wasn't there. John's short fuse burned to the end. "You know, all I got to do is talk and whatever it is you're doing is over before it starts."

Nicholas lifted his head but kept his eyes focused on the orange and yellow flames. After all he'd gone through, this little shit would not be his undoing. But Nicholas still needed Mary Surratt and simply killing her petulant son would complicate matters. Besides, his scrawny physique posed no physical threat—it was his mouth that had to be dealt with.

John watched in silence as Nicholas slowly leaned forward and reached down to his boot. Suddenly, a glint of firelight danced off the six-inch blade held firmly in Nicholas' hand. "You know how hard it is to cut out a man's tongue, boy?" Nicholas asked slowly. John's mouth fell open and his legs suddenly felt like stone. Nicholas took a sip of coffee to let the question linger. "It ain't as easy as you might think," he said, turning to look John Surratt dead in the eyes.

"You see, a man don't properly understand the value of his tongue until he's about to lose it. If he ain't motivated properly, he'll slip it right through your fingers leaving *you* with an inch of useless meat, and *him* with the chance to talk again. You can't feel too bad about it though. Everybody makes that mistake the first time they take a man's tongue.

"Now the second time, you know what a tongue can do when it's fighting for its own survival. So the second time, you bring along a pair of pliers. You make sure to pull that tongue way out and hold it firm before you put your knife to it. But that's when you make your second mistake. You see, this time you go in too deep. Oh you get the whole tongue alright but there's a whole lot of blood that comes with it—enough to drown a man. There's simply no fun in watching a man drown in his own blood. So, you try again.

"The third time, you pull that tongue out real tight and hold the pliers steady. But this time, you go in at an angle. You get that angle right, you'll get all the meat and only half the blood. You understand?"

John Surratt swallowed hard to ensure his tongue was still in place. His lip began to quiver. "I'm going to make something of myself," he said, unable to hold back the tears. He quickly stormed to the door and called over his shoulder. "I'll be more famous than you'll ever be! Everybody gets their start somewhere and mine will be something you'll never forget!"

Nicholas shook his head as he slipped the knife back in his boot. John Surratt was dumber than he looked. The last thing any operative wanted was fame but as Surratt's voice trailed off down the hallway, the memory of how Nicholas had found his start as a spy pushed its way to the surface. He stared into the flames...

*April 8, 1860 – 3rd Ward, Washington City*

"Nice work tonight, Charles," said the man in puffy green pantaloons.

"You, too. See you tomorrow," Charles said as he pushed his way through the stage door and out into the alleyway behind Canterbury Theater. Emerging onto Louisiana Avenue, he took a moment to get his bearings before turning left towards 4th Street.

Charles heard the commotion spilling out of Suter's Tavern well before he reached the front steps. He pushed through the swinging saloon doors and into the raucous and rowdy crowd. A piano man combined with a trombone player in the front of the tavern and blasted out makeshift music that had half the tavern on its feet dancing. Those who weren't dancing were talking at the top of their voice, or whooping and swearing for no apparent reason.

It was only the second time Charles had been to Suter's and he was only there because it was close to the theater. There must have been a thousand other bars in the City but Charles and his troupe would be moving on to Philadelphia soon so there was no point in wasting good drinking time looking for a better venue. The women and the beer were cheap at Suter's and that was good enough reason to come back.

Charles did love the finer things in life. He loved women in lace—especially those who were properly trained in the art of pleasure. He loved porcelain dishes and roasted pheasant. And he loved good whiskey—Maker's Mark if he had his choice in the matter, which he rarely did. He had only tasted Maker's Mark once in his life and that was only because a wealthy patron purchased a round for the entire cast. But there were no wealthy patrons tonight.

Charles found an opening at the bar and waited while the portly barman rushed from one demanding customer to the next. "What do you want?" he asked, finally getting around to Charles.

"He'll have a Maker's Mark." The voice was completely unfamiliar and Charles turned to see a clean-shaven man with leathery brown skin. The face was as unfamiliar as the voice. The barman looked skeptically at the stranger. He didn't look like someone who could afford to pay for Maker's.

Sensing the barman's doubts, the man pulled out a five-dollar bill and slammed it down on the counter. "Make it a double," he said. The barman reached for the bill but the man's thick hand pinned it firmly to the bar. "You keep 'em coming until this runs out. And then," the man paused as he opened his coat and flashed a wad of bills, "you keep 'em coming just the same."

The barman eagerly poured the drink and pushed the glass across to Charles. "Follow me," said the stranger.

Charles looked at the man curiously and then glanced down at the double Maker's on the bar. Listening to what some stranger had to say seemed like a small enough price to pay for such a reward. So he took the glass and followed the man to the table farthest away from the blaring trombone. Two men were already seated at the table but, upon seeing the threatening gaze of the stranger, they grabbed their beers and cleared out of the way without a word. Charles furrowed his brow as he watched the men scurry into the crowd. What the hell was going on?

The man sat down and poked a few strands of hair under his torn felt hat. Charles had always prided himself on being a good judge of a man but the figure seated across from him was confounding.

"You're Charles Cain," the man said in a voice as leathery as his face. "I've been watching you since you got into town. Been at the Canterbury every night and I swear I ain't never seen a better Lennox."

Charles was dumbfounded. This man didn't look like someone who would regularly attend the theater and he certainly didn't appear to be a Shakespeare connoisseur. Remembering the stranger's instruction to keep the Maker's coming, Charles saw no need to rush the conversation. "Thanks," he said simply.

"I've checked into you," the man continued. "I know where you come from."

Charles' curiosity got the better of him. "And why would you check into me?" he asked and then instantly changed his diction as if he were in a Shakespearean melodrama. "I'm just a poor itinerant actor from Richmond, Virginia."

The man grinned like a cat who had caught a canary. He'd found his man. The stranger leaned forward. "I'm William Harbin." Seeing the name didn't register with his new friend, Harbin added, "brother-in-law to Thomas Jones."

Charles' eyes got wide and he sat back in his chair. Every loyal Virginian had heard of Thomas Jones. The man was a legend. He had made his reputation smuggling anything and everything across the Potomac without ever being caught. The smuggler had grown so cautious that he hadn't been seen in public in years. If the man across the table worked for Thomas Jones, something quite unexpected was at hand and Charles Cain had a role to play.

Charles leaned forward and looked Harbin in the eyes. "You work for the River Ghost?" he asked, using Jones' well-earned nickname. Harbin answered with the hint of a smile. It didn't make any sense. What did the River Ghost want with an unknown actor from Richmond? Charles grappled with the question but couldn't make the connection. "What's that got to do with me?" he asked.

"Abraham Lincoln's going to win this election," Harbin said. "And as sure as the sun rises in the morning, that means we're headed to war."

Charles shot the double Maker's in one gulp. "I hate that son of a bitch," he said, slamming the glass on the table. "But I can't turn back the election and I wouldn't stop the war if I could. If the North wants war, it's war they'll get." Charles brooded over his empty glass for a moment. "But I'm just an actor," he said. "What do you want with me?"

Harbin smiled. "I want you to act," he said and then leaned in over the table. "When the war comes, information is gonna be the most valuable resource in the South. To get it, we need someone who can operate at every level of society—someone who is as comfortable with an iron worker as he would be with the President himself." Harbin paused to ensure he had Charles' full attention. "We need an actor," he said, sitting back in his chair. "We need you."

Charles had always known that, if it truly did come down to war, he would fight. His honor demanded it. But the idea of standing in an open field to face the Union guns had never sounded honorable to him—it sounded suicidal. William Harbin had just opened his eyes. He'd given Charles a way to join the struggle against Lincoln and satisfy his honor while maintaining a reasonable distance from the Northern guns. William Harbin had given him a way out.

Charles thrust his hand across the table. “I’ll do it.”

Harbin clasped his hand with a firm grip. “I knew you would.”

# Chapter 15

October 23, 1861 – 5th Ward, Washington City

Levi grabbed his coat and walked downstairs from the room he'd rented over Thurston's Barbershop. He glanced in the window as he passed by to see that the lights were off and the barber capes were folded neatly over the empty chairs. But that wasn't surprising. Like most of the shops in the City, Thurston didn't open his doors until the more respectable hour of nine.

Turning south on New Jersey Avenue, Levi pulled his gold coin from his pocket and turned it in his hand as his thoughts returned to the questions that had kept him up half the night. Who did the greasy and toothless man he'd met at Harvey's Oyster Salon work for? Abolitionists? A rival slaver to William H. Williams? There was no way to know for certain. The only thing Levi did know was that if Josiah was still locked away at Roby's Tavern, he wouldn't be there for long. Snatching freedmen off the streets was a risky business, even for someone as practiced as William H. Williams.

Assuming Josiah was locked away beneath the tavern, the options for setting him free were limited at best. The only time this City welcomed Justice for a colored man was when she arrived with a whip in her hand. Attempting to bring freedom to one of William H. Williams' captives bordered on suicidal but it was the only way to find Ellen Wolfe's killer.

Levi weighed his options and decided his best chance of success was to start with a ruse. Failing that, he always had the option of violence. The deception he had in mind required him to leave his uniform hanging in the wardrobe and dress in his best civilian clothes. Police were rarely welcomed into the underground slave trade.

Levi turned onto New Jersey Avenue where he saw the solid brick walls of Roby's Tavern and the white pillars of the Capitol's half-completed dome in the distance. The harsh irony of the image was impossible to reconcile. Just blocks away from the nation's source of law and justice, a notorious slaver stored his illicit stock beneath a house of ill repute. As the Capitol slowly faded from view behind Roby's brick facade, Levi realized the half-completed dome reflected the true reality of law and justice in this City.

Levi stepped into Roby's to see that, as he had hoped, the tavern was empty at this time of morning. James Roby was sweeping the back corner of the bar and didn't notice his first customer of the day.

Levi cleared his throat. "Excuse me, sir," he said, affecting his best Southern accent.

Roby looked up from his broom. "Can I help you?"

"I believe you can," Levi said, stepping further inside. "My name is Joshua Jones and I represent the interests of Mr. Stephen Duncan of Natchez, Mississippi. Mr. Duncan has sent me to see if he might conduct a little business with your Mr. Williams." Stephen Duncan was one of the wealthiest men in the South, with a well-known and voracious appetite for slaves.

Roby's eyes grew wide. The mere mention of Stephen Duncan's name had captured his full attention. In exchange for storing Williams' slaves, Roby received both a daily fee and a percentage of the sale price. Roby quickly leaned his broom against the wall and rounded the bar towards Levi. "Nice to meet you Mr. Jones," he said, shaking Levi's hand. "Mr. Williams isn't here but I'm sure he'd be interested in Mr. Duncan's business."

"Now hold on a minute," Levi said. "Who's to say there's any business to conduct?" Roby dropped Levi's hand and stared at him skeptically. "I'm here with the full authority of Mr. Duncan himself," Levi explained. "So talking to me is just like talking to him. And that means *I'm* the one to say whether there's any business to be done around here." Levi paused to let the message sink in. "I'm going to need to see your stock before *I* decide whether you've got anything worth buying."

Roby eyed Levi while he considered the argument. He had no idea who this Joshua Jones was or whether he could be trusted. But then, William H. Williams had ways of dealing with abolitionists and would-be thieves. Williams had once flayed a man's face to the bone for simply skimming ten dollars off the top of a sale. If this Joshua Jones was something other than what he said, Williams' boys would know exactly how to take care of him. For Roby, the chance of getting his hand inside Stephen Duncan's purse was more than he could resist.

"Well then," Roby said through a forced smile, "we'd better go see that stock."

Levi followed Roby through the back door and into a hallway that led to the alley behind the tavern. A narrow staircase at the end of the hall descended to a darkened room below. "Boys?" Roby called down the stairs. "I'm sending a Mr. Joshua Jones down to take a look around." There was no answer but Roby urged Levi towards the stairs with a nod. "The boys will take good care of you."

"They had better," Levi said with a confidence that masked his uncertainty. Levi had hoped Roby's greed would blind him to the truth behind his deception but, descending the darkened stairway, Levi was suddenly aware of the danger he was in. He was completely alone and, wearing a disguise as thin as a whore's gown, headed straight into an illegal slave pen to steal a freedman from William H. Williams. But it was too late for second thoughts. If he turned back now, Roby would have him for sure and William H. Williams would extract his revenge.

Levi's heart hammered in his chest as he turned the corner and disappeared from Roby's sight. With each new step, his view into the room below grew wider until two men suddenly appeared out of the dim lamplight at the bottom of the stairs. Though Levi was larger than either of the men, their combined effort would give them a firm advantage. Levi clenched his fists. If these men were looking for a fight, Levi was prepared to give them one.

One of the men lifted the oil lamp and Levi saw for the first time that both of their faces were deeply scarred. The man with the lamp was pockmarked from a festering skin disease, while the other carried the slash of a cavalry saber from forehead to chin.

Reaching the bottom step, the stench of stale air and human waste hung thick like a cloud. Levi's stomach wretched but he held fast. Slavers were used to the fetor of their trade and the slightest flinch could give him away. The men stared at Levi for a long moment before the silence finally broke.

"Who are you?" asked the pockmarked man.

"My name is Joshua Jones," Levi said, looking first at Pockmark and then over to Slash. "Personal representative of Mr. Stephen Duncan. I'm here on his behalf and with his authority to purchase up to five of your slaves, if, indeed, there are five worth purchasing." Levi tried to look further into the cellar but the men held their ground. "Now," Levi said through clinched teeth, "I suggest you men stand aside and let me get on with this transaction or I assure you Mr. Williams will learn exactly how you impeded our trade."

The demand lingered and Slash looked to Pockmark for the proper response. A wide smile spread over Pockmark's face. "Mr. Williams only deals in the finest of niggers," he said as he stepped aside and swept his hand to invite Levi into the cellar. "Come see for yourself."

When the men cleared the way, Levi saw that he was standing in a long, barrel-vaulted room that ran the length of the tavern above. A wall of iron bars separated the small landing area from the slave pen. Levi peered through the bars to see dozens of iron manacles dangling from the brick walls along either side of the room. The empty chains spoke of a time not so long ago when the slave trade thrived on the City's streets and Roby's slave pen was packed to capacity with human cargo. Since trading inside the City was now illegal, William H. Williams couldn't afford to put all his eggs in one basket. So this once thriving slave pen was now reduced to a mere six souls.

Levi narrowed his eyes and looked deep into the prison but the captives were no more than shadows in the dark. "Is this all you've got?" he asked.

"No," said Pockmark. "It's just all we've got here." He tapped a small leather-bound notebook in his breast pocket. "There's plenty more," he added, puffing up his chest with pride. "This is Mr. Williams we're talking about."

Levi stepped back from the bars. "I'm going to need a closer look to see if any of your stock is up to Mr. Duncan's standards. If not, then perhaps we can look into the others on your list." The two men wore blank stares and Levi noticed the keys dangling from Slash's belt. "Well?" he asked, nodding to the keys. "Are you going to open this door or am I to find another slaver more willing to do business?"

Slash put his hands on the keys and looked to Pockmark for direction. Pockmark considered Levi carefully. "Open the cage," he said. Slash turned the key and the door swung open with a grinding screech.

"You niggers stand up!" Pockmark yelled into the dark. Shadows on the floor began to move to the discordant sound of their own chains.

Pockmark held his lamp high and led the way into the damp, cold pen. Levi followed in the glow of the lamplight until it spread across the sallow face of the first captive. It was a young woman about the age of nineteen. Her short hair framed a pair of brown eyes that conveyed a depth of despair Levi could not begin to fathom. A pain in his chest urged Levi to reach out to her but reason held his hands in place. The slightest hint of compassion in this forgotten piece of hell would seal his fate.

"Mr. Duncan is looking for field hands," Levi said. "This one here won't do."

"Field hands, huh?" Pockmark said, leading Levi deeper into the dungeon. "Well then you're sure to like this next one." The lamplight slipped from the woman's face, leaving her in a darkness that mirrored her destiny.

They passed several sets of empty shackles before the profile of a man emerged out of the black. Pockmark came to a stop and raised the lantern up so that it was even with the man's face. "This here is Ben," he said. "He's known many a day in the field and he's stronger than an ox."

Levi slowly circled the man, looking him over from head to toe. He had broad, muscular shoulders and thick hands that were calloused from years of manual labor. When he completed his circle, Levi glanced to the side of the man's head to see that his right ear was quite in tact. Levi stepped back and gazed at the man as if admiring a fine painting.

"This one here's got some potential," he said. "How much does Mr. Williams want for him?"

"A thousand," said Pockmark.

"Oh really?" Levi said, nearly choking on the enormous fee. He pointed at Ben. "This one right here? A thousand dollars?"

"That's right," Pockmark said.

"You do know that's some two-hundred dollars more than Mr. Duncan paid for even his most prized field hand." Pockmark didn't respond. He didn't set the prices and had no authority to negotiate but it didn't matter. The man with the thousand-dollar price tag wasn't Josiah and Levi had no means to purchase him at any price.

Levi eyed the slave again, as if reconsidering. "He is a fine specimen," Levi observed. "Perhaps if you show me another one like him, we can find some common ground for doing business."

Pockmark smiled. "I know just the one," he said, cutting across the pen. "And he's right over here."

The light from Pockmark's lantern faded and Levi turned to follow. Reaching the opposite wall, the light fell upon a tall and handsome man with a broad chest and muscular arms that flexed beneath his thin white shirt. Levi circled the man to see a well-kept beard running down his jaw and up the other side of his face where it ended at a butchered and half-missing ear.

Levi's heart pounded hard against his breastbone. The odds of finding a colored man taken from the streets of Washington City were inconceivable. Levi held the man's gaze for a long moment. His deep brown eyes conveyed a confidence and pride the chains had yet to break. And with that, Levi knew. He'd found Josiah.

Blood surged through Levi's veins as excitement and relief welled inside. But just as it began to swell, Levi forced it back down. Finding Josiah was one thing—getting him out of this buried prison was quite another. The second half of Levi's plan was even more dangerous than the first.

Levi stepped back from Josiah and turned directly to Pockmark. "Do you think Mr. Duncan is stupid?"

The question caught Pockmark off guard and his face screwed up in confusion. "What?"

"It's a simple question," Levi said, his voice firm with anger. "Do you think Mr. Duncan is stupid?"

Pockmark shook his head, still confused. "I don't even know Mr. Duncan."

"Well then, let me tell you something about him. Mr. Duncan pays good money to know everything about the slavers he's dealing with and the slaves he's dealing in. That good money has purchased information that says this boy here is a freedman." The slaver's eyes widened in surprise as Levi pressed on. "Mr. Duncan isn't stupid enough to buy a freedman and he certainly wouldn't buy one at full price."

Pockmark was struck dumb and Slash blurted his way into the discussion. "He ain't no freedman," he said.

"Oh he ain't?" Levi asked, as he turned to see the lamplight playing tricks across Slash's deep scar.

"No," Slash said, looking to the floor for answers. Then an idea struck him. "When we got him he didn't have all his notes." The laws of Washington City required freedman to carry five sworn statements that would attest to their status. That Josiah didn't have his notes in order was surprising.

"Is that right, boy?" Levi said stepping to Josiah and looking him right in the eyes. "You walking around this City without your notes?"

Silence hung thick in the air and Josiah clenched his jaw. "No," he said. "That ain't right."

Pockmark clenched his fist and unleashed a sudden and ferocious punch to Josiah's jaw. "You shut your mouth, nigger! You ain't got nothing to say here!"

Levi raged inside but he kept it at bay. “Now hold on here,” he said, throwing his arms out to separate the men and calm things down. “The value of this here freedman is already in question. Beating on him will only serve to further diminish his appraisal.” Levi waited until Pockmark backed off before he turned back to Slash. “Now you say he didn’t have all his notes. Just how many did he have?”

“Four,” Slash said.

Uncertain what to do, Levi took his time to inspect Josiah once again. Finishing his circle, the leather-bound notebook in Pockmark’s shirt pocket came into view. The idea came to Levi in an instant.

“I don’t know,” Levi said, shaking his head. “I don’t know if Mr. Duncan would appreciate me buying a field hand with four notes in his pocket. That’s just a little too close to being free.” He stepped towards Pockmark and held out his hand. “Give me that book of yours,” he demanded. “I want to see if Mr. Williams has anything else on his list that might interest me.”

Pockmark fished the notebook from his pocket and handed it to Levi. “I seen most of the stock myself,” he said. “There’s plenty of good field hands to pick from.”

Levi opened the notebook and grabbed the pencil that was tucked inside. He flipped to the first blank page and started writing. Slash stood on his toes to try and look over Levi’s shoulder.

Pockmark stepped closer to see what Levi was doing. “What you writing in there?” he asked.

Levi continued in silence, making sure to keep the pencil steady and his writing legible. Pockmark took another step forward as Levi finished his writing and quickly tore the page from the notebook. He held the page up into the light for Pockmark to see.

"What's it say?" Slash asked eagerly.

"Now you know I can't read," Pockmark snapped.

"This here is a statement," Levi explained. "It says that Josiah is a freedman. I've sworn an oath to that effect and signed it at the bottom." Pockmark's mouth hung open as he tried to make sense of what had just happened. "This here is Josiah's fifth note," Levi continued, "which means he is no longer a slave but a sworn freedman under the laws of this City."

"You son of a bitch!" Slash said, finally realizing what Levi had done. Slash suddenly lowered his head and ran at Levi like a battering ram. Levi had anticipated the attack and quickly stepped to the side. Slash flew by and Levi grabbed the back of his neck to harness his momentum and propel him face first into the brick wall. The crunch of the impact echoed along the vaulted ceiling as Slash crumpled to the ground in a pile.

Levi stooped down and grabbed the keys off Slash's belt. Pockmark started towards Levi but Josiah stepped to the side to block his path. Levi stood and searched for the right key while Pockmark's jaw hung in disbelief.

"Now," Levi said, unlocking the first shackle, "me and this freedman are going to walk out of here." Levi unlocked the second shackle and the chains fell to the floor. "Or I promise you," he continued, "we'll make damned sure you never do."

Pockmark's mind swirled at the sudden turn of events. He didn't have an ounce of chance against one of these men, much less the two of them.

Levi took the man's silence as an answer. "Sounds like we have your word," Levi said. "Only I don't store much value in the word of a basement slaver." Levi kept his eyes squarely on Pockmark. "Josiah, what do you say to locking one of those shackles to

Pockmark and the other to his unconscious friend down there on the floor?"

Josiah smiled and gladly went about the task. When the two men were locked together, Pockmark finally found his tongue. "You boys ain't got away with nothing here! Mr. Williams' is gonna hunt you down like dogs. You ain't never gonna sleep peaceful again!"

Pockmark cursed and screamed as Levi and Josiah headed towards the stairs. When they reached the iron gate, Levi turned to look back into the prison. His gaze settled on the nineteen-year-old woman chained to the wall. Without a second thought, he tossed the keys at her feet.

# Chapter 16

October 23, 1861 – 4th Ward, Washington City

Nicholas Turner stared into the fire at Mary Surratt's boarding house as the memories of his past began to fade. Just then, the front door opened and his thoughts vanished in the flames. Nicholas turned to see a man of average build with long dark hair that was parted to the side and slicked over with an abundance of lard. He wore an unkempt suit that matched the state of his scraggly goatee. It was the man Nicholas had been waiting for all morning—it was George Atzerodt.

From the moment he was recruited, Nicholas had set about building his own network of spies and informants. He had started by enlisting barmen, stable boys, and other tradesmen. Men of that sort were often misjudged as simpletons with little capacity to understand the intricacies of politics and war. To men of a higher station, stable boys were invisible and of no concern when discussing matters of state. While the lower classes of spies were certainly useful, it was only recently that Nicholas had a true stroke of genius in building his network.

From iron, to cattle, to men, the war consumed everything in sight. But the true lifeblood of war was information; it pulled at the disparate parts and bound the war effort into a single coordinated movement. The speed of war demanded the efficient flow of information but the City's geography conspired against it. It was a mile and a half from the White House to the Capitol and a full three miles to the Navy Yard. Telegraph lines ran at full capacity day and night but there was far more information than the lines could carry.

To handle the overflow, the government hired hundreds of messengers to hand- deliver information to all parts of the City. Every day, the messengers carried with them the hopes, doubts, and fears of the Union at war. The messengers held the keys to unlocking the mind of the enemy and Nicholas was determined to make them his own.

Nicholas took his time identifying as many messengers as he could. He followed them to taverns and whorehouses. He bought them drinks and he got to know them. And finally, he found a man with as deep a love of the South as his own. Once Nicholas had his first recruit, it was easy to find others. Some of the most vital information in the City flowed through Nicholas Turner's network of messengers. One of those messengers was George Atzerodt.

George closed the door and walked directly to the empty chair beside the fire. He twisted nervously in his seat and glanced around the room to ensure they were alone.

"It's safe here," Nicholas said, anxious to get any news George may have. "Mary Surratt is a friend. Now, what news?"

Still nervous, George leaned forward with his elbows on his knees so that he could get closer to Nicholas. "I just came from the Navy Yard," he began in a voice just above a whisper. "I was sitting outside Admiral Dahlgren's office when word came in about the explosion at the Armory."

Nicholas' pulse quickened. The Armory attack had taken months to plan and he was eager to know what had happened. "Well?" he urged. "What of it?"

George cut his eyes around the room. "At last count, there was twenty-one dead. Most of them were women but some were burned beyond recognition so it's hard to say who else we may have got."

Nicholas leaned back in his chair. Attacking the powder stores would slow down the Union's efforts but it was the fiery death of those women that was the real victory. Striking defenseless women would put a stain of fear on the heart of the Union that would be impossible to wash away.

"But there's more," George said, leaning even closer. "Two of them bombs didn't go off." The statement wiped the smile from Nicholas' face and refocused his attention. George continued. "They know it weren't no accident. A couple of soldiers found them other bombs and reported it to Admiral Dahlgren. He sent word to that scoundrel Simon Cameron who ordered an all-out manhunt for whoever done it."

The manhunt was an inconvenience but Nicholas wasn't too concerned. Even if they somehow found Edmund Spangler, his co-conspirator would report that he worked with a man named John Haney. But John Haney never really existed and would never be seen again. Nicholas nodded. "Okay," he said. "Anything else?"

"Yeah," George said. "Some good, some bad. You know Billy Wright?"

Billy was the barman at Venerable's whorehouse and one of Nicholas' trusted informants. "I know Billy," Nicholas said. "What about him?"

George glanced around the room nervously. "Billy sent word that there was a policeman at Venerable's yesterday poking around about Ellen Wolfe." Nicholas was intrigued. The police didn't often ask questions about dead whores. "Anyway," George said, "Billy says the man's name is Levi Love from the 6$^{th}$ Precinct. He said to get word to John Haney."

"I'll be sure to tell him," Nicholas said. "Now, you said there was good news and bad news. I'd say a policeman poking around about Ellen Wolfe was the bad."

George nodded. "Sure was. I was saving the best news for last. So I was sitting outside Dahlgren's office and, just before news of the Armory explosion came in, I heard Dahlgren going on and on about all the trouble the Confederate Navy is causing with their blockade on the Potomac. And then something strange happened. His voice got all quiet and he told one of his men he should be getting an important piece of information from the War Department—information that could change everything.

"I knew right away that was some information you'd want and, seeing as how I was sitting right outside his door, I went in there and offered to go get it for him."

Nicholas couldn't believe it. Commander Glasson had used almost the exact same words when he mentioned the blockade. The Union clearly had a plan to break the Confederate Navy's back. And now, it seemed that George Atzerodt had obtained the precise information he was looking for. Nicholas leaned forward so that the two men were only inches apart from one another. "What was the information?" he asked anxiously.

"Oh I didn't get it," George said plainly.

"What?" Nicholas asked. "You just said you offered to get it for Dahlgren."

"I did offer," George said, "but he didn't let me." Nicholas slumped back in his chair and sighed. But as George went on, a flicker of hope came to light. "I know who is gonna get that message though."

Nicholas sat up in his chair. "Wait," he said. "You know who's going to deliver the message?"

"Better than that," George smiled. "I know when."

Nicholas felt the life surge back inside him. "What's this man look like?"

"He's got brown hair, average height, average build," George said. "But it ain't him you need to look out for—it's his horse." Nicholas shot him a confused look. "It's a brown and white Paint with a white circle around his right eye. Can't miss it once you see it."

A plan rolled into Nicholas' mind like thunder. "You stay right here," he demanded as he hopped out of his chair and shot up the stairs. Moments later he returned with a roll of paper in his hand. He unrolled the paper to reveal a detailed map of the City. He laid it on the floor in front of the fire and the men held the ends in place with their boots.

"The War Department is here," Nicholas said pointing with his finger. "And the Navy Yard is here." He pointed again and then slowly traced his finger along the roads that linked the two. After a long moment, his finger suddenly stopped and he tapped the map. "Here's where I'll get him."

"He won't be there until dusk," George said. "Dahlgren's got him on other business at the wharf until then."

Nicholas nodded. "Okay," he said, glancing at his pocket watch. "That gives me time to take care of some other business of my own."

Nicholas stood just as Mary Surratt entered the room carrying the tray of hot breakfast she had prepared for her guest. Without a word, Nicholas opened the front door and stepped out into the street.

Mary Surratt looked at the door and back to the breakfast she'd been laboring over. She appeared wounded. "I'll take them eggs," George said. Mary's face went from hurt to angry in an instant. She turned and left the room, taking her eggs along with her.

# Chapter 17

October 23, 1861 – 5th Ward, Washington City

The fallen leaves crunched under foot as Levi and Josiah cut across the lawn at the base of Capitol Hill. It was only a matter of time before James Roby went down to his slave pen to find the gate open and the two slavers chained to the wall. Levi hoped the other souls held captive in that dark dungeon had a chance at freedom but he didn't have time to linger on the thought. For now, he needed to get a safe distance from Roby's so he and Josiah could talk.

Up ahead, a Washington & Alexandria passenger train screeched to a stop in front of the Capitol. A handful of Senators and Congressmen mixed in with the crowd of laborers and support staff as they filed off the train and disappeared into the cloud of steam pouring from beneath the engine. Another busy day of legislation and backroom deals would soon begin.

Levi led Josiah into a small copse of trees and slowed to a stop. While Levi looked around to ensure no one was behind them, Josiah took a moment to try and process his unimaginable change of fate. Only minutes ago, he was in chains and destined for a life under the whip in the Deep South. There had been no way to get word to his wife and no hope of ever seeing her again. He had simply vanished from the face of the Earth and everything that made life worth living had been taken from him in an instant.

Standing in the darkened prison, a small voice in the back of his mind whispered the lessons of his past. If they take your pride, they will just as sure take your soul. Shackled to the wall of Roby's slave pen, Josiah hardened his heart and prepared to return to the man he used to be. But then, as if delivered by the hand of God, Joshua Jones appeared out of the darkness.

"I don't know why you did what you did, Mr. Jones," Josiah said, "but I'm thankful."

"My name's not Jones," Levi said. "And I don't work for Stephen Duncan either." Levi extended his hand. Josiah looked down at the hand suspiciously and then up at Levi. He had no idea who this man was but his eyes conveyed a sense of trust that Josiah found hard to resist. Cautiously, he reached out and shook the man's hand.

"My name is Levi Love. I'm an officer with the Metropolitan Police Department."

The shock of Levi's identity registered on Josiah's face. *A police officer?* The Metropolitan Police didn't give a damn about a colored man snatched off the streets.

Levi went on. "I'm investigating the murder of Ellen Wolfe."

At the mention of Ellen's name, Josiah's eyes fell to the ground and the memories of that night flooded his thoughts. Then, a question came to mind that was as inconceivable as it was confusing. Josiah looked up and smoothed his beard with a pull of his hand. His eyes narrowed on Levi. "Are you telling me you did all this on account of Ms. Wolfe?" he asked. "You went down into that slave pen and you risked your life on account of a murdered prostitute?"

Now that Josiah had said it, the whole thing sounded more foolhardy that Levi cared to admit. He decided to ignore the question. "I was told you were at Venerable's the night Ellen Wolfe was attacked."

Josiah nodded and looked down at his feet. "I was there," he said solemnly.

Levi subconsciously slipped his hand into his pocket for his gold coin. "I need to know everything you saw and heard that night, Josiah. Everything. So take your time and let's think it through."

Josiah pulled on his beard and looked into the thick branches overhead as the images of that deadly night slowly emerged. "The first thing I heard was the scream," he began. "It's the kind of thing you never forget. I ain't never heard a white woman scream like that before—like she was staring Death himself in the eyes. I knew she had one of her men in the room and Ms. Venerable had warned me to never disturb her ladies when they were working. But that scream," Josiah's voice trailed off as the blood-curdling sound rang in his mind. He shook his head to clear the memory away.

"I knocked and asked if she was okay but no one answered. So I put my shoulder to the door. When it broke through, he was standing right there waiting on me."

Levi couldn't believe it. Not only was Josiah there that night, but he had come face-to-face with the murderer. "Had you seen the man before?" he asked. "What did he look like?"

"I'd seen him before. He was one of Ms. Wolfe's regulars." Josiah pulled on his beard as he conjured an image of the man. "He's a big man. Tall and muscular. Brown hair. He's not a man you'd go looking to fight. There's a darkness in him you don't often see. But it's his eyes you can't forget. Eyes as black as night and cold as stone."

Levi listened in rapt attention as a vague picture of the man developed in his mind. Josiah's description was a start but it wasn't nearly enough to find a single man in this City of over a hundred thousand people. "You said you'd seen him around Venerable's before," Levi said. "Did you ever hear anyone say his name?"

Josiah nodded. "I heard him talking to a man the bar one time. He said his name was John Haney."

"John Haney," Levi repeated to ensure the name held firm in his memory. "Do you know anything else about him?" he asked, hardly able to contain his excitement. "Where he lives? Where he works? Anything?"

"I don't know where he lives," Josiah said. "But I do know where he works. He shoes horses at Howard's Livery."

"The one on G Street?"

Josiah shrugged. "I don't know where it is," he said. "I don't have much use for liveries."

"Okay," Levi said, searching for the thread of the conversation. "So you broke down the door and John Haney was standing there. What happened next?"

"He stared at me for a long time. He was thinking about my death as sure as I was thinking about his. Then something changed. He pointed at me and said he had something in mind for me that was better than death." Josiah glanced down at his feet. "When those Williams boys pulled me off the streets, I knew."

"You knew what?"

"I knew what Haney had meant. There's only one place to send someone that's worse than the grave. Haney was sending me to the Deep South. Until you came along, that is."

Just like that, a new piece of the puzzle appeared in Levi's mind. Only hours after Josiah witnessed the scene at Venerable's, someone had organized to have him snatched off the streets of this City in broad daylight. Pulling off an operation like that required men, organization, and practice. It required the type of skill and connections an ordinary farrier at Howard's Livery simply wouldn't have. Levi tried to fit all the pieces together but they wouldn't connect. There was something deeper going on with John Haney but Levi had no idea what it could be. Then he remembered something else.

"Do you know Christine Brandy?"

"Sure do," Josiah said. "She works at Ms. Venerable's."

Levi reached into his pocket and exchanged his gold coin for the small scroll of paper. "Christine gave me this," Levi said, holding the scroll out for Josiah to see. "Ellen Wolfe gave it to her and said that you would know what it means." Josiah took the scroll and a thought crossed Levi's mind. "Can you read?"

Josiah unrolled the scroll and stared at the writing.

STAF GGOG LCQB LMRN WURR
NKBB WZWK RWBS ATAV S

After a long moment, he shook his head. "I can read, Mr. Love," Josiah said, looking up at Levi. "But nobody can read that. Ms. Wolfe said I would know what this means?" He looked back down at the paper and pulled on his beard.

Suddenly, Levi saw a flicker of recognition in Josiah's eyes. "What is it?" he asked.

"Something I heard Mr. Haney say to Ms. Wolfe that night. He said, 'Reading that scroll won't change anything. What's done cannot be undone.'" Josiah thought for a moment. "If Ms. Wolfe gave this scroll to Ms. Brandy, it's a good guess Haney was talking about this scroll right here."

Levi thought it over. Something about what Haney had said was somehow familiar to him. "What's done cannot be undone," Levi repeated Haney's words. "He said it just like that?"

Josiah nodded. "Just like that."

Levi thought about it a moment longer but couldn't make the connection. He and Josiah had been standing in the open for far too long and Roby must have learned of Josiah's escape by now. Levi suddenly felt vulnerable. They needed to get moving. "Think, Josiah. Is there anything else you can remember about Haney? Anything at all?"

Josiah replayed the scene in his mind a final time. "Just one thing," he said. "When Haney pointed at me in the hallway, I noticed something on his finger. There was a small tattoo of some sort right here." Josiah lifted his hand and pointed to the inside of his index finger.

"A tattoo?" Levi asked. "A tattoo of what?"

Josiah pulled on his beard and shook his head. "Can't say. It was small and I only saw it for a second."

"Okay," Levi said, certain such a small tattoo would be impossible to spot out on the streets. "What about Ellen Wolfe? Anything else about her? Do you know if she had any friends other than Christine Brandy?"

"Not really," Josiah said. He had told Levi all he could remember and he was getting anxious to get home. "Mr. Love," he said, "I'm real grateful for what you've done for me and I won't forget it. But I didn't come home last night and my wife has to be in an awful state wondering what's happened to me."

"Of course," Levi said. "Before you go, would you mind telling me where you live? I may think of something else I need to ask you."

Josiah was reluctant to say but he wasn't sure why. Levi Love had saved his life. Surely he could be trusted with where Josiah lived. "I live in the second block on Blagden."

Levi nodded and extended his hand. “Thank you, Josiah.” Josiah shook Levi’s hand and then disappeared into the streets.

# Chapter 18

October 23, 1861 – 3rd Ward, Washington City

Nicholas Turner left Mary Surratt's boarding house and arrived at Center Market. The Market was strangely peaceful at this time of morning. The shops were all open but the first of the day's customers had yet to arrive. In a matter of hours, the Market would be jammed with merchants, carts, and customers scurrying in every direction. Walking through the empty market felt like the calm before the storm.

Nicholas cut through the fish market that backed up to B Street and the Washington Canal. The smell of the fish and the stagnant Canal formed a caustic mixture that stung his nose. He reached the muddied banks to see several fishmongers pulling cages of fresh fish from the putrid waters in preparation for the day's market. Nicholas reminded himself never to eat fish in this rotten City.

He walked along a narrow footpath towards a set of docks that he knew to be only a few blocks away. The tide was up at this time of morning, which meant the section of the Canal from the Potomac to Center Market was passable by boat, if only for a few hours. A handful of river barges, laden with stacks of wooden crates and burlap sacks, made the slow trek up the Canal. The lighter boats made their way by pushrod, while the heavier vessels required the help of barge horses along the opposite bank. The scene would have been quite tranquil, were it not for the smell.

The influx of fresh water from the tide had cut the stench in half but it was still awful. Like every other resident of the City, Nicholas hated the Canal and used every excuse to avoid it. But there were times when the wretched ditch was useful. Because everyone avoided the Canal, it meant those walking along its shores were assumed to have business there. The assumption that Nicholas belonged on the 10th Street docks was exactly what he needed.

Looking ahead, Nicholas saw a handful of wagons standing in a clump at the end of the docks. A dozen or more men hoisted sacks of dried goods onto their shoulders and hauled them from the barges to the wagons. The chaos of the scene was organized by the thundering demands of the boatmen and wagon drivers, whose voices filled the air and echoed off the water. Listening to the competing and contradictory orders, Nicholas wondered how the merchants ever received the actual goods they had purchased.

Nicholas wound his way through the dockworkers and wagons to the edge of the fray where several stacks of wooden boxes stood waiting for delivery. He grabbed the packing list sitting on the top crate and began to read it over. Nicholas had learned long ago that people rarely questioned confidence. If you acted like you belonged, people simply assumed you did. Glancing up from the packing list, he had a clear view of the foot traffic along Louisiana Avenue. Nicholas smiled. It was the perfect vantage point.

With several hours until Admiral Dahlgren's messenger would deliver the critical intelligence about the Southern blockade, Nicholas had some time to look into the little problem left behind by Ellen Wolfe. He had gone to unspeakable trouble to bury Ellen's body in the deepest bowels of the Canal and expected she would never be seen again. At worst, he thought it would take several weeks for some enterprising scavenger to uncover the body. But he was wrong. Ellen had been discovered in just three days and now a policeman was asking questions. If Levi Love was looking for him, Nicholas decided he had better go looking for Levi Love. His position at the 10th Street docks provided a perfect view of the 6th Precinct station house.

Nicholas waited around the docks for over an hour before he spotted the light blue overcoat of a Metropolitan Police uniform appear in the distance. His informant had described Levi Love as a man in his mid-twenties with broad shoulders and thick brown hair. To know if he had marked the right man, Nicholas had to get closer.

Glancing around, he grabbed a wooden crate from a nearby stack and lifted it to his shoulder. A merchant wagon loaded with goods jumped to a start and Nicholas waited for it to pass before stepping out onto Louisiana Avenue. The policeman's light blue overcoat flashed in and out of view as pedestrians and wagons cut across Nicholas' sightline. He squinted through the crowd but couldn't make out the policeman's features before he disappeared behind a passing wagon. Moments later, the wagon passed and Nicholas saw the policeman's broad shoulders and dark brown hair. His blood surged. Levi Love was only a half a block away and headed straight for him.

Nicholas set the crate on the ground and knelt beside it as if inspecting its contents. His heart pounded as his mind raced to make a decision. The man headed his way was asking questions about Ellen Wolfe—questions that threatened his very existence. Killing him would bring the problem of that worthless whore to a permanent end. And it would be all too easy. It was just a matter of timing.

Nicholas slowly slipped his hand inside his boot and felt the warmth of the blade strapped to his leg. He gripped the handle and prepared to strike. His muscles coiled. The slightest breath would set them loose and send his knife deep into the man's throat. His neck pulsed as his blood surged in anticipation of the kill. The light blue coat marking his prey was drawing closer with every second. The policeman was deep in thought and unaware that death was now only feet away. Nicholas flexed his grip on the blade. The moment was now.

And then suddenly, for reasons he didn't quite understand, Nicholas relaxed his grip and Levi Love slipped by in the passing crowd.

For a long moment, Nicholas lingered beside the crate in the road. Instinct had stayed his hand. Killing a police officer in the streets could be done but it was a bloody business that would only draw more attention and jeopardize his real mission in this wretched City. Levi Love was young, inexperienced, and looking for a man who no longer existed. Ellen Wolfe was dead and the trail for her killer was cold. Nicholas was safe.

Nicholas smiled as he stood and meandered his way along Louisiana Avenue. With any luck, he would never see Levi Love again.

# Chapter 19

October 23, 1861 – 3rd Ward, Washington City

Josiah walked along the muddied alleyway and began to cry. The rundown wooden tenements weren't much to look at, but together they formed a community bound in a common struggle to survive in this City. Josiah had never truly known how much the neighborhood meant to him until it was taken away. Now, by the grace of God he had returned and his heart longed for the home he never thought he would see again.

Turning the corner, he saw a door with layers of paint that had chipped and cracked over the years to reveal every shade of red, green, and black. At the sight of the door, Josiah's feet froze and he fell to his knees. Tears rolled down his face. His body trembled as he quietly sobbed into his hands and thanked God for sending Levi Love and for delivering him, once again, from a life in chains.

Suddenly, a familiar voice broke through his prayer. "Josiah!"

Josiah couldn't believe it. He closed his eyes tight so that God could hear him. *Please, Lord, tell me this isn't a dream. God, please let this be real.*

"Josiah!" came Anna's beautiful voice once again.

Slowly, Josiah dared to lift his head and open his eyes. A beautiful woman with tears streaming down her cheeks was running towards him. Her arms were open and her eyes were filled with worry and elation. She fell to her knees and grabbed the sides of his face to pull him close. "Josiah," she cried and kissed his lips. "My God, Josiah. Where have you been?" Anna kissed him again and then pulled him into the warmest embrace he had ever known. It wasn't a dream. Josiah was truly home.

The two of them held each other and wept until they had lost track of time. “Let’s go inside,” Anna finally said, breaking the embrace. They gently helped one another to their feet and walked inside. When Josiah closed the door, the full force of Anna’s emotions rushed to the surface once again. She pulled him tight and buried her face deep in his chest.

“I thought you were gone forever,” she cried. “I knew it. I just knew it.”

“It’s okay now,” Josiah said, holding his wife’s head as her tears soaked into his shirt. “Everything’s okay now. I’m home.”

He held her close and caressed her skin as his eyes drank in the home he thought he had lost. An orange fire glowed from the iron stove in the corner and cast its light upon the simple wooden table in the center of the room. A worn settee stood on the far wall beside the staircase leading to the bedroom above.

The sight of the staircase triggered a memory in Josiah’s mind. He rubbed Anna’s back before pulling her away so that he could look into her eyes. “Is everything okay upstairs?” he asked nervously.

Anna glanced over her shoulder at the stairs and then back to Josiah. She grabbed his arms and held them tight. “Everything’s okay, Josiah.”

A wave of calm washed over him but just then, a scream from somewhere outside shattered its relief. Anna’s eyes grew wide as she held Josiah’s gaze a moment longer. “Slave catchers,” she said.

Josiah turned to the front door. “Josiah, don’t,” Anna cried but Josiah opened the door and stepped outside.

Four white men stood in a half-circle in front of an open door a few houses away. The men were staring gleefully at the door as the screaming from within grew louder. Seconds later, the screaming grew to a fevered pitch and a man emerged from the door dragging a teenaged girl by her feet.

"Momma, don't let them take me! Don't let them take me!" she screamed over and again as she clawed desperately at the ground.

Her fingernails scratched deep into the mud as the man dragged her to the middle of the alley and dropped her feet into a puddle. The four men waiting outside swarmed around the girl, making it impossible to see. The men whooped and hollered as they went about their business. Seconds later, they stepped back to reveal the girl was hogtied and lying face down in the middle of the puddle. One of the men placed his boot in her back to hold her down as the girl struggled to keep her face just above the water.

"What the hell's taking Louis so long?" one of the men asked.

Another pointed to the door. "There he is," he said over the muffled screams that poured out of the house.

Josiah shifted his gaze to see a grizzled man in a black felt hat backing out of the door with his pistol drawn. As he stepped backwards into the alley, a man and woman appeared in the doorway. The woman was screaming and clawing at her chest.

"That's my daughter," she pleaded through her tears. "You can't take my little girl!" She fell to her knees and begged. "Please! Oh Lord, please don't take my girl from me!"

The grizzled man pointed the pistol directly at her. "She ain't yours," he said. He pointed with his other hand at the girl hogtied in the mud. "That there piece of property has been bought and paid for by Mr. Clement."

"But Mr. Owen," the mother cried.

"She don't belong to Mr. Owen no more," the grizzled man said. "She belongs to Mr. Clement. But don't you worry. Mr. Clement's got him a real nice sugar plantation down in the Deep South. You know how they love them pretty little girls in the Deep."

The mother collapsed on the floor and screamed at all the world. The father stepped forward. "Please, mister. We've been paying Mr. Owen every month for going on five years now," he explained. "Only eighteen dollars more and we get her papers. If Mr. Owen will only give us a little more time."

"I told you, boy," the man said, turning his pistol to the father. "Mr. Clement owns that little girl like he owns his own pigs." The men circled around the girl cackled and the grizzled man turned to face them. "Pick her up," he ordered.

The men pulled the girl from the puddle and the father stepped forward. "Please, mister. Please." Tears streamed down his face. "You can't do this. I'm begging you. You can't take my daughter. She's all we've got."

In a blink, the grizzled man spun around and smashed the butt of his pistol into the side of the father's face. The father's knees buckled and he fell to the ground. The man swung the pistol high in the air in case his message required a second blow. The father slowly got to his knees. He touched the deep cut over his ear and lifted his head. Blood streamed from the cut and mixed with the tears that poured down his face. His gaze fixed on the grizzled man with deep and penetrating hatred. But there was nothing he could do. He couldn't take all these men alone.

As he watched the scene unfold, Josiah's veins filled with rage. He shifted his gaze from one man to the next, searching for a weakness. All five men had guns but their attention was completely absorbed in their domination over this man and his little girl. Josiah focused on the closest man just twenty feet away. He was holding a rifle but his pistol was in its holster at his side. If he could just get that pistol.

He leaned forward but just then, a warm hand touched his arm and slowly tightened its grip. "You can't, Josiah," Anna whispered. "You know you can't. Not tonight."

Josiah looked back at Anna and then through their open front door. His eyes drifted to the narrow staircase at the back of their home and he knew Anna was right.

"Let's go, boys," said the grizzled man.

The father scrambled to his feet and ran to his wife's side. He dropped to his knees and buried her face in his chest to shield her eyes as the men gagged their only child and carried her away. They would never see their daughter again.

Anna put her arm around Josiah's waist and guided him back inside. She closed the door and Josiah walked slowly to the back of the room. The narrow staircase creaked under foot as he climbed to the second floor bedroom. Standing on the small landing, he stopped to listen for any sounds but the room was as quiet as a tomb.

"It's okay," Josiah whispered into the dark. "They're gone now. You're safe." He waited as is voice disappeared into the black. "You hear me? You're safe now."

From somewhere within, he heard the faint coo of a baby. Then, a tiny voice emerged from the dark. "I hear you."

# Chapter 20

October 23, 1861 – 2nd Ward, Washington City

After meeting with Josiah, Levi had gone back to his room over Thurston's Barbershop and changed into his uniform. He followed his usual route along Louisiana Avenue to check in at the 6th Precinct station house. Thankfully, Sergeant Corbett wasn't there, so there was no need for Levi to lie about his whereabouts or his plans for that afternoon.

Levi signed into the register and left the station house as quickly as he could. The traffic along 10th Street was moderate that afternoon and Levi passed the familiar shops and theaters without paying much attention. The conversation with Josiah had filled in some of the details surrounding the night Ellen Wolfe was murdered. While Josiah had gone so far as to provide the killer's name and his place of employment, Levi had his doubts. Was Ellen Wolfe's murderer really working as a stableman at Howard's Livery? And if so, what would he do when he discovered Levi was asking questions?

Levi exchanged greetings with Father Joshua Whitfield as he passed St. Patrick's Church and turned left on G Street. A few blocks later, he saw a sturdy brick building with a wide arched doorway. A sign over the arch said: JOHN C. HOWARD: HACK, HIRING, EXCHANGE, STAGE & STABLES. Out front, two men worked on a wagon that, with the addition of a brass boiler and yards of tubing, had been converted to one of the City's horse-drawn fire pumps. Closer to the front door, Levi approached a man with a thick white mustache who was busy saddling a black mare.

"Excuse me," Levi said.

The man tugged on the leather strap to tighten the saddle into place. "Can I help you?" he asked, still working the buckle.

"I'm looking for Mr. John C. Howard."

The man turned with a wide smile that faded when he saw Levi's badge and uniform. He cleared his throat. "What do you need with Mr. Howard?"

"I need to speak with him about one of his employees," Levi said.

The man's smile returned beneath the mustache. "In that case," he said, "I'm John Howard." He extended his hand, which Levi shook. "Who is it you're looking for?"

"I'm looking for a man named John Haney," Levi said.

Howard dropped Levi's hand. "Haney," he spat. "What did that no good thief do now?"

Levi was shocked. Was it possible Josiah's information was true? "Wait," he said. "You're telling me you know John Haney?"

"Know him?" Howard was incredulous. "Hell, I reported him to the police months ago. Much good it did me. You boys aren't exactly efficient in your administration of justice. "

Levi brushed away the insult. "Reported him for what?"

"For stealing my wagon, that's what," Howard said. The look on Levi's face indicated he was completely lost, which only exasperated Howard. "A couple months ago," Howard said, "this customer comes up and wants to rent a wagon for the day. John Haney went out there to bridle the horses and the next thing I know, the two of them are riding off with my wagon." Howard shook his head. "Never saw them or the wagon again."

Levi listened intently, trying to find a connection between the stolen wagon and Ellen Wolfe's murder. The wagon tracks that ran across the field to the Canal came to mind. "What does this John Haney look like?" Levi asked.

Howard closed one eye to get a better view into his memory. "He's a dumpy looking fellow. Fat with red hair and a permanent look of stupid on his face. You know what I'm talking about? The kind of man who never seems to breathe through his nose."

Levi's heart sank. It would be hard to describe someone more opposite from Josiah's description. He had almost given up the effort when an idea struck him. "Did you happen to get a look at the customer?"

"Oh sure," Howard said. "Every bit of money coming in and out of this place goes through me. You can't trust anyone these days." Levi stared at Howard to spur him to answer his question. "Oh, right, the customer," he said. "He was a big man—tall, not fat. Brown hair. But you know what I really remember?" Levi's heart beat faster. "I remember his eyes," Howard said. "His eyes were as black as night and cold as a winter shithouse."

There it was—exactly as Josiah had described. The customer had stolen Howard's wagon and John Haney's identity with it. And while using Haney's name, he had killed Ellen Wolfe. Whether the real John Haney was in on it or not didn't matter. Howard's story confirmed that Ellen's murderer was much more than an impulsive criminal. Adopting another man's identity took time and planning. It wasn't the sort of thing a one-time criminal would do. A pit formed in Levi's stomach. The man he was after was far more cunning, and far more dangerous, than he had ever imagined.

# Chapter 21

October 23, 1861 – 1st Ward, Washington City

Daniel Adams passed through the columned entryway and into the modest three-story brick building that housed the United States War Department. Just inside, the foyer was humming with activity. Uniformed officers walked urgently in every direction. Women in plain working dresses hurried across the room to deliver messages from the battlefield. Near the front of the room, a collection of soldiers, merchants, and politicians eagerly awaited their turn to meet with the high-ranking officials who worked in the building. It was a scene Daniel Adams had witnessed many times.

Daniel cut through the crowd and climbed the staircase on the far side of the room. Following the long corridor at the top of the stairs, he passed a variety of offices and meeting rooms before he heard the muted sounds of commotion filtering into the hall. He traced the sound to an unmarked door that he had visited at least once a day since the war began. Opening the door, Daniel stepped into the central nervous system of the Union's war machine.

Rows of telegraph operators sat at their stations and listened intently to the electric dots and dashes that arrived through a spider's web of telegraph cables hanging down from the ceiling. The operators scribbled furiously to translate the signals into meaningful messages. When the transmission ended and the translation was checked for errors, the operators held their slips of paper high in the air for one of the dozen or more runners darting along the aisles.

The operator nearest to the door lifted a new message in the air and a runner instantly appeared. Daniel stepped in behind the runner and followed her down the central aisle towards a long table at the far end of the room. Passing what must have been fifty operators translating messages from every corner of the

Union, Daniel marveled at how quickly technology had changed the way war was waged. Arriving at the table, the runner in front of him dropped her message in a collection basket and turned back down the aisle.

"Oh, Daniel," said a young woman behind the table. She took a moment to admire the handsome young officer's vibrant green eyes and waxed mustache before retrieving the collection basket for the latest messages. "Rebecca has your things ready for you."

"Thank you, Sara," Daniel said, flashing her a smile. The gold thread of his lieutenant bars sparkled as he walked to a desk in the corner of the room. An elderly lady behind the desk was busily organizing messages into stacks, which she bound together with lengths of twine.

"Good evening, Rebecca," Daniel said.

Rebecca looked up and smiled. "Hello, Daniel," she said, as she stood from her chair to get a better view of her desk. Her eyes traveled up and down the rows of bound messages. "Ah. Here it is," she said. She handed Daniel a set of papers, which he instantly leafed through.

The messages were all folded neatly and sealed with wax. Daniel examined the seals of each message until he saw a delicate imprint marking the letters BV. Seeing the stamp, Daniel smiled and tucked the entire stack into his leather pouch.

"You are as efficient as ever, Rebecca," he said as he turned for the door. Daniel had no idea what information was concealed beneath the delicate wax seal but he knew it to be important. Admiral Dahlgren had made Daniel promise he would not leave the War Department without the message bearing the mark of Brutus de Villeroi.

With the message in hand, Daniel left the building through the columned portico and walked directly to the side yard where his brown and white Paint was tied to the hitching post. He gave the horse a quick rub on the nose before loosening the reins and climbing up onto its back. The leather saddle creaked under Daniel's weight as he guided the horse out onto 17th Street and turned south towards the Navy Yard.

Half a block away, Nicholas Turner smiled. After deciding not to kill Levi Love, Nicholas had left the 10th Street docks and gone directly to a thriving little restaurant called Mini's Place. Though Mini was well known for her cooking, Nicholas had chosen the restaurant more for its location than the excellent fare. Sitting in Mini's window seat, Nicholas had an endless supply of fresh coffee and a perfect view of the War Department.

For the last several hours, he had been drinking coffee and watching the traffic coming in and out of the War Department's columned portico. He was starting to loose focus when he saw a brown-and-white Paint amble up the street. Nicholas shot up in his chair. The horse was exactly as his informant had described. Nicholas stared out the window as the man tied the horse to the post outside the War Department and walked casually inside.

With no way to know how long the man's business would take, Nicholas paid his bill and stepped outside to wait. Minutes later, he saw the brown-and-white horse trotting south on 17th Street. Nicholas climbed onto his horse and followed Admiral Dahlgren's messenger into the waning light of the evening sun. His trap was set.

# Chapter 22

October 23, 1861 – 3rd Ward, Washington City

Levi left Howard's Livery unsure what to do next. He had a vague description of John Haney but there wasn't much else to go on. Howard's story had confirmed that Ellen Wolfe's murderer assumed false identities, which meant even the name John Haney was almost certainly a dead end. Levi considered the facts of the case over and again as he walked the rest of his beat. There had to be something to connect all the pieces but each time Levi thought he had grasped it, the idea slipped through his fingers. By the time he finished his beat, he felt he was further away from catching Ellen's killer than ever.

He opened the door to the 6th Precinct station house to see Sergeant Corbett sitting at the front desk reading a newspaper. Levi could feel Corbett's deep-set eyes as they followed him through the station house to the wooden table that sat in front of the jail cells. Levi leaned over the table and picked up the pencil to sign the register. Still feeling the Sergeant's cold stare, Levi was glad to be signing out for the night and heading home.

Levi signed his name in the book but when he turned to leave his heart jumped. Sergeant Corbett was standing just a foot away and directly in Levi's path. Corbett's tobacco stained breath seeped out from beneath his greasy goatee. Levi stood his ground and held the Sergeant's gaze.

"My shift is over," Levi said.

A yellowed smile appeared from beneath Corbett's goatee. "I heard there was quite a commotion over at Roby's Tavern today," he said. Levi's stomach lurched and Corbett leaned in even closer. The Sergeant was a practiced interrogator. The slightest crack in Levi's façade would do him in.

"So?" Levi said as casually as he could. "Roby's is in the Fifth Ward. That's 8th Precinct territory, isn't it?"

"Story is some white man posing as an agent for a Mississippi slaver went into Roby's early this morning and stole one of Mr. Williams' slaves."

Levi's stomach twisted tight and he prayed it didn't show on his face. He was surprised that Corbett had already heard about Roby's but he shouldn't have been. Corbett was as connected to the underground slave trade as anyone in the City. Rumor was that William H. Williams himself fed Corbett half his information about runaway slaves hiding in the City.

Corbett took a step back. The lard pressed into his perfectly parted hair glistened as he eyed Levi up and down. "The white man they described was about your height, and your weight, and had pretty blue eyes," Corbett stepped forward so that he was only inches away. "Pretty blue eyes," he said again, "just like yours."

Levi's heart pounded in his chest as he waited for Corbett to complete his accusation. The silence felt like a vice, as the tension between the men grew ever tighter. If Levi struck his Sergeant, he would lose his position regardless of his personal connections. He held Corbett's stare a moment longer before breaking the connection and stepping to the side.

Corbett moved at the same time. "You ain't going nowhere, Lover," he said. "Not unless you pay the toll."

Levi stopped cold. "What are you talking about?"

Corbett's eyes shot down to Levi's pocket and back again. "I seen it the other morning when we brought that boy Raspberry in for his education." Corbett's tongue circled his chapped and rutted lips. "I seen you twirlin' that pretty gold coin."

Levi's hand instinctively went to his pocket. He would never give Corbett his father's gold coin. Even if he did, Levi knew it wouldn't matter. Corbett was going to do as he pleased with the information he had about Roby's, gold coin or not. Levi set his jaw. If Corbett wanted the coin, he would have to pry it out of Levi's dead hand.

The Sergeant roared and Levi was suddenly forced off his feet. Corbett's thick hands had Levi by the shoulders and drove him through the air. Just as Levi realized what was happening, a shock of pain shot through his body as his back slammed hard against the iron manacles hanging from the wall.

"Give me that fucking coin!" Corbett yelled.

With his shoulders still pinned to the wall, Levi wrapped his legs around Corbett's waist. In one swift movement he pulled Corbett close and threw his head forward. Levi's forehead crashed into Corbett's nose with an audible crunch. The Sergeant's hands shot to his face and the two men fell to the floor. Levi was still recovering when Corbett looked down at his hands to see they were covered in blood.

"You broke my fucking nose!" he screamed. "You're gonna pay for this, you son of a bitch!"

Levi was on his hands and knees catching his breath and preparing for another round when the door to the station house burst open. "Murder!" cried a man's voice. "Murder!" The man's voice trailed off as he looked around the seemingly empty room.

Levi scrambled to his feet and appeared from behind the front desk. "What are you talking about?" Levi asked. The man at the door was dressed in quality middle class clothing—probably a merchant of some kind.

"Murder!" the man screamed again.

"Yes," Levi said. "I heard you the first two times. Now tell me what the hell you're talking about. Who was murdered?"

The man shrugged his shoulders and looked confused. "How am I supposed to know who it is?"

"Alright then," Levi said with as much patience as he could muster. His blood was still up from the fight with Corbett. "How do you know there was a murder?"

"I saw the body," the man said urgently. "Saw it in The Division off of 14th Street."

At the start of the war, General Joseph Hooker attempted to reduce crime by rounding up all the brothels he could find and moving them to a six-block area between Pennsylvania Avenue and the Canal. To no one's surprise, except for General Hooker, the concentration of sex, gambling and alcohol only amplified the criminal elements that thrive on vice. This notorious section of the City was commonly referred to as Hooker's Division or, more simply, The Division. Like every police officer in the City, Levi knew the area well.

Levi glanced back at the Sergeant, who had climbed to his knees and was pinching the bridge of his nose to staunch the flow of blood. The conversation with Corbett was far from over but Levi knew well enough to delay its conclusion as long as possible. "Come on," he said, rounding the front desk. "Let's go see what you've found."

The two men hopped in the police wagon and Levi lit the oil lantern hanging on the post beside the bench. "The body is over by the 14th Street bridge," the merchant said. Levi slapped the reins and wagon rattled off into the night. The bridge was only a few blocks away.

The metal springs beneath the bench seat squeaked in protest as the wagon bounced over the rutted and bumpy road. North B

Street was commonly used to transport goods from the 6th Street Wharves to Center Market for sale. The combination of incessant traffic, heavy goods, and rain made it one of the worst thoroughfares in the City. Levi hated this road and avoided it whenever possible. As bad as the ruts and holes were, it was the proximity to the Canal that made him hate it so much. Tonight, however, B Street provided the quickest route from the station house to the 14th Street bridge.

The pull of the tides had transformed the Canal into a series of fetid puddles running from the Capitol to the Potomac. Levi diverted his gaze across the Canal to the red stone edifice of the Smithsonian Castle. The soaring turrets and pointed spires carved a majestic silhouette in the night and conjured images of nobler times that felt completely misplaced in this City of mud and war.

Levi blinked the thoughts away as the wagon crossed over 13th Street and the Castle passed from view. "What's your name?" he asked, suddenly realizing he had no idea who his companion was or how he came to find the body.

"Name's Michael," he said. "Michael Evans." His voice had a hint of an accent that sounded familiar.

"You Irish?" Levi asked.

The man looked around, as if his heritage was something he'd rather not discuss. "My parents are Irish. We crossed over when I was ten." Being raised in Ireland until he was ten made Michael Evans as Irish as a paddy's pig but Levi saw no need to poke at the man. "My father runs a wool trade out of Boston," Evans went on. "But with the entire Army camped in Washington City, he sent me here to see what I could do about the government's wool supply."

"So what brought you by the 14th Street bridge?" Levi asked.

"Well, you know," Evans said with a bashful smile.

Levi nodded. *Of course*, he thought. Why else would a young man be hanging around in Hooker's Division at this time of night?

Suddenly, Evans pointed up ahead. "There!" he said. "It's right over there."

The narrow wood and iron bridge was barely visible in the moonlight when Levi reined the horses in. He pulled on the brake and, as the creaks and rattles of the wagon faded into the distance, the night grew eerily calm. Levi didn't see a body anywhere. "Where is it?" he asked, peering into the dark.

"Over there," Evans said, pointing again. "Just down the embankment by the base of the bridge."

Levi hung the reins on the corner of the footboard and grabbed the lantern. "Stay here," he said, though it didn't appear that Evans had any intention of going anywhere near the body.

Levi jumped down off the wagon and held the lantern out as he crossed B Street towards the bridge. A faint chorus of bellows drew Levi's attention across the Canal to the thousands of cattle grazing around the truncated stump of the Washington Monument. The herd had arrived five months ago to help feed the massing Army. The stink of the cattle only added to the Canal's already abundant fragrance.

"He's just down there," Evans called. Levi glanced over his shoulder to see the Irishman shoeing him forward.

Levi turned back to see the black railing of the iron bridge appear at the farthest reach of the lantern's glow. Stepping forward, the dirt of the road gave way to a line of grass and weeds that ran down the steep embankment to the Canal below. He peered over the edge and squinted to the end of the light but he saw only clumps of grass clinging to the side of the hill. Levi sighed.

The moonlight reflected off the puddles of mud in the Canal as Levi tested his footing on the slope. One wrong move could send him tumbling down the hill into the noxious waters. Carefully measuring each step, Levi climbed slowly down the side of the embankment. He shifted his gaze between his feet and the Canal below until a shape emerged at the edge of the dark. With each step, the lamplight spread further down the hill towards the shape. And then Levi saw it—the soles of a man's boots. Levi hung his head. The Washington Canal had claimed two bodies in as many days.

With the lantern held high, Levi continued down the hill and knelt beside the body. His eyes traveled from the black leather boots to the blue wool pants and jacket. The gold insignia around the sleeve and on the man's shoulders indicated he was a lieutenant in the navy. A quick examination of the uniform showed no signs of struggle. Levi's heart beat faster as he turned his gaze to the man's face. What he saw made his blood run cold.

A dark purple bruise spread out beneath the chin. Extending the lamp further, a one-inch puncture wound appeared in the center of the black. Levi shifted his gaze to look beneath the man's perfectly waxed mustache. A dark stain of dried blood surrounded his mouth and ran down the side of his handsome face. Levi reached down and, knowing precisely what he would find, he slowly opened the man's jaw. A coagulated pool of black filled the cavity. The tongue was gone. Ellen Wolfe's murderer had struck again.

A surge of exhilaration rose in Levi's chest that was instantly doused with shame. The officer's death was a tragedy and Levi had no right to be excited when confronted with such a brutal crime. But there had to be something here—some detail that would lead him back to John Haney's trail.

Haney was meticulous and calculating. He didn't kill at random. There were thousands of officers walking the streets of this City but John Haney had chosen this one. What was it about this officer that drew Haney's blade?

Levi turned back to the body and noticed a thin leather belt running around the man's waist. He had never seen a naval officer wearing a belt over his jacket. Levi reached down and, as he pulled on the belt, the slack in the leather that had been pinned beneath the body gave way. Levi's heart raced. It wasn't a belt. It was the strap of a messenger's carrying case.

He threw his hand under the small of the man's back and grabbed the leather pouch at the end of the strap. Levi's blood surged as he opened the case and thrust his hand inside. There was nothing there. Levi scratched around every corner of the leather. But there were no messages, no papers to indicate why Haney had taken this man's life.

Hoping his hands had deceived him, Levi threw open the flap to peer into the case. The pouch was empty but something on the inside flap caught his attention. He turned the leather towards the light to see that it was branded with a message:

DANIEL ADAMS
FOR YOUR DEDICATED AND MOST TRUSTED SERVICE TO YOUR COUNTRY
ADM. J.A. DAHLGREN

Levi read the message again to make sure he had it right. He gazed across the Canal as he grappled with the conclusion that was written as clear as the words burned into the leather. John Haney had tracked down and killed the personal messenger of the most powerful naval officer in the Union: Admiral John A. Dahlgren.

The gravity of the discovery hit Levi like a cannonball to the gut. He reached into his pocket to retrieve the paper scroll Ellen Wolfe had entrusted to Christine Brandy. Unrolling it in the light, he stared at the jumbled letters, which suddenly took on a new meaning. Shifting his gaze across the Canal, he searched the moonlit pasture for any other explanation but it wasn't there. The man he was after used false identities. He killed without mercy. He hunted military messengers in the night. And he wrote in code. A southern spy was lurking in the City and Levi Love was on his trail.

# Chapter 23

October 23, 1861 – 3rd Ward, Washington City

Levi closed the shed behind the station house and threw the latch. For the second time in as many days, the dilapidated building provided a resting place for one of John Haney's victims. Unlike Ellen Wolfe, the discovery of a murdered naval officer required reporting to the proper officials, which, for Levi, meant informing Sergeant Corbett. Given the fight they'd had that morning, Corbett was the last person Levi wanted to see but he had no choice.

Levi rounded the corner of the station house and stepped onto the porch. Just then, the front door burst open and Corporal Townsend pushed past Levi with Sergeant Corbett right behind. When he saw Levi, Corbett stopped in his tracks. The tension of their fight, and the unfinished business it left behind, settled between them like a fog. Levi's muscles tensed. He stared into Corbett's eyes looking for the slightest sign of violence.

A cold smile spread beneath Corbett's greasy goatee. "Officer Lover," he said. "Just in time. I could use another set of hands." The gleam in Corbett's eyes told Levi everything he needed to know. He had caught Corbett and Townsend just as they were leaving on a raid. Corbett spun Levi by his shoulder and pushed him roughly towards the wagon.

"Where are we going?" Levi asked, knowing full well the answer didn't matter. If Levi wanted to remain in the Metropolitan Police, he would go where his Sergeant ordered.

Corbett grabbed a handful of Levi's coat and pulled him close. "We're going to the heart of the devil," he said through a wad of fetid tobacco. "We're going to Murder Bay."

Levi's eyes grew wide and Corbett laughed as he shoved him towards the wagon. Levi reluctantly climbed in back and a surge of disbelief coursed through his veins. In all his days in this City, he had never heard of police officers stepping foot into Murder Bay. Levi lowered himself down onto the wagon's hard bed and held on for the bumpy ride.

When Pierre L'Enfant designed Washington City, he envisioned a grand capital filled with public gardens and broad, tree-lined lanes. He designed the avenues to run diagonally across the City, which cut the landscape into blocks of every shape and size. When the land was finally put up for auction, speculators poured in by the hundreds.

Driven by unbounded greed, the landowners maximized their profits by dividing each City block into inner and outer rings. Lots along the outer rings faced the broad tree-lined avenues and were sold to the City's wealthiest white inhabitants and enterprising merchants.

For the inner ring, however, landowners had a different plan. That land was divided by a system of alleyways and reserved for the poorest black residents. Accessible only through the narrowest of gaps between the mansions and shops along the avenues, these blind alleyways were completely hidden from the view of respectable society and created a perfect place for crime and vice. Out of all the blind alleyways in the City, Murder Bay was the most notorious and the most violent.

At any given moment, there were probably a hundred reasons why a police officer was needed in Murder Bay, but Corbett wasn't going there to keep the peace. Levi's stomach began to knot. Somewhere in a dark corner of the alleyway ahead, a slave was hiding for his life and praying to make it to freedom. That prayer had been heard. But tonight, it wasn't an angel of God speeding his way to Murder Bay.

Corbett reined the horses and the wagon bounced to a stop. He threw the brake and Levi looked around to get his bearings. A lone gas lamp cast just enough light to see they had stopped near the corner of 13th and C. It was the outer ring of Murder Bay, where the streets were wide and lined with a collection of middle-class shops and taverns. Levi studied the handful of men in working-class dress as they stumbled along the lane in search of the nearest whorehouse or tavern. *Where was Corbett taking them?*

"Let's go, Lover," Corbett said. Levi looked up to see the Sergeant and Corporal Townsend standing beside the wagon. "We ain't got all day," he said.

A wide, almost lustful smile appeared through Townsend's beard as Levi climbed down off the wagon.

"Corporal," Corbett snapped. "Get that lantern." Townsend's smile vanished as he jumped at the order. He grabbed the lantern from the post at the front of the wagon and followed Corbett down C Street with Levi close behind.

The street lamp soon faded into the distance and reduced their field of view to the reach of the Townsend's lantern. Levi peered into the shop windows as they passed through the circle of light. Levi rarely saw this part of the City and, knowing what was ahead, he would have been glad to have never seen it at all.

"There it is," Corbett said.

Levi looked ahead to see Corbett pointing to a tannery near the middle of the block. *Why the hell would Corbett bring us to a tannery in the middle of the night?* But just as the thought entered Levi's mind, he realized Corbett wasn't pointing at the tannery at all. He was pointing to the dark and narrow gap between the tannery and the neighboring feed store.

Corbett drew his nightstick. "I suggest you boys get ready."

Anxious to defend himself, Townsend quickly turned for his stick. But as he did, he swung the lantern wildly towards

Corbett's face. The hot metal seared into the Sergeant's flesh. "Fucking, fuck!" Corbett screamed as his arm reflexively batted at the lantern, which slipped from Townsend's grip and crashed to the ground. Corbett held his throbbing ear as he looked down at the broken lantern and then back at Townsend. "You stupid shitbird!" Corbett yelled.

Levi looked to the ground in time to see the last flicker of the lantern's light extinguish into a trail of smoke.

Townsend looked down the narrow passageway, which had plunged into darkness. "Maybe we should turn back," he said.

Corbett rounded on Townsend and gave him a long look before stepping to within inches of his face. "We ain't turning back," he said. "Now get in there." He pushed Townsend down the alley and eyed Levi to ensure he knew the threat wasn't meant for Townsend alone.

The men clutched their nightsticks as they stepped into the narrow alleyway. Further inside, the light and sounds of the outside world faded into nothing. Darkness was all around and Levi heard only the sounds of his own breathing and footfalls in the dirt. Soon, faint noises arose from somewhere in the distance. Levi strained to hear sounds that vaguely recalled the midway at summer carnival. The sounds grew louder with each step until finally, a hint of light breached through the night. The men followed the light to the end of the alley where they entered into a hidden and forgotten world.

The narrow passageway opened up into a wider alley some thirty feet across. The scene was utter pandemonium. Ragged and dirty youngsters darted around their elders who were whooping at one another while playing cards or throwing dice. Two boys in badly broken shoes danced beneath a gaslight to the tune of a toothless fat woman picking at an old guitar. The sounds of the guitar mixed with faint tribal chanting that rose from some hidden pocket of darkness. In a distant corner, Levi watched a drunken man bury his head in a buxom woman's chest until a scream drew his attention to a fistfight just across the alley. Levi had never seen or heard anything like it.

"This way," Corbett said, charging his way into the commons.

The moment they crossed into the light, a man on a nearby porch began playing a solemn tune on his harmonica. Seconds later, a woman standing watch cried "Police! Police!" The woman's warning was relayed and echoed down the alleyway and the raucous scene that had been playing out before them evaporated in an instant. Women and children ran for their homes. The boys that had been dancing disappeared, leaving the fat woman to fend for herself. The men gambling on the porch dropped their cards and banded together in an obvious show of force against the uninvited officers.

Seeing the gathering mob, Townsend grabbed Corbett's arm and yanked him to a stop. Corbett rounded on Townsend but stopped short when he saw the fear in the Corporal's eyes. He turned down the alley to see the group of ten or so men standing together in a knot.

The muscles in Corbett's jaw tightened as he shifted his gaze to Levi and then back to Townsend. "Them boys are just trying to scare you," he said through clenched teeth. "They ain't going to do nothing but stare. We're going down this alley until we get to that second block." He pointed with his club. "Now let's go."

The men plunged deeper into the alley. As the distance from the gang of men grew, a thin layer of tension melted away and allowed Levi to take in his surroundings. Murder Bay was like nothing he had ever imagined. Cheap wooden dwellings covered with felt and tar were cut into odd shapes and wedged into every inch of space along the alley. Doors to the tiny apartments appeared in every conceivable place and Levi wondered how many people lived in these wretched conditions.

Corbett came to a sudden stop. "Alright, boys. There it is," he said. Levi turned to see a door with years of paint that had chipped away to reveal a kaleidoscope of colors. "Get your sticks ready," Corbett ordered.

Townsend instantly cocked his arm, ready to strike. Corbett inched closer to the door and counted down in a low voice. "One...two." Corbett raised his leg. "Three!"

He kicked hard and the brittle wood around the knob shattered as the door flew open without a fight. A shrill scream rang out as Corbett and Townsend rushed through the door. Levi stepped to the doorway but the combined mass of the two officers blocked his view. There were sounds of a struggle—the scuffling of feet, the screech of chair legs sliding over wood. Suddenly, the light blue uniforms disappeared behind the open door and Levi saw inside. An empty wooden table sat in the middle of the room in front of an iron stove. A narrow staircase in the back corner led to another room up above.

"Where are they?" came Corbett's voice. Levi peered deeper inside but his view was blocked by the cracked front door. His heart was pounding. He took a deep breath and closed his eyes as the scene on the other side of the door played out in his imagination.

"Close that door, Lover!" ordered Corbett.

The image in Levi's mind vanished but when he stepped inside and closed the door, it appeared once again. A woman stood hard against the wall, her neck stretched to its limit by the press of Townsend's baton. Her eyes were filled with concern for the man beside her whose head was pinned to the wall under the weight of Corbett's arm.

"I asked you a question, boy," Corbett said in a cold voice laced with experience in violence. "Where are you hiding Mr. Beauchamp's niggers?"

The man's voice was strained to a whisper under Corbett's crushing weight. "I don't know what you mean," he said.

Corbett swung his baton and it smashed through the thin wall just above the man's head. "Don't you lie to me, nigger!" Townsend cackled with anticipation. Corbett grabbed the man's shoulder and spun him around before pinning him back against the wall. He leaned his thick forearm into the man's neck, forcing his head to the side. Corbett shifted his weight for more leverage and Levi saw the man's face for the first time.

Levi broke into a cold sweat. His eyes fixated on the side of the man's face where only the vestige of an ear remained. Levi couldn't believe it. Corbett was after Josiah.

Townsend grabbed a handful of the fabric across the woman's chest. "Bet he'll talk if we take a look at what's under his woman's dress." Josiah's eyes grew wide and he clenched his powerful fists.

"Hold on now, Corporal," Corbett said. "That one there belongs to Mr. Arthur Blake."

"So?" Townsend said.

"So, you go damaging Mr. Blake's property," Corbett explained, "and Mr. Blake's gonna come looking for restitution."

Townsend screwed up his face. "Resti, what?"

"Payment, Corporal," Corbett said. "He'll come looking for payment for the damage you done to his property. But this one here," Corbett pressed his forearm hard into Josiah's neck, "this one here's a freedman, ain't you boy? And from what I hear, this freedman is hiding slaves right here in this very shack. All we got to do if find them."

Sweat beaded on Corbett's brow as he leaned close and whispered in Josiah's butchered ear. "I'm gonna find them, boy. I'm gonna find them and I'm gonna make them pay in ways you ain't never dreamed of. And when I'm done with them, it'll be your turn to pay."

Townsend cackled.

"Officer Lover," Corbett said. The haze that had settled in Levi's mind disappeared in a blink. "Get up them stairs and find me some pigs." Levi nodded and stepped slowly towards the stairs. "Lover," Corbett said, stopping Levi at the base of the staircase. "When you're done searching, you better know I'll be up there to make sure you done it right."

Levi hesitated as the Sergeant's threat hung in the air. Then, without a word, he turned to the narrow stairway and disappeared from sight.

The soft wood creaked under Levi's weight as he slowly made his way towards the room above. At the top of the staircase, a dim lantern hung from a nail in the wall. Levi turned the knob to extend the wick and a yellow light spread across the room. A mattress covered with an intricate quilt sat on a wood frame against the opposite wall. To the right of the bed, a small wardrobe held what Levi guessed was every strip of clothing Josiah and his wife owned.

Levi stood on the landing for a long moment and slowly scanned the room for any signs of life. Everything was still and quiet. He took a cautious step into the room and suddenly stopped. A faint sound filtered through the air. Levi held his breath and strained to listen over the heavy beat of his own heart. There it was again. A tiny scratching sound like fingernails on wood. Levi's eyes shot to the wardrobe. The sound was coming from just on the other side.

Careful not to make a sound, Levi stepped further into the room. The wardrobe was within reach when he stopped to listen again. The scratching continued from the small space between the wardrobe and the wall. Levi took a deep breath and prepared himself for what he might find. His pulse throbbed in his temples. With a final breath, he swung his body around the wardrobe. Just then, a giant rat scurried from the shadows. Levi jumped and his body hit the wardrobe, which screeched as it inched across the floor from the impact.

"By God! What the hell's going on up there?" Corbett yelled from down below.

Levi closed his eyes and leaned against the wardrobe to catch his breath. "It was just a rat," he breathed to himself. "It was just a rat," he repeated so Corbett could hear.

Levi pushed off the wardrobe and was turning towards the door when a flash of color caught in the corner of his eye. Looking back, he saw a narrow gap in the wall where the wardrobe had once been. Levi stepped closer and when he peered into the gap, his body went completely numb. There, crammed into a tiny space in the wall, a young woman of no more than twenty stood clutching a baby so tight to her bosom that it could hardly breathe. Levi looked into her eyes and a pulse of electricity shot down his spine like lightning. It was a look of terror like he had never known.

"What the fuck is going on up there?" Corbett yelled. Moments later, heavy footfalls echoed up the narrow staircase. Corbett was coming.

Levi's eyes grew wide with panic. The law made this woman and her child criminals but exposing them would mean unspeakable torture for the mother and worse for her child.

"What is it, Lover?" Corbett demanded as he made the top landing and stepped into the room.

Levi spun, unable to wipe the panic from his face.

"Well, well," Corbett said, "you're white as a ghost."

Levi's mind raced. "A rat," he said, panting. Corbett looked confused and Levi quickly found confidence in his story. "A rat," he repeated. "It jumped out and scared me." Just then, the rat scurried from beneath the bed trying to make a break for the stairs.

Corbett saw the rat and began to stomp madly at the floor. His heavy boot thundered to the ground over and again as the rat ran circles beneath his feet. Finally, the boot made contact and the rat's head shattered in a tiny pool of red. "Jesus Christ, Lover," Corbett said, looking down at the twitching corpse under foot. "You really are a lily white coward, ain't you."

He lifted his foot and took another step into the room. "Did you search this place good?" Levi nodded. Corbett glared out of the corner of his eye as he got down on his hands and knees to look under the bed. Standing, he looked at the wardrobe and then to Levi. Corbett rounded the bed and stood in front of the wardrobe's wooden doors.

Levi clutched his baton so tight he thought it might splinter. The slightest sound from mother or child would end their lives, and his. Corbett narrowed his eyes as he slowly reached for the wardrobe doors. With a sudden jerk, he threw open the doors, which crashed to a stop against the sides of the cabinet. He stared into the space for a long moment.

"You really are a coward," he finally said as he turned from the wardrobe and headed for the stairs. "Let's go," he ordered.

Without risking even a glance at the mother and child, Levi followed the Sergeant down the stairs. In the room below, Josiah and Anna were sitting at the table. Josiah's eyes were pinned to Townsend, who was holding a blade to Anna's throat.

"No one here," Corbett announced as he crossed the room to the broken front door. The lustful gaze slipped from Townsend's face as he reluctantly dropped his blade and followed Corbett outside.

Josiah shifted his eyes to the last officer in his home. Levi saw the flash of recognition, which Josiah immediately wiped away. If Levi had helped hide the fugitives upstairs, his life was in as much danger as anyone's in that house. Without a word, Levi stepped from the house and quietly closed the door.

# Chapter 24

October 23, 1861 – 1st Ward, Washington City

The barmaid slid the pint of beer across the table, sloshing the frothy head over the side. "Need anything else?" she asked suggestively.

At any other time, the woman's large breasts and wanton eyes would have drawn some consideration, but not tonight. "Privacy," Nicholas Turner snapped, reaching for the glass. The woman left in a manner that suggested she was unlikely to return.

Nicholas eyed the tavern over the rim of his mug as he took a long drink. The White Horse was busy that night, but not so busy as to crowd his table, which was tucked away in the back corner. A banjo player near the front door picked at a tune that had most of the bar distracted. The others were busy playing cards or getting drunk or both. No one was paying Nicholas any attention or had any idea that just over an hour ago he had removed the tongue of Admiral Dahlgren's personal messenger.

He took another drink to wash the memory away before turning to the messages. Somewhere in the stack of paper there was information that could change the tides of war. Nicholas untied the twine and flipped through the stack. There were six messages in all, each sealed with a wax stamp. He took the first message and, seeing no need to keep the full weight of the evidence in plain sight, he set the remainder of the stack on the bench beside him. The wax seal on the first message was marked: CAPT. J MOORE. The stamp was meaningless to Nicholas, so he tore it open and began reading.

*October 20, 1861 – Cairo, Illinois*

*Admiral Dahlgren,*

*Captain Winslow took command of the gunboat Benton at St. Louis on October 12th. Departed for Cairo, Illinois and ran aground on a sandbar. During attempted salvage, a link from a broken chain left Captain Winslow badly injured and unable to continue his command. Benton is harbored safely on the Ohio River and awaits further orders. Please advise.*

*Respectfully,*

*First Lieutenant in Command, John Moore.*

Nicholas thought through the message but could make no connection between the loss of a captain along the Missouri River and the southern blockade of the Potomac.

Setting the first letter on the bench, Nicholas quickly read the contents of the others. The messages came from officers of varying ranks and provided the Admiral with information on supplies, field promotions, and casualties from distant battles at sea. Nicholas finished the fifth letter and let out a sigh as he dropped his hands to the table. Thus far, he hadn't learned anything of interest or concern.

Nearing the conclusion that his informant had fed him bad information, Nicholas took a sip from his mug and reached for the final letter. He glanced at the wax seal and was about to tear it open when he stopped and gave it a second look. The seals of the other messages had all been marked with the heavy block letters commonly used by Union officers. But this seal was different. Pressed deep into the red wax were graceful, curved lines marking the letters **BV**. Nicholas' pulse surged as he carefully broke the seal and unfolded the letter.

*October 23, 1861 – H Street, Washington City*

*Dearest Admiral,*

*I am writing to inform you that we have completed our tests and the Scrubber has met your every requirement. We have determined it is fit for service. Shipment to your facility is underway. Scrubber should arrive by this evening at the latest.*

*Your Faithful Servant,*

*Brutus de Villeroi.*

Nicholas reached the end of the letter and read it again. This had to be the message his contact had told him about. But still, the letter raised far more questions than it answered. Who was Brutus de Villeroi? What was a *scrubber,* and what did it do? Nicholas was well versed in military armaments and he had never heard of such a thing. He stared at the word for a long moment and then decided it had to be some sort of codeword. The Union had grown more cautious since the start of the war and their use of codes had become increasingly common.

No matter what the *scrubber* was, its existence was disturbing. Admiral Dahlgren was known for developing some of the most deadly weaponry on earth. If the Admiral was personally involved, it meant this device was designed to lay waste to anyone in its path. There was no way to know whether the de Villeroi letter had anything to do with the southern blockade but it was unquestionably significant. Nicholas had to find out what this new weapon was and what it could do.

Determined to learn everything he could from the letter, Nicholas read it again. He paused at the last two sentences and allowed them to turn in his mind. *Shipment to your facility is underway. Scrubber should arrive this evening at the latest.* The largest research and development facility in the Union was located at the U.S. Navy Yard, right here in Washington City. That had to be where de Villeroi was shipping the device, which only made things more difficult. The Navy Yard was fortified and guarded at all times by hundreds of troops. Even if Nicholas somehow found his way into the Yard, there was no guarantee he could find his way out. There had to be an easier way.

Nicholas lifted his mug for another drink when he suddenly realized the answer to his problem was written right there at the bottom of the page. His mug hung in the air as he whispered the words, "Brutus de Villeroi."

There were two people in the world who held the information he needed: Admiral Dahlgren and Brutus de Villeroi. Dahlgren lived on a guarded compound inside the Navy Yard, which made getting to the Admiral virtually impossible. But de Villeroi was another matter. The letter indicated he lived in one of the grand mansions along H Street. Nicholas was surprised. While playing the part of Edward Huff, he thought he had met, or at least heard of, every resident along H Street. But Brutus de Villeroi was a mystery.

Nicholas drained his mug as the obvious conclusion settled in his mind. To find out who de Villeroi was, and what he was doing with Admiral Dahlgren, Nicholas needed someone who could move comfortably among the wealthy and elite residents of H Street. Nicholas needed Edward Huff.

# Chapter 25

October 23, 1861 – 3rd Ward, Washington City

Josiah sat at the table and gazed at Anna while she retrieved the kettle from the stove and poured him a cup of tea. Anna had always been a strong woman, but after seeing the strength and courage she had shown during the raid, Josiah looked upon her in a new light. As she returned the kettle to the stove, he wondered if she was ever really afraid of anything in this world.

Anna was almost to the table when a sudden knock at the door stopped her cold. Josiah's heart jumped and he instinctively glanced at the staircase before spinning in his chair towards the door. For a long moment, he sat motionless, praying his ears had deceived him. Seconds passed without a sound. Then, another rap at the door pierced the silence. Josiah gripped the side of the table and slowly stood from his chair. He looked back to see Anna's determined gaze. Whatever was on the other side of that door, they would face it together.

Josiah stepped across the room and cautiously removed the board he had used to bar the broken door after the raid. Holding the board in one hand, he slowly opened the door. Anna's heart raced as Josiah stood in the open doorway for what felt like an eternity. Who was he talking to? She was about to call out when Josiah finally stepped aside and Anna saw the man on the other side.

A sudden mix of fear and confusion coursed through her. Just hours ago, the man standing calmly in her doorway was forcing his way through her home in search of fugitive slaves. When the raid was finally over and the men had gone, Josiah had told her that one of the three police officers was the man who had saved him from Roby's tavern. Despite the sincerity of his voice, Anna found it hard to believe. But now, seeing the same man standing alone on her front step, all of Anna's doubts melted away.

"Come in," Josiah said, holding the door open. Levi stepped inside and waited while Josiah barred the door. "Anna," Josiah said, turning to his wife, "this is the man I told you about. This is Mr. Levi Love."

Levi turned to see Anna's eyes were filled with tears. She rushed forward to grab Levi's hand and cradled it in her own. A tear fell from her face and wet Levi's fingers. "Mr. Love," Anna said, looking up at Levi with her beautiful brown eyes, "I don't know how to thank you for what you've done for us. God himself has sent you into our lives, Mr. Love, and we are so thankful you're here."

The depth of Anna's gaze and warmth of her heart left Levi at a loss for words. "You're welcome," he finally said, squeezing her hands in his own.

Josiah stepped to Anna's side and put his arm around her. At the feel of Josiah's touch, she smiled. "I know you've got some things to talk about," she said. "I'll go on upstairs and leave you to it." With a final squeeze of Levi's hand, Anna turned and walked up the narrow staircase to the room above.

"You want to sit down?" Josiah asked, motioning to the chair by the table. Levi sat down and Josiah crossed the room to the stove. "Can I get you some tea?"

"Please," Levi said.

Moments later Josiah arrived with an empty mug and began to pour what appeared to Levi to be not much more than hot water. "I'm sorry for the tea," Josiah said, tracing Levi's gaze. "These old leaves have been poured over too many times. I'm afraid they don't have much left to give."

"That's okay," Levi said, as Josiah set the kettle on the stove and sat down across the table.

A heavy silence fell between them. The two men hardly knew one another but there was so much to say that neither knew quite where to begin. Levi felt his hand go into his pocket. A moment later, Josiah looked down to see a gold coin spinning through Levi's fingers. It was more money than he had ever seen in one place. That kind of money would change Josiah's life in an instant.

Josiah shifted his gaze to the steam rising off the dull water in his mug. "I want to thank you again for all you've done. I can't understand why you've done it but I'm thankful."

Levi nodded silently and stared at the coin a moment longer. "I was raised to respect both God and the law," he said. "The law says that woman and child you're hiding upstairs belong to someone else. The law says you're stealing."

Josiah looked over at the stranger sitting across from him and a thousand questions crowded his mind. Why had Levi Love saved him from Roby's slave pen? Why had he kept quiet after finding the woman hiding upstairs? And why had he returned here tonight? Josiah felt his entire life hang on the answers.

Levi watched as the alternating images of the coin spun through his fingers. "Do you have any idea what a woman like that would cost?"

"Five hundred dollars," Josiah said without hesitation. Levi held the coin and looked up at Josiah. "A woman like that costs five hundred dollars," Josiah said again. There was a certainty in his voice that spoke of a deeper understanding. Levi sat back in his chair and waited.

Josiah's eyes drifted back to the steam rising over his mug. "Mr. Blake wants five hundred dollars for Anna. We've been paying every month for going on five years now. We're almost there. But that girl upstairs," Josiah's voice trailed off for a moment as he stared into the steam, "she don't have nobody left to pay for her."

Josiah took a sip of the hot water and returned his mug to the table. His eyes glazed over.

"Ester found a man she wanted to marry down in Louisiana," he began. "But no one does a thing on Mr. Beauchamp's plantation without his say. Ester asked if she could marry but Mr. Beauchamp said no. He said he only bred the best of his slaves. He said he wouldn't let her man Peter lay with his dog, much less one of his women. So Ester and Peter got married in secret. Mr. Beauchamp never knew.

"But then the baby came. Ester lived in fear day and night as her belly grew. One day, there was no way to hide it anymore. Someone must have told Mr. Beauchamp because he came in there one night and drug her out of bed by her hair. Beat her real good wanting to know who the father was. Ester tried to blame one of the drovers but Mr. Beauchamp knew better.

"Next morning, he called the whole plantation together, even his own wife and children. He lined up all the colored men and boys beside the whipping post. Then he dragged Ester out in front of everyone and demanded to know who done it. But no one said a word. So Mr. Beauchamp grabbed the first one in line. The boy wasn't no more than twelve years old. No way that young boy was the father but Mr. Beauchamp tied him to the post anyway.

"The boy was shaking. He was so scared he could barely stand. The first crack of the whip split his back from top to bottom. But it was his screams that done it. That boy's screams brought Peter to his knees. Mr. Beauchamp drug Peter across the yard and tied him to the post. He whipped that man until he was hanging there limp. Then he kept right on whipping.

"He couldn't beat Ester any further without losing the baby so he promised every man and child in that yard that he would sell Ester one way and her child another. But God wouldn't allow it. And neither would Anna."

A long silence fell in the room. Levi had heard of stories like this before but listening to Josiah was like hearing it for the first time. He felt like he was standing over a dark abyss. The depths of man's depravity were beyond understanding.

"Will Ester be okay?" he asked.

Josiah shook his head. "The things she's seen won't ever be forgotten. She'll be hunted like a dog the rest of her life. But the child won't remember," he said, pulling thoughtfully on his beard. "Maybe he's got a chance."

"Things are changing, Josiah," Levi said. "Rumor is that Lincoln may even free the slaves one day."

"The law can't change a man's soul," Josiah said. "Rumors about freeing slaves only makes it worse. Those rumors got white people scared. They're selling their slaves to the Deep South faster than they've ever done. People are torn from their houses every night in this City, Mr. Love. A white man won't ever see a colored as his equal. The law can't change that." Josiah took another sip from his mug. "We'll still be fighting this war a hundred years from now."

Levi had never thought of it that way and a sinking feeling in his stomach told him Josiah was right. Suddenly, something in Josiah's eyes changed. It was as if he had just arrived back in the present moment. "You know what I can't decide?" he asked. "I can't decide if you're doing all this for John Haney or Ms. Wolfe."

Levi's eyes returned to his coin. "Ellen Wolfe," he said quietly to himself. He shook his head and laughed at his own foolishness. "I didn't even know what her name was."

Images that Levi had struggled to bury rushed to the surface. Ellen sat at a white table in an elegant dress. Rays of sunlight reflected off her deep amber eyes as she flashed her beautiful smile and laughed. Levi gripping her hand tight so that he could feel it was real for just one moment longer. Ellen's promise to see him again before pulling her hand away and disappearing into the crowd.

"I saw her on the street one day," Levi began. "She was walking towards me in a crowd but when I saw her, it was like no one else was there. In my whole life, I had never seen anything like her. She stepped closer and looked my way. I tried to speak but I couldn't form the words. I didn't know what to do, so I followed her for a couple of blocks before she finally stopped in front of Mini's Place.

"I knew if I didn't say something she would slip away forever. Somehow, I found the words to ask her for a cup of tea. She looked right into my eyes and considered my invitation for what felt like hours. *Just one cup*, she said." Levi smiled at the memory. "We must have had three pots that day. I spent the whole afternoon trying to find out who she was or where she lived. But she just smiled and turned the conversation to wine or art or travels to Paris. I listened for hours as she described places I'd never been and things I'd never seen." Levi's voice trailed off, lost in his own memories.

"You loved her," Josiah said.

Levi shook away the idea. "No," he said. "Maybe I thought I did."

"And then you found out she worked at Ms. Venerables," Josiah said. Levi thought on it for a moment and then nodded. "You know," Josiah said, drawing Levi's attention, "love don't care where a woman works or what she does to make it in this world."

Josiah's words pierced Levi's defenses and the images of Ellen rushed through his mind again. Finally, Josiah asked the question that had been on his mind since the first knock at the door. "So why did you come here tonight?"

"I'm going to find John Haney," Levi said, his voice steady and determined. "But I need your help." Levi looked up to see the surprise on Josiah's face. "You've seen him," Levi explained. "You've looked into his eyes and you know who he is. John Haney's name is meaningless now. A man can change his name and even change his appearance. But he can't change his eyes. You've seen his eyes, Josiah. You've seen them up close and you'll know when you see them again."

Josiah pulled on his beard. After all that Levi had done for him, he didn't hesitate. "What do you need me to do?"

"I need you to meet me at the 10th Street docks first thing in the morning."

Josiah had no idea what Levi had in mind but it didn't matter. "I'll be there."

# Chapter 26

October 24, 1861 – 6$^{th}$ Ward, Washington City

Levi slapped the reins and the horses kept pace with the light traffic as the wagon rolled down Louisiana Avenue. He had arrived at the station house before sunrise in hopes of collecting the horses and hitching the wagon before Sergeant Corbett was even out of bed. As a rule, it took the Sergeant until well into the morning to sleep off his whiskey and this morning was no exception.

The sun was bright and the air crisp as Levi neared the end of the avenue and the 10$^{th}$ Street docks came into view. A handful of wagons waited in a knot while dozens of workers unloaded the canal barges and organized the first of the day's shipments. Levi scanned the crowd around the docks but didn't see anyone that even resembled Josiah. He was just beginning to wonder if his entire plan was lost when he saw Josiah standing at the corner of Ohio Avenue. Levi wove the wagon through the plaza and pulled to a stop.

"Morning," Levi said.

"Morning, Mr. Love," Josiah said.

The metal leaf springs groaned from beneath the bench as Josiah climbed onto the wagon. With Josiah settled in beside him, Levi slapped the reins and the wagon rattled off across the plaza towards the Canal. The horse hooves clanged against the iron bridge as they crossed over the stagnant waters and continued south along 12$^{th}$ Street.

On the left side of the road, elegant winding pathways cut through a manicured lawn and led to the grand edifice of the Smithsonian Castle. On the other side of the street, the stump of the Washington Monument stood in a field of mud and manure where thousands of cattle awaited their demise at the nearby slaughterhouse. The image along 12th Street spoke of everything the City tried to be and everything it actually was.

As the wagon bounced along the road, Josiah's mind was filled with too many questions to notice the inherent contradictions of the City. Where was Levi Love taking him? What did he expect Josiah to do once they got there? The longer the wagon rattled on, the tighter the knot in Josiah's gut became. The wagon had just crossed South B Street when Levi suddenly pulled it a stop. Josiah turned to see the Smithsonian's red turrets towering in the distance over Levi's shoulder.

"You're probably wondering why I've asked you to come with me this morning," Levi said.

"It had crossed my mind," Josiah said.

"It started with something you said to me last night," Levi said, thoughtfully. Confusion spread across Josiah's face. He had said a lot of things last night. Levi continued. "You said, *A white man won't ever see a colored as his equal.*" Levi paused to think through Josiah's statement and confirm his own conclusions. "I believe you're right," he said. "Prejudice is woven into the very fibers of this City. Colored people go about the work of this country without the least bit of notice or concern from the white folk around them." Levi turned in his seat to face Josiah. "That got me to thinking. If a colored man is going about his business and doing what he's supposed to do, he could cross the floor of the United States Senate without ever being seen."

A flash of understanding shone in Josiah's eyes. "So you want me to go somewhere you can't," he said, pulling on his beard. "Somewhere dangerous."

Levi nodded and looked at Josiah with penetrating sincerity. "You don't have to do any of this, Josiah. You're free to go right now if you want. Maybe I find a way through on my own, maybe I don't. But the choice is yours right here and now."

Josiah thought for a brief moment before shaking his head. "Wherever we're going, it can't be any worse than that sugar farm I was headed to before you came along. I'll go with you, Mr. Love," Josiah said. "I'll go with you until I can't go no more."

Levi smiled and squeezed Josiah's shoulder. "I was hoping you'd say that."

Levi slapped the reins and the men rode along to the rhythmic jangle of the wagon until a question that had been on Josiah's mind forced its way to the surface. "I couldn't help but see that coin you was turning last night," he said. "You mind me asking what it is?"

Levi's heart jumped. He had been asked about his coin many times in the past and he had never given an answer. Most men had only asked out of greed. They were trying to size Levi up and see just how determined he was to keep the coin in his possession. But something about Josiah was different. He wasn't asking out of greed. He was just curious to get to know the man who had been thrust into his life. Slowly, Levi's defenses melted away and he stared off into a distant memory.

"I was born in Ireland," he began. "I grew up working a potato farm that had been in my family for generations. When the blight came in '45, it destroyed the farm and took everything we had. Then it destroyed the next farm and then the next. We'd go for days without much more than a slice of ham and a handful of beans to eat. Soon enough, the whole country began to starve. My father saw his family slowly wasting away. So he reached out to our cousin, Allan Pinkerton, in Chicago."

Josiah was surprised. Allan Pinkerton was a private detective who had gained national notoriety after uncovering a plot to assassinate Lincoln in Baltimore. Pinkerton was also a well-known abolitionist. Rumor had it that his home in Chicago had even been used as a station along the Underground Railroad.

"President Lincoln's security man?" Josiah asked, just to make sure.

Levi nodded. "Allan went straight down to the steamship company and paid to bring us over. He gave us a place to live. He trained us in his business and gave us work. When Lincoln asked him to come to Washington City, he brought me along and got me this job." Levi's mind returned to the gold coin in his pocket.

"Years ago Allan was tracking some train robbers out of Missouri. Somehow, he found out the men were hiding in a shack buried deep in the Ozarks. We saddled our horses and rode in to find them. We searched the mountains for days before we finally came upon the shack.

"We left our horses in a clearing about a mile away and started walking. The trees were so thick it must have taken us an hour before the outline of the shack appeared in the distance. Me and my father crouched down in the brush and waited for Allan to circle around back. It felt like forever waiting in those trees. My heart was beating so loud I was sure it would give us away. I barely dared to breathe.

"My father finally turned and put his hand on my shoulder." Levi dropped his head and closed his eyes while the scene played out in his memory. "He pressed a Colt revolver in my hand and looked me square in the eyes. His voice was barely a whisper. He said, *Son, we don't know how many of them boys are in there. I need someone to stay right here in these trees and keep an eye out. I need someone to watch over me.*

"I looked down at the pistol and gripped the handle tight to stop my hand from shaking. 'I'll watch over you, Pa.'"

Levi opened his eyes and his gaze returned to the distant horizon. The rhythmic rattle of the wagon filled the air as the memory slowly faded. "I'll watch over you, Pa," Levi said, returning to the present. "That was the last thing I ever said to my father."

"What happened?" Josiah asked gently.

Levi shook his head. "I don't really know. I remember watching through the trees as my father crept up to the shack. But then everything went black.

"I don't know how long I was out before Allan brought me around. When I finally woke, I saw the tears in his eyes and I knew. Allan killed three of the robbers as they ran out the back but the man who snuck up on me and killed my father got away.

"When Allan finally got me to my feet, he handed me one of the gold coins the men had stolen from the train. He told me it would help me remember there are things in this world worth fighting for—things worth dying for."

Josiah listened intently to the story, which reminded him of the sudden violence that had taken his own father all those years ago.

"There it is," Levi said, separating Josiah from his thoughts.

Josiah looked up to see a large three-story building with a sweeping archway cut directly through its center. Uniformed soldiers stood guard on either side of the archway, which was blocked by a heavy iron gate. Known as Latrobe Gate, the imposing structure served as the main entrance to the Washington Navy Yard.

"What are we doing here?" Josiah asked.

"Just follow my lead," Levi said quietly as the wagon slowed to a stop in front of the gate.

A young soldier with bright red hair pulled the rifle off his shoulder and held it at the ready. "What's your business?"

"I'm here to see Admiral Dahlgren," Levi said.

The soldier chuckled. "I'll bet you are," he said, glancing over at Josiah and then back to Levi. "The Admiral ain't said nothing about no visitors."

Levi had anticipated some resistance. He reached back to the bed of the wagon and grabbed the leather pouch he had found on the murdered lieutenant's body. Assuming the soldier couldn't read, Levi opened the flap and pointed at the inscription. "That there says: *Daniel Adams, for your dedicated and most trusted service to your country*. And do you see this?" Levi asked, pointing to the name at the bottom of the inscription. "That says: *Admiral J.A. Dahlgren*."

The soldier shot Levi a look he might have given to a traitor. "Where'd you get that?" he asked.

Levi touched the silver badge hanging prominently on his chest. "I'm a police officer," he said. "I found this pouch on Lieutenant Adams' body near the 14th Street bridge. We have important information for Admiral Dahlgren that he's going to want to hear."

The soldier looked over at Josiah. "What's he got to do with it?"

Levi narrowed his eyes. "This man is a witness to the crime," he said in a low and threatening tone, "and if you don't let us pass, I will ensure the Admiral knows you've interfered with the investigation of his personal messenger's murder."

The soldier eyed Josiah and the wagon for a moment longer. Levi could almost see the gears in the soldier's head turning. Finally, he called out to the men on the other side of the archway. "Open the gate!" The soldier waited for the heavy gates to start moving before turning back to Levi. "Follow the road around the bend," he said. "It'll take you to the Admiral's place."

The soldier backed away and Levi pulled the wagon through the stone archway and into the compound. The U.S. Navy Yard was the heart of the Union's military manufacturing and Levi wasn't surprised to see it was buzzing with activity. A line of horses pulled heavy loads of iron from a nearby warehouse. A brick smokestack rose out of the neighboring foundry and spewed black clouds into the air. Men and wagons went in every direction, carting supplies to the dozens of other buildings scattered across the landscape. The entire Yard sloped down to a series of massive boathouses that lined the shores of the Eastern Branch. In the distance, a handful of ships and steamers trolled the turgid waters.

Levi followed the dirt road to the middle of the Yard before it turned towards a two-story colonial house. Nearing the house, Levi pulled to a stop beside two other wagons and set the brake. He took a quick look around before turning to Josiah. "I'm going inside to see what I can find out from Dahlgren but there's something I need you to do while I'm in there."

Josiah listened carefully and pulled on his beard as Levi explained. "I think John Haney killed Dahlgren's messenger for a reason. I think there may be something here at the Yard that he was after. Something hidden. If we're ever going to know where to find Haney, we need to know what he's looking for." Levi motioned towards the interior of the Yard. "There are countless men, both white and colored, working around here—men of all types and trades. You're a carpenter, Josiah. You can blend in with the other tradesmen and wander this Yard without anyone being the wiser."

Josiah took an uneasy look around. It wasn't the idea of wandering the Yard alone that made him nervous. At one point or another, the Navy had hired every skilled tradesman in the City to work at the Yard. Josiah had worked on several of the warehouses in the past and knew his way around. But he had never walked the Yard in an aimless search for secret information. He pulled on his beard. "What am I supposed to be looking for?"

Levi shrugged. "I don't know," he said. "We're looking for anything that seems out of place." Josiah furrowed his brow, trying to think what that might mean. Knowing there wasn't much to go on, Levi provided the best advice he could. "Just look busy, keep your eyes open and don't get caught."

With that, Levi jumped down from the wagon and headed towards Dalhgren's house. At the top of the stairs, he glanced over his shoulder to see that Josiah was walking directly into the Yard as naturally as any other worker in sight. Levi smiled as he turned back to the house and knocked on the front door.

Moments later, the door opened to reveal a dignified looking man wearing the gold stripes that marked him as a sergeant. "Can I help you?" he asked, looking curiously at the silver Metropolitan Police badge pinned to Levi's chest.

Levi held out the leather case with the flap open. "I'm the police officer who found the body of Lieutenant Adams last night," he said. "I need to speak with Admiral Dahlgren."

The sergeant's eyes grew wide. "What's your name?" he asked.

"Levi Love."

"Wait here," he said and closed the door. Seconds later, he opened it again. "The Admiral will see you now."

The sergeant stood aside and Levi stepped into a small foyer with simple wooden benches lining the walls. "This way, please," the sergeant said, sweeping his arm to a set of paned glass doors.

Levi stepped through the open doors to see a man with thick sideburns and a thin mustache shuffling papers from behind a heavy oak desk. A narrow patch on either of the man's shoulders carried the gold stars and anchor of a United States Admiral.

"Mr. Levi Love is here to see you Admiral," the sergeant said before retreating from the room and closing the doors.

Levi waited patiently as the sounds of the Admiral's paper shuffling filled the silence. Apparently satisfied with the chaotic organization of his desk, the Admiral stopped and looked up at his visitor. "So you're the one who found Lieutenant Adams?" he asked. His eyes were determined and stern. This was a man who got his way instantly and without question.

"Yes, sir," Levi said. "I found him beneath the 14th Street bridge."

The Admiral nodded. "I thank you for taking care of his body until we could collect it. There are plenty of men in this City who would have left him on the banks of the Canal to rot."

"Yes, sir," Levi said, unsure what else to say.

Dahlgren looked down at the leather pouch in Levi's hands. "I see you've got his case with you."

"Yes, sir," Levi said, handing it across the desk.

Dahlgren took the case and opened it. He glanced at the inscription on the flap before plunging his eyes inside. "It's empty," he said sharply.

"Yes, sir," Levi said.

"When you found this case, were there any messages in it?"

"No sir," Levi said.

Dahlgren set the case on the desk and mumbled as he shuffled through his papers. Levi strained to listen but he could only make out every few words. "It's not here… should be here. Scrubber…someone's got it…de Villeroi…scrubber." Suddenly, Dalhgren realized Levi was still standing in his office. "Anything else?" he said.

Levi hesitated as he reached into his pocket and felt the paper scroll Ellen Wolfe had entrusted to her friend before she died. "Yes, sir," Levi said. "There is one other thing."

# Chapter 27

October 24, 1861 – 6th Ward, Washington City

With his long and confident strides, Josiah blended in naturally with the other workers going about the business of the Navy Yard. In truth, he had no idea where he was going or what he was doing. Heading down towards the water, he wove through the sprawling complex of workshops and unmarked warehouses as Levi's instructions turned in his mind. How was he supposed to find something when he had no idea what it was? Where was he supposed to look? He recognized the broad wooden building that housed the Navy's carpentry workshop. With no other ideas coming to mind, he turned towards the shop's open barn doors.

"Hey, you!" someone called out. Josiah's heart raced as he looked around to see a skinny young soldier pointing at him. "Yeah, you!" he said. "Come over here."

Josiah's eyes darted around the busy Yard searching for any sign of what the soldier might want. Had he been caught already? His pulse pounded in his neck as he slowly turned and walked towards the beckoning soldier.

"Yes, sir?" Josiah asked, trying not to look at the tiny white pustules that covered the soldier's face.

"We need some help in there," he said.

The pit that had formed in Josiah's stomach suddenly vanished. He hadn't been caught. The soldier just wanted his help, though with what he had no idea. Josiah looked around. "You need some help in where, sir?"

The soldier pointed. "In there."

Josiah followed his outstretched finger to a long, L-shaped warehouse where a team of men stood alongside a thick center mast. Josiah began to sweat. Setting a center mast on a ship was a long, hard job that would make it impossible for him to look around the Yard. It also made it more likely that someone would ask questions he didn't want to answer. He had to find an excuse.

"What're you waiting for?" the soldier asked.

Josiah's mind raced and he said the first thing that came to mind. "The foundry."

The soldier screwed up his face. "What about it?"

"I'm supposed to be fixing the roof," Josiah said. His story was gaining confidence.

"Says who?" the soldier asked, scratching at his festering skin.

"Captain Johnson," Josiah said, remembering the name of the foundry's commanding officer. "He sent me down here to get some supplies from the carpentry shop."

The soldier looked at Josiah skeptically but it quickly passed. Captain Johnson was known for his short temper and harsh discipline. He would happily punish any man who impeded the full and efficient operation of his foundry. "Well then," the soldier said, "why are you wasting the Captain's time standing around here? Get on with it!"

"Yes, sir," Josiah said but the soldier had already turned to recruit the next man walking by.

Josiah turned towards the carpentry shop where the sounds of hammering and scraping spilled out through the open barn doors and echoed across the Yard. Reaching the doors, Josiah cautiously peered inside. Twenty or more men were hard at work around a series of benches that filled the middle of the shop. Milled wood of every dimension and variety was stacked along the length of one wall. On the opposite wall, an assortment of carpentry tools hung neatly above crates of nails, clamps and other metal supplies used in the trade.

Josiah slipped inside and slowly picked through the supplies. Moving from one crate to the next, he stole glimpses of the men in the center of the shop. A variety of projects were underway. From shaping a thick wooden beam to fashioning the spokes and handles of a new ship's wheel, the men were hard at work building an armada to crush the South. Josiah scanned the rest of the workbenches but nothing appeared out of place.

Turning his attention back to the supplies, the frustration of his impossible task welled inside. His eyes settled on an open crate of nails. The Navy Yard was simply too big with too many buildings to search. It was like trying to find a nail in this stack of nails. Then suddenly, something about the crate itself sparked the flicker of a thought. Josiah turned to look out the shop's barn doors and then back to the crate. It was open. They were both open. So open, in fact, that Josiah had simply walked into the carpentry shop without notice or question.

The conclusion landed like a hammer. If the Admiral Dahlgren was working on something secret in one of these buildings, he wouldn't leave the doors wide open for anyone to see. Josiah smiled. He didn't have to search every building in the Yard—he only had to look for areas that were restricted. Josiah's smile faded as the next thought entered his mind. How was he supposed to search inside a restricted area? Deciding it was best to solve one problem at a time, he turned from the supply crates and left the shop.

Josiah's eyes darted around the collection of wood and brick buildings outside the carpentry shop. He needed a way to wander through the Yard without being conscripted for another mast-setting project. The clang of metal on metal rang out from across the dirt path and drew Josiah's attention. Two men were standing at the back of a wagon and securing a load of copper pipes with a length of rope.

“I think that’s got it,” one of the men said before disappearing back into the warehouse.

As the other man climbed onto the wagon and grabbed the reins, Josiah had an idea. He didn’t know where the wagon was going but if he could find a reason to follow it, he could search the Yard without being bothered. But what excuse did he have to follow a wagonload of copper pipe?

The driver slapped the reins and the wagon rattled and clanged to a start. Josiah had to think of something. Turning into the carpentry shop, he grabbed the first sealed supply crate he could find and then walked quickly out the door. If someone asked, he was delivering the metal clamps needed to secure the pipe. He’d just have to hope no one asked him to open the crate.

The wagon pulled away from the warehouse and Josiah hesitated a moment before stepping out onto the dirt path and following it deep into the Yard.

# Chapter 28

October 24, 1861 – 2$^{nd}$ Ward, Washington City

Edward Huff looked at the full-length mirror in Quigly's dressing room and checked every detail of his appearance. He pulled his tailored coat tight and buttoned it before straightening his tie and setting his top hat firmly in place. Leaning into the mirror, he pressed on the edges of his beard and confirmed that all traces of the adhesive had been removed. He stepped back and, with a final satisfied glance, he grabbed his cane and stepped out of the dressing room.

Entering the showroom at the front of the tailor shop, Edward found the proprietor, Charles Quigly, leaning over his worktable and tracing a pattern onto a rather fine length of wool. "Good morning to you, Charles," Edward said, his diction polished and perfect.

Quigly looked up from his work and smiled. "And to you, Mr. Huff."

The bell released its tinny ring as Edward opened the door and stepped out onto 14$^{th}$ Street. The mid-morning sun cast its rays across a blue sky and Edward glanced casually into the shop windows as they passed by. He was anxious to get where he was going but he couldn't show it. A man of Edward Huff's wealth and status always carried a sense of leisure as he went about his day. Nicholas Turner may rush about the City but Edward Huff took his time.

He had stayed up half the night at Mary Surratt's boarding house reading over the letter he stole from Dahlgren's messenger and planning how best to investigate Brutus de Villeroi. Surely one of Edward's friends would know the man. But the more he thought about it, the more Edward realized that simply asking one of his wealthy contacts was out of the question. He needed to be discrete and inquiring within the upper class would be like shouting from the rooftops. No one gossips quite like the wealthy.

What he really needed was someone familiar with the City's elite but who was also far enough down the social ladder so as to be below their consideration. With that in mind, the answer to his problem suddenly became quite obvious. There were only two places where the City's ruling class hid their secrets—the Nicholas Room at Mary Ann Hall's whorehouse and the lobby of Willard's Hotel. Given the early hour, Edward decided the Willard was a more suitable place to start.

Turning the corner on Pennsylvania Avenue, the Willard had just come into view when Edward saw two beautiful women in fashionable silk dresses walking directly in his path. The tight bodice of their dress pressed against their young breasts and sent them rushing to the surface. It took every ounce of Edward's will to keep his eyes above their shoulders as he stepped to the side and touched the rim of his top hat.

"Good morning, ladies," he said with a polite bow.

The women made brief eye contact and smiled before passing by in a deluge of giggles. Edward looked after them with narrowed eyes. The social pretensions of upper-class women could be truly nauseating. Without their family's money, those women were just as likely to be on their backs at Venerable's as anywhere else.

Edward arrived at Willard's Hotel where a bellman in a green livery and gloved hands greeted him at the door. "Good morning, sir," he said, with a hint of surprise at seeing Edward Huff at that hour of the morning. "May I help you?"

"I believe you may," Edward replied. "It would be a great help if you could tell me whether John has arrived at work this morning."

"John the barman?"

"Yes," Edward said. "That's the very one."

"Yes, sir," the bellman said. "I believe he arrived about thirty minutes ago. If you'll follow me, I'll make sure you're comfortable while I go and get him for you." They crossed the cavernous room to the fireplace where the bellman showed Edward to a leather armchair. "Would you like for me to have John bring you anything, Mr. Huff?"

"Coffee would be splendid," Edward said.

The bellman disappeared, and for a long moment Edward enjoyed the odd silence of Willard's grand lobby in the morning. He glanced at his gold pocket watch. In less than ten hours, the room would be so crowded with the City's ruling class that one would hardly be able to move.

Edward broke from his thoughts when the barman appeared around the corner holding a silver tray and matching coffee pot just over his shoulder. "Good morning, Mr. Huff," he said as he set the tray on a table beside the chair. John was a rosy-cheeked boy of about twenty. Willard had polished the boy's speech but not so much as to completely cover his rural upbringing.

"Good morning, John," Edward said. He waited patiently for the barman to fill his cup and add just enough cream to turn the color. The staff's ability to remember how each guest preferred his coffee was beyond Edward's comprehension.

John's eyes darted around nervously as he extended the cup and saucer towards the wealthy gentleman. "I was told you wanted to see me, sir."

Edward noticed a slight tremble in the barman's hand. "Nothing to be worried about, my boy," he said, taking the cup. "You've done nothing at all wrong. I'm simply working on a little mystery that I believe you might help me solve."

The boy was visibly relieved. "I'd be happy to help if I can, Mr. Huff," he said hopefully. Edward wasn't surprised. Service was in this boy's blood, which is precisely why Edward had chosen to speak with him.

Edward leaned forward and shot a conspiratorial glance around the room. "You see, I'm throwing a bit of a surprise party for a friend of mine," Edward said, turning back to the boy. "I've arranged invitations for all the guests except for one that is escaping me. My friend has mentioned his name several times and I'm embarrassed to say that I don't know a thing about the man or where I might send the invitation."

Edward took a sip of his coffee and looked up to see John was waiting eagerly to assist. Setting the cup back in the saucer, he said, "Do you happen to know of a man named Brutus de Villeroi?"

John's eyes flashed with recognition. "Yes, sir," he said enthusiastically. "I know Mr. de Villeroi."

"Wonderful," Edward said. "I knew I'd come to the right place. What can you tell me about him? I've never seen him here at the Willard."

"Oh you wouldn't see Mr. de Villeroi here," John said. "He's a private man and mostly keeps to himself. The only reason I know of him is that he only hires his help from the Willard."

Edward was a bit confused. "He doesn't have his own staff?"

"No, sir," John said, shaking his head. "I imagine it's because he's a Frenchman and is only in town for a little while."

De Villeroi's private nature and temporary residency explained why Edward hadn't ever heard of the man or seen him about town. But he still needed to find out where de Villeroi lived. He felt a sudden urge to grab this skittish boy by the collar and demand de Villeroi's address but he pressed it down. "He sounds rather intriguing," Edward said. "I can see why my friend finds him so interesting. So tell me how you were fortunate enough to meet the man."

"Like I said, Mr. de Villeroi only hires his staff from the Willard. About a month ago, he hired me to help serve at one of his dinner parties."

Edward couldn't believe his luck. "You served one of his dinner parties?" he asked. "Was the party at his house?"

"Yes, sir," John said. "He's renting one of them mansions up on H Street while he's in town." John squinted at the oak-paneled ceiling for a moment and then shook his head. "I can't remember the number but it's a big gray house with blue shutters."

Edward couldn't recall the house off the top of his head but he was sure he could find it. He took a sip from his cup. "Can you remember who it was that attended the dinner party?"

John shook his head. "Not really," he said. "It was mostly navy men and they all look the same in their uniforms." He thought about the uniforms for a moment longer and added, "There was an Admiral there though."

Edward's eyes shot up from his cup. "Could it have been Admiral Dahlgren?" he asked.

John snapped his fingers. "That's it," he said. "Admiral Dahlgren." John was suddenly puzzled and screwed up his face. "How'd you know that?"

Edward set his cup back on the tray and stood. "You've been a great help, John," he said, slipping a dollar into the barman's hand. "A great help, indeed."

# Chapter 29

October 24, 1861 – 6th Ward, Washington City

Levi stood in Admiral Dahlgren's office with his hand buried in his pocket. Feeling the paper scroll in his fingers, his stomach tightened. The message hidden inside held a secret that had cost Ellen Wolfe her life and Levi had to know what it was. But what if the Admiral took the scroll and refused to give it back? Levi silently cursed himself. Why hadn't he thought to make a copy?

Levi suddenly began to question why had he decided to show the Admiral in the first place. When Ellen gave the scroll to Christine Brandy, she hadn't said a thing about Admiral Dahlgren or anyone else in the navy. She had simply said that Josiah had the key to understanding what it meant. But Ellen was clearly mistaken. Josiah had no more idea how to read the scroll than Levi. The only connection to Dahlgren was that the man who wrote the cryptic message also happened to have murdered the Admiral's messenger.

Since receiving the scroll from Ellen's friend, Levi had spent hours staring at its string of random letters. But no matter how hard he tried he couldn't make any sense of them. He had hit a dead end. The frustrating conclusion brought Levi back to Admiral Dahlgren. If he didn't share the scroll with someone, how would he ever know what it meant?

"You're wasting my time, son," the Admiral snapped.

The room suddenly came back into focus. "Sorry sir," he said. "I'm investigating another murder that I believe may be connected to the death of Lieutenant Daniel."

Dahlgren sat back in his chair and made a steeple with is fingers. "What other murder?"

"It was a woman named Ellen Wolfe, sir." At the mention of Ellen's name, an unexpected surge of emotion coursed inside, but Levi held it back. Any sign of his personal feelings for Ellen would cause the Admiral to doubt his motives and question his conclusions.

"Ellen Wolfe," the Admiral repeated, searching his memory. "Never heard of her. What does she have to do with Lieutenant Daniels?"

Levi took a moment to organize his thoughts. "Well, sir," he began, "I believe the murders are connected by a couple of things. First, there are similarities in the killer's method. The unlimited supply of guns in this City means that almost everybody we find these days has been shot. But both of these victims were found with identical stab wounds beneath their chins. That fact alone makes these two murders rare, but there's something else that ties the bodies to the same killer: both Ellen Wolfe and Lieutenant Daniels had their tongues removed."

Dahlgren sat up in his chair. Levi had his full attention. Reaching into his pocket, Levi removed the scroll and held it up for Dahlgren to see. "And then there's this."

"What's that?" Dahlgren asked.

"Ellen Wolfe gave this to a friend of hers before she died. I believe it's something she took from the murderer."

Dahlgren took the scroll and flattened it out on his desk. Seeing the message, his eyes shot open. "My God," he said under his breath as he leaned forward to get a closer look.

Levi's heart raced. Could Dahlgren actually make sense of it? Levi watched in silence as the Admiral studied the paper for a long moment. Finally, he sat back in his chair and the paper snapped into a coil. "You say the man who wrote this message is the same man who killed Lieutenant Daniels and stole my letters?"

“Yes, sir,” Levi said. “I believe it’s the same man.”

The Admiral stared down at the tiny scroll and nodded. “I’m sure you’ve already guessed that the message written in that scroll is a Confederate code.”

Levi nodded. “That was my guess.”

“Well then,” Dahlgren said, opening a desk drawer, “you can’t read it, without one of these.” He held out a strange device for Levi to see.

Levi couldn’t believe it. Not only did Admiral Dahlgren know exactly what the scroll was, but he also had a way to read it. “What is that?” Levi asked, stepping closer to get a better look at the unusual contraption. The device was made of two concentric wooden wheels with the letters of the alphabet carved around their outer edges. The smaller wheel sat on top of the larger one so that you could clearly see the letters carved into both.

“Every Confederate spy uses one of these to encode their messages,” Dahlgren explained. “That way, if the Union ever intercepts the message, like the one you’ve got here, we won’t be able to read it. This device is called a cipher disc.”

Levi looked at the scroll and back at the cipher disc. “I don’t understand, sir,” he said. “I thought you said we could read the message if we had the disc.”

“That’s not at all what I said,” Dahlgren corrected. “I said you can’t read that scroll *without* one of these. The cipher disc only gets you half the way.”

Levi sighed. When he had first seen the disc, he thought the murderer’s message was within his reach. But just as he closed his grip, it had slipped through his fingers like smoke. “Alright, sir. What gets us the rest of the way?”

"The codeword," Dahlgren said. "Rebels encipher their messages using a codeword known only by the sender and the recipient. And before you get any ideas," he added, "you should know the codeword could be literally any word or phrase in the entire English language."

Levi reached for the scroll still sitting on Dahlgren's desk. "May I?" he asked.

The Admiral sat back in his chair and swept his hand out. "By all means."

Levi unrolled the paper and studied the jumbled letters. He could guess at code words and phrases for the next hundred years and never decrypt the message. But still, he wanted to learn as much as he could about the cipher disc. "Before I go, sir," Levi said, "would you mind showing me how the disc works?"

Dahlgren glanced over at the small clock on his desk. "I'll give you five more minutes."

# Chapter 30

October 24, 1861 – 6th Ward, Washington City

The copper pipes rattled and clanked as the wagon rolled along the dirt path towards the river. Josiah followed at a safe distance and adjusted the heavy crate in his hands. He wished he had taken the time to find a lighter box. Squinting against the sun, he scanned the wooden workshops and storehouses along either side of the path. Everything appeared normal. Men and soldiers wandered freely in and out of the buildings as they went about the daily tasks of the Navy Yard. There were no guards stationed at any of the doors or any other signs of secret activity. Josiah kept his eyes moving as the wagon slowly made its way down to the river.

A collection of warships and supply skiffs were moored along the docks that stretched far out into the Eastern Branch. Throngs of horses, carts, men, and supplies moved in synchronized chaos along the shoreline. Fresh supply skiffs had arrived and lines of men instantly formed to unload everything from wooden beams to barrels of whiskey. On another dock, a team of men resupplied a battered frigate with fresh gunpowder and cannonballs. Wagons cut across the entire scene and parted the crowds like the sea as they pushed their way along the waterfront.

Though the docks were bustling, the center of activity was the towering boathouse at the edge of the water. Inside, the USS Hartford sat in dry dock for emergency repairs. Men were crawling all over the ship like ants. Some were dangling at the end of ropes as they scraped the side of the hull, while others were cleaning the heavy deck guns, inspecting the rigging and repairing a broken blade on the ship's enormous brass propeller.

The USS Hartford was one of the Union's newest and fastest warships and her absence from the seas only made the Confederate blockade that much stronger. Admiral Dahlgren had ordered the men to work day and night until the powerful screw sloop was back in the water. Josiah marveled at the sight until it finally slipped from view. The efforts men made to destroy one another were almost inconceivable.

The wooden box cut into Josiah's skin and he shifted his hands to relieve the pressure. With the boathouse behind him, he turned his attention back to the waterfront. The only building near the docks was a long warehouse with a series of wooden doors topped with arching windows. Josiah studied the traffic along the docks to see that the steady stream of men and supplies flowed directly from the mouth of the expansive warehouse.

Weaving slowly through the crowds, Josiah peered through the open doors. What he saw was exactly as he had expected. Wagons were being loaded and unloaded while supply lists were checked and verified. From what Josiah could see, there was nothing unique or even vaguely interesting going on inside. Whatever Levi was looking for, it wasn't happening inside the warehouse.

Josiah sighed as the warehouse passed from his field of view. With so many people around, it was hard to imagine how the Navy could be doing anything secret near the waterfront. But then again, from what he'd seen, the entire Yard was full of people and activity. Josiah couldn't think of a worse place to try and conduct some sort of secret activity. Maybe Levi had gotten this entire thing wrong. Glancing up, he saw the wagonload of copper pipe pushing to the edge of the crowd.

Reaching the far side of the docks, the wagon continued its rhythmic plodding towards an unknown destination. The air grew quiet as the bustling activity of the waterfront gave way to a collection of smaller buildings nestled into the hillside. Suddenly, the quiet rattle of the wagon formed a pit in Josiah's stomach. Hiding amongst the hundreds of men around the waterfront had been easy. But here, only a dozen or more men wandered the pathways between the scattered buildings. Josiah tightened his grip on the crate to steady his nerves.

He looked up the hill and saw that the dirt path led up to a ridge where it split in two. One path continued up the hill towards the Admiral's house and Latrobe Gate. The other turned back towards the river and disappeared over the ridge.

Josiah took a deep breath and tried to think but he couldn't shake the feeling that Levi had asked for the impossible. He had nearly circled the entire Yard and hadn't seen a single thing out of place. If something secret was going on, it was well hidden. Josiah simply didn't have enough information to know where to look. Shifting his gaze back up the hill, he decided to follow the wagon to the fork in the road and then continue on to Admiral Dahlgren's house where he would find Levi and deliver the bad news.

Josiah had hoped to follow the wagon the entire way but when they reached the fork in the road, the driver pulled the horses to the right and the wagon crested the ridge to begin its slow descent back towards the water. Sticking to his plan, Josiah turned to the left and continued up the hill.

As the rattle of the wagon began to fade, he found himself all alone and completely exposed. While his story about carrying brackets for the copper pipes had been rather thin, it had at least provided an excuse for his wandering around the Yard. Now, his only cover was a wooden crate and he didn't even know what was inside.

Josiah picked up his pace. His eyes traveled nervously up the road where the ridgeline curved around towards the heavy stone wall marking the eastern boundary of the Navy Yard. Suddenly, an idea broke through like a ship piercing the fog. Josiah stopped in his tracks. Narrowing his eyes, he traced the ridgeline back to the road and down to the waterfront. Josiah's pulse quickened as the realization took shape. The ridgeline he was standing on surrounded a sunken pocket in the landscape that was completely hidden from the rest of the Navy Yard.

Josiah cut his eyes around the Yard as a question formed in his mind. Where was that wagon going with all that copper pipe? Shifting his gaze back to the road and over the ridge, he quickly scanned the hillside. The wagon was nowhere to be found. Where had it gone? Unlike the rest of the densely populated Yard, there were no buildings on the other side of the hill—just a large copse of trees down by the water. With nowhere else to look, Josiah stared into the thick trees.

Slowly, the outline of a long building emerged behind the dense branches. The wagon appeared to have stopped beside an open door near the front of the structure where a handful of uniformed guards were checking the load of pipe and questioning the driver.

A pulse of energy shot down Josiah's spine. This was it. He'd found Admiral Dahlgren's hiding place.

# Chapter 31

October 24, 1861 – 4$^{th}$ Ward, Washington City

"Your coach is here, Mr. Huff," said the bellman as he opened the thick doors to the cool mid-morning air.

"Thank you, Martin," Edward said, slipping the boy a dollar as he left the grand lobby and stepped out under the covered portico in front of Willard's Hotel. A neatly dressed coachman stood beside the sleek, black carriage. He opened the door as Edward approached.

"Good morning, sir," he said.

"New York and H," Edward said. "And let's not dawdle."

"Very good, sir," the coachman said with a nod.

Edward stepped into the richly appointed cabin and rested his cane on the empty seat beside him. He watched through the glass windshield as the coachman climbed up onto the bench and grabbed the reins. With a quick slap, the horses jumped to a start and the coach pulled out onto 14$^{th}$ Street. Edward stared out the window as the City rolled by. The repetitive clop of the horses' hooves lulled Edward deep into thought.

The meeting with the Willard's barman had proved to be even better than he had hoped. Not only did he learn the description of Brutus de Villeroi's home on H Street, but he had also confirmed that the intensely private de Villeroi had deep connections with the Union's military leadership. Admiral Dahlgren was notoriously anti-social but even he had attended Brutus de Villeroi's dinner party. Confirming de Villeroi's connections to Dahlgren had only strengthened Edward's resolve.

He reached into his coat pocket and removed a folded piece of paper. Edward had virtually memorized de Villeroi's letter to Dahlgren but he scanned the text as he thought through his plan one more time.

> *October 23, 1861 – H Street, Washington City*
>
> *Dearest Admiral,*
>
> *I am writing to inform you that we have completed our tests and the Scrubber has met your every requirement. We have determined it is fit for service. Shipment to your facility is underway. Scrubber should arrive by this evening at the latest.*
>
> *Your Faithful Servant,*
>
> *Brutus de Villeroi.*

This *scrubber*, whatever it happened to be, was the key to understanding whether and how the Union could break the Southern blockade. As it was, the blockade forced the Union to divert its naval resources to the narrow strip of water off the coast of Washington City. But if the Union broke through the southern guns, Edward feared the Confederacy's days of competing for the high seas would come to an end. If Brutus de Villeroi's *scrubber* helped the Union's war efforts in any way, Edward had to find it and either destroy it himself or get word to those who could. But first, he had to figure out what it was.

The coach turned right onto H Street and Edward opened the small panel in the windshield so that he could speak to the driver. "Here we are, Matthew," he said. "We're looking for a large gray home with blue shutters. Keep an eye out and just give me a signal if you see it."

The coachman nodded and Edward sat back in his seat. Peering from one side of the coach to the other, he studied the opulent mansions that occupied this elite section of the City. Up ahead, he saw a familiar three-story brownstone with a bright red door. Edward smiled knowing that, hidden in the mansion's carriage house, Nicholas Turner's clothes and identity were tucked away in a dusty trunk and awaiting Edward's return.

The smile vanished at the sound of the driver's knuckles rapping on the window. Edward leaned forward to open the panel. "You see it?" he asked.

"Just ahead on the left-hand side," the driver said in a tone that was barely audible over the clapping hooves.

Edward strained to see the mansion through the front windshield. "Slow down so we can get a good look," he said. Moving his cane out of the way, Edward slid across the leather bench to the left side of the coach. Moments later, a large gray home with blue shutters came into view.

Like the other mansions along H Street, de Villeroi's home was symmetrical in design. It had a blue front door in the center and two large windows on either side. The placement of the windows was mirrored on the second and third floors, which terminated in a steep slate roof.

"What should I do?" asked the driver as the coach reached the corner of $10^{th}$ Street.

Edward kept his eyes on the home, studying its every feature. "Take a left here," he said. The coachman turned north onto $10^{th}$ and Edward continued his examination of the home until it passed completely out of view.

"Want me to make another pass?" the driver asked.

"No," Edward said, collecting his cane. "Just pull over." The coach came to a stop and Edward stepped out. "Circle the block and meet me back here," he instructed. The driver nodded and slapped the reins. Putting his cane to ground, Edward retraced the coach's path down 10th Street until he stood across the street from the gray mansion.

There were two ways to go about the business of searching de Villeroi's home. The preferred method would be to wait until the home was empty and then quietly slip inside. Failing that, he was more than willing to force his way in at the point of a knife.

A heavy stone wall about five feet tall extended from the back of the mansion, providing privacy for the back yard and security for the carriage house. Edward's eyes traced the wall around the perimeter of the property. It wasn't the security for the carriage house that had captured Edward's attention, but the privacy the wall provided. He crossed the road and walked along the gravel carriageway that ran behind the wall. A low wooden gate at the far end of the property provided access for de Villeroi's carriage and a perfect view of the mansion.

With its central door and symmetric windows, the back of the home looked very much like the front. But where the front door was exposed to the street, the thick wall completely shielded the back door from view. Edward rested his hands on the top of the gate to test its height before returning his attention back to the door. He guessed that he could jump the fence and be up to the house in under ten seconds. He had found his point of entry.

But where would de Villeroi keep his papers? The mansion was large and searching the entire thing would take too much time. Edward peered into the windows hoping to catch a hint of what was in each room. Just then, there was motion in one of the lower windows. Edward quickly lowered his head and spun behind the stone column beside the gate. Removing his top hat, he slowly turned to peek around the corner.

Two men were standing next to one another and examining a rather large sheet of paper. Their discussion appeared to be both civil and formal. One of the men laid the paper out on a table while the other leaned over and pointed to something on the page.

The arrival of the men brought both good news and bad. The good news was that Edward had identified where the search of de Villeroi's home should begin. The bad news was that the search would have to wait. He couldn't go barging into the mansion knowing that at least two men were inside. It hadn't yet come to that.

Keeping his head low, Edward turned back down the carriageway towards 10th Street. He would give the two men some time to leave the house before making his return. Edward sensed the handle of the blade strapped to his leg. If the men were still home in a few hours, he would to turn to other means of getting inside.

The coach arrived just as he reached the end of the carriageway. The driver hopped down from the bench and opened the door. "Where to now?" he asked.

Edward stood in the door until a sudden tightening of his loins told him exactly where to go. "I believe I could use some time at Mary Ann Hall's."

# Chapter 32

October 24, 1861 – 7th Ward, Washington City

Levi crouched down beside the wagon wheel and tested each of the red spokes with his hand. After leaving Admiral Dahlgren's office, he had been waiting by the wagon for Josiah's return. He felt more suspicious with each passing minute and decided he had better find something to make himself look busy. He took his time rearranging the collection of debris in the back of the wagon but it hadn't taken very long. Hopping down from the wagon, he looked for something else to do. When nothing came to mind, he began checking each of the wooden spokes, though for what he had no idea. Levi was wondering whether the sick feeling in his stomach was from nerves or frustration when a dark shadow crossed his path.

"Something wrong?"

Levi's heart jumped and he spun around to see a familiar, broad-shouldered man pulling on his beard. "Good God, Josiah," Levi said. He dropped his head to catch his breath. "You scared the hell out of me." Knowing that his companion was okay, Levi's nervousness vanished and frustration quickly set in. "What took you so long?"

Josiah cut his eyes around the Yard. "Maybe we should get out of here first," he said with a knowing look. Levi glanced around. Josiah was right. It was time for them to leave.

The bench seat creaked as they climbed into the wagon and Levi slapped the reins. Weaving through the steady traffic in the Yard, they rode along in silence until they passed through the archway at Latrobe Gate. The guard that had given them such trouble on the way in opened the gate and allowed the wagon to pass without a second glance. Levi pulled out onto M Street as the heavy iron gate crashed to a close behind them.

Levi glanced over his shoulder to see their growing distance from the Navy Yard. "So what did you see?" he asked, unable to wait a moment longer.

"I found it, Mr. Love," Josiah said with a hint of excitement. "I found the hiding place."

Levi's mouth gaped open in disbelief. "How do you know?" he asked.

Josiah looked around as if to ensure one of the soldiers hadn't found his way into the bed of the wagon. "I walked that entire Yard," he said in a low voice. "There are more men working at that place than you can count. Keeping a secret like the one you're talking about is a hard thing to do in a place like that. I figure the only way to do it is to keep all those people as far away from that secret as possible."

Levi nodded. Josiah's logic was hard to dispute. "Makes sense," he said. "So what was it? What did you find?"

"Like I said," Josiah continued, "I walked that entire Yard and didn't see a single building in the whole place that wasn't crawling with people—except for one." Levi's eyes lit up and he turned to get a good look at Josiah.

"Most of the Yard slopes down to the flat by the waterfront," Josiah continued. "That's where all the buildings and people are. The main road leads around through the waterfront and then follows a ridge back up to the Admiral's house. But on the other side of that ridge, tucked in where you can't see it from the waterfront, there's a building all by itself down by the water."

Levi's excitement was growing by the second. "Did you get a good look at it?"

Josiah shook his head. "No," he said. "Too many trees. But I saw enough to know there are guards down there checking every wagon and man that comes within a hundred feet of that building."

Levi couldn't believe it. He had sent Josiah into the Yard without any real hope of finding anything. It was a dangerous task and Josiah had no help or any information to go on. Levi had asked for the impossible and that's exactly what Josiah had accomplished. He clasped Josiah's leg and smiled. "That's got to be it," he said. "Whatever it is that Ellen's murderer is after, it's got to be in that building."

"I don't know if it is or it isn't," Josiah said. "But if it is, he's going to have a hard time getting to it. There are soldiers all around and they're checking the wagons."

Levi thought for a moment. "So you saw a wagon go down there?"

"Sure did," Josiah said. "I followed it all the way around the Yard."

"Did you see what it was carrying?"

Josiah shrugged. "Just a bunch of copper pipe."

Levi slowed the wagon to allow a merchant pushing a heavy cart to pass. He wasn't sure what to make of the copper pipe and had no idea what the Navy was doing inside the secret building. It really didn't matter much to Levi. What did matter was catching Ellen's killer. But the Navy was building something inside that secret building and if John Haney was after it, he would have to find a way inside. Levi narrowed his eyes and tried to put himself in Haney's shoes. "Was there a dock down by that building?" he asked.

"I'm not sure," Josiah said. "The trees were too thick to see much of anything. But I suppose there could have been one," he added.

Levi aimlessly turned the wagon onto 3rd Street as two recurring questions turned in his mind. What was the Navy doing in that building? And did John Haney intend to do anything about it?

"So what did the Admiral say?" Josiah asked, cutting across Levi's thoughts.

Levi blinked to clear his head. He reached into his coat pocket and pulled out a contraption like nothing Josiah had ever seen.

"What is it?" Josiah asked.

"The Admiral gave this to me," Levi said, holding the strange object out for Josiah. "It's called a cipher disc."

Josiah took the disc and studied it for a moment. There were two wooden wheels with the entire alphabet carved around their edges. Josiah grabbed the outer wheel, which spun freely around the smaller wheel in the center. He couldn't make any sense of it. "What do you do with it?" he asked.

"You know that scroll I showed you?" Levi asked. "The one Ellen gave to her friend at Venerable's?"

"I remember," Josiah said.

"The reason we can't read the scroll is because John Haney used one of these discs to turn his message into a code. But the only way we can decode the message is to know the codeword Haney used to create the message in the first place."

"So what's the codeword?" Josiah asked, though he had already guessed at Levi's answer.

"No idea," Levi admitted. "It could be literally anything. And that doesn't just mean any word. Dahlgren said the Confederates sometimes use entire phrases to encode their messages."

Josiah pulled on his beard. With limitless possibilities for a codeword, they may as well try to walk on water as to read that message. “So what do we do now?” he asked.

Levi shook his head. “I’m really not sure.”

The wagon rattled along 3rd Street where it passed a clearing filled with the same white canvas tents that occupied every other open space in the City. Levi peered into the camp as the wagon rolled slowly by. Soldiers were scattered around the tents cleaning their guns, telling jokes, or playing cards. Someone scratched out a familiar tune on a fiddle. Given the bloody conflict that had brought the men together, the atmosphere was surprisingly cheerful.

Levi was glancing down another row of tents when something familiar caught his eye. The image formed a sudden pit in his stomach. He spun his head to get his bearings but the knot only tightened. Without knowing it, Levi had guided the wagon to the one place in this City that he swore he would never visit again.

“You alright, Mr. Love?” Josiah asked, sensing the sudden change in Levi.

“This is where we found her,” Levi said, softly. “This is where we found Ellen.”

Josiah looked down at his feet. Last night after Levi left his home, Josiah had remembered something else about Ms. Wolfe that he had so far kept to himself. Whether Levi admitted it or not, he loved Ellen Wolfe and Josiah had seen no reason to share information that would further erode Levi’s feelings. But now, even with everything they had learned about Dahlgren’s secret building and the encoded scroll, the investigation to find Ellen’s murderer had run cold. Protecting Levi’s feelings meant withholding information that could help in their search for John Haney. Josiah knew in his heart he had to say something.

"You know, Mr. Love," he began. His voice was gentle and calm. "The man we're after, this John Haney or whatever his name is, I got a good look at him. I saw those black eyes as cold as death. And I'd know him if I saw him again." Josiah hesitated. "But Ms. Wolfe," he said, "Ms. Wolfe knew the man."

The thought of Ellen lying with a murderous spy turned Levi's stomach. He didn't want to think of it or hear another word but Josiah's quiet understanding put Levi at ease. Whatever Josiah was about to say, Levi knew it was important. He squeezed the leather reins to steady his nerve.

"There's still a chance Ms. Wolfe told someone who John Haney really is," Josiah said.

"We already talked to her best friend at Venerable's," Levi reminded him. "If Ellen was going to tell someone, wouldn't she have told her?"

Josiah looked down at his feet again. "Ms. Wolfe didn't just work at Venerable's," he said. The knot twisted in Levi's gut. He looked over at Josiah and clenched his jaw in anticipation of what he was about to hear. "Ms. Wolfe also spent some time at Mary Ann Hall's place."

Levi dropped his head. Though he already knew Ellen was a prostitute, the news that she worked at multiple whorehouses made the sting of it all that much worse.

He closed his eyes tight and the leather reins grew slack in his hands. The horses began plotting their own course through the streets as Levi struggled to dredge images of the Ellen he knew to the surface—the brightness of her smile, the penetrating gaze of her amber eyes. The memories grew and spread like a fine mist rolling over a hillside. And then somehow, ever so slowly, the woman he knew Ellen Wolfe to be made peace the woman she actually was.

Levi opened his eyes and thought about what Josiah had said. "So you think Ellen may have told one of her friends at Mary Ann Hall's who John Haney really is?"

Josiah remained quiet as the conclusion set in. Slowly, Levi began nodding his head. "Okay," he said, sitting up and pulling the slack out of the reins. At the next corner, he turned left onto C Street.

"Where are we going?" Josiah asked.

Levi's eyes glowed with a renewed determination. "We're going to Mary Ann Hall's."

# Chapter 33

October 24, 1861 – 7th Ward, Washington City

“The usual, Mr. Huff?”

Edward looked up to see Mary Ann Hall’s polished barman holding out a fresh bottle of Maker’s Mark. “Yes. That will do just fine,” Edward said. The bartender stepped away and returned seconds later with a tumbler of bourbon.

“Thank you, Robert,” Edward said as the barman set the glass on a square of white cloth. Taking up the glass, Edward held it under his nose and breathed in the complex aromas of vanilla and cinnamon. It was always nice to be Edward Huff.

He took a small sip and smiled as he returned the glass to the bar. For the first time in days, Edward felt completely relaxed. His investigation into Brutus de Villeroi was going exactly as planned and his time upstairs with Renee Rose had released any of the remaining tension that had built over the past few days. Renee hadn’t quite acquired all the skills of Ellen Wolfe but Edward didn’t mind. In fact, he found a certain sense of pride in knowing that, from time to time, he could teach a whore a thing or two. While he took his time to complete Renee Rose’s education, he enjoyed the tight curves of her body and the taught skin that formed around her nipples at the slightest touch of his tongue.

“I’ve been looking at you for fifteen minutes now.”

The deep male voice felt like a bucket of cold water in a warm bath. Edward looked over to see the man who had so abruptly interrupted his thoughts. He wore a handlebar mustache and a wide smile. Glancing at the man’s dusty, middle-class suit, Edward wondered how he had gotten by Mary Ann Hall’s rather particular doorman.

"Name's Mitchell McCrea," the man said, thrusting his hand out. "I'm from Fort Worth, Texas. You ever been to Fort Worth?" he asked, his hand still hanging patiently in the air.

Driven more by propriety than interest, Edward reached out and shook the man's hand. "No," Edward said blankly. "I've never been to Fort Worth."

"Great town," McCrea said, giving Edward's hand a vigorous shake. "Fort Worth's got wide open skies and wide open women." McCrea laughed heartily at his own wit and Edward used the excuse to extract his hand from the man's grip. Oblivious to Edward's social cues, McCrea continued his boisterous speech. "Probably best to wait until this infernal war is over before you visit but it's hard for me to complain. This war has made me a richer than a nickel-night whore with a ten-dollar bill!"

Edward immediately sensed something about Mitchell McCrea that he didn't like. While his brash manners and harsh language had no place at Mary Ann Hall's, it was something else entirely that had struck Edward about his new companion. McCrea hailed from a Southern state and yet here he was in the capital of the North carousing with whores and bragging of newfound riches. Edward narrowed his eyes. "May I ask how it is that the war has made you rich?"

McCrea's wide smile reappeared under his thick handlebar mustache. "You've seen that flaccid stump of a monument they've thrown together to honor George Washington?"

"I have," Edward said, now genuinely curious where the man was taking him.

"More like an insult than an honor if you ask me," McCrea scoffed. "But if you've seen the monument then I'm sure you've seen all the cattle that are grazing around that useless pile of rocks. How many cattle you think there are out there?" McCrea asked.

Edward took his time with a sip of bourbon. "I haven't the foggiest of ideas," he said, returning his glass to the bar.

"There are 2,828 head of cattle in that pen," McCrea answered without the slightest attempt to hide his swelling pride. "Damn near every one of those heads came from my ranch."

Edward stared deep into McCrea's eyes and his blood began to boil. His mind rushed to control his temper but Edward's disciplined emotions somehow slipped from his grasp. "So you're a Southern rancher who turned on his own country to get rich by bringing food and aid to the North."

McCrea's wide smile slowly fell from his face until his mouth gaped open. Edward got a hold of himself but allowed the tension linger a moment longer before correcting course. "Just joking, my boy!" he said, slapping McCrea on the shoulder. "Let me buy you a drink!"

The smile that returned to McCrea's face was even wider than before. "You sure had me going there, mister."

"My name is--"

"No, wait," McCrea said, holding up his hand. "Don't tell me. That's why I came over here in the first place."

Confusion shone on Edward's face. "Oh?" he said.

"That's right," McCrea said. "I'll tell you something. There are only a few things in this world that I know. I know cattle. I know a good whore when I meet one. And I know a man's face when I've seen it before." McCrea gestured over his shoulder. "I've been sitting right over there staring at you for going on fifteen minutes now and I know I've seen you somewhere before."

Edward's heart began to thump as he searched deep into the recesses of his mind. Mitchell McCrea wasn't a man who blended into his surroundings. He was loud, brash and uniquely memorable. If Edward had ever met this man before, he would certainly remember.

"Now I can usually put a name to face like that," McCrea said with a snap of his fingers that recaptured Edward's full attention. "But for some reason, I couldn't quite place yours. Hell, I'd even started to doubt that I'd seen you before. But then I saw your eyes." McCrea's chest puffed with the pride of someone who had discovered a hidden treasure.

Edward's mind reeled and he tightened his grip around his glass. How was it possible that a cattle rancher from a thousand miles away had any idea who he was? Then an even more terrifying question came to mind. Who was it that Mitchell McCrea thought he recognized? Was it Edward Huff or someone else entirely?

Edward forced a smile. "You must be mistaken, Mr. McCrea," he said. "I'm certain I would remember if we had met before."

"I didn't ever say we'd met," McCrea corrected. "I said I was sure I'd seen you before. And then I remembered where." Edward felt his blood pressure rise. He took a sip of bourbon to calm his nerves as McCrea continued. "I came to Washington City back in April of last year trying to sell some of my cattle to the government. With the threat of war breathing down their necks, the Army was looking for any suppliers they could get. We struck a quick bargain and I went out to celebrate. That's when I wandered into the Canterbury to get a drink."

A jolt of electricity shot down Edward's spine like lightning. His muscles coiled as his eyes drifted up from his glass and locked in on McCrea. How could this be possible?

"I remember it was pretty crowded that night," McCrea said, continuing his story without any notice of his companion's change in demeanor. "There was lots of whooping and hollering for the actors up on stage. Soon enough a character named Lennox comes out and gives a speech like nothing I'd ever heard. By the time he was halfway through, that place was as quiet as the grave."

Memories of that night at the Canterbury swirled in Edward's mind like a tornado. His chest felt like it was going to explode. Mitchell McCrea didn't recognize Edward Huff—he recognized *him*. Edward kept his eyes pinned to McCrea's and he waited.

"When the show was over, I asked around to find out who it was that had delivered that speech. Finally, I found the boy running the curtain backstage and he told me the man's name was Charles Cain."

Edward's pulse throbbed and the blood rushed to his head. He hadn't heard his real name spoken out loud for longer than he could remember. But there it was. And now, something had to be done. Edward set his jaw. He would never allow this traitorous cattleman from Texas to undo everything he had worked for. His black eyes went cold as he pictured the blood pouring from Mitchell McCrea's severed throat.

Just then, a shaft of light from the front foyer cut through the darkened interior. Edward glanced over McCrea's shoulder to see the doorman escorting another man towards the bar. The dim light of the surrounding lamps cast shadows over the man's face but as he drew closer, his handsome features and thick brown hair slowly took shape. A sudden flash of silver pulled Edward's eyes towards the man's chest like a magnet. And then he saw it—the unmistakable badge of a Metropolitan Police officer. A quick glance to the officer's face confirmed what Edward already knew. Levi Love had just arrived at Mary Ann Hall's and he was headed Edward's way.

# Chapter 34

October 24, 1861 – 7th Ward, Washington City

The wagon bounced over a deep rut in the road and Josiah braced himself against the sideboard to keep from tumbling out. Regaining his balance, he looked out over the collection of broken down and tar-papered shacks along Maryland Avenue. Just ahead, a pack of feral dogs chewed on a hog's carcass. It was hard to believe that Mary Ann Hall's luxurious whorehouse was anywhere within a hundred miles of this place.

"You sure you know where you're going?" Josiah asked.

"I'm sure," Levi said. The wagon rattled along for several more minutes before Levi pointed. "There it is."

Josiah squinted down the road to see a beautiful, two-story brick building with a wrap-around porch. The building looked as out of place in this neighborhood as a colored man in Congress.

Levi pulled to a stop in front of Mary Ann Hall's and was instantly met by a barrel-chested man in a tailored black suit. "You lost?" he said abruptly.

Levi looked down to see the man was standing right beside the wagon. His stern visage warned Levi to keep his hands on the reins and his ass on the bench. But in Levi's experience, there were very few people willing to follow their words with violence, and even fewer able to actually do so.

He dropped the reins and stood in front of the bench so that he towered over the valet. "I'm here to see Mary Ann Hall," he said, stepping forward to jump down from the wagon.

Seeing Levi's boot directly overhead, the valet took a quick step back and Levi landed exactly where he had been standing. With the men on even ground, the valet's confidence returned. He balled his fists but before he could make use of them, Levi gripped the handle of his rosewood club. At the same time, Josiah slid across the bench to make his presence felt.

The valet's eyes bounced between Levi and Josiah for a long moment before he finally set his jaw and spoke through clenched teeth. "I'll walk you inside," he said, locking eyes on Levi. "But your boy here," the valet pointed up at Josiah, "he ain't going nowhere."

Levi looked up at Josiah. "I don't mind staying right here, Mr. Love," Josiah said before shifting his gaze to speak directly at the valet. "And I will stay right here."

Levi smiled at the valet. "It seems we have an arrangement," he said.

With a final stare that conveyed more defeat than intimidation, the valet turned and led Levi along the paved walkway to the covered porch. He opened the oak front door leading to an antechamber within. Another man in a black suit appeared in the doorway and looked to the valet for an explanation.

"This *officer* is here to see Madame Hall," the valet said, spitting the word *officer* like a bad oyster.

The doorman gave Levi a quick once-over that ended with an incredulous stare. Mary Ann Hall's wealthy and powerful patrons had always ensured the Metropolitan Police kept a respectable distance from her establishment. And now, not only was a policeman standing on the porch, he was asking to see Madame Hall herself. The doorman's mouth fell open but the words caught in his throat as he tried to organize his protest.

Levi quickly filled the void. "I'm here investigating the murder of one of Madame Hall's ladies. We think there might be someone out there looking to murder all of Ms. Hall's female employees, which, I imagine, would make it rather difficult for her to afford a doorman and a valet." Levi cut his eyes to the two besuited men. He had thought of the lie on the spot and hoped the doorman's personal interest would overcome his sense of duty.

Silence hung in the air a little longer than Levi had hoped before the doorman finally spoke. "You can wait for Madame Hall at the bar, where you will pay for a drink whether you want one or not."

Levi nodded his agreement, though he had no intention of giving a single penny to further Madame Hall's operations. He stepped into the windowless antechamber where the ornate chandelier overhead only hinted at the extravagance beyond. Months ago, Levi had gone to Willard's Hotel to return a bag that he had recovered from a notorious cutpurse. Stepping into Willard's lobby, Levi thought he had entered into the most opulent room on earth. But now, as the doorman opened the antechamber's interior door, Levi knew he had been wrong. The excesses of Mary Ann Hall's surpassed anything he had ever seen.

The doorman led Levi to the bar at the front of the room. "You wait right here," he ordered before disappearing through another door.

Levi glanced over at the barman who refused to acknowledge his presence. He continued surveying the room and was trying to absorb the lavish décor when his attention was drawn to a sudden *SLAP* on the bar. A few feet away, a loud and rather obnoxious man with a thick handlebar mustache pounded the bar while laughing at his own joke. The man's behavior may have been welcomed at the White Horse or some other saloon, but at Mary Ann Hall's it fit in like a turd on a dinner plate.

Levi craned his neck to see the man's bearded and bespectacled companion staring directly down at his glass without the slightest hint of a smile. In fact, the man appeared annoyed, if not downright angry. Levi was leaning further to get a better look at the man when a silky voice caught his attention.

"I hear you're looking for me."

Levi shifted his gaze to see a stunningly beautiful woman in an embroidered silk dress. She had long blonde hair and her unflinching blue eyes conveyed a deep confidence and even deeper intelligence. This had to be Mary Ann Hall. Levi stifled a smile as an image of the last Madame he spoke to came to mind. The contrast to the morbidly obese, and terminally obtuse, Madame Venerable could not have been greater.

"Madame Hall?" Levi asked just to be certain.

Mary Ann bowed her head slightly but didn't break eye contact for a second. "At your service, officer?" her voice trailed off, inviting Levi to fill in the blank.

"Love," Levi said. "My name is Levi Love. Is there somewhere private you'd like to talk?"

Mary Ann smiled at the question. "Honey, I can assure you there are far more shocking things that go on around here than whatever it is you've got to say. And trust me," she said, touching Levi's arm in a way that ensured his full attention, "everything that happens in here is private."

Levi glanced around to see the barman had retreated to the other end of the bar and the man with the handlebar mustache was still monopolizing his companion's attention. Satisfied no one was listening, he turned back to Mary Ann Hall. "I'm investigating the death of someone who worked here upon occasion. Do you know a woman named Ellen Wolfe?" Looking into Mary Ann's eyes, Levi knew the answer before she had a chance to speak.

"Yes," she said without a hint of surprise or emotion. "Ellen was a beautiful and remarkable woman. She would moonlight here upon occasion when we had extra people in town or when she was specifically requested by one of the guests." Levi suppressed the unpleasant images that accompanied the remark as Mary Ann continued. "But I can assure you that all of my guests enjoyed Ellen's company far too much to do her any harm." Mary Ann placed a suggestive hand on Levi's arm. "I do believe you're looking in the wrong place, Officer Love."

Levi glanced down at Mary Ann's hand. The obvious attempt to cut the interview short wasn't surprising. Police officers rarely enhanced the whoring business and Madams typically did whatever they could to get them out the door. But Levi wasn't finished. "Have you ever heard the name John Haney?"

Mary Ann looked towards the ceiling and took a deep breath that heaved her abundant breasts to the outer limits of her bodice. "It doesn't sound familiar," she said in a breathy voice laced with growing frustration. "But like I said, everything that goes on in here is private."

Levi had expected the answer. There was little chance a man with the description of John Haney could even get as far as the front porch at Mary Ann Hall's. "One more thing, Miss Hall," Levi said. He waited for Mary Ann's piercing blue eyes to settle on him once again. "I know Ellen Wolfe had some friends here and I'm going to need to talk to them."

"Ellen was a private and particular woman," Mary Ann continued. "She was particular about her guests and even more particular about her friends. In fact," Mary Ann added after a moment of thought. "I can only think of one of my intimates that she ever talked to at all."

"Who was it?"

"Renee Rose."

"Is she here now?" Levi asked, glancing quickly around the room as if he could identify the woman on sight.

Mary Ann's eyes traveled casually over the two men at the bar before sweeping up the staircase. "She sure is," Mary Ann said. "And I believe she is currently unoccupied."

# Chapter 35

October 24, 1861 – 7th Ward, Washington City

Edward gripped his glass so tight that he thought it might break. He had arrived at Mary Ann Hall's wanting nothing more than a comfortable place to wait for Brutus de Villeroi to vacate his home. He had planned on a brief interlude with Renee Rose and a quiet drink at the bar but he had gotten far more than he bargained for.

Edward had a decision to make. Both Mitchell McCrea and Levi Love posed a unique danger to Edward's life and his plans for Brutus de Villeroi. There was little doubt that both would need to be dealt with. What was less clear was which of the men posed the most immediate threat. Edward thought it through and quickly decided that everything hinged on one very important question: How close was Levi Love to discovering Edward Huff's connection to Ellen Wolfe?

"I'm telling you," McCrea blustered on, "I don't know a single person who can put a face to a name as well as I can. Yessir, my memory's as water-tight as a fish's asshole!" McCrea slapped the bar and roared with laughter. His brash nature alone was nearly enough to sway Edward's thoughts but he couldn't make his decision on emotion.

Edward stared deep into the bourbon at the bottom of his glass. Focusing every ounce of his attention on Levi Love's voice, the sounds of the pestilent Texan slowly faded into the background. "Do you know a woman named Ellen Wolfe?" he heard Levi ask.

Mary Ann Hall's voice was no match for McCrea's, which completely drown out her response. But it didn't matter. If there was one thing in this world a man could count on, it was Mary Ann Hall's discretion. She wouldn't give Levi any information that Edward wouldn't give himself. Besides, Levi's question brought with it some good news. The policeman had arrived at

Mary Ann Hall's looking for connections to Ellen Wolfe, not Edward Huff.

Moments later, he heard Levi's voice again. "Have you ever heard of a man named John Haney?" Edward suppressed a smile and relaxed his powerful grip on the glass tumbler. Levi could search until the end of his days and never find another trace of John Haney. That he would even ask Mary Ann Hall about a lowlife tradesman like John Haney was laughable. Levi Love was operating in a world of which he knew nothing about.

Levi's voice broke into Edward's thoughts once again. "I know Ellen Wolfe had some friends here and I'm going to need to talk to them." Edward strained to hear Mary Ann's answer but it was buried beneath McCrea's incessant storytelling. When McCrea finally paused to take a breath, Mary Ann's voice broke through for an instant.

"Renee Rose."

Edward's heartbeat surged and his hand tightened around the glass as he silently cursed himself. Why hadn't he seen it before? Ellen was friendly with Renee, who no more than an hour before had been pressing her naked body against his own. Renee had never met John Haney but she certainly knew Edward Huff. Edward's mind was racing. Could Levi Love somehow use Renee to make the connection between him and John Haney? Out of his peripheral vision, he saw Mary Ann lead Levi up the stairs and directly towards Renee Rose. What was he to do?

Just then, McCrea's voice forced its way back to the surface. "Come on, Charlie," he said, "give me just a little bit."

The silence hung in the air too long and Edward was compelled to respond. "I've told you, Mr. McCrea," he said, having no idea what McCrea had just asked him to give, "my name is Edward Huff. I've never heard of this Charles Cain fellow."

McCrea's lengthy silence pulled Edward's eyes from his glass and over to the blustery Texan. "See there," McCrea said, lifting his glass, "it's all in the eyes, Charlie."

And with that, the decision was made. Edward could do nothing to stop Levi from talking to Renee and there was still a good chance it would lead to nothing. But Mitchell McCrea had spoken Charles Cain's name one too many times. He would not speak it again.

Edward shot the last of the Maker's and returned the glass to the bar. "Mr. McCrea," he said, dabbing his beard with the small white cloth, "what do you say we get out of here and find a place with a little more spirit?"

McCrea slapped the bar. "You read my mind! This place has less action than a whore in church." Edward was standing to leave when McCrea said, "But how about we have one more drink here before we go?"

Edward balled his fists in frustration. He gave a quick glance up the stairs before settling his eyes back on Mitchell McCrea. This man was infuriating at every turn. Knowing he couldn't very well grab the annoying cattleman by his shitty suit coat and drag him screaming from the building, Edward calmly returned to his seat at the bar. "Just a short one then," he said.

# Chapter 36

October 24, 1861 – 7th Ward, Washington City

Levi followed Madame Hall up the stairs to a wide hallway lit by crystal chandeliers. Three velvet settees with matching side tables were evenly spaced down the right side of the hall. Levi briefly wondered why anyone would sit in the hallway until he noticed that each of the settees was arranged opposite a hand-painted door. Levi could only presume the doors led to the bedrooms where Mary Ann Hall's *intimates* conducted their business. Mary Ann led Levi down the hall to the third door, which was painted with a winding rose bush in full bloom.

She knocked on the door and waited a few seconds before opening it to reveal an elegant bedroom. On the far wall, a sweeping oil painting hung over a small dining table and an inlaid writing desk. Fine leather chairs sat on an ornate rug in front of the fireplace to create an intimate seating area. Beneath the marble mantle, a warm fire crackled and cast its orange glow across a heavy oak bed.

"Renee?" Mary Ann called into the room as she crossed the threshold.

"Yes?" came a female voice from somewhere within. Seconds later, the woman stepped out from behind the door and a pulse of electricity shot across Levi's body. The woman's olive skin, dark hair, and wide green eyes were stunning and exotic. She was tightening a light blue robe around her waist but the sheer silk left her dark nipples in plain view. Levi felt his mouth drop.

"Renee," Mary Ann said, "this is Officer Levi Love. He's investigating Ellen's death and has a few questions to ask you."

Renee's green eyes glistened at the rather harsh reminder of Ellen's murder but her voice remained steady as she extended her hand towards Levi. "Nice to meet you Mr. Love." Levi got the feeling that, under any other circumstances, his last name would have drawn a playful titter from Ms. Rose.

Levi took her hand and shook it gently. “Nice to meet you as well, Ms. Rose. May we sit down and talk for a moment?”

“Please,” Renee said, stepping aside and motioning towards the chairs by the fire.

Mary Ann Hall started across the room but Levi stopped her. “Madame Hall,” he said. Mary Ann spun in place and narrowed her eyes to a menacing stare. She knew what he was about to say. “I believe it would be best if I talk to Ms. Rose on my own.” Mary Ann held her stare as if trying to penetrate his mind. Levi shrugged. “Or I could just spend the rest of my day downstairs. I’m sure your patrons wouldn’t mind a police officer observing them during their day’s entertainment.”

Levi waited patiently but Mary Ann’s stern visage remained. “Ms. Rose has another appointment in thirty minutes,” she finally said through clenched teeth. “You will be out of this room and out of my house before then.” With that, Mary Ann crossed the room to the door but as she stepped over the threshold, she suddenly stopped and looked back at Levi. “I have connections of my own, Mr. Love,” she said, “and I promise I can make your life far more difficult than you can make mine.” The look on her face as she closed the door left little doubt that Mary Ann Hall meant every word of it.

A long silence filled the room that was broken only by the crackle of the fire. “I suppose we had better get started,” Renee Rose finally said. She rounded a leather chair in front of the fireplace and motioned for Levi to do the same. Levi crossed the room towards the fire and lowered himself into the chair. Looking up, he opened his mouth to speak but the words caught somewhere deep in his gut. The edge of Renee’s silk robe had fallen open so that it lay just over her nipples, leaving the body of her breasts fully exposed. The fire painted her skin with an orange glow that had made it impossible for Levi to speak.

"Mr. Love?" Renee said, drawing Levi's attention up from her chest to her full lips and then finally to her eyes. "You have some questions for me about Ellen?"

"Yes," he said, clearing his throat and shifting slightly in his chair. "There are a few things I'm hoping you might help me with. Madame Hall said that you were friendly with Ellen Wolfe."

"We were more than just friendly," Renee said as her eyes began to glisten. "Ellen was my best friend."

Levi allowed Renee a moment to collect herself. "I'm terribly sorry," he said. "Did Ellen ever mention a man by the name of John Haney?"

Renee's eyes drifted towards the fire where they stayed for a long moment. "Not that I can remember," she said, shifting her green eyes back to Levi.

"Maybe you saw him but didn't know his name," Levi suggested. "He's a tradesman. Larger than average build with brown hair and dark black eyes."

Renee smiled. "Tradesmen go to the Blue Goose or the Devil's Own, Mr. Love. They don't come here. Mary Ann only allows the rich and the powerful through her doors. And eventually," Renee added with a knowing smile, "they *all* come through her doors.

Levi had more questions about Haney but Renee's comment sent Levi's mind in another direction. Without thinking, he pulled the gold coin from his pocket and turned it in his fingers. *All the rich and powerful come through Mary Ann's doors.*

The memory of Admiral Dahlgren looking into his messenger's empty leather case rose to the surface. "*It's not here,*" Dahlgren had mumbled. "*Should be here. Scrubber...someone's got it...de Villeroi...scrubber.*" Levi had no idea what the *scrubber* was but de Villeroi sounded like someone's name. Somehow, this de Villeroi character was connected to the important message that Admiral Dahlgren had been expecting and that John Haney had killed to obtain. The more Levi thought about it, the more he saw that de Villeroi was at the center of everything that had happened.

A tenuous conclusion formed in Levi's mind. If de Villeroi operated anywhere near the same circles as Admiral Dahlgren, then perhaps he was the type of rich and powerful man Renee Rose was talking about. *Eventually, they all come through her doors.*

"Have you heard of a man named de Villeroi?" Levi asked.

"Brutus?" Renee laughed. "Everyone around here knows Brutus."

"So he comes in here?" Levi asked excitedly.

Renee shook her head. "No," she said with a smile that hinted at the images playing in her mind. "Brutus is intensely private. He's got an arrangement with Madame Hall though."

"What sort of arrangement?"

"His man comes in once a week to select a couple of *intimates* to come and entertain that dirty old Frenchman." The word *dirty* came across as a playful compliment rather than an insult.

"So if he doesn't come here," Levi said, "where do the ladies entertain him?"

"At his home," Renee said as if the answer should be obvious. "He's got a wonderful mansion up on H Street."

Levi's hands gripped the arms of the chair tight. "And you've been there?" he asked.

"Of course," she said. "All of us have at one point or another."

"So which house is it?"

"It's the gray one at the corner of $10^{th}$ and H Streets."

Levi closed his eyes to picture the mansions along H Street but he couldn't quite conjure an image of the house at the corner of $10^{th}$. Moments later, he gave it up and stood from the chair. "Thank you Ms. Rose," he said, returning the gold coin to his pocket. "You've been a big help." Levi had started across the room when Renee called out to him.

"I was just thinking," she said. Levi turned back to see Renee was now standing in front of the fire where the orange flames cast the shadow of her figure against her thin silk robe. "This man John Haney—the one that you described."

"Yes," Levi said, his pulse surging. "What about him?" In the excitement of learning about Brutus de Villeroi, he had almost forgotten their unfinished conversation about Haney.

"I don't know anyone by the name Haney but something you said reminds me of a man Ellen used to see." Renee glanced towards the ceiling as she pieced the images together. "It's what you said about his eyes," she said. "There's a man that comes in here from time to time. He's larger than most men like you said but he's got the blackest eyes I've ever seen."

Levi stepped back across the room so that he could read Renee's face. "What else do you remember about him?"

"He's rich," she said. "Incredibly rich."

That didn't sound at all like John Haney but it didn't matter. The man who had masqueraded as Haney could be anyone by now. "What about his appearance?" Levi pressed. "Is there anything else particular about him? Anything at all?"

Renee thought for a moment. "There is one thing," she said. "It's quite silly, really. He's got a little tattoo on the inside of his finger."

Levi's heart raced. "Are you sure?" he asked. "He had a tattoo on the inside of his finger?"

"Oh, I'm sure," Renee said, "I asked him about it one time but he just pulled his hand away and changed the subject."

It was just as Josiah had described. "So you've been with this man before?" Levi asked.

Renee nodded.

"Then you know his name."

Renee nodded again. "Edward Huff," she said.

Levi dug deep into his memory but the name Edward Huff was nowhere to be found. His thoughts soon returned to the tattoo. "What did this tattoo of his look like?"

"It's a little tail," Renee said.

Levi was bewildered. "A tail?" he asked. "What kind of tail? Like an animal tail?"

"No, not an animal. It looked more like a bug." Renee shrugged. "I didn't see it for long but it looked to me like a scorpion's tail."

"A scorpion's tail," Levi repeated to himself. "Are you sure?"

“No,” Renee admitted. “Like I said, I didn’t see it for long.”

Levi nodded. “Can you remember when you last saw this Edward Huff?”

Renee cast Levi a bashful look that seemed ill fitted for a woman of her profession. “I saw him this morning,” she said.

“What!” Levi snapped, his voice rising. “You saw him this morning? When?”

Renee’s eyes grew wide at Levi’s sudden outburst. “Well,” she said nervously, “he left just before you got here. He said he was going to the bar for a drink.”

Levi’s mind raced back to the men seated at the bar when he arrived. “Does he have a beard and wear glasses?”

Renee nodded. “Yes,” she said but Levi was already sprinting across the room.

Throwing open the door, Levi darted from the room and ran down the hallway. His heart was pounding when he reached the stairs and stepped out onto the landing that overlooked the luxurious room below. His eyes shot to the front of the room and scanned the length of the bar. Reaching the end, he scanned it again as a pit formed in his stomach. On his third pass, the devastating reality of what had happened set firmly in his gut.

Just a short time ago, he had been standing at the bar talking to Mary Ann Hall when, no less than five feet away, Ellen’s murderer calmly sipped a glass of bourbon. But now, the bar was empty and the man was gone. There was no doubt in Levi’s mind that Edward Huff had seen him arrive and heard him asking questions about Ellen Wolfe. Edward Huff was gone and he would not be back.

Levi closed his eyes and hung his head. Ellen's murderer had walked the City streets convincingly as both a tradesman and a member of high society. He could be anyone, anywhere, at any time he chose. A crushing sense of defeat pressed hard into Levi's chest. But then, as thoughts of giving in began to spread, a thin ray of hope broke through. Levi lifted his head.

*Josiah*. He must have seen the man leave. He would know what type of coach Edward Huff was driving and in which direction he had gone. He had to get to Josiah. Levi gripped the railing as he took the stairs two at a time and sprinted for the front door.

# Chapter 37

October 24, 1861 – 7th Ward, Washington City

The coachman held the door of the sleek black carriage as the unknown man with the handlebar mustache stepped up into the cabin. Waiting until the man was well inside, the driver cut his eyes nervously towards Edward.

"We'd like to go to the Wilted Rose," Edward said with a look that was both confident and terrifying.

When Edward had recruited Matthew to drive his coach, they had worked out a series of code words. At the time, Matthew found them to be quite silly but now, as Edward stepped into the coach, laughter was the farthest thing from his mind. The request to go to the Wilted Rose meant only one thing and it sent a cold shiver down Matthew's spine.

The coach started with a jump but then settled in at a good pace as it turned onto South F Street. "Come on Charlie," McCrea said, twisting his mustache. "There's no one else here. You can tell me now."

Edward left the statement hanging in the air and glanced casually out the window as the carriage continued through the slums of South Washington. For a moment, he stared at the threadbare clothes hanging on a line between two shacks. Seeing the filthy and pathetic sight, Edward wondered for the hundredth time what the Union was fighting for.

The clothesline soon passed out of sight and the pressing issue of Mitchell McCrea returned to mind. Given where they were, Edward needed to keep McCrea distracted for another ten minutes or more. The long silence in the cabin spurred him to say something. "My family hails from the silver mines of Georgetown, Colorado," Edward began. A well-rehearsed family history followed that continued on for quite some time before McCrea broke in again.

"Okay. Okay," he said. "I can see you're not going to admit who you really are. I tell you what," McCrea twisted the end of his mustache while he conveyed the terms of his proposal. "I won't go on about your real name if you'll give me just a few lines of that Macbeth."

McCrea's emphasis on the *Mac* in Macbeth sent Edward's fingernails deep into his own leg. He couldn't remember despising anyone so much or so fast as he did Mitchell McCrea.

"Come on, Charlie," McCrea insisted. "Just one line then."

The steady clip-clop of the horses began to slow and Edward glanced out the windshield. They were close. A familiar calm fell over him as he visualized the struggle he knew to be only moments away.

McCrea waited for Edward's response but noticed his companion's attention was focused on something out the window. He turned to find the object of his new friend's curiosity and was surprised to see that the coach had stopped well outside of town near the banks of the Potomac. A deep crease formed in McCrea's brow and he leaned towards the door to get a better look.

Edward silently slipped his hand down to his boot.

"I don't see any Wilted Rose around here," McCrea murmured under his breath. "Hey Charlie," he said, still staring out the window. "I think you might need to get yourself a new driver." A wide smile spread across McCrea's face as he turned back towards Edward.

Just then, a flash of silver arced across the cabin and a searing pain shot through McCrea's throat as Edward's blade lodged deep beneath his jaw. McCrea's smile vanished as his eyes filled with fear and his mouth with blood. He gasped for air but only drew the thick metallic liquid deeper into his lungs. His body convulsed and a violent cough sent a mouthful of scarlet across the cabin where it spattered the windshield. Suddenly, the cabin door flew open and Edward heaved McCrea's body out of the carriage and down to the tall grass beside the river.

McCrea gasped and kicked in the grass as Edward calmly emerged from inside the coach. The driver was still holding the door and Edward shot him an irritated look as he stepped to the ground. A gurgle and kick in the tall grass drew Edward's attention back to the traitorous man writhing underfoot. Edward looked down in mild amusement as Mitchell McCrea engaged in a desperate struggle to retain a soul he never had. Slowly, McCrea's legs stopped kicking as he devoted the last of his life to his still-beating heart.

With the convulsing safely behind them, Edward knelt down in the grass and lazily pulled his blade from McCrea's throat. Edward stared deep into the man's eyes for a long moment before leaning in so close that McCrea could hear him whisper, "Stars, hide your fires; Let not light see my black and deep desires."

McCrea's eyes grew wide and then the light went out.

Edward looked down on McCrea as the wind swept off the Potomac and chilled the air pushing through the tall grass. Reaching down, he pried McCrea's mouth open and fished out his tongue. "You know, Matthew," he said, talking to his driver just a few feet away, "you need to work on your execution."

The edge of Edward's blade cut through the muscle binding McCrea's tongue as if it was slicing butter. Edward stood and walked over to the coach where Matthew recoiled at the site of the dangling chunk of meat in Edward's hand. "It's all about timing, you see," Edward said but Matthew's eyes were pinned to a drop of blood still hanging from McCrea's severed tongue. "When I say we need to go to the Wilted Rose, I expect you to promptly open the door once the coach is stopped."

Seeing he didn't have his driver's full attention, Edward turned and flung the tongue towards the river, where it landed with a splash. "Look at this," Edward said, pointing into the coach where McCrea's blood was congealing on the inside of the windshield. "You're going to have to clean that up."

Sometime later, Edward finally took his seat and the coach jumped to a start. The driver turned north onto 12$^{th}$, destined for the fine mansions of H Street.

# Chapter 38

October 24, 1861 – 7$^{th}$ Ward, Washington City

Levi jumped off the porch at Mary Ann Hall's and sprinted towards the street. He quickly scanned the surrounding area but Josiah was nowhere in sight. Reaching the end of the walkway, Levi spun the valet in place and grabbed him by the lapels. "Where's my wagon?"

The valet gripped Levi's wrists with his thick hands. "Madame Hall won't have a piece of shit wagon like that sitting out in front of her place."

Levi didn't give a damn about appearances at Mary Ann Hall's. "Where the hell is it?" he demanded, pulling the valet's coat even tighter.

"I had your boy move it around the corner."

Levi looked over the valet's shoulder and, seeing the familiar faces of the two horses he'd bridled a thousand times, he dropped the valet's coat and ran into the street.

Rounding the corner, he saw Josiah waiting patiently on the bench and a wave of relief washed over him. Levi rushed to the side of the wagon. "Did you see anyone leave here?" he asked with heavy breath.

"Sure did," Josiah said, startled by the urgency of Levi's question. "Someone left here about ten minutes ago."

"What did he look like?" Levi demanded. "Did he have a beard and glasses?"

"I couldn't really tell, Mr. Love." Josiah swept his hand out to direct Levi's attention. "It's hard to see much from here."

Levi glanced over his shoulder to see that Josiah was right. From where the wagon was parked, he could just make out the barreled figure of the valet standing out by the street. He turned back to Josiah. "You said you saw someone leave ten minutes ago," Levi said. "So what did you see?"

"I saw two men getting into a coach. But I only saw their backs."

*Two men*, Levi thought. It had to be the men at the bar. "Did you get a good look at the coach?" he asked.

"Sure did," Josiah said, pulling on his beard as he tried to remember the details. "It was black and real short."

"Short?" Levi asked.

"It was one of those that looks like it's been cut in half."

"A coupe?" Levi asked, climbing up into the wagon and grabbing the reins. "Are you sure?"

Josiah nodded. "I'm sure," he said. "You don't see too many like that."

Levi smiled. Josiah was exactly right. Though carriages were ever-present in a City populated well beyond its capacity, coupes were still relatively rare. That Edward Huff drove a coupe gave them an edge. "Did you see which way they went?" Levi asked.

"They went that way," Josiah pointed, "towards the river." Levi slapped the reins and drove the horses until they reached a steady clip. Josiah held onto the sideboard. "Who are we after, Mr. Love?"

Levi realized he hadn't told Josiah a thing about what had just happened. He quickly recounted the story of the men at the bar and his conversation with Renee Rose. When he finished, he looked over to see Josiah staring off into the distance.

“This man we’re after,” Josiah said solemnly, “he sounds more like a ghost.”

Had he not seen Edward Huff with his own eyes, Levi may have agreed. “I assure you, Josiah,” he said, “Edward Huff is very real.” Levi slapped the reins to keep the horses motivated. “Now let’s just keep our eyes out for that coupe.”

Levi scoured the streets for the black coach as he drove the wagon hard towards the river. But something wasn’t right. The roads between Mary Ann Hall’s and the Potomac ran directly through the worst slums in Washington City. While it was rather obvious why a wealthy gentleman would find his way to Mary Ann Hall’s, there was no reason to go any farther into this neglected and dangerous section of the City. So why were Edward Huff and his friend headed towards the river?

Levi had no sooner asked the question when they reached the end of F Street and he saw the breaking waters of the Potomac through the tall grass along the shore. He pulled the wagon to a stop and ran his eyes as far along the river as he could see but there were no signs of the black coupe or of anything else that could lead to the murderer within. Peering into the distance, Levi let out a deep sigh. Perhaps Josiah was right. Perhaps Edward Huff really was a ghost.

Levi listened to the water lapping the shoreline until Josiah finally asked the question that Levi had been asking himself. “So now what?”

Levi slumped forward with his elbows on his knees and shook his head. “I don’t know.”

“What about that Frenchman?” Josiah asked.

“Brutus de Villeroi,” Levi said looking out over the Potomac. “He’s about all we have left.”

“H Street is clear up on the other side of the City,” Josiah said hopefully. “Maybe we’ll see that coach somewhere along the way.”

“Maybe,” Levi said without much conviction. He tightened the reins and turned the wagon towards the mansions on H Street.

Just a few feet away, the tall grass blew in a passing breeze and danced over the lifeless body of Mitchell McCrea.

# Chapter 39

October 24, 1861 – 4$^{th}$ Ward, Washington City

Edward Huff walked casually along the gravel carriageway where the gray mansion's upper windows and dark slate roof were visible over the top of the stone wall. A thin line of smoke trailed up from a chimney near the back of the house. Edward watched the smoke coil and disappear in the air as he made his way towards the low wooden gate at the far end of the wall.

He had hoped de Villeroi's house would be completely empty but apparently that was not to be. But it wasn't all bad news. The smoke wasn't rising from the grand chimneys in the middle of the house but rather the smaller one near the back. If de Villeroi was at home, the larger chimneys would almost certainly have been lit. Smoke rising from the smaller chimney signaled nothing more than a kitchen maid preparing a broth for dinner.

Arriving at the far end of the wall, Edward didn't hesitate. He reached over the gate and dropped his cane into the yard before swiftly hurtling to the other side. Stooping to retrieve his cane, he made his way to the back door as leisurely as a gentleman out for a tour of the gardens. When he arrived at the house he lifted his cane and glanced at its ivory lion's head handle before rapping it firmly against the glass paned door.

A shadow passed somewhere within and, seconds later, Edward heard the metallic scraping of someone fumbling with the lock. A heavy click followed as the bolt fell out of the way and the door opened to reveal a rather fat and flustered kitchen maid. "I, I'm so sorry, sir," she stammered. "I didn't hear the front door."

Gentleman in tailored suits and top hats did not arrive through back doors. Edward understood her confusion and pressed it to his advantage. "I've been ringing the front door for what must have been ten minutes now and you're telling me that you didn't hear it?"

The woman shook her head in a manner that left her fleshy jowls unsure as to which way to go. “N…no, sir,” she said earnestly. “I, I’m sorry, sir.”

“I’ve no time for your stuttering,” Edward said. “I have urgent business with Mr. de Villeroi and I must see him immediately.”

The woman’s confusion turned to concern. “Mr. de Villeroi ain’t here. He, he won’t be home until this evening.”

“That can’t be,” Edward said. “He assured me he would be here when I arrived.”

“I’m s…sorry, sir.”

“Your apologies do me no good. Now make me some tea and show me to Mr. de Villeroi’s study. I’ll wait for him there.” Edward tried to step around the maid’s doughy frame but she refused to give ground. “What do you think you’re doing?” he asked, his feigned frustration now becoming quite real.

“M…Mr. de Villeroi don’t let no one into his study unless he, he’s there with them.”

Edward forced a thin smile and glared at the woman. “Well then you’ll allow me the pleasure of waiting in the library.”

The maid’s jowls quivered. “N…no, sir,” she stuttered. “Mr. de Villeroi.”

An instant and boiling anger raged inside Edward such that he could no longer hear what the woman was saying. He took a half-step back and glanced at his cane. In a blink, the ivory lion’s head was arcing through the air and hurdling towards the woman where it crashed into the side of her face. The heavy blow sent the woman staggering backwards. She screamed and reached for the bloody gash as her body outpaced her legs and she toppled to the floor.

"Oh Lord! Oh Lord!" the woman squealed, holding her face and rolling around on the ground like a stuck pig.

Edward stepped quickly inside and closed the door to barricade the woman's cry. He looked quickly around to see that he was standing in a well-appointed kitchen with a long cutting table at its center. A butcher knife sat in the middle of the table beside a pile of half-chopped vegetables and a heavy copper pot.

"Oh Lord! Oh Lord!"

Edward glared down at the blubbering woman. He couldn't think with all her wailing. Stepping to the table, his hand hovered briefly over the butcher knife before reaching for the copper pot. The woman's eyes were closed tight as he cocked the pot in his arm.

"Oh Lord! Oh!"

*CLANG!*

The pot rang out like a gong as it made contact with the woman's skull. Edward looked down to see the maid's eyes closed and her mouth silenced. He placed a hand on the pot to muffle its resonant chime and the room suddenly fell quiet. Edward closed his eyes so that he could listen deep into the mansion. For a long moment, he shut everything else out but all he heard was the tranquil gurgle of a broth bubbling on the cast iron stove.

Satisfied he was alone, Edward placed the pot back on the table and left the room without a second glance at the bloodied maid on the floor. The fat and loathsome woman had caused him enough delay.

Just outside the kitchen, Edward paused in the hallway to get his bearings. Earlier that morning, he had been observing the de Villeroi mansion when he saw two men appear in the windows on the right hand side of the home. The men had been discussing the contents of an oversize sheet of paper. It was the odd size of the paper that Edward remembered. The men hadn't been discussing a letter or a manifest, but something quite out of the ordinary. With very little else to go on, Edward turned to the right in search of the paper and the room in which he saw it.

Stepping down the hallway, he glanced at the odd assortment of personal photographs and oil paintings along the wall until he reached the first of two closed doors on the right side of the hall. Inching close, Edward placed his ear to the door while his hand hovered over the knob. All was quiet.

Turning the knob, the door opened with a long screech that ended abruptly when the door hit the wall. Inside, the room's light blue walls and floral upholstery carried a sense of femininity that was ill-suited for the conversation he had witnessed from the carriageway. Still, Edward took a moment to look around the room. A quick glance over the bookshelves and through the writing desk drawer confirmed his intuition. This was the wrong room.

Stepping back into hallway, he made his way to the second door and repeated the process of listening before turning the knob. Again, the door creaked as it swung open but this time, Edward smiled.

In stark contrast to the room next door, de Villeroi's study was steeped in masculinity. The room centered on a massive oak desk that faced two dark green leather chairs and a wall of big-game trophies. Behind the desk, floor-to-ceiling shelves held hundreds of leather-bound volumes. Edward's eyes hung on the shelves as he stepped inside the study. He knew nothing of Brutus de Villeroi personally but gazing at the titles in his collection was more intimate than a private conversation over cognac and cigars. For every book in a man's collection provides a quiet glimpse into the man himself.

Edward dragged his finger lightly across the spines as he cataloged the titles in his mind. *The Physical Geography of the Sea* by Matthew Fontaine Maury, *Experimental Researches in Electricity* by Michael Faraday, *Principles of Geology* by Charles Lyell and *On the Origin of Species*, by Charles Darwin. At the far end of the shelves a marble table was stacked high with periodicals such as *The Military Chronicle and Naval Spectator* and *The American Mechanic's Magazine.* In all, the collection left little doubt that Brutus de Villeroi was a serious man of science but the topics were too varied to determine Admiral Dahlgren's interest in the man or what it was that de Villeroi could possibly be doing for the Navy.

Beside the table stood a wide cherry-wood cabinet with a dozen or more shallow drawers. Edward's hand hung on the top drawer while he studied its dimensions. It was precisely the width one would need to store the oversize paper he had seen the two men discussing through the window. Grabbing the handle, he slid the top drawer open to find a stack of nautical charts detailing the waters off of Maine, New Hampshire, and Massachusetts. Opening the next several drawers in turn, he discovered similar maps for each of the states along the eastern seaboard and around the Florida coast into the Gulf of Mexico. It was an immense and highly valuable collection that was surprising to find in private hands. So why did de Villeroi need such detailed maps of the coastline and ocean floor?

Edward made a mental note of the question and reached for the next drawer, which held yet another stack of oversize papers. But when the top drawing came into view, Edward was taken aback. He sprang upright and squinted at the page. Expecting to find more nautical charts, it took a moment to see that the drawing depicted the parts of what appeared to be an engine or pump of some kind. Flipping quickly through the stack, he saw page after page of detailed mechanical drawings and specifications. The tingling sensation of discovery spread across his back and down his arms. This was it. This had to be it.

Edward reached into the drawer and grabbed the entire stack of papers. Stepping to de Villeroi's desk, he sat down and poured over the first drawing.

# Chapter 40

October 24, 1861 – 4th Ward, Washington City

"That must be it," Josiah said, staring up at the palatial home. He had seen the mansions along H Street before but he could never make much sense of them.

"Guess so," Levi said after glancing around at the neighboring homes to see that none of the others matched the description. Deciding they were at the right place, he set the brake and rested the leather reins on the footboard before looking over at Josiah. "You had better stay here," he said, "but keep your eyes open."

Josiah looked at the line of fancy houses along the road. This had to be the safest and quietest street in the entire City. "What am I looking for?"

Levi cut his eyes up and down the street. "No idea," he shrugged. "Just let me know if you see anything."

Levi hopped down from the wagon and followed the paved walkway towards de Villeroi's house. Glancing in the windows, he was surprised to see there were no lights or fires burning inside. Perhaps Brutus de Villeroi was still out for the day. He found the string beside the heavy blue door and pulled the front bell. A delicate jingle sounded from somewhere inside.

℘℘℘℘

Edward's heart pounded as his eyes shot up from the stack of drawings. *Was that the doorbell?* He froze in place and waited, hardly daring to breathe. Silence. A sinking feeling in his gut forced him away from the desk and out into the hallway.

Treading lightly, he walked the length of the hall to the kitchen, where a quick glance confirmed the maid was still out cold. He peeked around the corner towards the interior of the mansion and was relieved to see a comfortable sitting room with no direct sightline to the front door. Stepping to the other side of the room, he placed his back against the wall and took a deep breath. Edward peered slowly around the corner and an impressive foyer came into view. Just then, the bell rang for a second time. A tingle of anticipation spread to his extremities as his eyes fell on the front door.

℘℘℘℘

Levi listened through the door as the front bell's chime faded away for the second time. Cupping his hands around his eyes, he peeked through the narrow window beside the door. The foyer was elegant, with marble floors and yellow upholstered chairs on either side of a carved, gold-leaf table. Levi swept his eyes deeper into the house where he saw parts of the dining area and a sitting room beyond. There were no signs of life anywhere inside.

℘℘℘℘

Edward recoiled around the corner and his breath caught in his chest. *This can't be happening*. How could Levi Love have tracked him to de Villeroi's home? His mind raced over the details of his day. The only people who could connect him with the insidious Frenchman were his driver and the barman at Willard's Hotel but neither seemed a likely source of Levi's information. Matthew had been driving him around town for months and was implicated in almost as many crimes as Edward himself. And as for Willard's pre-pubescent barman, Edward had chosen him precisely because he was so obscure he was beyond notice. Edward was obviously missing something but he didn't have time to find it. He needed every remaining second to locate the vital information buried somewhere in de Villeroi's study.

℘℘℘℘

Levi dropped his hands to his sides and backed off the porch to get a better view of the house. Mansions like de Villeroi's didn't operate by themselves. There was always at least one servant around to keep the kitchen running and the thieves at bay. But for some reason, de Villeroi's home was completely empty. Levi squinted up at the third story windows.

"No one's home?" Josiah asked from the street.

"I guess not," Levi said, still scanning the windows. "Let me know if someone comes out," he instructed. "I'll take a look around back."

Levi stepped off the walkway and crossed the small front yard to 10th Street where he turned towards the back of the house. He followed the heavy stone wall around the perimeter of the property and along the gravel carriageway to a low wooden gate at the far end. De Villeroi's backyard was quiet and empty.

Levi swept his eyes over the surrounding homes. The neighborhood was so peaceful, Levi felt as if he were somewhere far removed from the limits of Washington City.
He was turning back towards de Villeroi's when something on the next street over stopped him cold. The early evening sun was low in the sky and Levi strained to make out the image. A pair of black horses. A set of spoke wheels. And the truncated body of a black coupe carriage.

Levi's heart beat hard against his chest as he spun back to de Villeroi's mansion. He quickly surveyed the yard and the back of the house. Throwing himself over the gate, Levi charged towards the back door.

℘℘℘℘

Edward quickly scanned the document and then tossed it off the desk where it added to the pile on the floor. Each of the drawings he'd seen so far provided detailed instructions for manufacturing a particular part of a much larger and complex machine. So far, the drawings were all useless. Unless he knew what the machine did and how it might break the Southern blockade, there would be nothing the Confederacy could do to stop it.

Page after page fell to the ground as he frantically worked through the stack of drawings. A gear. A valve. A seal. A pump. *Wait!* Edward's hand froze on the page. Rather than individual parts, the drawing before him appeared to show a fully assembled machine. Edward's eyes shot to the large block letters at the top of the page: SCRUBBER – COMPLETE ASSEMBLY. A surge of excitement pulsed through his body. This was it!

Looking down at the drawing, a handwritten note appeared along the margins. Edward turned his head to the side and leaned over the desk to get a better view.

*Project Alligator – Boathouse F – Delivered October 23, 1861.*

Edward stood and immediately thought of the stolen message de Villeroi had sent to Dahlgren: *Shipment to your facility is underway. Scrubber should arrive by this evening at the latest.* Edward had presumed the intended *facility* was somewhere at the Navy Yard but the complex was so vast that conducting a search on his own was next to impossible. But now he didn't have to search the entire Yard. Now, Edward knew precisely where the *scrubber* would be—*Boathouse F.* The shadow of a plan began to form in his mind.

ஐஐ

Levi arrived at the back door and looked through the paned glass window where his eyes were instantly drawn to a large woman lying in the middle of the floor. Seeing the small pool of blood beneath hear head, Levi's last remaining doubts vanished in an instant. A sudden shot of adrenaline surged through his veins. Edward Huff was here.

His hand raced to the knob but the door was locked. Leaning back, he threw his shoulder into frame. Again and again he rammed the door but it refused to budge. Stepping back, he looked at the glass panes covering the top half of the door. There was no other option. Levi sharpened his elbow and threw it into the glass. The pane shattered and sent a shower of glass crashing down to the stone floor inside the kitchen. Protected by his thick wool coat, he punched out the razor sharp teeth still clinging to the frame and reached inside.

℘℘℘℘

Edward stood bolt upright as the sounds of broken glass echoed down the hall. His time was up. Grabbing the drawing, he folded it roughly into shape before opening one of his buttons and sliding the paper beneath his shirt. His eyes shot to the door as he fixed the button to secure the drawing. Leaving de Villeroi's mansion the way he had arrived was not an option. Levi could be here at any second and hand-to-hand combat in a narrow hallway would play to no one's advantage.

He spun around and, seeing the only other way out, he ran to the far side of the room. The window opened with ease and Edward had one leg outside before he saw his shining black top hat sitting on de Villeroi's desk. After a second's pause, he darted back inside. The hat bore the mark of Charles Quigly and Edward couldn't afford another loose end. With the hat in hand, he climbed deftly out the window and sprinted for the gate.

℘℘℘℘

Levi burst into the study where the scattered papers and open drawers left a trail to the open window on the other side of the room. Levi darted to the window. Placing his hands on the sill, he looked out to see a man in a black suit preparing to jump the back gate. Just then, the man paused to look back at the house. He wore a dark beard and a pair of round glasses that failed to disguise his coal black eyes.

A sudden rage surged through Levi's veins as he gripped the sill tight and threw his leg through the open window. Hanging halfway into the yard, he glanced up to see Edward Huff flash a contemptuous smile before disappearing over the fence.

℘℘℘℘

Edward's feet hit the gravel carriageway with a crunch. Had everything gone to plan, he would have strolled casually back to his carriage and returned to the comforts of the Willard to plan his next move. But things had not gone to plan, and the carriage was now out of the question. Edward simply couldn't risk leading the police to his driver. He had always known the only one he could ever truly rely on was himself and, until this mission was complete, he promised to do just that. Edward glanced over his shoulder to see Levi dropping from the window into the backyard. His decision was made.

Edward spun in the gravel and was off like a shot. Sprinting down the carriageway, he suddenly realized he had no idea where he was going. Edward Huff's time in this City was running short but where could he go? And who would he be when he got there? The pressure of Levi chasing after him made it difficult to concentrate. Until something came to mind, he would simply have to keep moving.

Edward rounded the corner at the end of the carriageway and ran. Glancing over his shoulder, he caught a glimpse of Levi jumping over the gate and into the gravel. Edward suddenly felt completely exposed. A man sprinting down H Street with top hat and cane would attract more curious eyes than a public hanging. He had to get off the streets.

Edward's legs churned at full speed as the grand mansions on H Street soon gave way to a collection of modest clapboard homes. The cool evening air chilled his lungs as he sprinted by one house after another. His eyes scoured each house for something, anything that would help him escape.

Up ahead, a small gap appeared between two of the houses. Edward had no idea where it led but he didn't care. He darted from the street and straight into the gap where a narrow walkway ran between the two houses. His body bounced off the side of the house as he changed course and sprinted down the path. A short picket gate blocked the end of the pathway. Edward hurdled the gate with ease but, landing on the other side, his foot caught on the uneven ground and he fell hard to one knee.

Pain shot up his thigh as he looked around to see that he was in a small backyard with a clothesline running from the house to a weathered woodshed along the back fence. The clothes on the line flapped in a passing breeze. Edward's eyes shot between the clothesline and the shed and a plan fell instantly into place.

He jumped to his feet and fought through the shooting pain in his knee as he crossed the yard and snatched a dark gray shirt from the line. Running to the shed, he opened the door and threw in every item that marked him as Edward Huff: his top hat and cane, his spectacles and his splendid wool coat that he would never see again. Slamming the door, he grabbed the gray shirt off the ground and hurdled the back fence into the neighboring yard.

The rough gray wool slid easily over the fine cotton of his custom dress shirt. He jogged across the yard where he slowed alongside a thick herb garden beside the house. There was still one last trace of Edward Huff that remained. Gritting his teeth, he grabbed a handful of his prosthetic beard. With a swift and hard pull, he tore the beard from his skin. A searing and familiar burn spread across his face as he stuffed the wad of hair to the bottom of a thick rosemary bush.

With the beard hidden away, he quickly rounded the house to a white gate that opened out onto 11th Street. Edward reached for the gate but then stopped to look over his shoulder. The two backyards he had just stormed across were as quiet as he had found them. Levi Love was nowhere in sight.

Pressing on his shirt, he felt the stiff resistance of the folded drawing against his skin. Edward smiled, opened the gate and stepped casually out onto 11th Street.

# Chapter 41

October 24, 1861 – 4th Ward, Washington City

Levi bent over and put his hands on his knees to catch his breath. The traffic along the busy corner of 11th and G Streets enveloped him as the adrenaline seeped from his body with the last of his hope. Edward Huff was gone. He was no match for this man.

From the moment he pulled Ellen Wolfe from the Canal, Levi had been three steps behind. John Haney had disappeared into thin air before Levi had even learned his name. At Mary Ann Hall's, he had been standing so close to Edward Huff that he could have reached out and touched him. But none of that mattered now. Edward Huff would never again walk the streets of Washington City. Levi was back to where he started. Josiah was right. Levi wasn't chasing a man—he was chasing a ghost.

"Mr. Love?" Levi heard the faint voice over the din of the passing crowds. "Mr. Love?"

Levi raised his head and slowly stood. He turned towards the familiar voice and was relieved to see the red spokes of the police wagon with Josiah at the reins. Stepping towards the wagon, he noticed several in the passing crowd staring up at Josiah. Their faces filled with confusion, and some even revulsion, at the sight of a colored man driving a wagon by himself. Even Levi had to admit to the strangeness of the sight.

Josiah slid across the bench to make way for Levi as he climbed up onto the wagon. Seeing a police officer in the wagon seemed to allay the growing suspicions and the crowd slowly moved on. Levi didn't say a word. It was obvious that Edward Huff had gotten away, so Josiah kept his eyes forward and his thoughts to himself as the wagon rattled north along 11th Street.

"I lost him again," Levi finally admitted.

Josiah nodded. “This man we’re after,” he said, hanging his head to compose his thoughts, “he’s dangerous and he’s smart—too smart for the two of us.” So far, Josiah hadn’t said anything Levi didn’t already know.

“I’ve been thinking on it,” Josiah continued. “There ain’t no way we’re going to catch this man by chasing his tail. If you want to catch a dog, you got to grab him by the neck.”

“And how are we supposed to do that?” Levi asked.

“You got to know where the dog’s going and what he’s going after,” Josiah explained. “The trick is, you’ve got to know where the dog’s gonna be before the dog has a chance to get there.”

Levi looked over. Josiah had his full attention. “We know this man is after something to do with the Navy,” Josiah continued, “but we don’t know what it is or where it is.”

“What about the secret boathouse you found at the Navy Yard?” Levi asked.

Josiah shook his head as he pulled on his beard. “We know there’s something down there but there ain’t no way to tell if it’s got something to do with de Villeroi. Whatever it is that Edward Huff is after, it may be down in that boathouse or it may not. We don’t know because we don’t got any idea what was in that message sent to the Admiral. But that Frenchman who sent the message, he knows. He knows what he said and whether it’s something worth killing folks over. And I bet he knows if it’s got anything to do with that secret boathouse.”

As the words slowly sank in, Levi knew Josiah was right. Chasing Ellen’s murderer had gotten him nowhere. But if he knew precisely what Edward Huff was looking for and where he could find it, then he could get there first and simply wait for Edward to come to him. Levi silently nodded. Brutus de Villeroi held all the answers.

Levi pulled to a stop in front of the gray mansion and set the brake. "Mr. Love," Josiah said. "It's getting dark out now and I need to be getting on."

"You don't need to worry about the Codes tonight," Levi said. "No one's going to come for you if you're with me."

The Black Codes were a set of local laws that forbade colored people from a wide variety of activities that were quite normal for the City's white residents. The laws prohibited everything from gambling to dancing without a proper license. They even set out special punishments if a colored person happened to break a lamp or damage a public water pump. Anyone caught breaking the Codes was subject to fines, imprisonment, public flogging, or all three combined. Levi assumed Josiah was concerned about getting off the streets before the assigned curfew.

"It ain't the Codes I'm worried about," Josiah said. "I've got to get back to." Josiah's stomach twisted and he stopped himself short. The reason he had to leave was enough to get him hanged in this perverted City. He couldn't believe he had almost told a white police officer where he was going. "I got to get home to Anna," he said simply. "She's been worried about Williams' catchers pulling me off the streets again."

In truth, Levi had been worrying about that himself. William H. Williams was the most powerful slaver in the City and he virtually owned the underground market. He had money, power, and connections and Levi feared it was only a matter of time before he used them to find Josiah and reclaim his property. Levi hated to see Josiah leave but he understood why he had to go.

"You go on home then," Levi said quietly. "I don't want Anna to worry."

The two men climbed down from the wagon and Levi was headed towards de Villeroi's house when Josiah called out. "Mr. Love?"

Levi turned around and met Josiah in the street. "What is it?"

"You're doing a good thing here, Mr. Love," he said. "I don't know anyone that would do what you've done on account of a," Josiah stopped himself. "On account of Ms. Wolf or on account of a colored man he ain't never met." Levi looked down at his feet as Josiah continued. "I got to go right now but I want to help you if I can." Levi looked up. Josiah had provided far more than help over the past days. "I'll be down by those docks on 10th Street tomorrow morning. If you need me, you just come and get me."

"Thank you, Josiah," Levi said, extending his hand.

Josiah looked down at Levi's outstretched hand for a long moment before he reached out and gripped it tight. "I'll see you in the morning then," he said.

Levi watched Josiah disappear into the night before turning to de Villeroi's house. Arriving at the front door, he pulled the string to ring the bell. He was considering going around to the back door when he heard the heavy click of the lock. The doughy maid that he had last seen on the floor of the kitchen appeared at the door with a bloodied rag held tight against the side of her face.

"Y, yessir?" she stammered.

"I'm Officer Levi Love and I need to come inside."

The maid's eyes flashed to Levi's badge and then back to his face. "Y, yessir," she said, opening the door and waddling aside. She closed the door and turned to Levi expectantly.

"The man that did that to you," Levi pointed to her face, "came here looking for information stored in this house by Brutus de

Villeroi. I believe that information is in Mr. de Villeroi's study and I intend to go look." The maid's fleshy jaw hung open. "Now before you try and stop me," Levi said, "you should know that this man has already killed at least two people in this City and I suspect he's not done yet. Now the longer you delay me, the farther away he gets. Do you understand?"

"Y, y," the maid tried to talk but kept swallowing the words. "Y, yessir," she finally said with what appeared to be extraordinary effort.

Levi left the maid in the foyer and walked directly to de Villeroi's study. The room was exactly as he had left it. Papers were strewn around the desk and across the floor. The window, which only a short time ago aided Edward Huff in his escape, was still open on the opposite side of the room. Levi stepped around the scattered papers and closed the window against the cool night air.

Turning back to the room, he wasn't sure where to begin. He stepped to the nearby chest and opened a drawer at random. A detailed nautical chart of South Carolina appeared at the top of a stack. Levi closed the drawer and tapped his finger on the top of the cabinet as he surveyed the room. Seconds later, an obvious conclusion finally struck him. His search should start exactly where Edward Huff's had ended.

Levi stooped down and collected a handful of papers off the floor. Laying them out on the desk, he studied each of them in turn. Drawing after drawing brought the same frustrating result. The gears and gauges depicted on the pages meant nothing to him. He sat down behind the desk and let out a heavy sigh as Josiah's words turned in his mind: *the Frenchman knows.* Levi would just have to wait for Brutus de Villeroi to return home.

Levi sat back in his chair and was reaching for his gold coin when he felt a hard object press against his side. Digging into his pocket, he pulled out the wooden cipher disc Admiral Dahlgren had given him. He studied the overlapping wooden wheels with the alphabet carved around their outer edges and wondered who would even think to invent such a thing. With nothing better to do to pass the time, he pulled the paper scroll from his pocket and opened a desk drawer to find a pencil.

On the back of one of the drawings, he copied the scroll's text out in careful block letters.

STAF GGOG LCQB LMRN WURR
NKBB WZWK RWBS ATAV S

Dahlgren had explained that the few Southern codes they had managed to break were enciphered using common military terms, such as the names of Confederate commanders. The first commander that came to Levi's mind was Robert E. Lee. Following Dahlgren's instructions, Levi repeated the codeword *Robert E Lee* beneath the encoded text.

If *Robert E Lee* was the right codeword, the disc would translate the encoded message into plain text. With the codeword in place, Levi picked up the cipher disc and spun the outer wheel.

Using the *A* of the inner wheel as a pointer, he lined it up with the first letter of the presumed codeword, *R,* on the outer wheel. If he had guessed the correct codeword, the letters on the inner wheel should now show the deciphered letter corresponding to the first letter of the scroll. Levi looked to see the first letter on the scroll was *S.* He found the letter *S* on the outer wheel and, seeing that it lined up with the *B* on the inner wheel, he wrote that letter down.

Moving to the next letter, he set the *A* of the inner wheel with the second letter in the presumptive codeword, *O*, in *Robert.* The disc was now aligned to decode the second letter in the scroll. Finding the *T* on the outer wheel, he saw that it lined up with the letter *F* on the inner wheel. He wrote that letter down beside the other decoded letter and stared at it: *BF.*

Levi sighed. He couldn't think of a single word in the English language that started with the letters BF. *Robert E Lee* was clearly the wrong codeword.

Undeterred, Levi gripped the pencil and made a list of a dozen or more potential codewords along the margin of the page. He would try every Confederate military term he could think of—at least until de Villeroi returned and told him what the hell was going on.

# Chapter 42

October 24, 1861 – 7th Ward, Washington City

Edward whistled the cab to a stop and jumped inside. He needed to get as far away from H Street and Levi Love as he could and called out the first destination that came to mind. "The Castle," he said.

"As you like," said the driver.

Minutes later, the sound of horse hooves over metal drew Edward's attention out the window and down the embankment to the very place he had left Lieutenant Daniel Adams to rot. He had risked everything to learn of de Villeroi's *scrubber* but there was still dangerous work left to do. The problem was, Edward had no idea how to do it. What he needed now was a new set of clothes and a safe place to think. As the cab pulled to a stop by the Smithsonian Castle, Edward knew there was only one place left for him to go.

"10th and D Street," he yelled out at the driver.

"But you said the Castle," the driver called back.

"Well now I say 10th and D!" Edward barked.

The driver shrugged and slapped the reins. As the carriage continued its rhythmic course towards the south side of the City, Edward took the opportunity to close his eyes and clear his mind. He had almost drifted to sleep when the carriage hit a rut that bounced his head off the side panel. Rubbing the sting out, he saw the carriage had arrived on D Street.

"This'll do," he called to the driver. The carriage pulled to a stop and Edward stepped out.

"You want to get out here?" the driver asked, glancing around.

"Obviously," Edward said, paying the man just enough to cover the fare.

The driver looked down at the meager fee and frowned. "Suit yourself," he said and then whipped his horses down the road.

Edward had to admit, the corner was rather desolate but it was far enough away from his actual destination to ensure the driver stayed safely out of his business. Edward kept his head about him as he passed the odd assortment of taverns, churches, and dilapidated shacks that lined this stretch of D Street. But as he walked among the nameless men staggering from one tavern to the next, a sense of loss and detachment descended upon him like a fog. It was as if his senses had left him for some far away place. A single question gripped his body and consumed his mind: *Who am I?*

He had no idea how long he had been walking before he felt the presence of the knife tucked in his boot. Strangely, it was all he could feel. With every stride, it dug deeper into his skin and it slowly reminded him of who he really was. He was a patriot and a messenger from God who was placed on this Earth to preserve the rightful order of this world. He wasn't John Haney or Nicholas Turner or even Edward Huff. All pretenses, all identities had been stripped away. He was laid bare.

Looking down at his hand, he rubbed the inside of his finger as if he could feel the ink set deep beneath the skin. By shedding his last identity, he was finally free. He was finally The Scorpion. And he would no longer fear his own name. Charles Cain was a patriot and spy for the Confederate States of America. And he would never hide again.

Just then, like a signal from God, a silver cross appeared over the surrounding rooftops. Charles Cain turned down 9$^{th}$ Street where the stained glass windows of Grace Episcopal Church provided the only source of color and hope in this forgotten part of the City. He followed the peeling clapboard exterior to a wrought iron fence that marked the perimeter of the parish cemetery.

Cain reached for the gate but, seeing the worn and rusted hinges, he reconsidered. A passing wind cut through the night and drew his attention to the line of oak trees surrounding the cemetery. Grabbing a branch overhead, Cain swung himself over the fence and into the yard where he landed softly in the grass. He crouched low in the dark and listened to the stillness of the night. Convinced he was alone, he went to find the man who had had sealed his fate those many months ago.

Cain wove through the tombstones without glancing at the names until he reached a small block of gray granite surrounded by much larger headstones. Kneeling beside the marker, he reached out and ran his finger across the name carved deep into the stone: KEVIN JOHNSON STANLEY.

He had hoped to go the rest of his life without visiting this man's grave but that was not to be. Kevin Stanley had been the personal messenger of General John Joseph Abercrombie. When Cain set out to build his network of spies in the City, Stanley had been his first recruit and his biggest mistake.

At first, Stanley had proven not only willing, but eager to help the Southern cause. The intelligence he provided was abundant. And it was treacherous. His false information led countless Southern men to meet their maker and for that, Kevin Johnson Stanley had met his own. Cain remembered standing over the man as he gasped and choked on his own blood. A rage boiled inside like he had never known. Stanley's traitorous tongue had done more damage than a thousand Union guns. As the last of the man's life seeped from his neck, Cain made a decision. Kevin Stanley's body was surely going to Hell but his tongue was staying right here.

The memory dissolved and Cain took a long look over the graveyard's shadowed tombstones. Then, digging his fingers down into the dirt, he gripped the bottom of the granite block and heaved the gravestone from its resting place. Groping in the dark where the stone had been, his hand fell across something waxy and soft. A thin smile appeared as he quietly pulled the object from the hole and set it in his lap.

The leather bag had been buried in the ground for almost a year but its wax coating and the heavy gravestone had kept it perfectly in tact. Untying the leather strap, Cain unrolled the bag and laid its contents out on the grass: pants, shirt, belt, coat, money and rough felt hat that was wrinkled and squashed. Reaching into the bag for a final time, he pulled out a dark leather sheath. He gripped the ivory handle and tested the dagger's razor-sharp edge with his thumb. It was everything he needed.

Cain stripped down to his underwear and quickly changed into the new clothes. He secured the dagger in the small of his back and punched the felt hat to give it some shape before pulling it tight over his thick brown hair. Glancing down at his feet, he stuffed his old clothes roughly into the leather bag before dropping it back in the hole and replacing the gravestone. A cold chill ran over his body as his hand hung on the rough granite. The last remains of Edward Huff had finally been laid to rest.

Cain crossed the graveyard and dropped down onto 9$^{th}$ Street where questions about Brutus de Villeroi and the Navy Yard surfaced once again. He needed a place to rest and to think. Halfway down the block, he was almost knocked over when a pair of swinging doors burst open and two men tumbled out into the street. Cheers and laughter from inside the establishment grew to a fevered pitch as one man gained the advantage and proceeded to pulverize the other.

Cain glanced at the wooden placard hanging over the door. There were no words to indicate the name of the tavern, only the carving of an arched bridge with a red devil standing at its center. Filled with thieves, cutthroats and conmen, The Devil's

Bridge was arguably the roughest tavern in the City and the last place a policeman would dare to go. It was the perfect place hide.

"What'll you have?" barked the greasy barman over the din of swearing and drunken laughter.

"Gimme a Schell's," Cain said, slapping a coin on the bar.

The barman turned to pull the beer but his eyes remained fixed to the mirror that kept watch over his back. Cain didn't share the barman's concerns. In fact, at this very moment, he was almost hoping for someone to pick a fight.

The mug landed hard on the bar and Cain carried it to a distant table. He took a long drink and then turned his mind to the problem of breaking into the most guarded military facility in the country. His beer grew warm as he turned the problem over and again. Every place, like every man, had a weakness.

He turned up the last of his beer and stared down into the empty mug. The site triggered a memory of Mary Ann Hall's and something Commander Glasson had said over a tumbler of Maker's Mark. *"The only way to manage the Navy Yard is with whiskey,"* he had said. *"The stuff arrives every morning in fifty barrel lots."*

*Fifty barrel lots*, Cain repeated to himself. And then it hit him. He had found his way in.

# Chapter 43

October 24, 1861 – 4th Ward, Washington City

Levi dropped the pencil to the desk and sat back in the chair with a sigh. The oversize piece of paper was littered with scratched out codewords and failed attempts to decipher the scroll. Admiral Dahlgren's suggestion to break the code with Confederate military terms had Levi running in circles. He was out of ideas. Levi closed his eyes and pinched the bridge of his nose to relieve the headache that had started to form in the back of his brain.

How could he have come so far and still feel like he was standing still? He allowed his thoughts to wander over the events of the last few days until they finally landed on Josiah. He hoped his friend had made it home safely.

*Josiah*. Levi's eyes shot open and he sprang up in his chair. *Josiah*. Thoughts collided in Levi's mind so fast that none of them made any sense. Still, buried somewhere in the wreckage, the idea was there. It was distant, like a small spark in the back of a long dark cave, but it was there. Levi struggled to separate his thoughts and grasp hold of the idea before it disappeared.

When Ellen gave the scroll to Christine Brandy she said something about Josiah. Levi squinted to get the wording just right in his head. *"Josiah has the key to understanding what the scroll means."* Levi whispered her words so that he could hear them out loud. He repeated them again, only this time he focused on the first four words. "Josiah has the key."

*The key*, he thought. His eyes drifted to the list of scratched out codewords on the paper. A codeword is a key that unlocks enciphered text. The conclusion took firm root in his mind. *Josiah has the key*. Somehow, Ellen Wolfe believed that Josiah knew the codeword to unlock the scroll.

Levi had just started to ask himself how that was possible when the second thought that had crashed in his mind came into focus. Standing on the Capitol lawn after escaping from Roby's slave pen, Josiah had said something that only now stood out in Levi's mind. *"When Haney pointed at me in the hallway, I noticed something on his finger. There was a small tattoo of some sort right here."* Josiah had pointed to the inside of his index finger.

Josiah couldn't remember what the tattoo looked like but Renee Rose could. *"It's a little tail,"* she had said. *"I didn't see it for very long but it looked to me like a scorpion's tail."* Levi slowly whittled her words away. *It's a little tail. A scorpion's tail. Scorpion.*

Levi leaned forward and picked up the pencil. Could it be? Finding a blank space on the paper, he wrote out the message from the scroll and filled in the codeword *Scorpion* beneath each letter.

His pulse ticked up a beat as he reached for the cipher disc and set the wheel in place. As he had done countless times already, he decoded the message one letter after another. Setting the wheel for the last time, he wrote down the final letter and stared down at the page.

His eyes raced over the string of letters but their arrangement into groups of four made it difficult to make any sense of them. Levi's heart pounded against his chest. He took a deep breath and forced himself to slow down and concentrate. A long moment later, the first word rose slowly to the surface. And then another. And another. Levi's mouth hung open as his eyes drifted up from the page. He couldn't believe it. It was impossible and yet there it was right in front of him. He had done it. He had broken The Scorpion's Code.

Levi blinked to snap out of his haze and looked back down at the page. Picking up the pencil, he found the beginning and end of each word and drew a line between them. When he reached the end of the message, he put the pencil down and lifted the paper off the desk. His pulse surged through his fingertips and shook the edge of the page as he read the entire code for the first time. “Oh my God.”

“What is the meaning of this?” came a booming voice in a thick French accent. “Who are you? What are you doing in my house?”

Levi looked up to see a squat man with thinning hair and a waxed mustache standing in the doorway. Seeing the drawings strewn all over the floor, the man’s face turned from outrage to concern. He looked like a man who had lost his child. “My papers! What have you done to my papers?”

Levi stood behind the desk but made no attempt to cross the room or shake the man’s hand. He needed absolute control of this discussion and he wouldn’t yield an inch. “Sit down, Mr. de Villeroi,” Levi said, motioning towards one of the green leather chairs opposite the desk.

De Villeroi appeared to be holding back tears as he slowly crossed the room. Nearing the desk, he stooped down and lovingly collected a handful of drawings before collapsing in the chair. “What have you done?” he asked, prying his eyes from the papers.

Levi tapped the silver badge on his chest. “I’m a police officer, Mr. de Villeroi,” he said. “I didn’t do any of this.”

De Villeroi glanced at the badge and threw his hands up. “Well then? Who did?”

Levi leaned over the desk to stare the Frenchman directly in the eyes. “A Confederate spy,” Levi said.

De Villeroi’s reaction to these three words was instantaneous. His eyes went as wide as saucers and his hands flew to his sides as he tried to extract his bulky frame from the chair.

"Sit down!" Levi roared.

The Frenchman paused and shot Levi an incredulous stare. He was not a man who was used to taking orders, and certainly not in his own study. He retreated back to the chair but was poised to spring at a moment's notice.

Levi pressed his position. "A Confederate spy has taken an interest in your work, Mr. de Villeroi, and you're going to tell me why."

De Villeroi shook his head violently. "No," he said plainly. "I cannot tell you a thing. It is an absolute secret."

Levi slammed his hand on the desk. "Don't you understand?" he roared. "Nothing in this room is a secret anymore. This man has seen everything!"

De Villeroi was silenced as he sat back in his chair to consider it. Moments later, he lifted his chin in defiance. "It is just one man," he said. "What can one man do against the entire Union?"

The blood in Levi's veins finally boiled over. "This!" he yelled as he slammed his hand on the desk again. He spun the paper with The Scorpion Code so that de Villeroi could read it. "One man can do this!" De Villeroi leaned forward and read the decoded message.

ARMORY ATTACK WEDNESDAY CNO EXIT CONFIRMED

"What does this mean? Armory attack Wednesday," de Villeroi asked, sitting back in his chair.

Levi stared down at him, his anger now forced into a calm, steady voice. "Have you not heard about yesterday's explosion at the Armory that burned twenty one women alive?"

"Yes, of course," de Villeroi said. "But the newspapers say it was an accident."

Levi's finger landed heavy on the deciphered code. "It was no accident," he said. "This message was written days before the explosion by a man we know to be a Confederate spy."

"So?" de Villeroi said, though without much conviction. "This man is a saboteur. Nothing more. What does this have to do with my papers?"

"It has everything to do with your papers," Levi answered. "This spy, this Scorpion, broke into your home to learn about your machine so that he can destroy it or find a way to stop it."

De Villeroi waggled a condescending finger in the air while clicking his tongue through pursed lips. "You have no idea what you are talking about," he said. "My machine is in the safest place in the entire world. Walls and men and guns surround it at every angle. There is no way your Scorpion could ever get near it."

Levi dropped his head. It was obvious that de Villeroi wouldn't cooperate but he had heard enough to know what he had to do. And to do it, he needed Josiah.

# Chapter 44

October 24, 1861 – 2nd Ward, Washington City

Josiah stepped through the narrow passage and he instantly knew something was wrong. The alleyway that was typically so full of life was completely deserted. From somewhere in the distance, a faint noise echoed down the commons. Josiah held his breath and closed his eyes to listen. A tingling sensation spread across his body. The harmonica's song was a signal to all who could understand and it hit Josiah like a punch to his stomach. Slave catchers were here.

Josiah's pulse raced as he sprinted down the alley. Every door he passed was closed and every window curtained but he didn't see them. His every thought, his every movement was focused on his wife and the two fugitives hidden behind his wardrobe. Josiah rounded the corner and heard voices emerging from the distance. *Where were they coming from?*

He stopped in his tracks and his ears pricked up. From somewhere behind him, men were laughing and cursing and talking over one another. Josiah placed his back flat against the wall and peered back around the corner with one eye.

A band of at least five white men emerged at the other end of the alley. The man in the front carried a lantern to ward off the shadows while the others brandished heavy clubs and guns. The color of their skin and the weapons in their hands left no doubt as to who the men were and why they were here. Josiah's brow dripped with sweat as he spun from the corner and sprinted to the home with the kaleidoscope door.

"Anna," Josiah said, knocking fast and quiet. "Anna, it's Josiah."

A second later, he heard someone remove the heavy board barricading the door before a hand grabbed his wrist and pulled him inside. Josiah had hardly blinked before he felt the comforting warmth of his wife's embrace. "Josiah!" she said, stepping back to look at him, "they're coming."

Anna's eyes were filled with the firm determination Josiah had seen so many times. But somewhere deep within, he saw the trace of something he couldn't quite touch. Whether fear, or love, or foreboding he didn't know but time was running short.

"I know," he said. "Ester has got to go tonight."

He stepped towards the stairs but Anna reached for his arm. "There's something else," she said.

"Anna, the catchers are coming," Josiah said firmly. "They're just down the way. Now I've got to get Ester and that boy outta this house or we're all gonna hang."

"Josiah!" Anna pleaded as her husband disappeared up the stairs.

Josiah reached the landing and ran straight to the wardrobe. Heaving it aside, he found Ester soaked in sweat and tears with Peter held tight to her breast. "They're coming," he said. "We've got to go right now."

Josiah dropped to his hands and knees and threw his arm beneath the wardrobe. Groping in the dark, he felt a pad of wax holding a folded set of papers to the underside of the wood. He tore the papers from the wax and got to his feet. "You ready?"

Ester gazed down at the baby boy tucked in her arm and then back to Josiah. She was terrified. Josiah placed his strong hands on her shoulders. "Ester," he said. His voice was gentle and firm. "Everything that Peter is or ever will be depends on what you do right now. You stay strong, stay quiet, and move when I say, and I promise your boy's got a long life ahead of him in the North. You understand?"

Ester nodded and tears dripped from her chin.

“Good,” Josiah said. “Now we got to go.” Ester nodded again as Josiah grabbed her arm and led her down the stairs where Anna was peering out the window through a crack in the curtains. “You see them?” Josiah asked.

“Not yet,” Anna said, dropping the curtain. Josiah led Ester to the door and lifted the board that held it shut. “Josiah,” Anna said.

“Them catchers are coming, Anna,” Josiah repeated. “Now we’re going.”

“Josiah!” Anna’s desperate plea finally broke through and Josiah turned to face her. Tears rolled down her cheeks and fell upon her dress. Looking into her eyes, Josiah finally saw what it was that lay behind her quiet determination. It was fear, it was love, and it was foreboding all at once.

“I’m pregnant.”

Josiah went numb. The world stood still and he suddenly forgot everything he had ever known. Then, as if the dam holding back the oceans had finally broken, a flood of emotions surged inside him that made it hard to breathe. It was fear. Love. Foreboding. And it was determination. Determination to give his child a chance to grow and to live. It was the very chance he was determined to give to young Peter.

He ran to Anna, desperate to hold her and feel her reassuring touch. He pulled her tight and they embraced for far too long before Anna finally said, “You’ve got to go, Josiah. You’ve got to go. But you come back to me.” Josiah stepped back. His wife’s image blurred through his tears. “You hear me?” Anna asked. “You come back to me.”

Josiah nodded. “I will.”

Josiah wiped his eyes and turned to the window to look through the curtain. Everything was quiet. He stepped to the door where Ester was waiting. "Give me the child," he said. Ester glanced down at Peter, who let out a peaceful coo as he was tucked away in Josiah's powerful arm. "Let's go," he said.

Josiah opened the door and they stepped out into the cool night air. For a moment, everything was still and then a sudden burst of laughter echoed down the alley from around the corner. The catchers were close.

"Come on," Josiah said.

Ester followed close behind as Josiah led her down the deserted alley and away from the voices. The alleyways of Washington City were a confused labyrinth of interconnecting common areas, darkened passages, and dead ends. They were designed to confine and hide colored people from the world so they could be more easily forgotten. It was an uncharted world that was completely unknown to the rest of the City. But for Josiah, it was home.

Ester struggled to keep up as Josiah ran towards a dark and narrow passage between two tar-papered shacks. Josiah slid between the buildings and looked back to see Ester several steps behind.

"Someone's running!" called a voice from somewhere down the alley.

"Get 'em!" yelled another voice. "Billy! You boys go around to the other side!"

Josiah's eyes went wide and his adrenaline surged. He didn't have to say a word. Ester knew her life and the life of her newborn son hung in the balance. So they ran. They ran faster than they had ever run in their lives, twisting and turning through one passage and down another. They ran so long that Ester began to wonder if it would ever end.

*Three more blocks*, Josiah repeated to himself. *If you can only make it three more blocks*. It wasn't the distance that concerned him—it was the curfew. The Black Codes made it illegal for colored people to be out on the streets after ten o'clock without a white escort. The Codes weren't enforced in the City's hidden alleyways but to get where they needed to go, Josiah and Ester would have to cross the busiest thoroughfare in the City.

The dim glow of a streetlight appeared up ahead. At the end of the passageway, Josiah held his arm out to stop Ester at the edge of the shadows. Handing Peter back to his mother, Josiah pressed his back hard against the wall. His lungs were starved for air but there was no time to waste. The streetlight cut across his face as he leaned slowly from the shadows and looked out onto Pennsylvania Avenue.

"Hello nigga."

The catcher appeared out of nowhere and was on top of him in a second. The sudden weight of the man's body threw Josiah off balance and the two men toppled over backwards into the darkened alley. There was a spark of silver and a slash of pain before Josiah caught the man's arm and froze the blade in midair. The catcher swung his free hand wildly until he grabbed Josiah's throat and began to squeeze. Josiah pushed and clawed but the man's grip only grew tighter around his neck.

Josiah looked from the blade to the catcher's crazed eyes and back again. He couldn't breathe. A faint darkness appeared in the corners of his vision and he struggled to hold the knife at bay. The darkness began to spread and his muscles grew weak. The knife drew ever closer. A baby cried from somewhere in the distance and thoughts of the child he would never know floated through Josiah's mind.

*CLUNK!*

The catcher's grip faltered and Josiah caught a quick gulp of air.

*CLUNK!*

He gasped and blinked to clear the darkness from his eyes.

*CLUNK!*

The catcher fell away and Josiah looked up to see Ester standing overhead with a cut of heavy firewood in her hand.

The catcher moaned and Josiah slowly got to his feet. The man was rolling in the dirt holding his hip with one hand and his shoulder with the other. Josiah coughed and rubbed his neck as the catcher writhed on the ground. The man rolled to one side and Josiah saw a glint of silver. Still coughing for air, Josiah quickly grabbed the knife and glanced over his shoulder at Pennsylvania Avenue.

"On your feet," Josiah said, his voice raspy and forced. The catcher didn't respond until he felt the cold steel of his own blade against his throat. "I said on your feet," Josiah repeated.

"Josiah, no!" Ester pleaded. "What are you doing?"

Josiah lifted the catcher to his feet with the edge of the blade. "Colored people can't cross that street at night on their own," he explained. Josiah leaned in so close that he could feel the catcher's breath. "But we ain't on our own now, are we."

The knife was so tight against the man's jaw that he was forced to speak through clenched teeth. "You niggers are gonna die for this," he said. "You hear me?" His eyes narrowed with hatred. "You gonna die."

"Maybe," Josiah said. "But not tonight." He spun the man around and shifted the knife to the side of his ribs. "One wrong move. One sound out of your mouth and I push this blade straight to your heart," Josiah said. "You can nod if you understand."

The catcher gave a quick nod.

"Ester," Josiah said, keeping his eyes tight on the catcher, "go get Peter and you walk right behind us to cover this knife from view."

With a poke of the blade, they stepped from the shadows and onto Pennsylvania Avenue. The catcher quietly led Josiah and Ester through the late night traffic and across the Avenue to an alley on the other side. Stepping out of the streetlight and back into the shadows, Josiah lowered the blade and spun the catcher around.

"You think you got away with something here, boy?" the catcher asked. "You ain't got away with shit. William H. Williams don't forget. He ain't never gonna forget about you and he ain't never gonna forget about what you've done."

In a flash Josiah grabbed the man's head and slammed it into the side of the building. A small gash opened on the side of his skull.

"Josiah!" Ester exclaimed in a whisper.

Holding the catcher up with one hand, Josiah slammed his bloodied head into the building a second time before dropping him to the ground like a sack of grain.

Ester stared down at the man's limp body and pulled Peter tight to her breast. "What have we done?"

Josiah lifted Ester's chin and looked deep into her eyes. "Don't you think on it. You're going North now. By tomorrow night, you and Peter will be far away from here. But we've got to keep moving, you hear? We're almost there now."

Josiah took Ester's arm and pulled her away from the catcher who would have gladly slit both of their throats. Staying in the shadows, they walked quickly through the next alleyway until they emerged in a middle-class neighborhood on F Street. Josiah scanned the nearby houses until his eyes landed on a modest, two-story brick home about half a block away.

"There it is," he said over his shoulder. "Stay with me."

They crossed the street and walked quickly to the house where Josiah knocked on the door in a rapid burst. Seconds later, a heavy bolt sounded and a man with gray hair standing on end appeared through the crack in the doorway.

"What the devil," the man said but stopped short. Looking Josiah and Ester up and down, he set his jaw and opened the door. "You best get inside." Josiah and Ester stepped over the threshold and the man glanced outside before quickly closing the door and setting the bolt.

"Mister," Josiah said, unsure where to start, "My name is Josiah Johnson and this here is Ester Epps and her boy Peter." The man kept his eyes on Josiah. "Mr. Bigelow," Josiah swallowed hard and started again, "Mr. Bigelow, he told me if I was ever in trouble that I should knock on your door. He told me I should trust you."

"Catchers?" the man asked, sensing that time was short.

"Yes, sir."

"How many?"

"At least five that I saw but we took care of one of them."

The man nodded but didn't ask for details. "Are they Williams' boys?"

"Yes, sir."

"Then we best get moving." The man motioned to Ester and Peter. "You got any papers for these two?"

"Yes, sir," Josiah said. "Right here." He reached into his pocket and handed the man the papers that had been stuck beneath his wardrobe.

"Okay then," the man said, opening the wax seal on the papers. "Josiah, go out that back door and hitch up my wagon. We'll be right behind you."

Josiah cut straight across the house and out the back door, leaving the man alone with Ester and Peter. The man held the papers up for her to see. "Can you read?"

Ester shook her head. "No, sir."

"Well then you had better listen good. These here papers say your name is Emma Brown and your boy's name is John. You got that?"

"Emma Brown. Yes, sir."

"Ester Epps is gone, you hear? And she's never coming back." Emma nodded. "Alright then." The man led Emma and John out the back door to the wagon where Josiah was buckling the last of the straps.

"Get in," the man said, pointing to the bed of the wagon.

"Where you taking her?" Josiah asked.

"Best if you don't know," the man said. "Best if you forget her and the boy. And it's damned sure best if you forget me or ever stepping foot on my property."

Josiah nodded and Emma suddenly grabbed him and held him tight. "Thank you, Josiah," she cried. "God bless you and Anna for what you done."

Josiah hugged her and then laid a gentle hand on her boy's face. "You done good, Peter. Your daddy'd be proud of you."

"Time to go," the man said.

"Thank you," Emma said as she climbed in the wagon. "God bless you, Josiah. God bless you."

# Chapter 45

October 25, 1861 – 7th Ward, Washington City

The 6th Street Wharves reached out over the Potomac like fingers. Scores of ships and barges used the busy terminal as a stopping point along the dangerous stretch of river between Washington City and the forward bases of the Army of Virginia. The food and supplies that fueled the war went out from the wharves, while the dead and the wounded came in. Today, the dead and wounded numbered in the hundreds. The Battle of Ball's Bluff had exacted a heavy price on the Union Army.

Charles Cain leaned casually against the side of the warehouse and surveyed the scene. A steady stream of wounded ran from the water's edge to the shore. Pale and helpless soldiers lined the ground with bloodied rags tied around their heads, arms, and legs. The faded blue of their uniforms was doused with ever-growing pools of red. The wounded were lined shoulder-to-shoulder in every space available. They laid on old blankets or quilts if they could find them, the bloodied grass if they couldn't. And they waited. They waited silently for someone to notice them and for someone to care. The war was hardly six months old but the City had already grown calloused and cold. The wounded were too many and the attendants too few.

As Cain observed the scene before him, the silence of the men's suffering was almost unnerving. A man who could bury his pain so deep as to not let out a cry was a man to respect and to fear. Given the opportunity, he would gladly slit every one of these men's throats but still, their silent courage was admirable.

Just as the thought entered his mind, a bloodied soldier not ten feet away screamed out loud. Cain shot him a narrowed stare as the man continued to wail. There were men with far worse injuries in every direction. Cain wanted nothing more than to pull his knife and carve the cowardice from the man's heart but he had more pressing matters at hand.

The timing of the day's events was critical. Earlier that morning, he had sent a message to his friend, Solomon Drew, to warn him of things to come. The message had set a series of events in motion and had put Cain on the clock. If his timing was off, all would be lost. He had to get moving.

Stepping through the soldiers and supplies, he wandered down towards the docks. His eyes scoured the boxes and barrels stacked along the length of the warehouse and down to the river. There were supplies of every kind imaginable but Cain was only interested in one thing: whiskey.

Near the end of the wharf, he spotted an old man and a young boy wrestling a heavy barrel onto a flat-barge loaded with other supplies. Cain studied them for several minutes as the two struggled to load their cargo. No one came to their aid or paid them any mind. The two were working alone. Then, with a wide and friendly smile, Cain wound his way to the end of the dock.

"Can I give you a hand?" Cain asked.

The old man was pushing on a crate that appeared to outweigh him two to one. Upon hearing Cain's voice, the man rested a forearm on top of the box and looked up at the kindly stranger. His face was worn and leathered from decades in the sun and Cain guessed he was somewhere around sixty years old.

"I'd be much obliged if you did," the old man said. His muscles flexed in defiance of the surrounding skin, which sagged with age.

Cain reached down and grabbed the other end of the box. Together, they carried the heavy load down the gangway to the deck of the barge.

"Right over here," the old man grunted. They arranged the crate neatly beside another that looked just like it.

"Whew!" the man said, wiping his brow. "That was a heavy one. I sure do appreciate the help." He tipped his hat back on his head to get a clear view of his new friend. "Name's Nathanial but everyone calls me Catfish," he said, spitting a mouthful of tobacco juice overboard and wiping his mouth with his sleeve.

"I'm Charlie," Cain said. He threw his hand out and Catfish gave it an almost violent shake. Cain took note of the man's grip. Despite his advanced age, Catfish could clearly fend for himself.

Just then, a young boy of around fourteen arrived from the front of the boat. His blonde hair looked like it had been hacked away with a dull knife. Catfish threw an arm around the boy's shoulder. "This here's my grandson, Turtle." The boy spit over the side of the boat but his inexperience left most of the brown juice dribbling from his chin and soaking into his shirt.

*Turtle and Catfish*, Cain thought, glancing back and forth between the two before pointing up to the dock. "What're you hauling?"

"Oh a little of this, little of that," Catfish said. "Hardtack, rope, nails, horseshoes, mail. Half them barrels up there got gunpowder and the other half got whiskey."

*Whiskey*. The fates of Catfish and Turtle now hung on whether they were intending to drive their barge up river towards the Navy Yard or down to the Canal. "Well it looks like you boys have quite a job ahead of you," Cain said. "I'd be willing to help you load up if you could give me a ride up river."

"How far you going?" Catfish asked.

"My uncle Farlow Smith's got a farm just past Cool Springs Road. He needs my help pulling in the harvest."

Catfish exchanged glances with Turtle. "Sounds like we've got ourselves a deal."

Cain smiled and headed up the gangway to grab a barrel. “I’m much obliged,” he said, turning the barrel on its side and rolling it carefully down to Turtle.

With Cain and Turtle loading the boat, Catfish decided he’d earned a break. He sat down on a nearby crate and covered his eyes with his hat.

“How far up river you headed?” Cain asked, handing the boy another box.

“As far up as Edward’s Ferry,” Turtle said. “Northern Army broke through there last night. We got to get these supplies up river so they can keep their foot right up Johnny Reb’s ass.”

“You watch that mouth, Turtle,” said Catfish from beneath his hat.

To get to Edward’s Ferry, they’d have to drive this barge directly past the United States Navy Yard. Cain turned to get another barrel and smiled. This was just getting better and better.

# Chapter 46

October 25, 1861 – 3rd Ward, Washington City

The gold coin glinted in the morning sunlight as Levi turned it anxiously between his fingers. Josiah had promised to be at the 10th Street docks first thing in the morning but he was nowhere in sight. As Levi scanned the burgeoning crowd, his nerves began to fray. *Where was Josiah? Had he made it home last night? Did he break curfew?* And then the worst came to mind. *Did William H. Williams find him?*

Levi spun in his seat and looked around for the hundredth time. Finally, peering up Ohio Avenue, he saw Josiah's broad shoulders and thick beard appear in the passing traffic. Levi breathed a sigh of relief but it passed in an instant. There was trouble written on Josiah's face.

"Morning, Mr. Love," Josiah said. His voice was strained and tired.

Levi studied his eyes. "What's happened?" he asked.

Josiah winced as he pulled himself up into the wagon and sat on the bench. "Everything's alright now," he said, keeping his eyes forward so that Levi couldn't see them. "Ain't nothing you need to worry on."

It was plain to Levi that there was plenty to worry about. Just as obvious was that the busy intersection in front of the 10th Street docks was the wrong place to discuss it. He picked up the reins and held his questions until the wagon crossed over the Canal and the Smithsonian Castle came into view. "What happened, Josiah?"

Everything Josiah had ever known told him to stay quiet. In all his life, he had never known a white man to understand a black man's heart. Josiah reached up to touch his mutilated ear and the memory of the day he bought his own freedom burst into mind. The very man who had carved his ear away had also handed him his freedman's papers. *These papers don't mean a thing,* the man had said. *You're a nigger. You'll always be a nigger. And there ain't a white man alive who will ever see you any different.*

Josiah glanced over at the man sitting beside him—the man who had risked his life to set him free from Roby's slave pen—and he saw something different. He saw concern and remorse. He saw a good man walking the finest of lines in this wretched City. He saw a friend. Josiah turned his gaze down the road and into the distance.

"Catchers came last night," he said. A heavy pit formed in Levi's stomach but he stayed quiet. "Williams' boys," Josiah continued. "They were already in the alley when I got home. I don't know who they were after but they found me."

"Do they know who you are?" Levi asked.

"You mean, do they know if I'm the one who escaped from Roby's?" Josiah asked. He shook his head. "I don't know. There were five or more of them but only one got a good look at me. I ain't never seen him before but that don't matter much. If he saw my ear, that'd be all he needs."

Levi glanced at what was left of Josiah's ear. His head was spinning with questions and worry. "What about the others? What about Anna?" he asked.

Josiah looked at Levi with eyes that had carried a heavy burden. "They'll be okay," he said. "I think they'll be okay."

Levi wanted to know every detail but couldn't bring himself to ask. He could only imagine the horrifying night that Josiah had been through and forcing him to relive it somehow seemed cruel and heartless. It was enough to know that, despite everything,

Josiah was here. Levi turned to thank him and saw Josiah still touching his ear, his mind trapped in some far off place.

"Josiah," Levi said gently, "what happened to your ear?"

The question cut through the fog in Josiah's mind and brought him back to the present. With his eyes still fixed on the horizon, he said, "I was born on a cotton plantation outside Macon, Georgia. John Fitz Jarrell got the plantation and the slaves after his daddy died. Mr. Jarrell was a kindly man. He had a local teacher come every morning before sunup to teach reading and writing to any slaves who wanted to get up an hour early to learn. Sick or tired, it didn't matter. I got up every morning.

"I guess that got Mr. Jarrell's attention and one day he asked me if I'd like to learn some carpentry. He said his overseer, a man by the name of Casper, could use some help building a new barn in the back half of the property. Learning a real skill wasn't nothing I ever heard of from a slave. And then Mr. Jarrell said something that I ain't never heard from a white man. He put his hand on my shoulder and said, *'Josiah, you learn some carpentry, you show me you can earn a living and I'll let you buy your freedom.'*"

Josiah wiped his eyes. "Can you believe that?" he asked Levi. "Right there. Just like that, Mr. Jarrell gave me everything a man could ever want." The rattle of the wagon filled the void until Josiah continued.

"I went down to the barn straight away but Mr. Casper, he didn't want coloreds knowing nothing but how to pick cotton from the boll." Josiah paused as the edges of the memory grew clear. "The look he gave me, I'd seen it before. Casper wanted blood. But I hadn't done nothing but show up like Mr. Jarrell said. Casper stared at me for a long time before he thought of what to do.

"'*Fetch me that skew former,*' he said. I ain't never heard of such a thing but Casper wouldn't say another word. I stood in front of those tools and I couldn't tell one from the other. But I knew what he was doing. Even if I picked the right one, Mr. Casper would have said it was wrong. So I just grabbed the first one off the top. When I took it to him, Casper was ready.

"'*You dumb nigger,*' he screamed. He grabbed me by my ear and dragged me over to the tools. '*I told you to get me the skew former.*' I was looking down at those tools when Casper pulled his knife and sliced clean through my ear.

"The pain took me to my knees. And no matter how hard I pushed, I couldn't stop the blood. When I looked up, Casper was standing over me with my ear in his hand. '*What's the point of having ears if you can't hear shit anyway,*' he said. Then he dropped my ear in the dirt and walked away."

When Josiah's story ended, Levi's stomach was tied in a knot so tight he felt like he might get sick. "My God," he said in a whisper. It was all he could muster.

The wagon rattled on for some time—each man lost in his own thoughts. "What did Mr. de Villeroi say?" Josiah finally asked.

"He didn't say much," Levi said. He pulled the scroll from his pocket and handed it to Josiah. "But he didn't have to."

Josiah took the scroll and unrolled it. The last time he had seen it, the scroll contained a single line of seemingly random letters. But this time, there were two additional lines of text. Josiah studied the first line and saw that the word *scorpion* was repeated several times. He then turned his gaze to the second line.

At first, the odd grouping of the letters made it difficult to read but the words soon rose to the surface. "Armory attack Wednesday CNO exit confirmed," Josiah said. After a beat, his eyes grew wide and he looked over at Levi. "Is that what Ms. Ellen's code says?" he asked, hardly able to contain his excitement. "Armory attack Wednesday CNO exit confirmed?"

Levi smiled. “That’s what it says.”

Josiah’s eyes shot back down to the scroll. “Scorpion,” he said. “The codeword was scorpion.” Levi nodded. “But how’d you know that?”

“I knew it because of you.” Josiah was understandably confused until Levi explained how he had connected Haney’s tattoo to his conversation with Renee Rose and then back to the scroll.

Josiah pulled on his beard. “So Ms. Ellen was right,” he said. “I did have the key.”

Josiah read the message again before looking off at the horizon. “Armory attack Wednesday,” he said quietly as he thought it over. “This Scorpion,” he began, “he’s the one who burned up all those women at the Armory?”

Levi nodded. “Sure looks that way.”

“So what’s the rest of this mean? *CNO exit confirmed*?”

“Hard to say,” Levi shrugged. “But it’s got to have something to do with the attack on the Armory.”

Josiah nodded and pulled on his beard. “Makes sense,” he said. “So where we going now?”

“We’re going to catch the dog by the neck,” Levi said with a smile.

“We’re going to that boathouse, ain’t we,” Josiah said.

“We are.”

“How do you know that’s the place?”

Levi thought for a moment to silently confirm the logic of his conclusion. “When I went back into de Villeroi’s house,” he began, “his study was littered with all sorts of mechanical drawings for some kind of machine. I stared at those drawings for an hour and couldn’t make any sense of them. When de Villeroi got home, I told him about the Scorpion and asked him why a Confederate spy had taken such an interest in his machine. But he wouldn’t tell me anything. The only thing he said was that his machine was stored in the safest place on Earth. He said it was surrounded by walls and men and guns at every angle.”

Josiah made the connection in an instant. “The Navy Yard.”

“Exactly,” Levi said. “Now you walked that entire Yard and there was only one place that answers to de Villeroi’s description.”

Josiah pulled on his beard. “I believe you’re right, Mr. Love,” he said. “Let’s go catch us a dog.”

# Chapter 47

October 25, 1861 – Potomac River, Washington City

Cain set the pole into the mud and pushed hard to keep the barge steady in the current. It had taken the better part of two hours to load the remaining cargo and secure it to the deck but the boat was now drifting lazily south under the mid-morning sun. Cain had taken up Catfish's pole and worked one side of the deck while Turtle worked the other. The boxes and barrels were stacked so high between them that Cain only caught glimpses of the boy as he skillfully piloted the boat downstream. As for Catfish, he had kept his seat at the front of the boat, content to rest his eyes in the shade of his hat while his mouth ran at full speed.

"Where'd you say you was from?" Catfish asked.

Cain hadn't said one word on the topic but, given the circumstances, he saw no harm in telling the truth. "Richmond, Virginia."

Catfish sprang up and nearly fell off his crate as he lifted his hat. "Richmond?" It was, after all, the capital of the Confederacy.

"Yes, sir," Cain said. "Born and raised there."

"What in tarnation are you doing here?"

"Acting," Cain said.

Catfish's leathery face twisted in confusion. "Huh?"

"I'm an actor," Cain repeated. "I came to Washington City to act."

For some reason, the revelation set Catfish at ease. He leaned back on the crate and placed the hat back over his eyes. "Well how'd you end up here?" he asked.

"I was part of a Shakespearean troupe that was travelling north when the war broke out," Cain said. "I just never went home." Having spent months burying his past beneath layers of false identities, the moment of honesty left Cain feeling strangely liberated. It was like he had suddenly shed a hundred pounds he didn't realize he was carrying. Still, there was no need to dwell on the topic.

"So how'd you get the name Catfish?" Cain asked.

"You ever been noodling?" Catfish asked.

"Can't say I even know what that is," Cain replied, setting the pole in the water and giving it a firm push.

"Catfish are smart," the old man said from beneath his hat. Of all the descriptors Cain thought to apply to a fish, smart didn't come to mind but he held his tongue. "They ain't like all them other fish that just swim around in circles waiting to get et'," Catfish continued. "No, sir. A catfish digs himself a deep hole in the riverbanks. Then he backs his self in there where them other fish can't see. When one of them dumber fish swims by, the catfish pops outta that hole quicker than shit from a goose.

"Now noodling," he said, turning to the point of his story, "noodling is when *you* get to outsmart the catfish." The old man's chest puffed out as if outsmarting a catfish was a momentous feat. "First thing you gotta do is wade out into the water and drag a stick along the banks until it finds one of them hiddin' holes. Then, quick as you can, you throw your hand down that hole and right into the fish's mouth. You grab it by the gill, yank him outta there and throw him up on the grass."

Cain had never heard of such a thing and was genuinely fascinated. "Don't they bite?"

Catfish laughed and spit his tobacco juice without aim. “Hell yeah they bite!” he said. “They come outta there madder than a nest of hornets. But anyone who noodles knows that from the start. If you ain’t willing to get bit then you best not play the game.”

Cain stared out over the water and thought about all that he had done and dangerous job still ahead. Catfish’s simple wisdom was just as true about spying as it was about noodling. “What about Turtle?” he asked. “How’d he get his name?”

Catfish belted out another laugh and another stream of tobacco juice. “Couple years back, we was noodling up on Four Mile Creek when Turtle’s stick found a hole deeper than a whore’s kitty.” Catfish chuckled. “Anyways, Turtle figures he’s about to pull the biggest fish he’d ever seen. So he wades over there and throws his arm right down in that hole. But it weren’t no fish living in there. It was the biggest, meanest snapping turtle you ever seen. That thing got hold of Turtle’s little finger and sent him screaming to the shore like he was on fire!”

Catfish laughed so hard it roused a wet cough that sent him gasping for air and farting at every exchange. The fit lasted until a wad of mucus broke loose in his lung and he spit it out onto the deck. “Been calling him Turtle ever since.”

Cain stuck his pole out to push off from a nearby rock and noticed a shift in the current. He looked off the front of the boat and realized they had reached the wide peninsula that divided the headwaters of the Potomac and the Eastern Branch. Known as Greenleaf’s Point, the peninsula marked the halfway point in the journey from the 6th Street Wharves to the Navy Yard. It was also the site of the U.S. Arsenal where, only days before, Cain’s carefully planned attack destroyed tons of munitions and the women who built them. Cain squinted into the sun to try and catch a glimpse of the damage.

“Coming around!” Turtle yelled as he deftly planted his pole in the mud.

The combined currents of the two rivers shifted the barge beneath Cain's feet and knocked him off balance. His stomach lurched.

"Push!" Turtle yelled.

Cain grabbed hold of the cargo to regain his footing and quickly threw his pole in the water. The opposing currents pushed the backend of the barge one way and the front end another.

"Push!" Turtle yelled.

Cain's pole struck bottom and he pushed with everything he had. With a second and third long push, the barge slipped from the pull of the Potomac and entered the calm waters of the Eastern Branch. Cain pulled his pole from the river and leaned against the cargo to catch his breath. Glancing towards the front of the boat, he saw that Catfish was still reclining on the crates as calm as if they were standing still.

Turtle navigated to the far shore and the tranquil rhythm of the boat soon returned. Cain and Turtle planted their poles in turn and slowly worked the barge upstream. With the excitement of the headwaters behind them, Cain's thoughts shifted to the business at hand. The turn at Greenleaf's Point meant the Navy Yard was less than an hour away. From here, the success of Cain's plan depended on timing.

They continued upriver as the sun beat down and turned the water gold. A half hour later, Cain squinted into the sun to see a schooner and two barges disappear into the glare. When they emerged on the other side, the current would push them far downstream in a matter of minutes.

Cain worked his pole to the back of the boat and shifted his gaze downriver. Staring into the distance, he could just make out the shape of another supply boat fighting the currents at Greenleaf's

Point. Glancing upriver, the glare of the sun was almost blinding. Cain smiled at his good fortune. The boat turning at the Point couldn't see a thing. In a matter of moments, he would have Catfish and Turtle all alone.

Cain turned his attention to the cargo stacked high in the middle of the deck. Peering between the boxes and barrels, he caught fleeting glimpses of Turtle as he worked the other side of the barge. Cain marked Turtle's position at every pass and slowly adjusted his pace so that he was working the front of the boat when Turtle was working the back. They made one pass after another until their rhythm was set. Now, the closer Cain got to Catfish, the further away he was from Turtle.

Cain's senses spiked as his world shrunk to the size of the river barge. Pulling his pole from the mud, every sound, every motion was suddenly magnified—the sway of the boat, the gentle lapping of the water on the hull, the creak of the rope as it strained against the cargo. Cain reached the front of the boat to see that the morning sun and sounds of the river had lulled Catfish to a deep and peaceful sleep. There would be no struggle.

He set his pole and marked his steps towards the other end of the deck. The next pass would be his last. At the back of the boat, Cain hesitated a half a second to ensure his timing was perfect. Then, turning towards the bow, his hand slipped to the ivory handle hidden in the small of his back. With his eyes fixed on the cargo that concealed Catfish from view, Cain walked slowly down the deck.

The old man's boots appeared from behind the crates and Cain lifted his pole from the water. Laying it silently on the deck, he kept a steady pace towards his prey. The feel of the knife in his hand slowed his heart and focused his mind. The sudden calm that warmed his body was familiar and reassuring. It reminded him his cause was just and that God was always watching.

Cain stepped to the end of the crates and set his back against the wood. Peering around the corner, he saw Catfish was still fast asleep in the sun. By now, Turtle had surely reached the far end of the barge and was making his turn. It was time. Cain gripped the ivory handle tight and circled around the crate. Inching closer, he stepped in front of the sun and his dark shadow fell upon the unsuspecting old man.

"We there already?" came a leathery voice from under the hat. Cain's heart jumped as Catfish lifted the brim of his hat. The old man recoiled at the site of the hulking stranger standing over him. A sunbeam flashed and Catfish shifted his gaze to see the knife in Cain's hand. His heart hammered in his chest and his feet scratched for traction but the heavy cargo blocked his retreat.

Cain lunged and thrust his blade. The old man screamed, "Turtle! Run!" but his cry was cut short as Cain buried the knife deep under the old man's jaw.

Something shifted nearby and Cain turned to see Turtle standing only feet away from the grizzly scene. Wide-eyed and open mouthed, the boy stood paralyzed at the site of his grandfather writhing in pain and clasping his neck to staunch the flow of blood.

Turning his cold rage on the boy, Cain clutched the knife hidden in his boot. The sudden movement woke Turtle from his trance and he turned to run. Cain pounced but the boy ducked and disappeared behind the cargo.

Cain thundered after him and was gaining ground when Turtle dove headlong off the back of the boat and splashed into the river. Grabbing the boy's pole from the deck, Cain swung it wildly into the water where he made contact with something hard. When the splash fell away, he peered into the murky depths. Had he struck the boy or something else? Cain's breath caught in his lungs as he waited for a ripple in the water or a splash on the shore. Nothing came. The boy was gone.

# Chapter 48

October 25, 1861 – 6$^{th}$ Ward, Washington City

Levi slowed the wagon as they approached the sweeping archway of Latrobe Gate. A handful of supply wagons formed a line in front of the iron gates while the guards checked their cargo and questioned the drivers. One by one, the wagons were granted entry into the Navy Yard and the line inched slowly forward. When Levi and Josiah reached the front of the line, they saw the same quarrelsome soldier that had given them so much trouble the last time they had come to see Admiral Dahlgren.

"You two again, huh?" the soldier said. He removed his cap and scratched at his bright red hair like it was infested with lice, which it likely was. Replacing his cap, he glanced at his fingernails before looking up at Levi. "Suppose you're gonna tell me you're here to see the Admiral."

"That's right," Levi said. "We've got some new information on the murder."

"What kind of information?"

"The kind of information that's none of your damned business," Levi said. "Are we really going to go through all of this again?"

The soldier scratched at his head through the top of his forage cap as he thought it over. Finally, concluding both his scratching and his thinking, he called out to the other guards. "Open the gate!"

Levi drove the wagon through the arch and followed the dirt road into the Yard. "You alright?" Levi asked, still concerned about everything Josiah had been through the night before.

"I'm alright," Josiah said but it wasn't entirely true. He had escaped from Roby's slave pen and beaten a catcher halfway to death. William H. Williams was surely coming for him but, for now, there was no time to think on it. "Now that we're here," he said, "what do you want me to do?"

Levi guided the horses around the bend in the road and the Admiral's two-story colonial house came into view. "I'm going to go and talk to Dahlgren but someone needs to keep an eye on that boathouse. Is there somewhere over there you can hide and keep watch over the place?"

Josiah slowly shook his head. "I can keep watch from a distance," he said, "but I can't get too close. There ain't nothing but wide open space between the ridge and them trees."

Levi pulled the wagon to a stop and set the brake. He placed a hand on Josiah's shoulder. "Just do what you can." Levi jumped down from the bench and started up the path to Dahlgren's house. Knocking on the door, he looked over his shoulder to see Josiah making his way into the Yard.

"Can I help you?" Levi turned to see a rather dignified looking sergeant standing in the door. "Ah, it's you," the sergeant said, seeing Levi's badge. "The Admiral is very busy this morning. He doesn't have time to discuss Lieutenant Daniels today."

"Neither do I," Levi said. "Just tell the Admiral I've broken the Confederate code."

The sergeant shot Levi a suspicious stare. "Stay here," he said and closed the door. Minutes later, Levi was considering knocking again when the door finally opened and the sergeant reappeared. "The Admiral will see you now."

Levi stepped into the foyer and walked directly into Dahlgren's office where the Admiral was leaning over his desk and signing a letter of some sort. His bald head shined in the gaslight until he set his pen in the ink bottle and leaned back in his chair.

"Sergeant Williford tells me you've broken the code," he said, getting right to the point. His skepticism was plain in his voice.

"I have," Levi said, pulling the scroll from his pocket and handing it across the desk.

The corners of Dahlgren's mouth curled with doubt as he took the scroll and laid it out on his desk. Seeing the three lines of text, his mouth grew slack and he dropped his head towards the scroll to get closer look. Dahlgren fell back in his chair, astonished. "Scorpion," he said. "The codeword was scorpion." He turned his wide eyes to Levi. "But how could you possibly know that?"

"It's a long story, Admiral but I think we should focus on the code and what it means."

Dahlgren leaned forward and read it again. When he finished, the scroll snapped back into a coil. "It doesn't mean anything now," he said. "The attack on the Armory has already happened. There's nothing we can do about it."

"I agree, sir," Levi said, trying to keep his frustration at bay, "but it does tell us that all of this is connected. The man who killed Ellen Wolfe is the same man who blew up the Armory, killed Lieutenant Daniels, and stole the message from Brutus de Villeroi."

Dahlgren was visibly shocked. "How do you know about Brutus?"

Levi took a deep breath. The Admiral was focusing on all the wrong details. "Sir," he said, "this spy we are after, this Scorpion, he's obviously after Brutus de Villeroi's machine. And I believe that machine is hidden right here at the Navy Yard."

Dahlgren leaned back in his chair and stared out the window for a long moment. "Officer Love," he finally said, turning back to Levi, "if such a machine existed, and if it were here at the Yard, there would be nothing for you to worry about. Look around you." Dahlgren swept his arms out. "The Navy Yard is the safest place on Earth. There are thousands of men here and the entire place is surrounded by walls and guns."

"Surrounded by walls and guns," Levi repeated, his frustration now boiling to the surface. "The Armory was surrounded by walls and guns. But that didn't stop this man from blowing it up!" Levi slammed his hand on the desk and the smug look on the Admiral's face faded. "The Scorpion is coming to the Navy Yard, Admiral. He's coming as sure as the night. Now what are you going to do about it?"

# Chapter 49

October 25, 1861 – 6th Ward, Washington City

"You boys mind throwing me a line?" Cain called across the water. One of the men working the supply docks found a coil of rope and threw it out to the barge. "Much obliged," Cain said but the man had already turned to collect a nearby sack of grain.

Cain tied the rope to the front cleat and slowly pulled the barge towards the docks. Following the disappearance, and likely death, of Turtle, he had poled the barge to the inlet of a nearby creek and tied off in a group of trees. His first order of business was to dispose of Catfish's body. Cutting a length of rope from the cargo, he tied the old man to a crate of horseshoes and dumped him into the river. Then, after washing away all the blood that hadn't already soaked into the deck, he took a quick inventory of the cargo and made a small pile of the barrels and boxes he might need. A half hour later, the Navy Yard's busy supply docks came into view.

With a final pull, Cain eased the barge to the dock and tied off. A man in a blue Army uniform appeared overhead. He was of average height and build but his eyes shone with an intelligence that belied his lowly rank of corporal. "Whatcha carrying?" he asked sharply.

Cain closed one eye against the sun and flashed a broad smile. "Oh you know," he said, "a little of this, little of that."

The corporal eyed him skeptically. "I ain't never seen you before," he said.

"I'd be surprised if you had," Cain said. "I'm just in from New York not two days ago."

"New York City?" the corporal asked.

"No. Haverstraw," Cain said, remembering the name from a newspaper article. "It's a little town on the Hudson."

The corporal stared down at Cain. "Well how'd you get to delivering supplies to the Navy after just two days in Washington City?"

The corporal's questioning was pointed and smart. And it was unnerving. Cain maintained a friendly smile as he wove his fiction from thin air. "My family owns a barge just like this up in Haverstraw," he began. "I been running stock and supplies up and down that river since the day I was born. But when President Lincoln called for volunteers, I came running."

The corporal glanced down at Cain's legs as if to make sure he had some. "Well you must not run too fast," he said. "Lincoln made that call months ago."

"I tried to enlist with Major Johnson's brigade in Yonkers," Cain said, his pulse rising, "but the Army wouldn't take me."

"Is that right," the corporal said, locking eyes with Cain. "The Army wouldn't take you? Now why is that?"

"On account of my lungs," Cain said, throwing out as little detail as he could manage.

The soldier glanced at Cain's chest. "Your lungs?" he asked. "What's wrong with them?"

Cain shrugged. Why was this corporal so damned inquisitive? "Don't really know. But if I walk too far or run too fast I start to coughing up blood and lots of it."

The corporal narrowed his eyes and held his gaze for a long moment. "That still don't answer my question," he said. "How'd you get from New York to polling this here barge in just two days?"

Cain's heart hammered in his chest. Up on the shore, and somewhere out of sight, hundreds of soldiers were patrolling the compound. The slightest signal from this vexing corporal would send them running. Cain forced himself to stay calm. "Well my cousin owns this boat. I'm here on account of him being sick."

"And who would your cousin be?"

"Nathaniel Flem," Cain said, making up a last name and hoping for the best. "You probably know him as Catfish."

The corporal's eyes opened a fraction upon hearing the familiar name. Without warning, he dropped down off the dock and onto the boat where he went directly to the cargo to poke around. He disappeared behind a stack of crates and was out of sight for a long minute before he emerged near the bow. Cain was relieved to see the corporal walking back towards him but then he suddenly stopped. Tracing his eyes slowly along the deck, the corporal stared at the dark stain that had set into the wood. It was the exact place where Catfish had breathed his last.

A surge of adrenaline coursed through Cain's body as the corporal got down on one knee and reached out to touch the stain. Wiping his fingers over the wood, he lifted his hand and smelled his fingertips. Cain's hand slipped towards the small of his back. If he was headed to the afterlife, this meddlesome corporal was coming with him.

"Private Terrance!" the corporal yelled, still staring down at the deck.

A boy around the age of seventeen appeared at the end of the dock with a rifle on his shoulder. "Yessir?"

"Private Terrance," the corporal stood and Cain's hand inched closer to his blade. "I need you to get some boys down to this boat right now." The corporal turned and looked directly at Cain. "Let's get this cargo unloaded."

Cain's hand hung behind his back and he forced a smile. "Much obliged," he said as the corporal climbed up to the docks.

Seconds later, a wooden gangway appeared along with six men who immediately set to unloading the boat. Cain stood near the back where he had set aside a portion of the supplies for his next stop. The dockworkers had the rest of the cargo off the boat in short order and one of the men reached for the barrel of whiskey beside Cain.

"The rest of these supplies are going upriver," Cain said. The man nodded and had turned towards the gangway when Cain stopped him. "But I wonder if you could help me."

"Will if I can," the man said, turning back.

"Commander Glasson has asked me to deliver these supplies to Boathouse F."

The dockworker squinted over Cain's shoulder. "Don't believe there is an F," he said.

Cain furrowed his brow. "You sure?" he asked. "Commander Glasson was real clear about it being Boathouse F."

"I'm sure," the man said. He swept his index finger along the shore as he counted off the buildings. "That's A, B, C and that one over there," he pointed to the last boathouse in sight, "that's D."

Cain immediately understood. It wasn't that Boathouse F didn't exist – it was that this lowly dockworker didn't know a thing about it. "My mistake," Cain said. The man nodded and climbed the gangway before drawing it up off the deck.

Cain traced his eyes to each of the boathouses along the shore and silently counted them off in his mind. *A. B. C. D.* The buildings were lettered in ascending order from left to right and that could mean only one thing: Boathouse F was hidden away somewhere just upriver.

A broad smile crossed Cain's face as he untied the boat, set his pole and cast off.

# Chapter 50

October 25, 1861 – 6th Ward, Washington City

Josiah followed the narrow wagon trail as it wound its way from Admiral Dahlgren's house through the open field in the center of the Yard. He watched as scores of soldiers arranged and rearranged the endless rows of cannon rolling out of the nearby foundry. The cannon appeared in every shape and size—each offering its own opinion on the most efficient destruction of the enemy.

Josiah studied the soldiers and the cannons until a sinking feeling drew his thoughts inward. The last time he wandered the Navy Yard, he had no idea where he was going or what he was looking for. Now, knowing both, the weight of his task somehow felt even heavier.

The thought hung in his mind as he left the field behind and the road wound through a dense collection of buildings and sheds. The sounds of tradesman hard at work filtered from the nearby workshops and filled the air with a rhythmic chorus of hammers and saws. Though the doors to the shops were open, Josiah kept his eyes on the ground. His last trip to the Yard had taught him that the slightest eye contact could invite unwanted questions and get him conscripted for some other task. Besides, there was no need to look around. The Scorpion was after de Villeroi's machine, which wasn't anywhere near the crowded workshops on the hill—it was hidden deep in the trees and far away from prying eyes.

Soon, the ground shifted and the road began its long descent towards the river. The dense collection of workshops gave way to a handful of sheds that dotted the open hillside. Josiah scanned the row of sheds along the ridgeline until he saw the heavy stone wall marking the eastern boundary of the Navy Yard. The sheds were all roughly the same size and shape with clapboard siding and a narrow door. There were no workers or tradesmen around any of the buildings, which led Josiah to guess they were simply used for storage of one thing or another.

Reaching the first shed, he opened the rough wood door and peered inside. Sunlight streamed through the door and cast Josiah's long shadow across room. The shed was littered with junk of every type and variety. There were worn out tools, stacks of wood, broken wheels, ropes, horseshoes, rusted pulleys, and even an old saddle collecting dust in the corner.

Quickly scanning the odd collection for a second time, Josiah closed the door and continued on down the path. He needed to find some sort of work to do that would appear natural and allow him to remain at the top of the ridgeline to watch over the boathouse. There was simply nothing he could do with a collection of old junk.

A cool wind blew in off the Potomac and rattled the tall grass as Josiah followed the narrow footpath to the next building. He opened the door and something glinted in the sun. Blinking against the glare, Josiah stepped inside to see an axe hanging on the far wall. It was then that he noticed the shed was filled with logs. Josiah smiled as he grabbed the axe and threw a dozen or more logs out into the grass. With winter fast approaching, no one would second guess a man chopping wood.

From the top of the ridge, Josiah could see the entire waterfront, which was bustling with activity. A line of livestock and supplies ran from the warehouse to a massive gunboat preparing for sea. Men climbed the ship's rigging to check the sails while others scrubbed the decks and polished the guns. A supply barge pushed off the docks and headed further upriver as another arrived from Greenleaf's Point. Josiah watched the activity for a long moment but everything appeared perfectly normal.

Josiah set a log on end. Heaving the axe in a long arc, the blade split the log in two and sent the pieces tumbling to the ground. As he picked up the pieces, he looked further upriver where his eyes fell upon the thick stand of trees that shrouded the secret boathouse from view. In contrast to the frenetic activity of the waterfront, the boathouse was as still as the grave. Four uniformed guards stood in a quiet clump near the corner of the building. They were talking and sharing a pipe as if there wasn't a care in the world. Josiah split another log and squinted into the distance but it was simply too far to make out the men's faces.

Frustration welled as Josiah set another log and swung the axe a little harder than required. He was close enough to see the boathouse but too far away to be of any use. At this distance, he couldn't tell one soldier from another. For all he knew, the Scorpion *was* one of those soldiers.

# Chapter 51

October 25, 1861 – 6th Ward, Washington City

The current swirled against the bow but, having offloaded most of the cargo, Cain poled the barge upriver with ease. Passing Boathouse D, the docks and ships and industry of the waterfront came to an end and the river returned to its natural state. The trees along the shoreline grew thick as grass and arched gracefully over the water as if trying to reach the other side. Cain kept the barge in the shade as his eyes swept slowly through the trees. Somewhere in the thicket, Brutus de Villeroi was hiding a machine that could dictate the fates of war.

Minutes later, a faint and familiar sound echoed through the trees. Cain pulled his pole from the water and closed his eyes to listen. For a moment he couldn't quite place it but then slowly, the sound formed an image in his mind. It was the sound of the current swirling around a heavy object. Cain set his pole to ground and pushed upriver. It could just be the water rolling over a rock or a dead tree or—Cain's thoughts stopped cold as the object appeared through the trees—*a dock!*

Cain peered into the woods as he poled the barge closer to the dock but the dense branches made it impossible to see where it went. Pushing further, he reached a break in the trees and caught his first glimpse of the quiet inlet where Admiral Dahlgren and Brutus de Villeroi had hidden their secrets from the world. The narrow dock ran from the rushing currents of the river into a calm pool of water. And there, on the far side of the dock, was the building Cain had sacrificed everything to find.

Boathouse F looked nothing like the massive structures found along the waterfront. The building was short and narrow. There were no windows to be found and the exterior doors facing the lagoon were closed tight. The lagoon itself was quiet and deserted, leaving Cain with an eerie feeling as the barge skimmed silently across its waters.

Cain set his pole deep in the mud and slowed the boat to a stop alongside the dock. The trees curled overhead and shrouded the lagoon in shadow. A tingling sensation spread over Cain's body. Things were too quiet and too easy. Sticking to his plan, he grabbed a barrel of whiskey and rolled it to the edge of the barge. He was heaving the heavy barrel off the deck when the sound of heavy footfalls rang out from the other end of the dock.

"You there!" cried a man running down the dock. "Stop right where you are!" Within seconds, Cain was surrounded by three soldiers with their guns drawn. "Who the hell are you?"

Cain looked up to see a man with a badly broken nose and a heavy purple bruise around his eyes. The man had obviously suffered a recent and massive blow to the head. Cain threw his hands in the air. The man poked Cain in the gut with his pistol and Cain saw the sergeant's stripes on his arm. "I asked you a question, mister," the sergeant said.

"My, my name is," Cain stuttered and stumbled for good effect. "I'm Charlie Cain. I'm just here to deliver some supplies."

The sergeant called over his shoulder at the two privates standing behind him. "You boys know anything about a delivery?"

"No, sir," the men said in unison.

The sergeant turned back to Cain. "The boys ain't heard nothing about no supplies coming in today."

"That's because this here whiskey is compliments of Commander Glasson," Cain said, feigning an uneasy tone and shifting his eyes nervously between the men. He looked every bit the man who had never had a gun pointed in his direction. "The Commander asked that I personally deliver these two barrels to the men in this here boathouse."

"Is that right?" the sergeant asked, skeptically. "Commander Glasson said all that, did he?"

"Sure did," Cain said, nodding vigorously.

The sergeant peered around Cain at the barrel on the dock. "Whiskey, you say?"

"Yes, sir," Cain said.

A crack appeared in the sergeant's façade. "I suppose it'd be a shame to disappoint the Commander," the sergeant grinned. "Best get them barrels inside then."

Cain smiled inwardly and turned the barrel on its side to push it down the dock. The sergeant pressed a heavy hand into Cain's shoulder. "Where do you think you're going?"

Cain was confused. "You said you wanted the barrels inside."

"You ain't going nowhere near that boathouse, boy," the sergeant said with a menacing stare. "The only place you're going is back down to your boat to fetch me that second barrel of whiskey."

Cain dropped his eyes to the sergeant's gun and then over to the other two soldiers. Given the battered state of the sergeant's face, Cain knew a well-placed punch would easily take the man to the ground. If he acted fast, Cain could probably take out one of the other soldiers but not both.

"Okay, okay," Cain said, dropping down onto the boat. "No need to get so rough." Reaching for the second barrel of whiskey, he eyed the other boxes and barrels stacked nearby. He had hoped the whiskey would be enough to get him inside the boathouse but, as it was, he would have to use alternate means.

Cain heaved the second barrel onto the dock and set his pole in the bottom of the shallow lagoon. Pushing the barge out into the Eastern Branch, he looked over his shoulder to see the younger soldiers rolling the barrels down the dock under the sergeant's watchful eye. Cain shook his head. It would have been much easier for everyone if the sergeant had simply allowed Cain to roll the barrels into the boathouse and take a look around. But Cain wasn't too discouraged. Where peaceful methods failed, violence often prevailed.

Staying close to the shore, Cain pushed the barge upriver until the lagoon and the boathouse disappeared in the trees. He continued on for several more minutes before lifting his pole and gliding the boat to a stop on the muddy banks of the river. Jumping ashore, he tied the bow rope to a thick tree and triple-checked the knot. If the boat slipped away, he would have no chance of leaving this City alive.

Cain jumped back onboard and quickly carried the remaining cargo to shore. Two small barrels of gunpowder and a box of supplies were all he had to get inside the most secure building in the U.S. Navy. They would have to be enough. He opened the crate to see a stack of canvas bags along with a flint and steel striker. Putting the striker and flint in one pocket, and the canvas bag in another, he crouched in the trees to get his bearings.

His gaze swept along the river and through the forest. The gurgle of the water and the sounds of his breath filled the air. All was still and quiet—but not for long. Cain heaved a barrel of gunpowder onto each shoulder and headed into the trees. A layer of dried leaves covered the ground and crunched under foot as he wove his way slowly towards the lagoon.

Minutes later, a distant voice cut through the air. Cain stopped in his tracks and knelt down on one knee. Turning his head towards the sound, he waited and listened. Muffled laughter filtered through the trees and was carried away in a passing breeze. Cain peered through the dense branches where the broken outline of Boathouse F appeared over a small rise in the landscape. He lowered the barrels from his shoulders and set them quietly on the ground. This was the place.

Cain cleared away the leaves and set one of the barrels on the small patch of dirt. Then, pulling the canvas bag from his pocket, he removed the stopper from the second barrel and carefully poured the black gunpowder into the small sack until it was about half-full. He tied off the sack and set it aside. Then, starting by the barrel of powder on the ground, Cain dragged the heel of his boot through the dirt to create a long, thin trail in the leaves. After double-checking the distance, he poured a heavy line of gunpowder all the way down the trail to the base of the other barrel.

Another burst of distant laughter sounded through the trees. Cain glanced towards the boathouse as he stooped to pick up the canvas bag. Somewhere on the other side of the building, the battered sergeant and his lackeys were enjoying an illicit cup of whiskey. Cain smiled as he pictured what the men's faces would look like only seconds from now.

He made his way to the far end of the trail and crouched down in the leaves. Pulling the flint and striker from his pocket, he slowly traced his eyes along the line of gunpowder to the barrel at the other end. Any gaps in the black powder would cut off his makeshift fuse and leave him stranded in the woods. Everything was in place.

Cain leaned over and held the steel striker beside the powder. Holding the flint over the metal, he closed his eyes and visualized the next thirty seconds in his mind. His blood surged and sweat collected on his brow. One spark from the flint would set everything in motion.

The flint crashed into the steel and a shower of sparks rained down on the powder. A white-hot flame erupted with a heavy hiss and coursed down the trail. Seeing the flames, Cain turned and was off like a shot. Ducking branches and rounding trees, he ran straight away from the coming explosion as fast as his legs could carry him. Just ahead, a heavy log cut across his path. Cain dove behind the log.

*KABOOM!*

The heavy concussion rattled the ground and shook the trees. By the time Cain peeked over the log, the soldiers had already rounded the building and were running into the forest. There was no time to waste.

Staying low to the ground, Cain got to his feet and cut through the trees. He had just reached the edge of the tree line when the boathouse door burst open and dozens of men poured into the clearing. A rush of questions erupted from the men.

"Did you hear that?"

"What the hell was it?"

"Sounded like an explosion."

"An explosion?"

"Where'd it come from?"

Cain stepped into the gathering crowd and pointed into the trees. "I think it came from over there!" he said. As the men pushed forward, Cain backed into the crowd and slowly melted away.

# Chapter 52

October 25, 1861 – 6th Ward, Washington City

A light rap on the paned glass door drew Admiral Dahlgren's attention. "Come in!"

The same sergeant that had questioned Levi upon his arrival appeared in the doorway. "Excuse me, Admiral."

"Yes, what is it?" Dahlgren barked. He had grown frustrated and tired of trying to convince Levi Love that this Scorpion of his didn't stand a chance in hell against the full might of the U.S. Navy.

"Sir, there's a man outside claiming an urgent need to speak with Officer Love."

Without waiting on the Admiral's reply, Levi rushed to the door. Pushing past the sergeant, he crossed the foyer and opened the front door to see Josiah standing on the porch.

"Mr. Love," Josiah said through heavy breath. He had obviously sprinted across the Yard and, from the look on his face, the news he came to deliver wasn't good.

"What's happened, Josiah?"

"There's been an explosion."

"A what?" Levi asked. "Where?"

"Down by the boathouse."

A heavy weight dropped into Levi's stomach. The look on Josiah's face told him precisely the boathouse Josiah was talking about and Levi's frustration with the obstinate Admiral rose to a fevered pitch. "Come with me," Levi said.

He led Josiah across the foyer and burst into Dahlgren's office. "What's the meaning of this?" the Admiral said, seeing the one-eared colored man standing in his doorway. "Who is this man?"

"This is Josiah Johnson," Levi said. "He's been helping me track the Scorpion." Levi turned to Josiah. "Tell the Admiral what you just told me."

"There's been an explosion," Josiah said. His tone was respectful but firm.

Dahlgren shot up from his chair. "An explosion?" he demanded. "Where?"

"Down at that boathouse of yours in the trees," Josiah said.

A layer of concern fell across Dahlgren's urgent expression. "You mean at the waterfront?" he asked, shooting a furtive glance at Levi.

"No, sir," Josiah said. "The secret boathouse you've got hidden off by itself in the trees." Seeing traces of doubt lingering on the Admiral's face, Josiah added, "It's the boathouse where you're building Mr. de Villeroi's machine."

Dahlgren's face was wiped blank and his jaw went slack. How in the world did a colored man, whom he had never before laid eyes on, know the details of the most secret operation in the Navy?

Josiah pointed to the window overlooking the Yard. "Sir, if you'll just look out that window, you can see for yourself."

Dahlgren stepped to the window and looked out across the Yard. The slope of the land prevented him from seeing the river or the boathouse hidden in the trees but it didn't matter. The thin line of black smoke trailing up into the sky told him everything he needed to know. He slowly turned to face the room.

"He's here, Admiral," Levi said. "The Scorpion is here."

# Chapter 53

October 25, 1861 – 6th Ward, Washington City

The men that had rushed from Boathouse F gathered near the edge of the woods and stared into the trees. Wild speculation about the source of the explosion continued as Cain drifted to the back of the crowd and slipped away.

Walking the length of the boathouse, his pulse quickened. De Villeroi's secret machine was just on the other side of the thin pinewood exterior. Cain's body begged to run to the door and burst inside but he knew he couldn't. Surrounded by enemies on all sides, the slightest flinch could give him away. So he focused his thoughts and kept a steady pace towards the door at the far side of the building.

Cain's heart hammered in his chest as he quietly opened the door and stepped over the threshold into the most secure building in the Navy. The competing and arrhythmic clang of hammers on metal filled the air and echoed off the ceiling. Cain turned from the door to see that he was in a long corridor that ran the length of the boathouse to a door on the other side. His eyes shot from left to right as he slowly made his way inside.

The walls were lined with supplies of every kind imaginable—sheet metal, bolts, copper pipe, lengths of wood, and rope. And then there were the machine parts. Cain's eyes drifted from one bin to the next and he couldn't believe what he was seeing. It looked like every one of de Villeroi's drawings had been produced ten times over and dumped into bins along the corridor. Something was going on in Boathouse F that was far greater than the *scrubber* Cain had discovered in de Villeroi's study. Whatever the Navy was building, it was massive.

Halfway down the hallway the wall of supplies stopped at a doorway that led to the interior of the boathouse. Cain slowed at the sound of voices spilling through the opening. Suddenly, he felt completely exposed. He was an unknown man walking the corridor alone with nothing more than a bag of gunpowder in his hand. If he was to play the part of an ironworker, he needed a prop to help him blend in.

Glancing around, he reached into the nearest bin and grabbed an iron gear about twice the size of his fist. It was the thinnest of all disguises that wouldn't withstand more than a single question from an inquiring worker but it didn't matter. If anyone questioned Cain at this point, all was already lost. He took a deep breath and listened to the voices on the other side of the doorway.

"I tell you what," a man said, "I ain't been that drunk since nickel night at the whorehouse." The other men burst into laughter.

Cain was relieved. If an overseer was within earshot of these men, they wouldn't be laughing and exchanging jokes about whores. Cain took a deep breath to calm his nerves. Then he stepped through the doorway and into the heart of Boathouse F.

Cain's stomach instantly turned and his face grew slack. He wasn't sure what he had expected to see but the site before him was far greater and far more dangerous than anything he had ever imagined. It was like nothing he had ever seen. Every inch of its surface was completely foreign and yet, somehow, Cain knew exactly what this monstrous machine was and what it was capable of doing. The blood raged through his veins and sent a tingling sensation to the farthest reaches of his extremities as he tried to process the complexity of the machine's design and the havoc it could bring.

The entire machine was made of metal that had been hammered into shape and bolted together in sheets. Its nose was long and pointed and flared out into a cone that measured at least six feet in diameter. The cone was bolted to a metal cylinder some fifty feet long. Ten small and circular windows were evenly spaced down the length of the metal hull, which tapered down to a large propeller at the other end. Cain stared at the machine in disbelief as his conversation with Commander Glasson rushed to the surface.

*"If you can't tell me what the Navy's solution to the blockade is,"* Edward Huff had said, *"perhaps you can at least tell me when I might see it."*

*"I can tell you this,"* Glasson had said, *"if things go right, you shall never see the solution at all."*

Cain had spent days trying to understand Glasson's meaning. Now, he finally knew. This wicked machine was designed to hide from its enemies' eyes. It lived and breathed just beneath the surface and consumed its prey in the dark. Brutus de Villeroi had built a machine inspired by the Devil himself. Brutus de Villeroi had built submarine.

As the undeniable conclusion set in, a jolt of panic came with it. How could the Confederacy defeat a machine they couldn't see? Merely knowing of the submarine's existence wouldn't help the Confederate Navy destroy it. Without more, the submarine could secretly patrol the Potomac and break the southern blockade that was slowly strangling this City. Cain's eyes ran down the length of the extraordinary machine. There had to be a weakness.

A pair of workers brushed past Cain as they stepped through the doorway. "You think it could have been the rebels?" one of them asked.

"Nah," the other said. "No way a rebel could get this close to the Yard."

Other workers began filing in and Cain knew his time was running short. His eyes darted around the boathouse. There had to be something here that could help the Confederates find and destroy the submarine. Just then, he spotted a narrow stairway that led up to an office overlooking the entire boathouse. If the submarine had a weakness, it would be hidden somewhere in the overseer's office.

Cain cut through a collection of worktables and ran up the stairs. Reaching the landing, he opened the door and stepped inside.

The overseer popped up from his desk. "What's the meaning of this? Who the?"

The heavy iron gear arced through the air and crashed into the man's face with a sickening crunch. The overseer's knees instantly buckled and he fell to the ground in a pile. Cain stood over the man, prepared to strike again but his body was as still as a stone.

Cain set the bloodied gear and the bag of gunpowder on the overseer's desk and went straight to work. Moving an oil lamp to the side, he saw several stacks of papers arranged neatly along the top edge of the desk. Cain grabbed the nearest stack and flipped through it. The papers rained down onto the floor as he quickly tossed them aside. There were timetables, supply lists, letters, and lists of workers. They were all useless.

He glanced out the windows to see more and more men returning from outside. Time was running out. Cain's body tensed as he spun in place and raked the office with his eyes. Passing over the series of cabinets, he saw a wooden table in the back corner covered in sheets of oversize paper. *Drawings.*

Cain stepped to the table and flipped violently through the pages. Drawings fell from the table and scattered across the floor as Cain's nerves began to fray. He had to get out before the entire Navy descended upon him. Casting a final page aside, his hand suddenly stopped and his eyes grew wide. The drawing showed the entire submarine as if it had been sliced down the center of the long axis. It showed every piece of the interior from the commander's wheel to the propeller. Cain glanced at the block letters at the top of the page: USS ALLIGATOR. This was it.

Cain folded the drawing and stuffed it into his pocket. Having found what he needed, his thoughts immediately shifted to his escape. He needed time. Glancing at the overseer's desk, Cain knew exactly how to get it.

Cain moved the oil lamp and the sack of gunpowder from the desk to the top of the wooden cabinets. Then, he collected as many papers as he could from around the room and stacked them high on the desk before grabbing the bag of powder. Opening the bag, he turned it up on its end. The gunpowder rained down over the papers and onto the floor like sand from a broken hourglass. Cain grabbed the lantern from the cabinet and stepped to the door. Raising the lantern high over his head, he took a final glance out the window. Cain narrowed his eyes and a shot of adrenaline coursed through his veins as he prepared to run.

The lantern flew through the air and the glass shade protecting the flame shattered on the side of the desk. Fueled by the gunpowder, the flame sparked a conflagration that tore through the papers and around the office in seconds. Cain shot out the door.

"Fire! Fire!" he yelled as he ran down the stairs.

The reaction around the boathouse was instantaneous. Every man dropped what he was doing and ran. Some ran for buckets and water, while others simply ran for their lives. Chaos and confusion rained down as Cain jostled his way to the far end of the boathouse and slipped quietly through the door.

# Chapter 54

October 25, 1861 – 6th Ward, Washington City

The scene around Boathouse F was frantic as Levi pulled his wagon to a stop in the middle of the fray. Men were yelling at one another and running in every direction—some towards the lagoon to fetch buckets of water, others simply ran for the hills. Levi glanced up from the confusion to see the dark cloud of smoke seeping through the boards and swirling from the roof of the boathouse.

“Fire! Fire!” yelled a panicked young private as he ran around in circles.

Levi and Josiah watched from the wagon as Admiral Dahlgren and his sergeant dismounted from their horses and took control of the scene. “You there!” Dahlgren yelled at an ironworker running up the hill. Seeing the stars on the Admiral’s shoulder, the man stopped in his tracks. “Where the hell are you going?” Dahlgren demanded. From the look on the man’s face, it was clear he had no idea.

“Fire! Fire!” yelled the private.

Dahlgren fought through the incessant chant and pointed the ironworker down to the water. “Get down to that lagoon and help those men!” The man nodded and ran towards the lagoon, though with less enthusiasm than he had for the hills.

“Fire! Fire!”

Dahlgren walked swiftly to the hysterical private and unleashed a backhand that silenced the man and sent him tumbling to the ground. “Get a hold of yourself, man!” The private blinked and appeared to snap out of the hysteria.

“Fire,” he said feebly.

"I'm well aware there is a fire, Private. Now get to your feet and go find more buckets," Dahlgren ordered. "You three!" he yelled, pointing at some other men. "You go with him." The men nodded and ran off towards the waterfront.

The Admiral walked through the scene spouting one command after another and slowly brought order to the chaos. Within minutes of the Admiral's arrival, buckets of water were flying from the lagoon towards the fire. The dark smoke pouring from the roof soon turned to gray as it mixed with the rising steam. The smoke faded with each passing bucket until, finally, it was gone.

"Come on," Levi said.

He and Josiah jumped down from the wagon and headed towards the boathouse. A thick haze hung in the air as they stepped inside and walked a long corridor filled with metal and supplies. The workers collected in clumps along the hallway and exchanged theories on how the fire could have possibly been started. Levi led Josiah through the crowds to the doorway in the middle of the corridor.

A knot of men had collected just over the threshold and Levi had to push his way to the other side. When he finally got through, he looked out across the boathouse. His face grew slack and his jaw dropped. The sight before him was unlike anything he had ever seen. It was almost inconceivable. He blinked hard to clear the smoke from his eyes and take another look.

"What is it?" Josiah asked.

"This is it, Josiah," Levi said, his voice distant, as if somehow trapped in his own thoughts. "This is what the Scorpion was after."

Josiah slowly traced his eyes down the length of the machine and around the room to the stairway and the blackened office overhead. Shifting his gaze between the office and the iron machine, the startling connection was clear. "I'll be right back," he said. Levi nodded silently, still lost in thought.

Josiah wove quickly through the crowds and out to the lagoon. It was clear as day that the fire in the overseer's office had been started as a diversion. Just as clear was that the Scorpion couldn't escape the Navy Yard through the front gate. His only way out was down the river.

Josiah swept his eyes up and down the water but the thick stand of trees made it impossible to see. Then he noticed the long dock that reached out across the lagoon to the edge of the trees. The currents of the Eastern Branch swirled around the wooden piers at its end. From there, Josiah knew he would have a clear view of the river.

The weathered boards creaked under foot as Josiah hit the dock at a full sprint. The sounds of the Eastern Branch drew closer with every stride but Josiah kept his eyes on the narrow strip of wood beneath his feet. Within seconds, the dock broke through the trees and the full breadth of the river came into view.

Josiah's lungs burned for air as he squinted against the sun and scanned the length of the river. Out of the corner of his eye, he caught a shadow as it crossed the golden glare in the water. Josiah spun in place and stared at the shadow to make out its shape. His muscles coiled as his body instinctively knew what his mind was still trying to understand. The thin shadow in the sun was an empty supply skiff manned by a single pilot. Despite the current already carrying the skiff down river, the man was setting his pole and pushing the craft as fast as it could go. There was no doubt in Josiah's mind—he had found the Scorpion.

Josiah sprinted down the dock and burst into the boathouse. "Mr. Love, come quick!" he yelled.

The urgency of Josiah's call snapped Levi to attention. "What is it?" he asked.

"He's on the river. He's headed back towards the City."

Levi's eyes grew wide. *The river. Of course.* "Come on," he said.

Levi led Josiah back outside and directly to Admiral Dahlgren, who was in the middle of a conversation with his sergeant. "Sir, the river," Levi interrupted.

Dahlgren's face twisted in annoyed confusion. "The what?"

"The river," Levi repeated, pointing through the trees. "The Scorpion is escaping down the river!"

Dahlgren gazed skeptically at the water. "Are you sure?"

"I saw him," Josiah said, stepping forward. "He's on an empty skiff running down river by himself."

Dahlgren eyed Josiah and then Levi for a long moment. Levi's muscles slowly tightened in frustration. Every second they stood idly by, the Scorpion drifted further from their grasp. "Sir," Levi began but the Admiral cut him off.

"Sergeant," he said.

"Yes, sir," snapped the sergeant.

"Gather some men and get down to the waterfront. Prepare a schooner for immediate departure."

"Yes, sir," the sergeant said and then immediately set out to conscript every man he could find.

Levi couldn't believe what he was hearing. A schooner was a multi-masted ship with a complicated setup. By the time a schooner was prepared to sail, the Scorpion would be around Greenleaf's Point and out of sight.

"Sir," Levi said. The look he received conveyed the Admiral's patience was nearing exhaustion but Levi pressed ahead. "Sir, preparing a schooner will take too long. The Scorpion is floating with the current. By the time you're—"

"Officer Love," Dahlgren interrupted. "While I'm sure your understanding of the sea is far greater than mine, I will remind you that I am in command here. This is a Naval matter, Mr. Love, and far beyond the purview of the Metropolitan Police. Me and my men will take this matter from here. Do you understand?"

Levi held the Admiral's stare for a long moment but there was obviously no point in arguing. "Yes, sir," Levi said.

As the Admiral turned to bark additional orders at his sergeant, Levi and Josiah drifted over to the wagon. Levi pulled the gold coin from his pocket and turned it in his fingers. "Where's the Scorpion going?" he thought out loud.

Josiah pulled on his beard and shook his head. "I don't know," he said.

"He has to have a plan," Levi said, turning to Josiah. "Think about it. This man has been three steps ahead of us since the moment we pulled Ellen from the Canal. He doesn't make things up as he goes along. He plots and he plans. He's always three steps ahead because he's already planned his next three moves before he takes his first step."

Josiah nodded. "You're right about that."

Levi continued his train of thought. "We've seen this man, Josiah. We know who he is. The Scorpion can't operate in this City anymore. It's too dangerous now and he knows it. He's got to get out and I'll bet you anything he already knows exactly how he's going to do it."

"Mr. Love, everything you're saying makes sense but there are a thousand doors that would lead a man out of this City. How are we supposed to know which one he's gonna pick?"

Levi suddenly clutched the coin in his hand. An idea rattled in his mind that he couldn't quite grasp. Finally, he got a finger on it and pinned it to the surface. "That's it!" he said. "A door."

"Huh?" Josiah asked. "What do you mean?"

"A door is a way out," Levi said.

"So?"

"So a door is an exit," Levi said, his eyes growing wide as his hand dove into his pocket to grab the scroll. "We're looking for an exit!" Stepping closer to the wagon, Levi flattened the scroll out on the bed and read the text. "There!" he said, his finger slamming down on the paper.

Josiah leaned over the bed and read the text aloud. "Armory attack Wednesday CNO exit confirmed." Josiah stood. "CNO exit confirmed," he said, pulling on his beard. "What's CNO mean?"

Levi's eyes filled with conviction. "It's not CNO, Josiah. It's C *and* O," he said. "He's talking about the Chesapeake and Ohio!"

Josiah's hand froze on his beard as the conclusion set in. His eyes grew wide. "The Canal," he said.

"Exactly!" Levi said, slapping a hand on Josiah's shoulder. "We thought the CNO exit had something to do with the attack on the Armory but it didn't. They were two separate messages. The Scorpion was telling the Confederates that the Armory attack was set *and* that he had received *their* message about using the C and O for his escape. The Scorpion's exit from this City is the Chesapeake and Ohio Canal!"

"That Canal is all the way across town," Josiah said skeptically.

"How do you catch a dog by the neck?" Levi asked, scanning the area around the boathouse.

"You get to where he's going before he gets there."

Levi spied the two horses the Admiral and his sergeant had ridden down to the boathouse. A smile spread across Levi's face. "You get to where he's going before he gets there," he said. "Come on."

Levi walked quickly to the Admiral's horse and put his foot in the stirrup. Josiah followed but then stopped short. "Mr. Love, I can't ride this horse."

Levi looked over at Josiah and dropped his foot to the ground. "Why not? You don't know how to ride?"

"Oh no," Josiah said. "I can ride just fine. It's just that they hang horse thieves in this City."

Levi stepped close. "You've got this all wrong, Josiah. You're an agent of the law in pursuit of a murderous Confederate spy. You're not stealing that horse, you're commandeering it for the public good."

Josiah glanced at the horse and back at Levi. The idea of commandeering the horse suited him just fine. "We best get a move on then," he said.

The men jumped into the saddles and spun the horses around. "Hey!" Dahlgren yelled. "That's my horse!"

Levi didn't hesitate. He slapped the reins and spurred the horse into a run with Josiah close behind.

# Chapter 55

October 25, 1861 – Chesapeake and Ohio Canal, Lock No. 1

Completed in 1850, the Chesapeake and Ohio Canal ran one hundred and eighty-four miles along the Potomac River from Washington City to Cumberland, Maryland. Unlike the Washington Canal, the Chesapeake and Ohio was a vibrant waterway used in the daily transport of goods towards the country's interior. The Chesapeake and Ohio also traced the Virginia state line, which meant that, so long as Charles Cain was on the Canal, he was never far from home. And that made the C&O the perfect escape from this God-forsaken City.

Cain polled the empty barge across the flat water at the mouth of the Canal. A handful of boys were minding their tow horses along the shore and waiting for a fare. "You there!" Cain called as his boat touched ground on the muddy banks. All the boys turned in unison. "How much for a tow?"

"Five cents a lock!" called several of the boys.

Hearing the demand of his competitors, one enterprising boy yelled, "Three cents a lock!"

Cain smiled at the boy. "Sounds like we've got a deal." The boy tugged at his horse and eventually got him moving. "What's your name?" Cain asked as the boy arrived on the shore.

"Maynard," he said. Maynard was a nice looking boy around the age of twelve. His clothes were threadbare and hung loose on his malnourished frame. Judging from the accumulation of dirt on his hands and face, the boy hadn't seen a bath or scrub brush in weeks. "How far up you going?" Maynard asked.

"The fourth lock," Cain said.

The disappointment was evident on the boy's face. With more than seventy locks along the C&O, he had been hoping to drag the empty skiff further up the Canal and make a little more money. But a deal was a deal and the boy dutifully tied the towrope to the cleat at the front of the boat. Cain leaned in close as the boy finished his knot.

"I tell you what," he whispered. "If you get me up to that fourth lock in under an hour, I'll give you a dollar."

Maynard's eyes shot open before his skepticism forced them down to a narrow slit. "You lying to me, mister?" Cain dug into his pocket and fished out a dollar bill. "Yes, sir!" Maynard said, his eyes resuming their wide stare. "I'll get you there in an hour."

"*Under* an hour," Cain reminded him.

"That's what I said," Maynard called back as he poked his horse in the flank with a stick. The horse plodded down the towpath and slowly pulled the slack from the rope.

Cain sat down at the back of the deck as the barge jerked to a start and then leveled off in the smooth waters of the Canal. He gazed up at the clear blue sky and thanked God for getting him this far. It hadn't been easy.

After setting fire to the overseer's office, Cain had darted from the boathouse and sprinted through the woods. Halfway to the barge, he spied someone moving in the trees. Peering through the dense branches, he saw the bruised and broken face of the sergeant he had encountered at the lagoon. Cain knew if the sergeant caught the slightest glimpse of him hopping the barge or floating down river, he would be dead in the water.

Using the trees for cover, he made a wide circle around the sergeant's position where he waited behind the thick trunk of an oak tree. It felt like an eternity before the crunch of the leaves sounded the sergeant's approach. Cain clenched his fist as the sounds grew closer with every step. When the sergeant was at arm's length, Cain jumped out from behind the tree and landed a ferocious punch to the center of the man's broken nose. The sergeant had barely hit the ground before the tempered steel of Cain's blade sliced through his throat.

The encounter with the sergeant was unexpected and had put Cain dangerously behind schedule. Earlier that morning, he had sent a simple message to his friend, Solomon Drew: *CNO exit at noon*. Cain was running late but, with the tow horse pulling him steadily up the Canal, there was nothing more he could do. So, he lay back on the deck and closed his eyes against the sun. As he drifted off to sleep, he hoped his friend was still waiting for his arrival.

"That'll be a dollar," came a voice from the fog. "Mister?" A nudge on Cain's shoulder brought him closer to the light. "Mister?" Cain cracked his eyes and squinted at the shadow hanging over him. "Mister, we're here," said Maynard. "I checked with the lock tender when I paid the toll. I got you here in fifty minutes."

Cain sat up and tried to look around but the boy's outstretched hand was in his face. "That'll be a dollar," Maynard said with a satisfied smile.

Cain got to his feet and handed the boy the money. Maynard's smile grew even wider as he inspected the dollar bill in the sunlight. "Thanks, mister!" he said, stuffing the money in his pocket and stepping to the front of the boat.

Cain studied his surroundings as Maynard untied the tow rope and coiled it neatly on his horse's back. The barge was moored on the far side of the fourth lock and behind a long canal boat that occupied more than thirty feet of the shoreline. Cain scanned the deck but it appeared that no one was aboard. A light breeze swept across the water and cut through the tall grass growing along the banks. All was quiet. Cain was looking back to check on Maynard when he noticed the stone house tucked in behind the trees.

To keep traffic and revenue moving, the C&O Canal Company required the seventy locks along the Canal to be manned twenty-four hours a day. To attract the men needed to operate the locks, the company paid its lock tenders $150 a year and provided them housing in the form of a simple stone cabin. Solomon Drew and his sons had been living in lock number four's stone cottage for more than twenty years but their Southern heritage extended far deeper into the past.

Cain stepped onto the shore and climbed the short embankment to the towpath where he stopped to scan the Canal. Looking back towards the City, he saw a tow horse emerge in the distance, its rope taught from the weight of the barge still hidden behind the canopy of trees. Cain didn't have to see the barge to know it was of little concern. If someone was chasing him, they wouldn't do it from the deck of a heavy supply boat. Shifting his gaze up the Canal and towards his destination, everything was calm and quiet.

Cain breathed a sigh of relief as he stepped off the towpath and followed the well-worn trail to the cabin in the trees. The cabin was simple in design with a plain, four-panel door at its center and two small windows on either side. Cain climbed up to the covered porch, which was too small to even shield a man from the rain, and he knocked on the door. Leaving nothing to chance, his hand drifted towards the knife in the small of his back.

The lock rattled and the door cracked open to reveal a sliver of a man's face. Layers of wrinkles surrounded a cornflower blue eye that darted nervously across Cain's visage. The man's lips curled into a smile that stretched at the deep ruts in his skin and revealed a mouth of yellowed teeth. Cain dropped his hand from the knife.

"Best get on in here," Solomon Drew said, opening the door and allowing Cain to step inside.

The lock house was small, perhaps thirty foot by eighteen, with a kitchen on one side, a bedroom on the other, and a heavy, brick fireplace in the middle. Solomon led Cain into the kitchen and glanced out the window. "You're late."

"Couldn't be helped," Cain said.

"Don't matter," Solomon reassured him. He pointed out the window. "We're gonna take that canal boat up to John Patterson's place at lock twenty-four. John's family's got a holding down in Drakes Branch. You'll be safe there."

Cain shook his head and thought about the difficult journey ahead. "That's got to be a hundred and eighty miles from here. How am I supposed to get there?"

Solomon pulled his eyes from the window. "You've got powerful friends, Charles," he said with a yellowed smile. "The River Ghost is gonna meet us at Patterson's lock. He'll take you from there."

Cain's spirits rose in an instant. It was the River Ghost's brother-in-law who had recruited Cain to be a spy in the first place. The River Ghost knew the Potomac River and the backwoods of Virginia better than God himself. If Cain could get to lock twenty-four and meet up with the River Ghost, he could cross the Potomac and disappear off the face of the Earth. But twenty-four locks was a long way to go.

"Best get going," Solomon said. "There's a bag in the bedroom for you. I'll meet you down by the boat."

Solomon stepped out the front door and Cain rounded the fireplace to the bedroom, which was furnished with nothing more than a bed, a side table, and a three-legged stool in the corner. Cain stepped to the bed and opened the leather satchel sitting on the mattress. Stuffing his hand in the bag, he took stock its the contents by feeling his way through the layers.

A fresh set of clothes covered two thick stacks of money, a knife, a canteen and a cold metal object that felt familiar but that Cain wanted to see for himself. He gripped the object and pulled it from the bottom of the bag. The Colt model 1860 was the latest, and finest, six-shot percussion revolver on the market. Cain weighed the pistol in his hand and checked to ensure it was loaded.

He reached back to tuck the gun in his belt but hesitated. To make it all the way to lock twenty-four, he had to play his new role perfectly. Lock tenders were notoriously nervous about doing business at the point of a gun, so canal merchants didn't often carry sidearms. Knowing he couldn't carry the gun in the open, Cain dropped it on top of the clothes and closed the flap. He would keep the bag close by.

Cain threw the satchel over his shoulder and stepped out into the bright midday sun. By the time he got to the Canal, Solomon had already harnessed his tow horse to the boat and pulled out the slack. "You're gonna need this," he said, meeting Cain at the boat.

Cain turned to see Solomon holding out a wooden handle connected to an eight-inch iron hook. "A meat hook?" Cain asked. "Why do I need a meat hook?"

Solomon smiled and pointed down to the boat. Cain followed the man's finger to see piles of slaughtered hogs stacked high along one side of the deck and sides of beef along the other. Save a narrow walkway down the middle of the boat, the butchered meat occupied every inch of space from stem to stern.

Solomon thrust the hook towards Cain. "You're a meat trader now, Charlie," he said. The look on Cain's face made it clear he'd rather be something else. Solomon let out a high-pitched laugh.

"You'll get the hang of it," he said as his laugh tapered off. "The important thing is, when we get to the locks, you got to look like a meat trader. That means you take this here hook and you walk up and down that deck arranging and counting your stock."

Cain reluctantly took the hook. "What do I do between the locks?"

Solomon slapped Cain on the shoulder. "Just be yourself!" Solomon laughed as he turned away and headed towards his tow horse.

Cain scanned the boat and, finding an opening between the carcasses, he dropped down onto the deck. Moments later, the boat slipped away from the banks and began its quiet journey towards lock twenty-four.

# Chapter 56

October 25, 1861 – Chesapeake and Ohio Canal, Lock No. 6

The horse wheezed and gasped for air as it turned hard onto the dirt road, cutting through the cotton fields. Rounding the corner, Levi glanced over his shoulder to see that Josiah was falling quickly behind. The race across town had driven their horses to near exhaustion and there wasn't much more they could give. But the race wasn't over yet.

The boys at the mouth of the C&O had sworn that, no more than an hour ago, a man on an empty skiff had been towed up the canal to lock number four. Levi and Josiah raced up the canal and had found the skiff but the lock house had been empty and the Scorpion was nowhere in sight. Levi stood at the lock and gazed over the Potomac at the dense forests of Virginia. If the Scorpion had gone overland, there was no hope of finding him. But if he had caught another boat and continued up the canal, there might still be a chance.

With no other options, they made a quick decision. Taking the road just off the river, they would push their horses as hard and as fast as they could. When the horses began to falter, they would find the nearest road, cut to the canal, and hope to God they had arrived in time.

Levi drove his heels into the horse's flank and scanned the road. Just ahead, the cotton fields ended abruptly in a series of open-air barns that were filled to capacity with the recent harvest. On the far side of the barns, a simple wooden bridge spanned a fifty-foot gap that had been carved deep into the landscape. Levi set his eyes, and his hopes, on the bridge—it was his last chance to catch the soulless man who had murdered Ellen Wolfe and eluded him at every turn.

Nearing the bridge, Levi turned off the road and cut across the field to the barn. He was tying the leather reins to a post when Josiah pulled his horse to a stop and jumped to the ground.

“What do you think?” Josiah asked.

Levi glanced at the horses, which were drenched in sweat and struggling to breathe. “I think this is as far as we can go,” he said. “Let’s take a look at that canal.”

Sunlight cut beneath the edge of the roof and played against the dust in the air as Levi and Josiah wove their way to the far side of the barn. Bales of cotton that had been wrapped in fabric and tied off with lengths of rope towered overhead like giant burlap caterpillars. Reaching the other side of the barn, Levi and Josiah stopped short to peer outside and take in their surroundings.

The barn was set back about ten feet from the rather precipitous drop-off that led to the canal below. Levi craned his neck but the canal was too far below the embankment to see anything. Looking down towards lock number four, the gradual slope of the land finally revealed a clear view of the water and the towpaths on either side. There were no horses or boats in sight. Shifting his gaze up the canal, he saw the wooden bridge just ahead.

“Ain’t much to do now but wait,” Josiah said, stealing Levi’s thoughts.

Staying just out of sight, they sat down in the warmth of the sun and stared out over the canal. After the recent harvest, there was nothing to see for miles around but dried cotton stalks standing at attention in the dirt like so many soldiers. They sat in silence for a long moment, their thoughts somehow stranded in the barren landscape.

“Ms. Wolfe would be thankful for what you’ve done here,” Josiah finally said.

Levi stared into the distance and shook his head. "I haven't done anything, Josiah," he said. "I didn't stop the Scorpion from doing those horrible things to her and I didn't catch him when I had the chance. All I've done is prove how much better he is at all of this than me. Nothing more."

Josiah pulled on his beard and nodded. "Maybe so," he said thoughtfully. "But there's one thing you can't argue." Levi looked over and met Josiah's gaze. "You saved me, Mr. Love. You saved me from a life of hell—a life away from Anna. And you gave me a chance to be father."

Levi sat up straight and his eyes went wide. "You're having a baby?"

Josiah smiled. "Anna told me last night."

Levi smiled wide and shook Josiah's hand. "That's great news, Josiah. Congratulations." Josiah looked off at the horizon and the light that had briefly flickered in his eyes faded away. "What is it?" Levi asked.

Josiah turned back to Levi and forced a thin smile. "Nothing you need to worry on, Mr. Love."

A moment later, Levi knew. "How far away are you from buying Anna's freedom?"

"Too far," Josiah said.

"And that means the baby."

"Our baby's gonna be a slave," Josiah said. "That's the law. Ain't nothing to be done about it. Like I said, Mr. Love, it's nothing you need to worry on." Levi had opened his mouth to press the question when Josiah's arm shot out and he pointed down the Canal. "Look there!"

Levi looked into the distance to see a man prodding a horse along the path with a heavy Canal boat in tow. Levi strained to see the deck of the boat. "How many men are there?" he asked.

"I just see the one," Josiah said.

"Can you see what they're hauling?"

Josiah slowly shook his head. "Not sure," he said. "Looks like it may be a slaughter boat."

Levi's pulse picked up. "One man on a slaughter boat?" he asked. "That doesn't make sense, does it?"

"No," Josiah agreed. "It don't make sense at all."

Even with a full complement of deck hands, hauling sides of beef was back breaking work. There was no way one man would set out on a slaughter boat all on his own.

"That's him, Josiah," Levi said. "That's got to be him."

Levi looked up to the bridge and then back to the slaughter boat before turning to Josiah. "We've got to stop that boat," he said plainly. A thin plan came quickly to mind. "I need you to get up the canal somewhere past the bridge. Find some cover behind one of those sheds up there and wait for the tow man to pass. Can you do that?"

Josiah nodded. "I can do that," he said. "But where are you going?"

Levi glanced down at the slaughter boat, which was getting closer by the second. "I'm going down to that boat," he said.

Josiah hesitated. "You sure?" he asked.

Levi's eyes shone with determination. "I'm sure," he said. "You just wait until the boat is past the bridge before you do a thing."

Josiah disappeared between the bales of cotton and Levi turned back to the canal. He glanced at the bridge and then down at the slaughter boat, which continued at a steady pace. In a matter of moments, the boat would reach the bridge and disappear behind the embankment.

Levi tore off his jacket and threw it into the barn. The jacket would only constrict his movement and slow him down. Levi had one chance at this, and his timing would have to be perfect.

The tow horse snorted as the driver's stick tapped out a rhythm on the path that kept the beast moving at a steady pace. Levi waited patiently until the horse and driver vanished behind the embankment. He then shifted his gaze to the bloodied deck of the slaughter boat where a man was diligently arranging the meat with the point of his hook. As the front of the boat slipped behind the embankment, the man released a side of beef and stood to stretch his back. His cold, black eyes glinted in the sun.

A sudden rage shot across Levi's body like lightning. His heart pounded as the world around him faded into nothing. There was no thought, no hesitation, no fear. There was only this place and this moment. As the anger coursed through his veins and drove deep into the fibers of his muscles, he knew. Someone was going to die today.

Levi gripped the side of the barn and coiled his body like a spring as the last of the slaughter boat drifted out of sight. Closing his eyes, he visualized the pace of the boat and its distance from the bridge. He took a deep breath and flooded his lungs with air as he waited just a second longer. His muscles tensed. *Now!*

Levi burst out of the barn and was off like a shot. Sprinting down the length of the barn, he fixed his eyes on the bridge and the edge of the embankment ahead. His heart thundered in his chest.

Waiting to the last second, he cut towards the canal and the slaughter boat suddenly came into view. A wave of panic clenched Levi's gut. The boat was moving too fast.

Levi's legs burned as he demanded every ounce of speed they could give. When his boots finally hit the road, the last of the slaughter boat was slipping beneath the bridge. There wasn't a second to waste. Levi's footfalls echoed off the wood as he hit the bridge at full speed and hurled himself over the side.

Levi was weightless. The wind whipped past his ears as his body sailed through the air. His arms and legs flailed in search of solid ground. Then suddenly, as if the bottom of the world had dropped away, Levi began to fall. Gravity had taken hold and it pulled him faster and faster towards the Earth. In a blink, he was hurtling down on the slaughter boat at a breakneck speed.

A shadow crossed the boat and the man on the deck looked up to see a massive object shooting down from the sky. The man threw up his hands but it was too late. Levi's boot crashed hard into his head. The impact sent the men tumbling down towards the bloodied carcasses stacked high along the deck.

Levi slammed down and all the air was forced from his lungs. He rolled flat on his back and fought to catch his breath. His pulse throbbed in his neck as he got to his hands and knees and forced his lungs to draw air. His chest burned like fire. Slowly, the air seeped back into his lungs and he turned to get his bearings.

He had landed on a pile of slaughtered hogs that lined the entire length of the boat. A narrow path down the middle of the deck separated the hogs from the stacks of beef on the other side. Levi ran his eyes slowly down the deck where they finally landed on the man who had murdered the woman he loved.

Levi's gaze drifted up to the Scorpion's face and fixed on his cold black eyes. Tracing the thin line of blood that ran down to the

Scorpion's chin, a searing hatred welled inside. There was far more blood to be spilled from this man.

A flash of silver in the sun drew Levi's eyes to the blade held tight in the Scorpion's grip. Levi's hand shot down for his rosewood club and his stomach suddenly tightened. The club wasn't there. Panic flashed in his eyes. The men were evenly matched but the knife in the Scorpion's hand gave him a firm advantage. Levi cast his eyes around the boat in search of anything to even the odds. Then he saw it. Ten feet away, dug deep into the side of a hog, the iron meat hook was his only chance.

"I must admit," the Scorpion said. The voice was startling and cold. Levi met the man's gaze but his focus remained on the hook. "I am delighted to see you, Officer Love."

Levi was surprised to hear his name but he shouldn't have been. The Scorpion had murdered dozens of people and infiltrated the most guarded building in the Union. It only made sense that he should know precisely who Levi Love was.

"It was an odd feeling, really," the Scorpion continued. "I had played my role beautifully and accomplished everything I had set out to do. And yet, as I made my grand escape, a nagging feeling persisted that there was another act to this play—some final scene that might draw a more satisfactory conclusion. And suddenly," he smiled, "here you are. Now, we are only left to write the ending."

Levi's jaw grew tight and he spoke through clenched teeth. "You murdered Ellen Wolfe."

The Scorpion's eyes went wide and he let out a sudden burst of laughter. "You've done all of this for Ellen Wolfe?" Seeing the hateful stare on Levi's face, he suddenly understood. "Why Officer Love, I do believe you loved her." The Scorpion let out another guttural laugh. "Ellen Wolfe was nothing but a whore—a traitorous and worthless whore."

The Scorpion's smile fell away and his knuckles grew white around the hilt of the knife. Silence fell as the men held each other's gaze. Levi focused his thoughts and rehearsed the next few seconds in his mind. The meat hook was simply too far away. The tingle of mortality spread across his body. He had to move.

Without warning, he coiled his legs and dove onto the pile of hogs. Grabbing a carcass by the jaw and the tail, he rolled towards the hook and thrust the hog high in the air. The Scorpion's silver blade pierced straight through Levi's shield until the hilt lodged against the bone. With the knife trapped deep in the flesh, Levi tossed the carcass aside. The Scorpion faltered as his weight was thrown off center and he tumbled down onto the deck.

Levi lunged for the hook and grabbed hold of the wooden handle as the Scorpion quickly regained his footing. Levi rolled off the hogs and had just landed on the deck when a searing pain shot across his arm. Staggering backwards, his foot caught on a carcass and he suddenly lost his balance. He swung the meat hook in a long and wild arc. The hook made contact with the Scorpion as Levi's heels hit the side of the boat and he toppled overboard.

Levi grasped the handle with an iron grip. The weight of his body set the hook deep into the Scorpion's back and locked the men together in free fall. Splashing down into the canal, Levi wrenched the hook hard into the Scorpion's ribs. Blood swirled in the water like smoke.

Suddenly, the Scorpion's boot hammered into Levi's stomach. The air shot from his lungs and bubbles raced to the surface in a violent storm. Levi's fingers slipped from the handle as his feet hit the bottom of the canal. His lungs burned and his vision grew dark. Pushing hard off the silt, Levi shot to the surface of the water and into the light. He coughed and gasped for air as he blinked to clear the water from his eyes. Scanning across the canal, he saw the Scorpion crawling over the muddied banks and onto shore—the iron hook set deep in his back.

Levi fought his way to the shore and pulled himself from the water. The slash in his arm burned in the cool air. Levi turned to see the Scorpion lying just feet away. A thick stream of blood ran out of his mouth and down the side of his cheek. The point of the hook had found its mark deep in the Scorpion's lung.

Levi climbed slowly to his feet and gripped his arm to staunch the flow of blood. Stepping down the shore, he stood silently over the Scorpion and saw that even Death himself couldn't warm the man's cold, black eyes. The Scorpion opened his mouth and coughed to clear the blood from his throat.

In a voice that strained towards a whisper, he said, "Cowards die many times before their deaths. The valiant never taste of death but once."

A shadow fell across the Scorpion's face as Levi leaned in close. "Make no mistake," he said. "There is only one coward here. And you are sure to taste death a thousand times when you find your place in Hell."

And then, with a long and gurgled breath, the Scorpion's life slipped away, leaving only the cold in his eyes behind.

Movement in the grass drew Levi's attention. He turned to see the warm face of the man who had stayed with him to the end—the man to whom he owed everything. Josiah smiled as he stepped through the grass and down to the muddied banks of the canal. Without a word, the men embraced like the brothers they were.

# Epilogue

October 27, 1861 – 2nd Ward, Washington City

Sergeant William Corbett licked his hand and pressed the mixture of saliva and tobacco juice into his hair as he stared across F Street at the modest, two-story brick home. "That's it," he said. "We gonna get us some niggers tonight." He pulled the rosewood club from his belt and turned to within inches of Levi's face. "And if a single one of them gets away," he said, his breath acrid and sour, "there's gonna be hell to pay. You got that Lover?"

Levi glanced at the house and then back to Corbett. His silence was all the answer Corbett needed.

"Good boy," Corbett said. "Now you stay right behind me."

Corbett led the way across the street and up the walkway towards the front door. Glancing over at Levi, he stopped just short of the door and looked down at Levi's hands. Corbett's anger welled. He slapped Levi's chest with a meaty hand and grabbed a fistful of his jacket. "You gonna go pig hunting empty handed?" he asked. Levi winced at the smell rising from Corbett's tobacco-stained goatee. "Walking into this here situation empty handed is making me doubt your sincerity, Lover," the Sergeant said. "Now you best get your stick out and get ready."

Levi reached down and took the club from his belt.

The Sergeant smiled and pulled on Levi's jacket. "Now every man, woman, and child in this house is either a pig or a thief. That means that every skull in there that moves is ripe for cracking. You understand?" Levi nodded and Corbett released his jacket.

Turning back to the door, Corbett counted out loud. "One…" he braced himself against the side of the porch, "two…" he raised his heavy boot high in the air, "three!" Corbett's boot crashed into the door. The frame splintered and the door flew open. Corbett rushed inside with Levi close behind.

Instantly, Corbett knew something was wrong. The crash of a front door was always punctuated by screams and the sounds of people scrambling for their lives. But, standing stock still in the living room, the only sound in the air was the pop and hiss of the embers dying in the fireplace. There was no one there.

"Looks like a bad tip," Levi said.

Corbett swung his stick around and pressed it to Levi's chest. "Shhhh." His eyes danced around the living room and back towards the kitchen. It wasn't a bad tip. No one ever left their house or went very far with a fire burning in the hearth. The fact that everyone was hiding only confirmed Corbett's instincts. They were here somewhere.

Suddenly, a shadow moved past the window facing the backyard. "There!" Corbett yelled, rushing to the back door and knocking over tables and chairs along the way. He threw open the door and ran outside. Scanning the backyard, he saw an old wagon half filled with hay and an old man holding a two-pronged pitchfork.

"What the devil?" the old man said, his gray hair standing on end.

Corbett didn't hesitate for a second. He grabbed the pitchfork from the man's hand and threw it across the yard. "Where are they?" he thundered, cocking his stick in the air.

Confusion flooded the old man's face. "Where are who?"

Corbett grabbed him by the shirt with his free hand and lifted the old man up to the tips of his toes. "The niggers you're sneaking out of town."

The old man's eyes plead his innocence. "I don't know what you're talking about."

Corbett's club arced down from the sky and smashed the man's collarbone. The shock of pain sent the old man straight to the ground where he rolled over in agony. Corbett leaned over the man and pointed at him with his stick. "You make one move to get off that dirt and I'll snap one bone after another until you don't never get up again. You hear me?"

The old man squinted in pain as he nodded his understanding.

Corbett turned to Levi and pointed with his stick. "You keep an eye on this one," he ordered. He waited for Levi to step within striking distance of the old man before turning to scan the rest of the yard. His eyes quickly landed on the wagon and the hay piled high in the bed. He stared at the wagon for a long moment before a thin smile spread across his face.

Corbett crossed the yard and grabbed the pitchfork before walking calmly back to the old man and crouching down beside him. "You think I'm stupid, don't you," he said.

"No, sir," the old man whimpered, holding his shoulder tight.

"So you're telling me right now that you don't think I'm stupid?"

"No, sir."

Corbett narrowed his eyes. "Alright then," he said. "I'll tell you what. If I walk over to that wagon and I stick me a pig with this pitchfork, as soon as I'm done sticking him," a lustful smile crossed Corbett's face, "I'm coming right back here to stick you."

Corbett stood and went straight to the wagon. Lifting the pitchfork high into the air he thrust it down into the hay where it collided hard against the bed. Corbett smiled. There was simply no sport in sticking a man on the first try. Over and again, the pitchfork rained down until Corbett had poked at every inch of hay on the wagon. Finally giving it up, he threw the pitchfork across the yard.

"I know they're here! Now where are they?" he screamed, slamming his fist on the bed of the wagon. In that instant, his eyes shot open and he spun in place. He stared down at his hand, still resting on the bed. Then, turning his knuckles, he wrapped on the weathered pine boards.

The hollow sound that rang out across the yard hit Levi like a punch to the gut. He knew precisely what Corbett had discovered but he prayed to God he was wrong. His hand grew sweaty around his rosewood club as he watched Corbett slowly release the metal pins that held the wagon's tailgate in place. The gate swung down on its hinge and slammed against the wagon's frame.

Levi's stomach tightened in a knot. The open tailgate revealed a hidden cavity that wasn't much more than a foot tall. Peering into the darkened space, Levi knew—God had refused his prayer.

"Well looky what we found here," Corbett said. His eyes were afire as he raised his club high in the air and slammed it down on the bed. "Looky what we found here!" he screamed as the club thundered down with every word.

Inside the hollowed space, the soles of four feet remained as still as the grave. Corbett's club dangled from the leather strap around his wrist as he reached into the dark and grabbed the first set of feet. Corbett gripped the ankles and the feet began to kick and flail.

"Kick all you want," he said. "Ain't nothing gonna save you now!"

He pulled the feet from the hole and the hem of a dress came into view. The sight hit Levi like a second punch. *God no*, he prayed. *Oh God, please, no.*

Corbett pulled at the woman's legs until her shoulders slipped off the end of the bed and her body fell hard to the ground. Levi's breath caught in his chest. God had failed him for the second time. He closed his eyes tight and the image before him went to black. When he finally forced his eyes open, his worst fear was confirmed all over again. It was Josiah's wife Anna.

"What are you waiting on, Lover?" Corbett asked. "Get over here and get this other one outta that hole."

Levi's mind reeled as he crossed the yard to the wagon and slowly grabbed hold of the second pair of feet. He started to pull on the man's ankles when Corbett said, "I got a bet for you, Lover." Levi stopped pulling and glanced over at the Sergeant. "I'll bet you that shiny gold coin in your pocket that the pig at the other end of them feet ain't got but half an ear."

Levi's body went numb. Every inch he pulled brought Josiah closer to the dark fate that awaited him. But what choice did he have? Levi's fingers tingled as he reset his grip and somehow found the strength to pull.

Corbett licked his lips and his eyes grew wider as the man's body slowly emerged from the dark. Seconds later, a pair of hands gripped the side of the bed and the man pulled himself out of the wagon and onto his feet. Levi stood in silence as he looked upon the face of his friend.

A bellowing laughter broke the silence. "I told you, Lover!" Corbett said. "William H. Williams never lies and he never lets a pig get away."

Levi glanced down to see Josiah clench his powerful hands into fists. Levi shifted his gaze to Corbett and back to Josiah. His heart began to beat again and the numbness faded from his body. Maybe they had a chance. Just as the thought entered his mind, Josiah took a step forward. In a flash, Corbett pulled a knife and stuck it to Anna's throat. Josiah stopped on the spot.

"I know what you're thinking, boy," Corbett said. The point of the knife formed a deep valley in Anna's skin. "You're thinking you'd like to kill me. I can see it in your eyes plain as day. But you make one more move and I gut your pretty little wife like the pig she is."

"Stop it! You can't do this! You can't!" came the hysterical scream from across the yard. Levi glanced over to see the old man sitting on the ground with his back against a tree. "You can't do this! You can't do this!" he screamed over and again.

Corbett kept his eyes locked on Josiah. "Lover!" he barked. "Get over there and shut his mouth or I swear I'll cut this bitch from tits to toes."

Levi's legs felt like they were set in stone. Staring at the knife in Anna's throat and the hate in Corbett's eyes, he couldn't move.

"You can't do this! You can't do this!" cried the old man.

"You better shut that nigger-lover's mouth!" Corbett yelled.

The Sergeant's scream broke Levi's feet from the ground. A torrent of questions and doubt flooded his mind as he slowly circled around towards the hysterical old man. The cancerous hatred that consumed Corbett's soul had seeped into this world through the cracks of Hell. Levi stared at the knife pressed to Anna's throat and for the first time in his life he understood—it wasn't Corbett holding that blade, it was the Devil himself.

The old man screamed over and again into the night and Levi gripped the rosewood club tight in his hand. There was only one thing left for him to do. Raising his arm high in the air, Levi lowered the club with every ounce of strength in his body. The club crashed into Corbett's head with a savage blow that buckled his knees and sent him tumbling to the ground.

Levi stood over Corbett's body and everything went still. A pool of deepest red formed beneath the Sergeant's head and slowly spread across the ground.

Levi couldn't move. He couldn't breathe. He just stood, waiting for something he couldn't quite place. Was it Justice? Was it God?

And then he felt it. A heavy but gentle hand fell on his shoulder. Levi slowly lifted his gaze and turned to see the tears welling in Josiah's eyes. Josiah pulled him close and held him in a long embrace. There were no words to describe the feelings they shared and there didn't need to be. They were brothers and that was enough.

"We got to get moving," came a sudden voice that broke the men's embrace.

Josiah looked over to see the old man standing nearby, still holding his shoulder. Turning back to Levi, his eyes were filled with concern. "What are we gonna do?"

Levi already knew the answer. He pulled his wrist from the leather strap of his club and held it out for Josiah. "You're going to need this," he said.

Josiah shook his head. "Mr. Love, I can't."

Levi pressed the club into his hand. "You have to, Josiah. It's the only way. There's no time for anything else. Just make it look good and try not to kill me."

Josiah looked down at the pool of blood around Corbett's head and he knew Levi was right. Slowly, he clasped his hand around the club.

Levi smiled. "There's one more thing," he said. He reached into his pocket and pulled out his father's gold coin. "I want you to have this," he said.

Josiah shook his head. "No," he said. "I can't."

Levi took Josiah's hand and placed the coin in his palm. Curling Josiah's fingers closed, he said, "Please, Josiah. Take it."

A tear rolled down Josiah's face as he tightened his fist around the coin. He closed his eyes and nodded his head.

"You take care, Josiah," Levi said, turning his back. "You take good care." A moment later, the club fell and the lights went out.

Josiah opened his hand and stared down at his palm as Anna stepped to his side. "My God," she said. It was more money than she had ever seen and it could change their lives forever. But then, Levi Love had already done that.

Josiah looked over at Anna, her loving eyes confirming his every thought. And then, kneeling down beside his friend, he tucked the coin deep into Levi's pocket.

Made in the USA
Lexington, KY
21 October 2017